# LEAR'S SHADOW

# LEAR'S SHADOW

*A Novel*

CLAIRE
HOLDEN ROTHMAN

PENGUIN
an imprint of Penguin Canada, a division of Penguin Random House Canada Limited
Canada • USA • UK • Ireland • Australia • New Zealand • India • South Africa • China

First published 2018
Copyright © 2018 by Claire Holden Rothman

www.penguinrandomhouse.ca

*Publisher's note: This book is a work of fiction. Names, characters, places and incidents either are the product of the author's imagination or are used fictitiously, and any resemblance to actual persons living or dead, events, or locales is entirely coincidental.*

Conseil
des arts
et des lettres
du Québec

LIBRARY AND ARCHIVES CANADA CATALOGUING IN PUBLICATION

Rothman, Claire, author
    Lear's shadow / Claire Holden Rothman.

Issued in print and electronic formats.
ISBN 978-0-7352-3425-3 (softcover).—ISBN 978-0-7352-3426-0 (electronic)

    I. Title.

PS8585.O8435L43 2018              C813'.54              C2017-907158-0
                                                        C2017-907159-9

Cover design: Terri Nimmo
Cover image: Danuta Nierada / Getty Images

Printed and bound in the United States of America

10 9 8 7 6 5 4 3 2 1

Penguin
Random House
PENGUIN CANADA

*For Samuel Leonard Holden*

*Who is it that can tell me who I am?*

—WILLIAM SHAKESPEARE, *King Lear*

# PROLOGUE

*KENT.*

*Alas, sir, are you here? Things that love night*
*Love not such nights as these.*

(3.2.42–43)

THE OLD MAN KNOWS he should watch the road, but he can't. His eyes keep drifting to the black churn of cloud overhead. Nightfall is still an hour away, but the sky is so dark he can't see the white lines on the pavement. He curses, gropes for the headlight switch, pressing buttons and turning knobs to no visible effect. The car plunges through the shadows down the final stretch of Pine Avenue, past the Royal Victoria Hospital and the grimy stone archway of the Neurological Institute. It weaves across lanes as though driven by someone crazy or blind or both.

As the old man rounds the curve onto Park Avenue, brake lights ignite in front of him. These he can see. He slams down hard and stops a foot short of an aging Pontiac. Behind him, another car squeals to a stop. All the way up Park Avenue cars are at a stand-still, their taillights blinking in frustration.

The old man kicks open his door. Above him, the sky is as oily and opaque as the asphalt. Wind slaps him, claws at his clothes, whips strands of hair across his scalp. He puts a hand over his eyes to shield them from the swirling grit and fights his way forward. Then he hears it: the beating heart of the chaos, a faint, steady patter of drums. Through the blur of wind and flashing lights he sees them: arms linked, laughing like drunks at a party.

They've choked the broad city street—they've brought him and everyone around him to a halt. And they're laughing.

The wind knocks him hard into a stopped car. He can see them clearly now. Youngsters, shirtless, their chests decorated with paint. Two girls are half-naked too, directly in his path, wearing bikini tops or maybe their brassieres. He moves closer, grabbing at the sides of vehicles for balance. One of the girls is fleshy, a pink-skinned child. The old man shoves her. He does it out of indignation, but also because she's the weak link in the chain. She comes unhooked from her companions and staggers, looking up at him with round astonished eyes. A boy shouts. A second boy spits at him, then grabs his arm and shakes it so hard his vision tunnels.

He breaks free and continues through the bodies, through the shoves and shouts and gusts of wind, until something makes him look up. Above him, a winged black enormity is etched against the sky's lesser blackness. He freezes. Then he realizes it's the angel—his angel—gazing down benignly, pointing the way home.

The sky lights up making the angel gleam. A second flash comes and the old man sees again the thing that he thought was a hallucination. A rope is tied around the angel's neck; someone is hanging from it.

The sky blazes and goes dark, blazes and goes dark: God playing idly with a light switch. At the end of the rope is a girl, a thick tail of hair swinging behind her like a demented metronome. Her feet brace against the angel's loins while one of her arms sweeps up and down, as if half of her were trying to fly.

Thunder cracks followed by shrieks. A drop of water hits the old man's forehead, then another. An instant later the sky opens, obliterating the girl and scattering the crowd. He tries to run but his limbs are useless, as in a nightmare. He collapses, first onto one knee, then onto his shoulder. For one electric moment as the pain sparks through him, his body fuses with the storm. The old man rolls onto his back. The last thing he sees, dimly, before closing his eyes, is a stricken angel in a drowned sky.

# ACT ONE

FOOL *[Singing].*
*He that has a little tiny wit—*
*With heigh-ho, the wind and the rain—*
*Must make content with his fortunes fit,*
*Though the rain it raineth every day.*

$$(3.2.74–77)$$

I.

BEATRICE ROSE STOOD in the kitchen of her apartment on Sainte-Famille Street, staring at the string of Christmas lights looping off her shelves. It was the end of May and the temperature was brutal, inside and out. Montreal was in the grip of the year's first heat wave. She glanced through the window at the darkening sky and back at her brave little out-of-season lights.

It was the day of her mother's birth: Deirdre McMaster Rose would have turned sixty-five. A pain flared in Bea's chest. Not a pain exactly, more a familiar squeezing, strong enough to block her breath. She knew it wasn't a physical phenomenon. It wasn't asthma, though years ago a pediatrician had concluded that it was and prescribed a puffer. And it wasn't her heart. That poor, flapping organ would survive, she knew, after decades of living with this squeezing. She'd visited her mother's grave at the Mount Royal Cemetery that morning. The grass around it had been lush, undamaged as yet by the sun. The first flies of the season had circled her lazily. She'd left a rose on the headstone instead of a rock.

Her mother had been dead now for more years than she'd been alive. She was killed in a car crash at the age of thirty-two. Bea's father, Sol, was at the wheel. He never spoke of it. After the car overturned at the intersection of Park Avenue and Pine, he'd climbed out with bruises and a graze on his left cheek where his beard hairs would never grow again. Her mother hadn't been so lucky.

The kettle chirped tentatively then opened into a full-throated wail. Bea took it off the heat and made herself a herbal tea: calming nettles. The bright orange stove coil faded to black. Her tension wasn't due entirely to the anniversary. There was a more pressing cause. She'd been invited to a party.

She glanced at the kitchen clock, a whimsical thing she and Jean-Christian had picked up at the dollar store, fluffy clouds floating in a blue sky, and took a sip that scalded her tongue. The evening was too hot for tea. Her body was a furnace. She put the cup in the sink, taking care not to spill its contents. She was in her party wear, a pink kameez, the most beautiful thing she owned, bought years ago in northern India. The neckline, low by Indian standards, was embroidered with shimmering threads of gold. She knew it looked good, even if the body it adorned was no longer young.

It was time to leave. She walked down the hall without turning on the lights. The apartment was typical of the Plateau Mont-Royal, long and narrow, with windows at either end, its middle cave-dark. Bea patted the wall at the bathroom doorway to find the light switch. Her face appeared in the mirror, lit up out of the darkness.

Jean-Christian had come in February for his belongings. Among the items he'd left with was the rice-paper globe that had once softened the bathroom light and made intriguing shadows. A naked bulb remained, dangling dejectedly from the ceiling. Also gone was the shower curtain with its bright motif of tropical fish. She'd been at work when he dropped by. He knew her schedule. It was easy to find on the studio website, but he knew it without checking: her schedule had been his. For seven years they'd managed Om Sweet Om together, offering yoga classes and workshops and running a popular teacher-training program. They were well known. Their studio had been one of the best. Not as big as the places downtown, perhaps, but reputable, respected. Even her father was impressed.

The light cast visible lines in the face in the bathroom mirror, especially around the eyes, from which they fanned like cracks in a windshield. Bea would turn forty this summer. No man, no money and a business on the point of collapse. She had spent the winter adrift.

She should have gone for counselling. That was what her sister, Cara, said. But Bea didn't have the money or, frankly, the desire for therapy. She didn't need a psychologist to tell her what was wrong. The breakup had hit her hard. Jean-Christian had given her no warning. There had been a third party; she never did find out who. Behind that pain was the deeper anguish of her mother, the old trauma, the ghost in the shadows. It didn't take a degree in psychology to see where the trouble lay. She would survive this loss, just as she'd survived the one in her childhood. She still had some fight left.

In any case, she couldn't waste energy thinking about her emotional state. Other matters required attention, like her failing yoga studio. Without Jean-Christian, Om Sweet Om was no longer viable. The clients were mostly women, whom Jean-Christian had held, literally, in the palms of his hands—large, capable hands with which he'd adjusted people's postures while reciting Persian poetry. The mix was devastating. He wasn't young anymore either, a full decade older than Bea, but no one ever guessed. Whereas Bea was short and wiry like her father, Jean-Christian was six three, with a dancer's build and hazel eyes so piercing they made you weak-kneed. Bea used to think that was a figure of speech. But at the first sight of Jean-Christian, she'd felt it. And she'd seen other competent, sane women turn red and confused when he looked their way. Within three months of his departure a third of her clients had left, and Om Sweet Om had begun to lose money.

Bea squared her shoulders and breathed. A deep breath, filling her belly. Whatever she'd once shared with Jean-Christian Dubois was over. It was time to move on.

Tonight would be the first step. She'd found a summer job working on a production of *King Lear*. A young actor named Jay O'Breen from one of her yoga classes had posted the notice three days before on the Om Sweet Om bulletin board. When Bea asked him about it, he told her the theatre company was desperate: rehearsals were slated to begin this Thursday, the last day of May. The pay wasn't great, but Bea supposed that was how things went in the theatre. One made sacrifices for art.

Jay was surprised that she was interested, but enthusiastic, promising to put in a good word. Bea dialled the offices of Bard in the Parks that very morning, as soon as her last class ended and she had said her goodbyes to the small group of loyal students who had shown up for the occasion. No one answered, but the next day, an eager-sounding woman telephoned her. Could she commit to June, July and August? the woman wanted to know. And did she have a valid driver's licence? There would be travel involved. Bea said yes to both questions. There was no mention of a CV or references. The only other question the woman asked was about cell phones. If she was surprised that Bea didn't own one, she didn't say so. Bea promised to buy a smartphone so she could receive emails as well as calls and texts. And that was that. The woman congratulated her and gave her the date and address for the company meet-and-greet. At first, Bea thought she'd misunderstood. But the woman had laughed—a pleasant, tinkly sound—and told Bea not to worry. They'd see each other at the party.

Was this how things worked in the theatre? You were given a job after thirty seconds on the telephone?

Still, it felt like a lifeline, a chance to pull herself out of the static and insular Montreal yoga community, where everyone knew everyone else's history. Her world would change. She would meet new people, visit new places. Not to mention that the production was being staged in municipal parks, so she'd get to spend the summer outdoors. Everything about the job was right.

And *King Lear*—now that was a play to conjure with. Bea had studied it back in high school and she remembered its power. She'd already begun rereading it. Working in theatre would be an entirely new venture. It would be her way forward.

She pursed her lips and stared into the mirror. The scar vanished briefly in the unforgiving light and reappeared when she released her breath: a tiny chain of pale skin descending from her left nostril to the cupid's bow of her upper lip. Her mother had referred to it as a trifle. Jean-Christian, in the glow of early love, had once called Bea "perfect in her imperfection." At the studio no one remarked on it, though occasionally a gaze would linger for a second on her mouth. Most of the time, she managed to forget it entirely. She was luckier than many people with clefts. She'd once met a girl whose whole face was skewed, her speech so impeded that Bea had struggled to understand her.

Bea's father had hunted down the best doctors and treatments. Only the best would suffice, even if the result would never be perfect. From birth to her teens Bea had borne one intervention after another—structural surgery, bone grafts, cosmetic surgery to the philtrum, speech therapy and, after she started school, counselling from a psychotherapist to help her deal with the teasing. The efforts had paid off. Her speech was normal, her face symmetrical. You had to get right up close to see the chain.

From the mirror, her nearly normal face watched her squeeze a dab of white paste onto her toothbrush. The dark hair and pallor, the slightly stubborn set of the mouth—it was her father's face, really.

2.

THE NOISE OUTSIDE her apartment was a shock. Ahead of her on Pine Avenue a police car sped past, its siren wailing, lights spinning wildly. Horns blared in the distance like an orchestra tuning up. At the first gap in traffic Bea sprinted across Pine and then stepped onto the footpath beside the Hôtel-Dieu Hospital. A wind was blowing, a strong one, the kind that promised rain. She'd heard storm warnings on the radio before leaving for the cemetery. Now gusts were throwing grit in her eyes and kiting old wrappers into the air. On Park Avenue the traffic was grid-locked—the source of the honking that filled the evening air. The street was jammed all the way to Mount Royal and beyond, as far up as Villeneuve, where her sister lived. Behind the car horns, fainter but insistent, was another sound. Bea stopped on the grass and listened. There it was: the clang of pots and pans. Of course. It was past eight. The *casseroles* were marching. She could see their banner in the wind.

For two months they'd marched every night in the streets of Montreal. To start with, it was students cutting classes in the unusually mild spring weather to protest tuition hikes. The *printemps érable*, they called it, comparing themselves only half-facetiously to the freedom fighters of the Arab Spring. But soon the protests had begun to transform. Young parents started showing up, pushing their children in strollers. Baby boomers joined in, nostalgic for the marches of their youth. The event turned festive, carnivalesque. The week before, half a million people had poured into the streets to celebrate the hundredth night of demonstrations. The organizers claimed it was the largest protest march ever held in the country.

Bea, too, had come out that night, not because of the tuition hikes—in Montreal, you could attend university for a fraction of what you'd pay in most places in the world, not to mention the rest of Canada—but simply to join in, to leave the apartment and be part of something bigger than her own woes. She had danced for three solid hours. The whole city seemed to be out, making music.

Across Park's clogged lanes she made out the contour of the angel, its great bronze wings outstretched behind as if it were about to take flight. It—she—held a laurel crown in her left hand. Bea's father, Sol, was the one who'd pointed out the laurels, which were easy to miss if you didn't stop and look. He'd spent his boyhood on Saint-Urbain Street, a block away. The grassy slope on which the statue stood had been his turf.

A human sea swirled around the statue, lapping against the pedestal, spilling onto the street. Some drivers were out of their cars. A couple of them were yelling. It sounded like things might turn ugly.

Bea began to walk again. The wind was getting stronger, shaking the trees and their newly unfurled leaves. A plastic bag flew by at eye level like an airborne jellyfish. A moment later drops fell, fat and heavy, dotting the pavement. Bea hurried on. She'd brought an umbrella, a collapsible one that was several years old. She fished it from her bag and opened it, but the wind grabbed it immediately and pulled it inside out. As she struggled to force the metal spokes back the right way, one of them snapped. She started running, holding the maimed umbrella in front of her face like a shield against the wind and the droplets.

The address was just up ahead. She was searching in her pocket for the slip of paper on which she'd scribbled the details when the sky opened. Water crashed down in a cascade, as if someone had overturned a gigantic pail. Around her, the world ceased to exist. The cars, the marchers, the angel, even Mount Royal itself, vanished.

She made it to her destination: one of the sedate grey stone triplexes on L'Esplanade that looked out at the mountain. She hurried up the outside staircase and stopped on the second-floor landing to catch her breath, partly sheltered by the arch over the door. Rain was still coming down in sheets, monsoon-like. Below her, L'Esplanade was a coursing river. The broken umbrella had been surprisingly effective. Her hair and kameez were damp but presentable. Her jeans, however, were soaked through, and her sandals were ruined.

Bea tried to look through the small square of glass in the door, but it was frosted. She rapped lightly. The rain was coming down so hard that all she could hear from inside the little alcove was the roar of water. Seconds passed. She rapped again. Either no one could hear her over the noise of the party or she'd gotten the address wrong. She was about to rap again when something moved behind the window. She took a step back and squared her shoulders.

The door opened to reveal a man of her height with a shaved head. They stared at each other for a second. Bea's hand went to her mouth.

"So it *is* you," the man said, opening the door wider. "On the crew list you're Bea, so I wasn't sure."

Bea's hand remained raised, shielding her mouth, a habit from years ago. Arthur White. She'd known him in childhood. It was absurd. He looked exactly the same as he had back then, only bald.

He glanced past her, as if expecting more people. "Good Lord," he said, his eyes widening when he saw how hard the rain was pounding. He took her arm and drew her in. Immediately they were swallowed up by party sounds—music, laughter— although she couldn't yet see anyone. They were in a sort of tunnel that served as a vestibule. A curtain hanging at the far end hid whatever lay beyond. It had the feel of a fairy tale. Or *Alice in Wonderland*—Bea at the lip of a rabbit hole.

"I changed mine too," Arthur said. He'd done the talking when they were young as well, jumping deftly over the pools of her silence. "I go by Artie now. You didn't make the connection when you saw my name on the company website?"

She had not, she said quietly. The truth was she hadn't thought to visit the Bard in the Parks website. Arthur—Artie—was watching her. As well he might. The company, she would learn hours later, after she'd made it back to Sainte-Famille Street and turned on her laptop, was under his authority. He was the artistic director of Bard in the Parks. She didn't quite know what that involved, but it certainly sounded impressive.

They hadn't seen each other since they were eight years old. It was a period that Bea had spent her adult life trying to forget. Not because of him. He'd been the one bright spot that terrible year, at least until he moved away. They'd been next-door neighbours on Melville Avenue, where Bea's father still lived. Their mothers had been friends. The two women whiled away many evenings on each other's front porch, weather permitting, drinking a glass of wine and watching their children play in the park across the street.

Arthur White wasn't like other boys Bea knew, boys who occupied their waking hours catching baseballs in sweaty leather mitts. He owned a mitt, and he had a soccer ball and an army of small green plastic soldiers, but these things bored him. He preferred stories. He and Bea spent many hours between the ages of four and eight re-enacting dramas from their favourite books and TV shows. Even simple games like tag or hide-and-seek had plots to underpin them.

Bea had been in love with him. His mother, who was British, had declared that they were "in each other's pockets," an expression that made Bea shy but also happy. When, at age five, they started going to the big public school down the street and Bea was teased by the other children, Arthur White remained loyal. It was as if he didn't see the scar or hear the way she spoke.

Artie's brown eyes were fixed on her, waiting for her to speak. His face was unreadable.

Bea's lips burned, a sensation she hadn't felt in years. It had happened all the time when she was young. Her mouth would grow hot with the pent-up desire to speak. She rubbed it.

Artie broke the silence. "You come highly recommended," he said. "Jay O'Breen," he added, when she looked puzzled.

So that was why it had been so easy. Jay had come through. She must find him tonight and thank him. Artie took her arm. He put her soaked umbrella on a bench and led her through the vestibule toward the curtained-off interior.

They emerged through the curtain into an expansive space full of noise and people. The lights were low. All Bea could see at first was a dark mass swaying to Bob Marley's "No Woman, No Cry," which was blaring from the stereo. As her eyes adjusted, she began to discern individual faces. They smiled at Artie; hands raised beer bottles as he passed.

He led her to the bathroom. "Make yourself at home," he shouted, passing her a towel.

Artie's bathroom was spare and orderly. His possessions were few: an emerald-coloured toothbrush in a transparent drinking glass, a tube of toothpaste lying beside it, rolled meticulously from the bottom up. Three clean towels were stacked on a shelf for the use of his guests. The surfaces were spotless. So was the toilet bowl, whose lid happened to be open.

"You want pants?"

She was having trouble hearing with the noise and wondered if she'd misunderstood.

He held up a hand, then disappeared. Bea looked in the mirror. Her hair was lank with dampness and her face was pallid. The rings beneath her eyes were so dark they looked like bruises. She scrunched her limp hair and pinched her cheeks. She was squeezing moisture from her pant cuffs when Artie reappeared with a pair of purple sweatpants.

"These ought to do," he said, holding them to her waist as if they were playing dress-up. "You can throw the wet ones in the tub."

He disappeared again, closing the door behind him. The sweatpants fit, and whether by fluke or from memory, he'd picked her favourite colour. They matched her kameez. She stepped out of the bathroom feeling restored.

Three women were standing outside the door, talking earnestly. They were young and beautiful, their shoulders bare in skin-tight party dresses. To Bea, they looked like an advertisement—for designer eveningwear maybe, or for hair products. It was like stumbling onto a fashion shoot. One of the women was Afro-Canadian, her head a cascade of ebony braids, a golden leaf dangling from each ear. Her dress was the boldest, a sea-blue African print that highlighted every curve and contour beneath. The other two women were white, equally stunning and model-like. One had chestnut hair with glints of henna, the other's was coppery red. Their dresses were almost identical: black and strapless, with hip-hugging skirts à la Marilyn Monroe. The three women fell silent when sweat-panted Bea stepped into their circle. After an awkward pause, the young black woman addressed her.

"And you are . . . ?"

Bea said her name.

The woman introduced herself as Margo Indongo. Her two friends, she informed Bea, were Ann O'Neill and Claire Johnson. "We're the princesses," she said, smiling. "Daughters of King Lear."

A mixed-race royal family; Bea was impressed.

Margo asked what role Bea was playing. When Bea answered that she was in production, Margo's smile diminished a bit. "In what capacity?"

Bea explained that she'd been hired to help a man called Dave.

Claire Johnson tilted her coppery curls to the middle of the room where the crowd was thickest. "Dave Samuels. He's over there. The tall guy with the hair."

Above the press of bodies, one head swivelled left and right like a periscope. The face was pale, encircled by a frizzy black halo. Bea saw a gleam of metal on his left eyebrow. Dave Samuels had piercings. Like the princesses, he was very young.

Margo's interest revived. "You must be the replacement." She turned to her friends. "Remember? Winston what's-his-name had an accident."

Bea liked Margo's voice, which was deep and unhurried, like a river. It put her a bit more at ease.

"Oh, right," said Ann. "The ASM."

Bea didn't know what that was. She shrugged with what she hoped would pass for happy insouciance, bid the three prin-cesses goodbye and headed off in the direction of her new boss, who was still periscoping in the middle of the room. With the princesses, she had felt like the odd man out. Now she was a swimmer in the ocean, pushing through the waves. Every couple of strokes she had to stop and recalibrate. She came level with the kitchen, or at least with a space in one corner of the big open-concept living area equipped with a sink, cooking appliances and a small island on casters. Hanging overhead from a metal frame were Arthur White's pots and pans.

He obviously liked to cook, because there were a lot of them, some with copper bottoms reflecting the light. Two fresh pizzas had been set out on the island to cool, sending up wafts of roasted garlic. Bea stopped and cut herself a square. She was chewing the soft, warm dough when a petite woman in a bright pink T-shirt and mauve pants wandered over. She was older than most of the people here, older even than Bea. Her hair was mostly brown, but silver streaks ran through it.

"I like your colours," she shouted, nodding at Bea's tunic and smiling. She had an accent, broad vowels, as if she were from the American South. But also something else. French, maybe. Or German.

"Mimi Meir," she said, offering her hand. Her grip was surprisingly firm.

So she *was* French. But the South was definitely in there too. When Bea said her own name, Mimi grinned. "Our assistant stage manager!"

Something dinged in Bea's brain. ASM. So that's what it stood for.

Mimi said that she herself had been an assistant stage manager. "Years ago." She waved her hand through the air like an orchestra conductor. Her voice was musical, even at top volume. "In my misspent youth!" *In mah misspent yooth.*

"My very first play was Shakespeare," she continued. "In a park. I thought I'd died and gone to heaven! The very first day, I declared to anyone who'd listen that I'd found my vocation."

"As a stage manager?" Bea asked hopefully. She still didn't know what Mimi's role in the production was, but she suspected, from all the arm waving, that she was an actress.

Mimi looked at Bea's face more closely. Then she laughed and turned her attention to the pizza. "Any good?"

Bea gave her a slice and they stood together, chewing and listening to the party roar around them. Mimi poured wine into disposable glasses. They clinked plastic rims and toasted the show's success. Then Mimi informed Bea that she was the show's director.

"Forget it," she said, when Bea began to apologize. "You're new, right? How were you supposed to know?"

Talk was a bit strained after that. Bea tried to revive it by asking Mimi about herself. French was, indeed, in her background. Her father, an acrobat and mime artist from Paris, had taught for years at the National Theatre School in Montreal, where Mimi herself now taught. Her mother, she said, had been a costume designer from Virginia. The noise made further divulgations difficult. Shouting over the music, Mimi suggested that they find Dave.

He was still in the centre of the room, his pale face shining above the crowd like a beacon. Bea walked behind Mimi, clutching her little plastic glass, still largely full, which she raised over her head, trying not to spill.

"Bea!" Dave cried when Mimi introduced her. He looked as if he'd been waiting all night for her to arrive.

Mimi explained to the people standing with him who Bea was. A pink-haired girl in torn black jeans who looked no older than fifteen shook Bea's hand warmly, and when she spoke, Bea recognized the voice that had conducted her telephone interview. Apparently she was old enough to run the Bard company office. Also in the group were the show's music director and two stage technicians: a tall guy named Bear and his assistant, Maggie. After

Mimi had done the introductions, Dave made a gesture over Bea's head as if blessing her and told the group they should fall on their knees. Bea, he said, had saved the show.

Talk turned to the young man Bea had been hired to replace— Winston Frankel—who'd broken his leg. Everyone in the group knew him. They asked Dave how he was doing, then started talking about their own experiences with broken bones. There were jokes about the old theatrical wish "break a leg." Dave said the expression simply meant take a bow. He demonstrated, bending one leg, stork-like, directly behind the other while simultaneously lifting both arms. Everyone clapped, including Bea, who was revising her initial impression. Dave Samuels might be young, but he had style.

After a few more minutes of shouting and gesticulating for the group, Dave pulled Bea off to one side. "So," he said, eyeing the jam-packed room. "What do you think?"

Bea shrugged. She didn't want to admit to being overwhelmed. It was all so different from the silence and emptiness of her yoga studio. "Big gang," she said, cautiously.

Dave grinned. "Always, with Mr. Shakespeare. It's your job and mine to look after each and every one of them."

Bea hesitated. "Um, what is it that I'll be doing, exactly?" She had no idea what a stage manager actually did, let alone an assistant. It sounded a little intimidating.

Dave looked at her a moment, then launched into a list of all the things she'd be helping him with—everything from looking after props to line-prompting and doing something called blocking, whatever that was. As he rattled off her duties she tried desperately to absorb them all. Finally he paused, performing the periscope motion again. "There are two kinds of stage managers, Bea. There are mothers, and there are sergeant-majors." He watched her reaction. "I'm a mother."

Bea laughed, but Dave's expression remained serious. "It's basically my only requirement of you."

"Motherhood?" said Bea. A boy with studs in his eyebrows was going to teach her, an unwed, childless woman on the brink of forty, about motherhood?

Lady Gaga was belting out her desire to marry the night. Dave kept talking, though Bea could hear only half of what he said. He was explaining how he'd gotten into stage management. Originally he'd wanted to be an actor. Didn't everyone? But auditions terrified him; he could never seem to get them right. So three years ago he'd crossed the floor. One day, he vowed, he would cross back.

His lips, which were claret red and which she'd been watching intently as if to read the words she couldn't hear, stopped moving. He had, apparently, said all he was going to say. In a small space beside the stereo, the three actresses Bea had met at the start of the evening—the princesses—were dancing. They looked beautiful, gyrating to the loud, simple beat. Margo Indongo's braids billowed suddenly, spreading out like the tentacles of a sea anemone in a current. A breathtaking sight. The song ended with all three royal sisters pumping fists and laughing.

Dave Samuels swung his periscope back to Bea. Her turn. Maybe this was the test she thought she'd bypassed on the strength of Jay O'Breen's generosity. After all, she hadn't signed a contract yet. They might want to reconsider. She swallowed and confessed, finally, that she had no theatre experience.

Dave's eyebrows shot up. "You didn't study it? I thought Jay knew you from theatre school."

She shook her head. "Yoga," she said, reddening. "I run a studio, or at least I used to run one. I just sold it, actually. Jay was my student." She'd always dreamed of working in the theatre, she added. That last part was a bald lie. She enjoyed going to the theatre. She even read plays on occasion. But in her nervousness, she was spinning tales.

She fell quiet. She should offer to withdraw. Rehearsals would begin Thursday. They still had a day. Bard in the Parks could surely find someone who actually knew what she was doing to jump in as Dave's assistant. No hard feelings. Bea understood completely; she would never have hired a yoga instructor with zero experience. She was wondering how to put these thoughts into words when a hand seized her shoulder from behind. Bea wheeled. Before her stood a man of impressive height, with gleaming white hair and a full white beard.

"Samuels," he boomed at Dave, not taking his eyes off Bea. "What are you thinking, keeping this ravishing creature to yourself? You're supposed to be looking out for us, not starving us of company."

Dave smiled sheepishly. "Bea Rose, meet Phil Burns."

The man stepped between them, ending the uncomfortable exchange about Bea's lack of qualifications. She wasn't sure whether to feel relieved or alarmed.

"Lear," he said, taking her hand. "As in the king." He bent and brushed the backs of her fingers with bristly lips.

Dave Samuels rolled his eyes. "Oh, God."

"No, David. Just *king*," Phil said. "For this run, anyway."

Mimi Meir, who'd been engrossed in a conversation with the music director, took a step forward. "Watch yourself, Phil," she said, in a tone that wasn't entirely jocular. Her head barely reached his shoulder, but he still took a step backward. She turned to Bea. "You watch out too. He's a big old flirt."

Bea believed it. Phil Burns was clearly well past sixty, but even so he was a monument to manhood. His hair was thick, his face square-jawed and dignified. He'd kept holding her hand, lightly, signalling that she could pull away any time. It was sort of sexy.

Bold, but not grasping. Not desperate. His fingers were smooth and dry. She began to disengage herself.

Mimi winked and returned to her conversation with the music director.

"Don't mind her," Phil said, releasing Bea's fingers. "She's just jealous." He scanned the room thoughtfully, then glanced down at Bea's glass. "What are you drinking?"

Before she could answer, he snatched it. "Empty," he said, to no one in particular. His voice cut through the ambient chatter as if amplified. Heads turned their way. "Rule number one," he boomed, holding her glass aloft. "Never let a girl run dry."

Bea gave him a look. "Girl" was more objectionable than flattering. And she was perfectly capable of getting her own drink.

"Rule number two," he continued, not registering her disapproval.

More heads had turned.

"Replenish frequently."

The people next to them laughed.

His fingers sought Bea's again and she found herself being pulled with surprising vigour out of the circle in which she'd been standing and back toward the kitchen. Bea turned to Dave Samuels, thinking she should stay with him, but he smiled pleasantly and waved. Mimi Meir frowned.

Phil Burns was a ship cleaving the waters. There was nothing to do but follow. They made it to the bar, where Bea watched as he refilled their glasses. White wine from a carton for her, burgundy for himself. Tonight was the first time in seven years she'd touched alcohol. Jean-Christian was an abstainer, and when they started living together she became one too. It was a yogic precept. No intoxicants to cloud the mind and make it heedless. Bea hadn't wanted to be rude to Mimi when she offered her the first glass, and now she didn't want to explain the whole prohibition thing to Phil, so she accepted a refill and followed him into the crowd. It was the start of a new life, after all.

Phil headed to the far side of the room, where Maggie the technician was sandwiched between Bear and another young man on a sagging leather couch.

"Get lost," Phil growled. He didn't smile and seemed only half in jest. "I'm twice as old as you. My back aches. My feet hurt. And," he added, winking conspiratorially at Bea, "I happen to be your king."

All three stood up right away, with no apparent hard feelings. Bea felt guilty, but not very. She was as tired as Phil Burns said he was. She hadn't slept well in far too long, and this couch seemed to be the only seat in the entire room. Her conscience diluted by the wine she'd drunk, she sank onto the leather with the show's lead actor. For a moment, neither of them spoke. But soon Phil turned to her and in his booming bass began to regale her with the films he'd been in, from *Silence of the Lambs* to *The Aviator* to *X-Men*. He'd worked with Leonardo DiCaprio, Penélope Cruz, Julia Roberts, Robert De Niro. He told funny anecdotes about all of them. And having brought the bottle of red from the bar, he kept topping up his glass as he talked. Bea was warmed by his attentions, even though the stories all centred on him. And she'd decided that Mimi was right. Phil was a ladies' man. He kept locking eyes with Bea and lowering his voice unexpectedly, as if they were intimates. He seemed to be an aging Lothario with a taste for sweet young things. Not that Bea could be called young anymore, or sweet. But Phil didn't seem to notice. Perhaps the pretty pink smock had fooled him.

His lips stopped moving. His eyes were on her wineglass. "You're not drinking," he said, his face so close that she could smell his sour-grape breath. Springs poked at her through the cushions. The couch was so old and droopy that their bottoms were inches from the floor. Bea sipped dutifully, feeling the alcohol's warmth rise to her cheeks. The taste wasn't so bad. She sipped again and began to tell Phil about Jean-Christian's booze embargo.

"Seven years?" he said, marvelling. The wine had coloured his lips purple.

She nodded, blinking as Jean-Christian's face rose in front of her. "But it's over now," she said, then instantly regretted it when Phil Burns leaned in closer.

Jean-Christian had been her whole life. The yoga studio they'd established together had been important. Om Sweet Om really was a home to Bea, her first since leaving the house on Melville Avenue where she'd grown up. Bea was the Rose family nomad. For most of her twenties she'd wandered through Asia, living out of a backpack, camping or renting cheap rooms in hostels and ashrams. There'd been companions along the way, men she'd loved with varying degrees of intensity, but only with Jean-Christian had she been able to land.

He too had spent the early years of his adulthood trekking through Asia. It was in India that she'd first heard his name, when she was studying to become a yoga teacher up in Rishikesh. A decade earlier, Jean-Christian had taught at the school where she was eventually certified. He was long gone by the time she'd arrived, but everyone who'd known him spoke his name with reverence. Five years later, they crossed paths in Montreal. Within a week, they became lovers.

In the end, the country that had brought them together drove them apart. For years they'd talked about going back to India, but whenever it came up either funds were short or one or the other had too much on their plate. And then, one day the summer before, Jean-Christian was asked to lead a retreat in Bodh Gaya. The invitation was for December, the week of the winter solstice. Jean-Christian asked Bea to go, but holiday airfares were exorbitant and anyway someone had to stay and manage the studio. Bea resigned herself. Not long afterward she saw an item on their company Visa bill: two round-trip tickets to New Delhi. When Jean-Christian came home that night she kissed him lovingly, thinking he'd secretly booked her a ticket. Instead of returning the kiss, he pulled away. Then the lies began.

"Rules are made to be broken," Phil said, drinking his wine.

She had to laugh. What rules hadn't been broken? What hopeful, earnest precepts of yogic living had Jean-Christian not violated, trying to hold her eye as he tangled himself in contradictions? She had stopped trusting him then and there.

Phil refilled her glass with red. She shouldn't drink anymore. She could feel the anger surging.

He placed the bottle on the floor and brought his hand up to her face. She thought he was going to brush away a stray hair. Instead, he crooked his index finger and stroked her upper lip. "What's this?" he asked.

Bea sat very still. She must have telegraphed her discomfort, because Phil withdrew his finger. Released from his touch, she recoiled, shifting positions on the uncomfortable springs and striking the couch's rickety back with her elbow. There was a loud crack and one side of the base gave way. She fell sideways onto Phil's chest, and together they slid into a crevice of snapped boards and springs. Her hands flew up instinctively. The contents of her glass rose too, in slow motion—a gleaming ruby pitching skyward against the white backdrop of a wall. The wine hovered for a moment, undecided, then came splashing down on their heads.

They were both flailing. Phil was the first to surrender. He pulled a handkerchief from his sports jacket and began to mop Bea's face with great tenderness.

Bea recoiled again. They must look ridiculous. Worse than ridiculous. Phil's handkerchief was a damp pink mess. She tried to take it from him, but he wouldn't let it go. The front of her kameez was spattered. Phil was dabbing her lap now, humming as he pressed his hanky to her thighs.

A flash of mauve caught her eye. Mimi Meir walked past briskly, glancing at them but then continuing on. No word of sympathy, no offer to help Bea clamber out of the trouble into which she'd inadvertently fallen. And did Mimi actually look angry? She probably thought Phil was making moves on Bea and not getting any resistance. That, Bea realized with horror, was what it must look like to anyone watching. Their heads were at knee level, hidden from general view by the dense crowd, but Mimi had seen them clearly enough. Bea snatched the handkerchief out of Phil's hand and put an end to the pawing. He *was* making moves on her. His eyes were soft and big, and his lips had stretched into a sloppy grin. He tried to refill her glass again, but Bea pulled away.

"Pish posh," he said, his face stern and mocking. The words came out slurred.

She could have slapped him, although that impulse was probably wine-induced too. Phil Burns was drunk. So, she realized with shame, was she. When she tried to stand up, her legs felt unsteady. She sank back into Phil's arms. And he was ready for her, his big body absorbing her weight, enfolding her in a boozy embrace.

Dave Samuels finally saw her struggling and came to the rescue, grabbing her hands and pulling her upright. Phil didn't seem the least bit perturbed. "Me too," he said, reaching up like an overgrown child.

Dave placed Phil's wineglass on a bookshelf. Then, grunting, he pulled the older man to his feet. Phil was less able than Bea to stand on his own. Dave had to hold him tightly to his side as if he were a war casualty or a long-lost friend. They walked away toward the bathroom, their trajectory in no way resembling a straight line.

Bea's mouth was bone-dry. Her right temple pounded. The

walls of the apartment appeared to be softly undulating. She needed air. Now that Phil was gone, no one was paying her the slightest attention. Without his commanding presence, they had all returned to their conversations. Bea had messed up. Instead of meeting people, forging friendships, making sure the company's first impression of her was good, she'd sat in a corner and gotten drunk with a lecherous old man. She'd gone passive, allowed herself to be pulled off course. And now Mimi Meir and Artie White and everyone else in the cast and crew were entitled to conclude that she was a flake, a pathetic groupie.

Bea plunged again into the crowd, heading for the way out. She seemed to bump into someone at every step. Over and over again she said she was sorry. At last she reached the vestibule curtain. All she had to do was slip through and the front door would be in sight.

She was pulling the curtain aside when Phil and Dave burst out of the bathroom, almost knocking her over. They were arguing.

Dave's face was white. He was holding Phil by the elbow. "Be reasonable, man."

Phil's nostrils flared. He shook himself free but then almost pitched over. "*Reason not the need!*" he shouted, his face red.

Dave grabbed his arm again. "You can't even stand up. No way I'm letting you drive."

Phil grimaced. In the dim light, his face looked even older.

Bea tried to duck past the curtain, but Phil spotted her. "Bea!" he boomed. "I'm leaving too. We'll go together!"

Every head in the room turned.

Dave looked at Bea. "Don't," he said. "He can't drive."

"Pish posh," said Phil, shaking free again. This time he stayed upright, supported by the wall and the roomful of eyes turned his way.

Dave didn't falter. "I won't allow it."

Phil's eyes opened wide, his lips flattening into a purple line.

"You'll take a cab," Dave said. He dug into his pocket and pulled out a wad of twenties bound with an elastic.

For a second, Phil contemplated the wad. "I was going to take her," he said, nodding at Bea. "Go for a bite to eat."

"Fine," said Dave. "Whatever. But you can go by cab."

Dave was, indeed, a mother. He held Phil tight and motioned to Bea to take Phil's other arm so he could phone for a taxi. He had to dial three companies before he found a dispatcher.

"It'll take a few minutes," he told them, hanging up. Demand for rides had surged with the storm. He looked pointedly at Bea. "You'll take him?"

Motherhood. Could she handle it?

"It's pouring," Phil said gruffly. "I'll make sure she gets home sound and safe."

Dave's eyes were pleading. There was really no choice.

So this was stage management. The old actor would get to walk out of the party with his pride intact and his physical safety assured.

Dave gave her Phil's address on Saint-Joseph Boulevard and squeezed her shoulder in gratitude. Then she noticed Mimi standing not far off. Their eyes met, and then Mimi dropped her gaze.

There was too much momentum to stop now, even if she wanted to. She caught a look of surprise from Artie. She still had his sweatpants on—her damp jeans were lying in his bathtub—but there was no time to rectify that either. Bear, the tech guy, waved as they left, but mostly the boisterous crowd ignored her, turning back to their party.

They made it down the staircase without incident, but once on the sidewalk, Phil's drunkenness seemed to overwhelm him. He'd put all his energy into leaving with dignity. Now that dignity evaporated. His resentment at Dave came out in a slurred growl. What right did some little punk from Montreal have, ordering him around?

Phil pointed at a motorcycle parked several metres away. It stood before them covered in a tarpaulin, bull-shaped and immense, dripping in the street. "My wheels," he announced, grinning.

Bea stared at the Harley, appalled. It was still raining, so they ducked under the front-door arch. Water lapped at the curb. L'Esplanade Avenue was a foul black river; the storm drains had backed up completely. Beyond the street, Bea couldn't see much. The protesters and cars on Park were long gone, she supposed, although there was no way of telling.

She was too scared to ride on the bike, she said. This admission seemed to calm Phil and settle their travel plans. He would play the hero and honour her fears. When the cab finally pulled up they had to wade through the water to reach it. They rolled west to Park Avenue, then north to Saint-Joseph.

Park Avenue was deserted, except for the odd police car that roared by, lights flashing. The earlier traffic jam had dissolved. On either side of them, the storefronts were dark. The streetlights too. Even the traffic lights had stopped working. The cab driver advanced slowly, by the glow of his headlights, stopping at each corner to check for other cars. Half the city, he told them, was without power.

"*Les arbres,*" he said by way of explanation, waving his hand at a great, splintered branch lying on the roof of a parked car. "*Ouf,*" he added. "*Quelqu'un va pleurer.*" The city was a disaster zone. The Quebec premier had just come on the radio, officially declaring it so.

When they reached the house on Saint-Joseph, Bea paid the cabbie with the money Dave had given her and roused Phil, who'd dozed off beside her. Instead of sobering him, his sleep had had the opposite effect. She and the driver had to wrestle him out of the taxi, and he leaned on her heavily as they walked to the house.

They passed through a small muddy garden and mounted the porch stairs. The power was working here, thank heaven. Inside, Phil's flat was unexpectedly pretty. A bronze milk can stood at the entrance with the crooks of several umbrellas sticking out of it, one in the shape of a duck's head. On one wall was a fifties-era Coca-Cola poster in which a buxom brunette smiled as she raised a bottle from the back seat of a red convertible. On the hall table Bea saw a framed photo of a stocky little girl in a polka dot dress, frowning at the camera. A stylish woman's raincoat hung from a coat rack, along with a pink canvas gym bag with the words BURN BABY printed in black on its side. Bea had a moment of anxious realization.

"This isn't your place," she said stupidly. Of course it wasn't. His home was in New York. He had told her so. He was only here for the summer. "I'll be going now," she told him, her hand on the doorknob.

Phil's eyes were swimming in their sockets. He seized her hand and drew her down a long hallway, pitching off the walls as he went. Whoever shared the flat with him seemed to be absent, which was a relief, but also not.

Bea felt no fear—Phil was hardly a threat—but she was uncertain what to do. What was the motherly way to take an old drunk actor home? Leave him at the door and hope for the best? See him safely to his bed and pray he didn't try to pull her in with him? She opted instinctively for the latter, wondering whether it would lead to trouble. Or the loss of her job.

They veered into an unlit bedroom, where Phil released her hand. He sat down heavily on the bed, sagged onto the pillow and began to snore. Bea stood there, feeling the tension in her body ebb. In the oblique light from the hall she could see that the bed was unmade. A suitcase lay open beside her, its contents strewn on the floor.

Bea swung Phil's legs onto the mattress. He was wearing old brown metal-tipped cowboy boots. She pulled them off, yanking hard, one at a time. Then she peeled off his soaked socks. His toenails needed clipping. He moaned softly and rolled onto his side, clutching the pillow like a child. She pulled the duvet over him and carried the cowboy boots to the front hall, where she left them on a mat near the door. Phil's flatmate clearly liked things neat.

The rain had diminished to a fine mist when she emerged from the house. Saint-Joseph Boulevard was deserted. Bea slipped through the gate and hurried west. The streetlights were working here, halos glimmering around them. She still couldn't make out the mountain, or the cross at its summit. Rain and cloud obscured them both.

Park Avenue was submerged. Occasionally a car appeared out of the fog, rolling by in a wash of filthy water and then disappearing again. Fallen trees straddled the caved-in bodies of cars; others lay in the street. South of Saint-Joseph, entire blocks were without power. As Bea continued down Park, a cyclist whipped by her on the sidewalk. For an instant they looked at each other. She saw a black helmet, and under it round, frightened eyes. And then nothing. He was gone.

She hurried home, sensing Mount Royal Park more than seeing it, retracing her steps through the waterlogged field abutting Hôtel-Dieu. A lake had formed outside her apartment building. She waded through it. Though she'd done it once already, the water was still a shock, cold and gritty against her bare skin. She found a stick and began hacking at the silty mass that blocked the drain. She forgot Phil Burns and the humiliation of the party. She forgot Artie White's surprised look as she left with Phil; she forgot the frown on Mimi Meir's face. She even forgot Jean-Christian and the empty bed waiting for her inside.

# 3.

BEA STOOD AT THE WINDOW of Om Sweet Om and looked down at the trench that had once been Laurier Avenue East. She rubbed her eyes. It was ten after seven in the morning. The rain had stopped at around midnight, but crews of city workers had been up all night, trying to clear the backed-up drains. Bea had been up all night as well, listening to the trucks and the sirens. Like most of the streets in the Plateau and Mile End districts, Laurier East was still submerged. To make matters worse it had been in the process of being repaved; all the asphalt and cement had been dug up and last night's rain had transformed what remained into a canal. A complex structure of planks and metal poles connected each doorway to a narrow, muddy footpath, so people could at least enter their homes and businesses.

Across the way, the little park in front of the Saint-Enfant-Jésus church was also in bad shape. The wind had half-torn a limb off one of its ancient trees, and now it hung perilously over a park bench. Workmen were grouped in a semicircle around it, having a smoke and discussing what to do. They'd even cordoned off the park with bright yellow danger tape.

Gaya Pal was late for their appointment, although after last night perhaps that was inevitable. Bea had never met Gaya in person, but she certainly knew about her. Everyone did. Gaya was the star of a new morning flow-yoga and Ayurveda show on MAtv. She was also a presence on YouTube; she posted a daily blog; and across the city, larger-than-life images of her in yoga and casual wear appeared in the display windows of Ragtag stores, an American chain that cultivated a local feel by hiring yoga teachers as its regional ambassadors. Gaya Pal was the face of Ragtag in Montreal.

A bright yellow umbrella bobbed into view, pausing at the gangplank to Bea's building. Across the street in the park, several city workers stopped what they were doing. When a woman like Gaya Pal came into view, men were bound to look. Bea watched them watching, her forehead cool against the glass. A minute later there was a knock on the studio door.

"It's crazy out there," Gaya said as Bea let her in. She was, if anything, more breathtaking in person than in her photos. Her cheekbones were chiselled, her lips generous. In the light that came through Bea's grime-streaked window, her skin had a golden glow. "I tried to call you," she said, "to let you know I'd be late, but there was no answer."

Bea realized she was staring at Gaya's face. She ducked her head and began searching for her cell phone in her knapsack.

"Dead battery?" asked Gaya when she found it.

Bea wasn't sure the phone was even working. It was new, purchased hours after the call with Bard in the Parks. The store clerk had said it might take forty-eight hours to shut down Bea's landline and switch the number to her cell.

Gaya was studying her with liquid eyes. Bea knew she would see the scar, the slight but telling asymmetry of her face. Her stomach tensed, that old need to protect. On bad days, it felt as though nothing else about her was visible.

"May I take a look?" Gaya reached out with graceful fingers and took the device.

The contract Bea had signed was for three years. She'd been taken aback, but the clerk said thirty-six months was standard. He also said that someday no one would bother with landlines anymore.

"I see the problem," Gaya said. Her voice was melodious. Bea had heard that she was born in Mumbai to an Indian father and a Chilean mother. But she must have come to Canada as a child, because she spoke with no accent Bea could discern.

Gaya pressed a button. *"Et voilà,"* she said. She handed the phone back to Bea. A dial tone buzzed. "Step one: turn the power on." She smiled charitably.

Bea tried to press the Off button and almost dropped the phone. Gaya looked tactfully away. "And what might *this* be?" she asked, walking over to a large tube-like structure in the middle of the studio. She was evidently feeling at home. The ends of the structure were tapered. In the middle was a bulge. It was made out of papier mâché and looked vaguely like a boa constrictor digesting an antelope. Gaya squatted down and gently rolled it toward her, revealing on its underside two Sanskrit Om symbols separated by the English word SWEET.

"A yoke!" Gaya said.

Bea nodded. "Yoke" was what *yoga* meant. Or so teachers in the West taught their students. The root was actually *yuj*, which meant "unite."

For Bea, this particular yoke was fraught with significance. Jean-Christian had made it seven years ago, when they'd opened the studio. It had hung over the door ever since, supposedly blessing all who entered. The passage of time had affected it, drying it out, making it fragile, as Bea had discovered while waiting for Gaya to arrive. It had stained her hands when she took it down.

"I love the colour," said Gaya, running her fingertips over the surface. Saffron: the colour of Hindu priests and sadhus, men

who had renounced sex and the entangling energies of the second chakra. "Do you think it's fixable?"

Bea had inadvertently poked a big hole in it that morning,
exposing its chicken-wire skeleton. She shrugged. "You want it?"

"I thought that was the deal."

Bea remembered the terms they'd discussed weeks ago over
the phone: Gaya wanted everything. All Bea had to do was sign.

This was harder than Bea had imagined. She read quickly
through the contract Gaya had prepared. Gaya would take everything in the studio, all the furnishings and equipment. In return,
she would pay the three months' back rent Bea owed and free
her from all future obligations to the landlord. Gaya had already
contacted the landlord by telephone to introduce herself and let
him know she was taking over the lease as of the first of June.
There had been no objections.

"Here we go," Gaya said, signing the three copies she'd had
the foresight to print up and bring along. Everything she did was
professional and organized. Bea sighed and signed her name
below Gaya's.

"Much gratitude for this," Gaya said. She patted her breast-
bone, letting her gaze sweep the room. "Blessings to you for
offering me this amazing space." Bea could see why people liked
this woman.

She fished the keys out of her bag and was about to hand
them over when a bell rang. She and Gaya looked at each other.
It wasn't the fire alarm. The sound was much softer, a reverberating gong with a delicate tinkling in the background. Were
those wind chimes?

Gaya touched Bea's arm. "It's you, Bea. You're ringing."

Then Bea remembered. The guy at the phone store had helped
her download a ringtone: "Winds of Tibet." She pulled out her
phone and began tapping at it. The chimes wouldn't stop.

After several seconds, Gaya took it from her. She pressed Talk and raised the device to Bea's ear.

A familiar voice called out. "Bea! Thank God!"

It was her sister, Cara, speaking very loudly. Bea took the phone and held it at arm's length while she searched for volume control.

"Have you seen the news?" Cara shouted. "Didier was arrested."

Bea dialled down the volume and brought the phone to her ear again. Didier Ignace Malraux was Cara's husband, an extroverted Parisian businessman, now a Montrealer.

"Arrested?"

"At the march last night. They got Gen-vie too, and Jérémie Canton."

Gen-vie was the chef at Crudivore, the raw-food restaurant Didier and Cara owned on Rachel Street. Jérémie Canton, leader of the biggest student protest group, was a regular customer. Over the weeks of the *printemps érable,* Crudivore had become the unofficial headquarters for the movement. Bea remembered the cars she'd seen stuck on Park Avenue honking in the storm. "I saw them," she said. "Not Didier, but the march. It was on Park, right?"

"Yes," said Cara. "It got ugly."

"Are they okay?"

"They survived. They spent the night in a holding cell up on Crémazie. I just drove them home, the three of them. Didier's in the shower."

Gaya was squatting on the floor beside her, pulling an iPad out of her triangular tote bag. She peeled back the protective case and began to type. Seconds later, she lifted the screen in front of Bea. It showed a photograph from that morning's *La Presse.* Manacled, dripping with rain, Jérémie Canton and Gen-vie were being pushed into a paddy wagon by two burly officers in riot gear. Didier, also manacled, was behind them.

Gaya lowered the iPad, leaving Bea to finish her call.

"You need help?" Bea asked her sister. In the background she could hear the high-pitched cries of her nieces mixed with music from a children's TV show.

"No, no. The sitter will be here soon." She yelled at the kids to pipe down, that their daddy needed quiet. "Sorry about the noise. They laid charges against him, Bea. Obstructing justice, just because he aired his views. He might end up with a criminal record. Hang on a second . . ." There was a muffled swoosh followed by a series of high-pitched shrieks. She held the phone away from her ear.

Cara was back a moment later. "Sorry. They're reacting to all the commotion." She paused. "I'm actually not calling about Didier. It's Sol. He's not answering his telephone."

Guilt pressed on the hollow of Bea's chest. Sol: the man she'd been doing her best to avoid since her life had begun to unravel. And yet at the mention of their father's name, the studio and all her turbulent feelings about the morning's transaction with Gaya Pal seemed unimportant. "Maybe he's out," she said.

"At eight in the morning? He's usually just waking up at this hour. And he wasn't answering last night either."

"He could have been asleep."

There was static on the line: a sound like crunching termites. Cara was Sol's younger daughter, born five years after Bea. She had inherited the good looks of the blond, statuesque mother she didn't remember. And she was Sol's favourite. Like him, she had a knack for business: a combination of brains and entitlement that opened doors whenever she knocked. Like him, she had a management degree from McGill. Like him, she was funny and well-spoken. But her status as Sol's favourite predated his discovery of these shared affinities. It dated back to her birth.

"Maybe he has a lady friend," Bea said, then immediately regretted it. Cara had little patience for the women Sol occasionally brought home, dismissing them collectively as "gold diggers." But if they were digging for gold, they never found any. Three decades, and not one of them had struck a nugget. Cara didn't have to worry; Sol needed no protection when it came to managing his money.

The crunching continued. Bea's feet were bare, and she could feel grit from the unswept studio floor on her soles. She had just signed her life away. It was hard not to compare herself to her sister, co-owner of one of the trendiest restaurants in town, mother of two beautiful little girls, married to a man who adored her.

"So you don't know where he is?" Cara asked.

"No." Bea tried to remember the last time she'd spoken to Sol. It had been weeks, perhaps a month. Her father had liked Jean-Christian, recognizing in him a fellow businessman, even if the field Jean-Christian had chosen was, in Sol's mind, marginal. Sol had actually told Bea that he approved of her choice. That was a first. When she announced after Christmas that she'd left him, Sol couldn't hide his disappointment.

Cara said she had to go; the kids were getting restless. Background whines escalated to yells. Cara began to shout too, and then the connection went dead.

"All done?" Gaya was watching Bea with interest.

Bea nodded and slipped the phone, which appeared to have turned itself off automatically, into her shorts pocket. This was a historic moment, not that Gaya Pal needed to know: Bea's first conversation on the first cell phone she had ever owned.

"I couldn't help overhearing parts of that," said Gaya. She seemed suddenly warmer. "You *know* Gen-vie Roy? Personally, I mean? She's a friend of yours?"

Bea had met Gen-vie only once, at Cara and Didier's condo on Villeneuve. She was an impressive young woman. She'd finished a degree in sociology at UQAM while working full-time as a cook. She wore her hair in dreadlocks, and it looked good even though she was white-skinned and blond. She was a tad earnest, but she was only twenty-two. "She works for my brother-in-law," Bea said noncommittally.

"Didier?" Gaya's eyes widened. "What a sweet man! I love that guy. Crudivore is, like, my second home."

Bea nodded. The restaurant was certainly a hub these days. Raw food was the city's newest discovery, and Didier had become its unlikely champion. Unlikely, because before discovering the raw movement on a trip to California, he'd been a hard-core carnivore. When Bea first met him, twelve years back, his dream had been to open a French bistro on Saint-Laurent Boulevard.

"I can't believe the police arrested them. For what? Walking in the rain? It's crazy. The authorities have gone haywire." Gaya reached into her bag and pulled out a small square of red felt: the *carré rouge*, a symbol of solidarity with the protest. *"Voilà,"* she said. She pinned it to the strap of her halter top. "I forgot to put it on this morning."

Bea didn't own a red square. She felt too old, for one thing, although people of every age seemed to be wearing them. Didier had just turned forty. He and Bea were born in the same year. Yet in the newspaper photograph Gaya had just shown her, there he was, climbing into the paddy wagon behind Gen-vie and Jérémie Canton. He wasn't shy about showing solidarity with the students.

Whatever Didier was doing, it was winning him points. And not just him. Gaya was looking at Bea with admiration. She smiled back uncertainly.

4 ·

THE REHEARSAL SPACE was in a building on Young Street in a district known simply as Le Sud-Ouest. Bea was unfamiliar with the area. When she arrived by bike at nine on Thursday morning, the first day of June, men were squatting on the sidewalk outside, tossing bottle caps into a Styrofoam cup. They stopped to observe her. One of them tipped his baseball cap. The building next door seemed to be a service agency for the homeless and unemployed. A sign hung over the door with the image of a tree burnt into its wood surface.

Bea secured her ancient Rallye racer to a railing. She wondered if, despite the bike's decrepitude—she had owned it since her twelfth birthday—and the fact that it was a girl's model, it might still be considered worth stealing.

The front door was unlocked. Bea walked in and then up a steep set of ill-lit dusty stairs. Dave Samuels was waiting for her.

"You make it home okay Tuesday night?" he asked, looking her in the eye. There didn't seem to be any innuendo. She nodded. He showed her where to stow her bag and gave her the grand tour.

The second floor was divided into two rooms. The first resembled a student flat. A large table stood in the middle, mismatched chairs pushed up along its sides. Two faded carpets covered the uneven floor. Immediately to the left of the entrance was a kitchenette, whose principal feature was a large coffee percolator, the kind one might see in a church basement, plugged in and grumbling. A box of doughnuts lay open on the counter beside the percolator, filling the room with a sugary smell. "I'll show you how to make coffee when we do the next batch," Dave said. "That'll be your first job every day. The minute you arrive."

Opposite the counter was a grim-looking sink. Beneath the dish rack, a rubber drip catcher bloomed with black mould. Dave pointed to a shopping bag full of ceramic mugs sitting nearby on the floor. "Those need washing and labelling," he said. He handed Bea a roll of blue gaffer tape and an indelible marker. "There are sixteen. Enough for the cast and director. You and I can make do with the chipped ones in the cupboard."

The second room was the size of a gymnasium. The wooden floor was blackened with rot in places where the roof had leaked. Plastic pails stood waiting to catch the drips. Aside from the pails, the room was bare. This was where rehearsals would take place.

"Here's your second daily job," Dave said. He pointed at a push broom propped against the wall. "Sweeping. We also mop once a week. I'll show you where the mop and bucket are."

Bea got to work scrubbing the sink and the mouldy rubber mat. Then she washed the sixteen cups, scraping off each dollar-store price tag with her fingernails. At nine-thirty Mimi Meir came in, passing Bea without a word. Philip Burns was the next to arrive. He came over to the sink. "And how are we this fine spring day?"

Bea smiled and kept scrubbing.

"Samuels has enslaved you already, I see. I'll have a word with him."

As if on cue, Dave came in from the other room, talking in low tones with Mimi. Phil stopped him. "David, my man. Top of the morning." He gave Dave two smart pats on the cheek, then leaned in with stentorian confidentiality. "Go easy on the new help, eh?" he said, nodding at Bea. "We like her."

"We?" said Mimi.

Phil ignored the implication, or missed it. He smiled. "The royal we, sweet one. I'm a king, remember? My wish is your command."

Bea had looked Phil Burns up online. His Wikipedia entry confirmed the roles he said he'd played in Hollywood movies. He had indeed rubbed shoulders with the greats, although his parts had been relatively small. His most significant credit was *Malice*, a television series in which he'd played an irascible father and ladies' man. He was, Wikipedia said, sixty-nine years old, born in LaSalle, Quebec, now living in Manhattan. He'd been married three times and had one child.

Mimi resumed her conversation with Dave and walked away to get a doughnut, leaving Phil and Bea at the sink.

"May I?" said Phil, picking up one of the cups drying on the rack.

They weren't labelled yet. Bea started to object, but at a sound from the door Phil turned from her, grabbing a second unlabelled cup off the rack to give to the next actor to arrive. "Gregory Pym," he told her over his shoulder, "the man who plays Gloucester, one of King Lear's oldest and truest friends."

Bea hurried through the rest of the washing to prevent further plunders. The other actors were arriving. The trio of princesses— Ann, Claire and Margo—came together. Phil introduced the next two actors as they showed up. The first was Stan Garroway, who played Lear's trusty servant Kent. Then Jack DeVries, the man who'd been cast as Edmund, bastard son of Gloucester and the villain of the play, strode in with a bicycle slung over one shoulder. Bea wanted to see where he'd put it, but there was no time. She had to finish the cups and then sweep.

She was headed for the rehearsal room when Dave called her name. "Mimi wants these in the other room," he said, indicating the twenty or so mismatched chairs. "We'll be reading in the hall today."

Bea told him she hadn't swept yet, but Dave was adamant. "Chairs first."

So Bea started moving them, two by two, into the big room. Phil Burns helped, and then Jack DeVries joined in. His bicycle was nowhere in evidence.

By the time Mimi walked in, the chairs were arranged in a large circle in the centre.

She frowned. "They're too close. Push them back a bit."

Phil folded his arms. "We'll be too far from each other, Mimi darling. You'll make us all shout."

Mimi didn't even look at him. "We're going to stand first," she said, "in front of the chairs. Trust me, you'll need the space." She was wearing mauve again, this time a sleeveless top that showed off surprisingly well-defined biceps. It was hard to tell how old she was. Bea guessed over fifty, but her arms gave nothing away.

Phil helped Bea rearrange the chairs. The room was stifling. Bea had chosen to wear a long-sleeved blouse, which she regretted. She was now perspiring freely. As she and Phil worked, Dave entered the rehearsal room with the rest of the cast. Mimi gave him a curt nod and told everyone to hold hands.

Phil made a squeamish face. Then he stepped between Margo Indongo, who was playing Cordelia, and Artie White, his Fool. "Kindergarten," he stage-whispered into Margo's ear. She smiled, but also stepped back reflexively. She had to advance again in order to take his hand. Stan Garroway, fiftysomething and trying hard not to look it in jeans and a canary yellow polo, took the hand of tall, blond Jay O'Breen, Bea's former yoga student. Jay was playing Edgar, Gloucester's legitimate son and heir, the play's youthful hero.

The circle broke near Mimi. It was as if some force were holding the actors back. Mimi gestured impatiently at Ann O'Neill and Claire Johnson—Goneril and Regan—who moved in on each side of her and closed the circle.

"And you two?" said Phil, lifting his chin at Bea and Dave, who were watching from the sidelines. He dropped Artie's hand and reached out to Bea. "Come, my lovely. You're part of this mad undertaking."

He said this with such authority that Bea didn't hesitate. She skipped forward and took his big hand and Artie's smaller one. Only then did she notice that Dave hadn't followed. His eyes were on the director.

Mimi did not look happy. Bea realized that Phil's invitation was a breach of protocol: he had publicly undermined the director's authority and, no less important, encouraged the technical and creative sides of the production to mix. Stage managers and their assistants were not entitled to join in with the cast's ritual hand-holding, it appeared. Bea's heart began to thump. To step back out of the circle would make things worse. Mimi solved the problem by nodding at Dave. He joined in and Mimi directed them all to shut their eyes and inhale. With relief, Bea complied.

"I want each of you to formulate an intention for the show," Mimi said. "Something you want to achieve both in your own life and also for the community."

Mimi's voice was lovely. She enunciated clearly, and there was that musical lilt: Southern belle meets suave Parisienne. Even after Bea opened her eyes, she could hear it. She liked Mimi. And the circle of breathing bodies reminded her of yoga class. Mimi asked them all to place, with their minds, their intentions in the centre of the ring.

Bea wished for success. Was Phil right when he'd said this was a mad undertaking? She hoped with all her heart that things would work out—for her, for Mimi, for the rest of them. In the hush of the room, the only sound was the distant plinking of the kitchen faucet. Bea hadn't been able to turn it off properly. Her mind hovered over the sink for a second before returning to her breath, and then it was done. One by one, the men and women in the circle dropped the hands of those on either side of them. Phil squeezed hers lightly before letting go.

Mimi instructed them each to step forward into the empty space inside the circle. And there, eyes level and chins raised, they pronounced their names. The actors did this with gusto, each in his or her own particular style. Bea could barely listen. For her, the task wasn't so simple. Perhaps this was why Mimi had wanted to keep her out. She wasn't an actor. She had hated speaking in public since childhood. She stared straight ahead as she waited for her turn, avoiding Artie's gaze. He had known her back then. Seconds ticked by. Then, after Phil had announced himself with trumpets, he gave her a nudge with his elbow. She stepped forward.

"Beatrice Rose." It was barely a whisper, but the room was so hushed it still resonated. When she stepped back into the safety of the circle, Artie smiled at her.

A few minutes later, after the naming ritual had ended and the actors were sitting down for the first read-through, Bea and Dave went back to the sidelines. She felt oddly jubilant, as if she'd passed some sort of test. She followed Dave to a work station he'd set up for them at the front of the room near the door. Two little school desks side by side. On the desks were ring binders containing scripts—his and hers. Next to one binder was a cup of freshly sharpened pencils and a yellow plastic pencil case, the kind kids used in primary school.

Dave sat down and unzipped the case. He pulled out wads of fluorescent Post-its, handed several to Bea, and began marking off scenes in his copy of the script with bright orange tabs. Bea chose pink. Talking was prohibited, so Dave couldn't tell her what to do. She had to learn by imitation.

Mimi Meir was addressing the actors. *Lear* was a masterpiece, she said, the jewel of the Shakespeare canon. The dramatic structure was pure brilliance, an architecture of symmetries and repetitions. And the themes of aging and parent–child dynamics were as relevant today as they had been in Shakespeare's England. *Lear* was one of the most poignant renderings of old age in all of literature. Mimi's hands beat the air like a bird's wings. Her voice was passionate, her pale face radiant, transformed.

Dave placed something on the script in front of Bea. An orange Post-it folded several times over. She opened it and saw his loopy, childish scrawl. "Watch out for Phil Burns." The writing continued on the other side; Bea turned it over. "He likes you." Dave was already scribbling out another orange note. "Careful not to step on toes of his ex."

Bea reread the last, truncated word, and looked up, confused.

Dave scribbled out a third note, fingertips white with pressure. He wrote like a little kid, like someone in grade school. "You mean you didn't know?"

When the expression of confusion failed to leave her face, he snatched the orange slip back from her and scribbled more words. "Mimi = Phil's ex-wife."

Bea's gaze lifted off the strip of orange fluorescence with its incendiary equation, and travelled across the room to Mimi, who was still expounding. She was an attractive woman; there was no disputing that fact even now. Back in the day, she would have been a knockout. Bea's glance shifted to Phil, who didn't appear the least bit interested in what Mimi was saying. His head was bent and his eyes were wandering sideways to Margo Indongo's hands, which she'd folded on her lap. With a stab, Bea remembered the soggy handkerchief and his hands patting her own lap at the party, just as Mimi had walked by. She recalled how he called drunkenly to her before she took him home. *Home*, she thought, a chill setting in as she remembered the woman's raincoat hanging from the coat rack, the umbrella with the duck's head. It must have been Mimi's flat.

Mimi would have been the one to leave him, not the other way round, Bea suspected. And what was their relationship now? Mimi must have invited him up for the summer, which explained why an actor of his calibre was playing Lear in a bunch of Montreal parks. It also meant that their relationship was still functional on some level. Bea doubted they were trying to reignite it, given how he'd pursued her so openly at the party. But anything was possible.

"Thank you," she finally wrote on a pink Post-it. She'd be more prudent from now on. Phil Burns would be handled with lead gloves.

Mimi told everyone to take ten minutes and fill their water bottles; the real fun was about to begin. They were going to go through the play from start to finish, with one short break.

When at last they got down to it, Bea was still thinking about her blunder. She needed to mend things with Mimi. Dave wasn't paying the actors much attention either. He was bent over his script, scrupulously pasting in his Post-its and labelling the tops and tails of scenes. Bea was too agitated to look at her own script, not that she knew exactly what the labelling was for. Backstage drama had eclipsed Shakespeare.

A few feet away from Bea, Margo Indongo stood up suddenly from her chair, seizing her attention. The first scene, which had gone by largely without Bea's being aware of it, was reaching its climax. Youngest daughter Cordelia was being disinherited. Silence descended on the room. Phil Burns stood up too. He threw down his script and kicked his chair away.

"Better thou had'st not been born," he said, looking into Margo's eyes, "than not t'have pleased me better."

Even Dave had stopped pasting and raised his head. Time faltered. Bea held her breath. In the stillness, she could feel her neck pulsing.

And then her phone rang. She didn't recognize the sound immediately, the gong and tinkly wind chimes she'd selected with the help of the guy at the store. Dave's head periscoped to the left. The actors turned too. Only after the second ring did Bea realize that the sound was connected to her.

She jumped up and pulled the phone out of her pocket, inadvertently hitting Talk.

A loud voice filled the room. "Bea?"

Bea couldn't react. Her fingers, weirdly, refused to move.

"Bea?" Cara's voice shouted from the device. "Are you there?"

Dave brought his hand to his ear to prompt her and the spell broke. She cupped her hands around the phone. "I can't talk," she whispered hoarsely. She handed the phone to Dave, who switched it off and placed it safely on the desk in front of him, as if she were a student caught playing with it at school. Bea resumed her seat and the actors turned back to Mimi, who was delivering a pointed little speech about electronic devices. Jack DeVries took out his phone and checked it. Ann O'Neill did the same.

Calm was restored, and after a minute or so the reading resumed.

At the break, Bea apologized to Dave. She wanted to apologize to Mimi too, but he vetoed the idea. "I wouldn't try that right now," he said, making a face. He took Bea's phone and reviewed the functions with her: how to put it on vibrate and on mute, how to hang up after a call. The guy at the store hadn't done this; he must have assumed everyone knew such basics. She felt like a child standing there with Dave, but she was grateful. He truly was a mother, even to the woman who was supposed to be helping him run the show. He pointed to a fire door at the far end of the room. "That's where you go when you need to talk."

She thanked him and went to investigate. The flat tar-and-gravel roof of the car wash next door was where smokers—a category to which most of the cast seemed to belong—assembled at break time. It was also where they checked their phone messages and made calls. Bea walked past the boisterous gang to a quiet corner. The heat was as oppressive as it was inside. After weeks of rain, June had brought sunshine to the city. To the north, Mount Royal shimmered. On the surrounding roofs, bitumen sparkled in the sun's glare.

A tangle of bikes leaned against a towering brick chimney in the roof's centre. Bea's thoughts went to her own bicycle, fastened to a pole down in the street. She looked over the side of the building, trying to locate where she'd parked it, but saw no familiar landmarks. So she went around the chimney, out of the others' sight, and practically collided with Mimi, who was hunching over her phone. Her face was unguarded, as was her voice; the drawl was more pronounced than ever. "Hang in there, honey," she told whoever was on the other end. "And remember, ah love you."

She reddened when she saw Bea.

"I'm so sorry," Bea said, but Mimi just waved her hand.

"No problem. I'm done." The vowels had turned hard again, more clipped and Canadian. She began to walk away.

Bea tried to stop her to apologize for the disruption in the rehearsal room, but Mimi's feet kept walking. "History," she said, her eyes not touching Bea's.

Bea squatted and tried to breathe. Then she dialled Cara's

number, twice—the first time getting it wrong. She was rattled and unaccustomed to the little touch screen. Her sister's phone rang many times before there was an answer.

"Never do that again." Cara's voice was flat with rage.

The sun was giving Bea a headache. Underfoot, the roof tar was gooey. "Sorry," she said.

There was a brief silence. "What were you up to that was so important you couldn't talk to me?" A siren wailed in the background. Cara was evidently outdoors too.

Without waiting for Bea to answer, Cara broke her news. "I found Dad."

He was in the emergency ward of the Samuel Rabinovitch Hospital. He'd been picked up on Park Avenue during Tuesday night's storm, bareheaded in the rain. "Somehow he got swept up in the march."

"With the *casseroles*?" Bea couldn't quite imagine it. Their father thought the students were crazy. He called them hooligans. "Is he all right?"

"He's conscious, at least. He wasn't when they found him. They think maybe he had a fall. It's all a mystery, because he couldn't tell them what happened. He couldn't even say his name, apparently. He wasn't carrying ID. That's why it took so long to track him down. He's awake now, but he's still confused."

Bea tried to picture it. "I don't understand. He walked over the mountain to join the protest?"

"He drove. They found the car abandoned in the middle of Park Avenue. It was only when I called the police looking for him that they linked the old man they'd taken in with the Range Rover. He just left it there. Can you imagine? His jacket was in the back with his wallet inside. It's a miracle no one took it."

Bea remembered the gridlocked cars on Park the night of the party. He must have been stuck in traffic and climbed out to investigate. Or to berate the hooligans. But that raised another question. "What was he doing out? Was he on his way to see you?"

"Are you kidding?" said Cara. "You know how he feels about this part of town." The sisters fell silent. Sol had taken it as a personal affront when first one, then the other of his daughters had moved east to the Plateau Mont-Royal. Had he really sweated all those years just so they could move back to the ghetto of his youth? It did no good explaining that the Plateau was now one of Montreal's trendiest neighbourhoods, or that the house prices rivalled Westmount's. Sol didn't want to hear it.

"Something weird has been going on with him," said Cara after a moment. Her tone was reluctant, as if she wasn't sure she should confide in Bea. "He's been coming by Crudivore. I don't mean for lunch, which he's done a couple of times, although he always complains about the food." She paused. "I mean late, after dark. It's happened twice now—well, twice that we're aware of. He hasn't come inside, just skulked around on Rachel Street, looking in the windows. One time he went around to the back, into the alley. Gen-vie caught him. He didn't say hello to her, even though he knows perfectly well who she is. He walked away without a word when she approached him. She was a bit spooked. She said that if she hadn't recognized him she would have called the cops."

"Maybe he was looking for you."

"Then why not call me, or come by the condo? I'm home with the kids every evening. He knows that. Anyway," she added, "whatever he was up to Tuesday night, he's been found. That's the main thing. He's safe." She paused again. "Although now he keeps talking about angels."

"Angels?"

"You have to see him, Bea. He's not himself."

For a moment, all Bea heard was heavy breathing. Then Cara said, "Sorry. The light was about to turn red. I'm up here now on Côte-des-Neiges. I've just come from him. How fast can you get over here? I've got to go and pick up the girls."

Sun-warmed tar was sticking to the soles of Bea's sandals. Every time she moved, it sucked at her.

"He can't speak to the doctors, Bea. He needs an advocate."

Bea was facing the chimney. Its bricks were ancient and porous. "I can't," she said.

"What?"

"I can't." Bea looked down at her toes. "I'm at work."

She told Cara that she had a new job and her number was linked to a cell phone now, not her old landline. It all sounded lame and frivolous compared to Cara's grown-up responsibilities: the kids, the restaurant, the search for Sol, whose trouble Cara had intuitively sensed in the first place. Cara was the super-daughter. The competent one. Bea couldn't even operate a cell phone.

The sun was hammering at her, singeing her scalp. The only shade was a sliver of darkness at the base of the chimney, where her toes were. Bea noticed suddenly how quiet it was. She looked around. The actors had disappeared. All that remained was a collection of cigarette butts on the flashing of the roof.

Dave Samuels appeared in the doorway and waved.

Cara, meanwhile, was being meaningfully silent, trying to guilt her into taking some responsibility. "I've got to go," Bea said. "I'll stop at the hospital tonight after work. I promise."

Dave gave her a last wave and retreated inside, shaking his black curls. Bea pocketed her phone and hurried after him. She couldn't leave in the middle of her first day of work. Her father was safe in the hands of doctors, in a hospital he trusted. In her hurry to get back inside, she slammed the door. The sharp sound startled everyone. At least they hadn't started reading again. Mimi would definitely not have appreciated that.

The reading ended at two-thirty, at which point Mimi went around the circle asking the actors to describe their characters and their primary motivations. The talking seemed to go on and on. Bea was past the point of listening. All she could think about was Sol and the minutes that stood between her and her bike. A packet of pink stickers sat on her desk waiting to be pasted into her script at the tops and tails of scenes, just like Dave had done, but she couldn't even look at them. Dave had finished with his script. He was chewing gum, looking up something on his phone and ignoring her, unaware of her real-life domestic drama. She could smell the gum's synthetic fruity fragrance layered over the onion whiff of his sweat.

When Mimi and the actors finally left at five, Bea told Dave about her father's situation. They still had a number of things to do, he said, including cleaning the single toilet that sixteen actors plus the director and two stage managers had used continually throughout the long first day of rehearsal. They'd all be back the next day by twelve noon sharp. He agreed to do the lion's share, but even so, when Bea finally got out onto the street, it was past seven. To her relief, her bike was just where she'd locked it. The pockets on the nylon carrier case had been unzipped, though, and her front and back lights were gone.

Above her, the sky was pale. The light would last another two hours, enough for her to get to the hospital. From there she could take the well-lit bike path along Côte-Sainte-Catherine Road to her home in the Plateau. Tomorrow she'd have to buy a new set of lights. Another expense, but a necessary one. She had a feeling she'd be cycling in the dark a lot this summer.

———

It took half an hour of hard uphill pedalling to reach the sprawling brown brick hospital on Côte-des-Neiges Road. Bea arrived sweaty and out of breath. There was no bike rack to be seen, so she attached her bicycle to a lamppost on a street corner.

The emergency ward was in the basement at the far end of the building. Bea navigated through twisting corridors, passing lines of overflowing laundry bins as she followed signs marked URGENCES above an arrow.

A crowd of people sat on straight-backed, uncomfortable-looking chairs in the triage zone. Some had bandaged limbs, others had less obvious complaints, but every face was greenish and miserable in the neon light. A plump, pretty girl in an over-tight T-shirt sat behind a Plexiglas partition at the reception counter. Bea knocked on it and asked for Solomon Rose. After the girl typed in his name, she gave Bea a cubicle number.

Bea was able to go through the big double doors directly into the ward itself. Beds lined both sides of the corridor. Many patients were already in blue hospital gowns, hooked to IVs. Most had relatives watching over them. *Family*. Their eyes met Bea's, curiosity flickering and dying as she continued on her way.

Things improved when she turned the corner. Before her was a large, windowless room with a human hive in the centre. Young people—nurses in candy-coloured outfits and doctors in white coats—swirled through it. The patients were out of sight behind curtains in cubicles that radiated in spokes from the hub.

Bea made her way to the cubicle number given to her by the receptionist. Her father's curtains were closed, but those of the patient to his right were open. An alert grey-haired man in his sixties with a large mole on his nose was lying in bed, speaking Italian to a woman of roughly the same age. A younger man was stowing clothes in a tray beneath the bed. All three turned as Bea hurried past them with an apologetic nod and pulled back the curtains on what she hoped would be her father.

He was on his side, curled in a fetal ball. His appearance was shocking. He had never been a large man, but lying there on the mechanical bed, clutching his hospital flannels in skinny fists, he looked like a shrunken caricature. Bea felt an urge to gather him in her arms and carry him away.

The neighbouring family of three was regarding her with hostility, as though she'd done something wrong, broken some command-ment: the unwritten one, perhaps stronger in some communities than in others, which holds that thou shalt not let thine aging, defenceless parent lie alone in an emergency ward all day. Bea stepped into Sol's cubicle and closed the flaps behind her.

Her father was asleep, emitting a soft *pahh* with each breath. She bent over him. His hair blended perfectly with the pillow-case, making him look bald. His eyelids were veined and quiver-ing. She'd barely seen him since Christmas, when Jean-Christian had left for India on his double air ticket. Sol had been so dis-appointed when he hadn't attended the family's annual winter brunch, as if somehow the failure was entirely hers. Now she regretted her own decision to stay away. How could this poor old man instill dread in anyone?

The eyelids kept quivering. Bea wondered what he was dream-ing. She became keenly aware of her own fatigue. It was late. She kissed her finger and laid it on his lip, realizing only as she touched him that she should have washed her hands.

He used to do this with her. It had been their ritual. The father's touch, followed by the extinguishing of the light. There was comfort in it, though as Bea grew older she'd wondered, Why not a plain old kiss? He'd kissed Cara, but with Cara he'd had to be a mother and father both.

Her father puffed again—*pahh*—and rolled onto his back. His lips widened into an enigmatic smile. A blue shadow showed beneath his left cheekbone. Other than that, there were no bruises or other signs of trauma. At least none that she could see. His sleep seemed sweet and serene.

Bea left the hospital soon afterward. She cycled back to the Plateau along Côte-Sainte-Catherine, as she'd planned. Dusk had fallen, bringing a slight respite from the day's heat. The road was illuminated by arched streetlights instead of a brutal, burning sun, and the insects were out. They collided with her in confusion, bouncing off her face and chest. Her mind went back to the Italian family in the cubicle next to Sol's, their disapproving looks, as though they'd sensed the difficulty of her kinship with her father. She pictured his poor shrunken face, the thin fists grasping his hospital smock like a baby. Through it all, her bicycle wheels kept turning, turning, like the ceaseless wheel of samsara, carrying her forward into the night.

5.

IN THE GLIMMER of the Christmas lights, Bea could just make out the black minute hand of the kitchen clock slicing a puffy white cloud. It was four in the morning. She was standing naked at the sink, waiting for two tiny sugar pellets to dissolve in her mouth. They felt like pebbles against the underbelly of her tongue. You had to dissolve them sublingually, for some reason, to get the full effect.

Four o'clock: an ultrasensitive hour, when the slightest sound might wake her up. The homeopath she occasionally went to said she was suffering from exhausted adrenal glands, a condition that afflicted many women in their forties, especially high-powered women with stressful lives. Bea wasn't forty yet, and she certainly wasn't high-powered. She suspected her insomnia was inherited. For as long as she could remember, Sol had had trouble with sleep. And who wouldn't have slept badly after the day she'd just had? Seeing Sol so shrunken and vulnerable at the hospital; the blunder with her cell phone in the rehearsal room; the director who wouldn't look her in the eye.

The coffea 200-strength pills prescribed by the homeopath came in a tiny cylindrical glass vial. They were so small that one could easily doubt they had any effect at all. Her father scoffed at any profession that ended in "path." Osteopath, naturopath, homeopath, all were the same, as far as he was concerned: char-latans, relieving the gullible of their hard-earned cash but never of their ailments. And yet, for Bea, homeopathy worked. Coffea often coaxed her back to sleep, and aconite reliably warded off head colds. She wiggled her tongue, rolling the pills in the saliva accumulating behind her teeth.

The white Christmas lights looked like puja flames on the Ganges. When she was living in Rishikesh she'd watched villagers gather on the banks of the river every evening as the sun was setting to send candles out into the waters on floating bowls. She'd loved this nightly ritual, the little flames blinking bravely in the dark. Jean-Christian loved it too. They had reminisced about it last November as they looped wire strands along their kitchen shelves in an attempt to brighten the room. It had turned out to be one of the last acts they would perform as a couple. A month later, Jean-Christian was gone.

Bea rubbed her eyes. The sugar pellets had dissolved, leaving a film on her teeth and gums. She rinsed her mouth with water from the faucet and wiped her lips on her arm. The air felt stag-nant. Molecules saturated with the night's heat seemed to be bouncing in slow motion off her skin.

In the flat across the way, a light went on in the kitchen. Bea crouched, shielding her breasts because the Christmas lights gave off enough of a glow to make her visible. She crept to her balcony door and positioned herself out of her neighbour's sight-line. Her neighbour was a small, hairy, middle-aged man. He entered his kitchen in his pyjama bottoms and walked to the sink to pour himself a glass of water. Civilized. His private parts cov-ered. No slurping from the faucet. Yet he too was on the prowl. She'd seen him up at this hour before.

Bea waited until his kitchen light went off and then returned to her bed, fumbling blindly down the pitch-black corridor.

Hours later, a cry broke through the layers of sleep. She sat up and looked around. She'd been dreaming of her father. He'd been right here on Sainte-Famille Street, a place he hadn't visited once in the seven years she'd lived here.

In the dream, Sol had been lying beside her on the futon. Bea stared at her sheets. Stray hairs and crumbs were visible in the unforgiving light of the new day. His eyes had been shut. He had nuzzled her like an infant trying to suckle. She had been naked, as she was now, but somehow, in the transgressive logic of dreams, that hadn't been an issue.

The cry came again. Only it wasn't a cry. It was the sound of wind chimes. She looked on the floor, and there, beside the futon, was the little device that had become her tormentor.

The moment she pressed Talk, Cara's voice assailed her. She was at the hospital. Their father was in crisis. Sol had awoken at four that morning, completely disoriented and demanding his car keys. When the nurse told him what time it was and suggested he go back to sleep he'd started to shout, rousing the patients around him. He had to be sedated.

Bea was wide awake now, although her brain still felt a bit slow. She sat up and planted both feet on the floor. The sun was already high above the roof of the apartment block across the street, glowing white hot in a dull grey sky. Beside her, the digital alarm clock displayed a row of four red lines. It took her a second to process the image: it was eleven minutes past eleven.

She jumped off her futon and began searching for clothes, holding the phone to her ear as Cara went on talking. Sol had been under sedation when Bea had looked in on him the night before. That was why he'd seemed so peaceful. He kept waking up raving and the hospital staff kept feeding him medication. By four o'clock that morning the meds had worn off again. He'd woken up confused and caused a code white, Cara said, which meant a patient was turning violent.

Bea thought of her own four a.m. insomnia: perhaps Sol had been trying to summon her. Then she thought of the Italian family in the neighbouring cubicle. Of course they'd been hostile. They had surely witnessed his unhinged condition right up close. They were bound to be suspicious of him and—for all they knew—his crazy daughter.

"He's got to have someone there," Cara said in the take-charge voice she sometimes adopted with children and employees. "At all times. Someone he knows. Otherwise it's total chaos."

The good news was that he now had his own room.

"Squeaky wheel," said Cara. After fifty-four hours in Emergency, he'd been moved to the geriatrics floor. A private room.

Bea found her underpants and tried to step into them while holding the phone. The little white pills, or her sister's call, had affected her balance. She tumbled sideways onto the futon, still clutching the phone to her ear.

"Bea?"

"Sorry."

"What are you doing? You're out of breath."

"It's nothing. I'm fine."

Cara lowered her voice. "You've got to get down here, Bea. I can't do this alone. Didier and Gen-vie are at the lawyer's office, so I have to supervise things at Crudivore."

The sunlight coming through the window lit up Bea's legs. They were pale, flecked with dark hairs. Her panties were around her calves like a hobble. She yanked them up.

"I can't," she said.

The clock read eleven sixteen. Bea had approximately forty minutes to get dressed and bike to the rehearsal room on Young Street. "I'm working today," she said. "The new job, remember?"

"They can't replace you? There must be other yoga teachers around."

"It's not yoga." She explained about Bard in the Parks.

"The Shakespeare thing?" Cara asked. "What, you're an actor now?"

"Stage manager." She didn't have the courage to specify that she was only a lowly assistant.

"You've got to be joking. They're all kids, aren't they? What are they paying you?"

Bea saw herself suddenly through Cara's eyes. It wasn't a dream job. She was doing menial work for a small summer theatre company and being paid next to nothing. The artistry, the nobility of the enterprise—the things that had briefly seemed so appealing—were the delusions of a lonely woman on the cusp of forty. She had jumped into the job blind. Worse than blind. With eyes wilfully shut. She'd been surprised that the company would gamble on an untrained outsider. But there was a reason why Bard in the Parks had hired her. As usual, she hadn't thought it through. The company was only a notch above amateur, as Cara now lost no time in pointing out. They were kids—Cara was right—fresh out of theatre school or, in the case of Jay O'Breen and Margo Indongo, not yet even graduates. Their shows were free of charge. Their financing came from government grants and the passing of a hat.

"I have to go," said Bea. She'd been pressing the phone to her face so hard that her cheek hurt. She felt awful. "I can visit him tomorrow."

She closed her eyes, imagining her sister's infuriated expression. Tomorrow was her first official day off. Bea opened her eyes again and squinted into the sunshine. "Cara?" There was no answer.

# 6.

THE SAMUEL RABINOVITCH HOSPITAL, an impressive brick-built complex stretching the length of a city block, stood in the heart of the Côte-des-Neiges district. For years, Sol Rose had sat on its board of directors. He'd been a generous donor. His name was inscribed on a plaque near the entrance, a plaque crowded with the names of Jews like himself who'd done well in Canada and made a point of giving back. He must have insisted that the ambulance bring him here—there were several hospitals closer to Park Avenue, where he'd been found. He'd had no memory of who he was, no ID to serve as a clue, but somehow he'd had the wits to insist on the Samuel Rabinovitch Hospital.

The initial theory was that he'd been beaten up and robbed. His cheek was bruised and he had no wallet. When the officers reached the scene, they found him wet and moaning, drifting in and out of consciousness, shivering with cold. He couldn't say what he'd been doing on Park Avenue in the downpour. He couldn't give a coherent answer to any question they asked. Despite his age, everyone assumed he was a protester. He did not mention the Range Rover, abandoned several hundred metres up the road.

The geriatrics ward was on a quiet upper floor of the hospital. The walls were a soothing custard colour, the corridor utterly still. The only noise was a whispered conversation between two nurses at a desk near the elevators. It was so quiet that when Bea stopped to ask for directions to Sol's room she could hear the scratching of the nurse's ballpoint pen. She could have been in a library or an empty church. No beds lined the halls here. Whatever misery existed was kept hidden behind closed doors.

Sol was crouching on the floor beside his bed when Bea walked in. Through the gap in his loosely knotted hospital gown his backside peeked out. He turned to face her, glaring. "They're gone."

Bea tried to smile. She had no idea what he was talking about, but at least he wasn't raving.

"They were here," he said, getting to his feet. He pointed under the bed. "There was a shelf." He bent again, displaying withered buttocks and shockingly thin legs.

Bea tried not to stare. Guilt flushed through her. In the months she'd spent avoiding him, her seventy-nine-year-old father, steadfast pillar of the community, appeared to have cracked.

"There's no shelf here," she said, crouching down beside him to investigate the bed's underside herself.

"There was one. That's where they put them. I'm sure of it."

"Put what?"

He looked at her with scorn. "My clothes," he said, as though it were obvious.

Suddenly she understood. "That was in Emergency. The beds there are on wheels." She pictured the econo-size orange garbage bag that someone, Cara most probably, had stuffed with his belongings and stowed in the space for that purpose under the bed.

He gave her a strange look, his forehead creasing with mistrust. Then he straightened up and started to shout, accusing the doctors and nurses of stealing, of keeping him here against his will. Accusing Bea of helping them, jabbing a finger at her, waving spindly arms.

She began to panic. "Look," she said, stepping around him and pointing at a metal locker in the corner. "That looks like a place for hanging clothes. Let's see if they're in there." She walked over to it theatrically, taking long deliberate strides that she hoped would distract him and defuse his energy. The yelling stopped, but when she opened the locker it was empty.

"I've been robbed," Sol said calmly. Then his arms started waving again. "Call the authorities!"

"I'll find the nurse," said Bea. She wasn't entirely sure Sol recognized her. He hadn't addressed her by name or said anything to indicate he knew her. And although he wasn't raving, he certainly wasn't in a normal state. She walked quickly out of the room and into the corridor. It felt good to put some distance between herself and her father, to collect her scattered emotions. The corridor was as deserted as ever. At the nursing station a young man had joined the nurses. He was standing in a back cubicle bending over one of them as she sat at the computer. Both of them were laughing. They looked like high school students collaborating on a project. They saw Bea and turned toward her, still enjoying their joke.

The eyes of the child-doctor widened. "Bea!"

She stood there for a moment, trying to place him. He approached her, grinning and holding out his hand. "Om Sweet Om," he said cheerfully.

She remembered him now—the warm, wide smile. A few years ago he'd taken her Sunday morning beginner's class. His hamstrings had been so tight his fingers could barely reach his knees, but that wasn't the main reason he was there. He was in medical school at the time, and was trying to reduce his stress.

"Michel," he said, as they shook hands. The tag on his chest displayed his last name: Allaire. He turned to the two young nurses who were watching them. "Bea turns people into pretzels."

"I teach yoga," Bea explained, realizing as she spoke that the words were no longer true.

Michel was smiling. "I loved that class, although the only pose I was halfway good at was the one where you lie on your back and go to sleep."

The nurse at the computer laughed. "The corpse?"

Michel looked at Bea with a frown. "You had another name for it."

"*Savasana,*" said Bea. "But she's right. In English, it's the corpse pose.'"

The young doctor smiled wryly. Bea remembered how sweet he'd been in class, despite the stiffness of his legs and lumbar region. He asked what she was doing on the ward.

"My father." When she told him the room number, he and the nurses exchanged a glance. Bea asked them about the missing clothes.

Michel Allaire retreated behind the reception desk and pulled an orange plastic bag out of a large drawer. He handed it to her. "Take out whatever he needs."

"I thought I'd bring him the whole thing."

"Not a good idea," said the nurse in the cubicle.

"He'll split," Michel explained. "He's already tried twice today, even without his clothes. He's not our most contented customer."

Bea left the bag at the nursing station and returned to her father's room with Michel, who brought along a clipboard. He was, he told her, a specialist in geriatric psychiatry.

He rapped sharply on the door before pushing it all the way open. "Good morning, Mr. Rose. How are you today?"

Sol didn't answer. He was back in his bed, which had been cranked up like a chair. His flannel top sheet was thrown back and his hospital gown had ridden up. His legs were hairless and twig-like. The toenails were so long they curled.

Michel Allaire didn't seem troubled by Sol's appearance, or by his failure to respond. He entered the room, motioning for Bea to do the same. Then he introduced himself and asked if he could take Sol's history.

Sol frowned. "I don't need that. What I need," he said slowly, as if addressing a child or a person with an intellectual deficiency, "are my clothes."

"I'm afraid I can't help you with that," Michel said. "I know the gown isn't very fashionable, but the rule is, you have to wear it during your stay."

Sol's jaw clenched. "My stay is done." He cocked his head at Bea, who was hovering silently by the bed. "She's come to take me home."

Michel smiled. "Soon, Mr. Rose," he said. "Very soon. But not quite yet, I'm afraid." He spoke in soothing tones, paying no heed to the signs of Sol's growing fury. "We have more tests to do. Nothing complicated, but they'll help us figure things out so we can help you."

Sol grabbed at the bedside table and upended it. Bea jumped back, narrowly avoiding being crushed as it fell to the floor with a crash. She bent down and tried to right it. The thing was on casters, so heavy at its base that even when Michel leaned in to give her a hand, it was a challenge.

"You're a strong man," Michel observed brightly. "How did you do that, Mr. Rose?"

Bea regarded her father with amazement. He *was* strong. And also dangerous. The table was upright now, but as Michel stooped to pick up a box of tissues from the floor, Sol swung himself off the bed and tried to knock it over again, this time onto the young doctor's back. Bea let out a cry.

"Easy," said Michel, turning to face him. Although he was young, he wasn't agile. No match, it seemed, for the obstreperous old man. "Please, Mr. Rose," he said. "I've got to do my job."

This logic seemed to touch Sol, or perhaps it was the young man's saintly patience and good humour. Whatever the reason, he allowed Michel Allaire to seat him in a chair. And Bea allowed herself to exhale.

"This won't take long." Michel pulled one of the visitor's chairs forward for himself and laid his clipboard on his lap. "I need to ask you some questions, and then we'll do a quick test. Nothing too complicated. For a man of your intelligence, this should be easy. If you cooperate, you'll be out of here in no time."

Before Sol could object, Michel fired off his first question. "Do you remember the storm last Tuesday?"

Sol crossed his arms. His lips were pursed with mistrust.

"Mr. Rose?" said Michel. "Do you remember why you took the car out that night? Where were you off to?" He checked his papers. "Were you trying to go and visit someone? Your daughter, perhaps?" He smiled at Bea, fiddling with his plastic ballpoint. It bore teeth marks on its end and had only a little ink left in its transparent body. "There was a storm warning that night. What made you go out in your car? Had you not heard the warning on the news?"

Sol's lips remained pursed. His beard was unkempt. Bea could see breakfast crumbs in it. He scowled at the young doctor, but the scowl could have been a cover for confusion.

"Mr. Rose?"

Sol waved a dismissive hand. "Of course I remember. I went out, that's all. For a drive." He smoothed his gown on his knees. "Now you answer me something, Doctor whatever your name is. You're not English, I take it."

Michel explained that he was from Abitibi, in northern Quebec. He had grown up speaking French.

"You know this is a Jewish hospital," Sol said, looking directly at him.

Bea reddened, but Michel didn't register any resentment at the implicit slur. "It was founded by the Jewish community," he said amiably, "but its doors have always been open to everyone. We have patients and staff here from lots of different backgrounds. That was the institution's mission from the start."

"The Jewish doctors were kicked out of the French hospitals. They weren't allowed to sit on the boards. The English hospitals weren't a whole lot better. That's why we founded this one. So Jewish doctors could practise their profession. I know," said Sol, sitting straighter. "I grew up with them."

"And where was that?" asked Michel.

Sol closed his mouth resolutely. Bea recognized that stubborn look. She turned to Michel and provided the answer. "In a row-house on Saint-Urbain." The place was still standing. She didn't mention what an eyesore it was, a shabby structure that surprised her with its dark ugliness every time she passed it.

Michel paused for a moment, thinking. "Were you going back there the night of the storm?" he asked, watching Sol closely. "Do you go visit sometimes?"

Sol scowled.

"Maybe it was the march," said Bea. This was what Cara had suggested. "My sister's husband was there. He's part of that whole movement. He goes every night." She turned to Sol. "Was it Didier you were going to see, Dad?"

Her father didn't move.

"So you wanted to see your son-in-law, Mr. Rose? Was that why you went out?"

Sol closed his eyes as if trying to shut out the whole interrogation.

Michel softened. "It's okay if you don't want to talk," he said quietly. "No one is going to force you. I'm just trying to piece it together. This whole thing is a bit of a mystery."

To Bea's surprise, Sol opened his eyes and leaned forward confidentially in his armchair. "You know the angel?" he said.

Michel looked unsure for a second. "You mean the Cartier Monument? The one on Park Avenue?"

Sol shook his head. It was hard to tell if he was disagreeing with the doctor, or trying to dispel painful thoughts. "Did you see what they did to her?" he whispered. His head was no longer shaking. His fists were clenched. "Criminals," he said. "That's what they are, despite all the trappings. It's an outrage."

Bea searched his face. Was this the raving Cara had spoken of? Was their father having visions? She put a hand on his arm. "Dad, what—" She never finished the sentence. He glared at her with such distain that she didn't dare.

Michel jumped in and rescued her. "Your other daughter told me you're a businessman. A successful one," he added, offering Sol a smile.

Sol didn't answer, but the mention of his professional success had an effect. Sol's demeanour softened. The doctor went on asking admiring questions about his accomplishments, and little by little the arms came uncrossed. The jaw relaxed. Like a swimmer getting used to chilly water, Sol was hesitant at first. Then he began enjoying himself. He told Michel about his stores.

"You *own* Rosebud?" Michel said. The respect in his voice sounded genuine. Rosebud was Montreal's best-known women's retail chain, a rare winner in the city's moribund clothing sector.

"I founded it," Sol said.

Bea had heard the story many times: the penniless boy from Saint-Urbain Street who built a fashion empire out of nothing, rising through the ranks as a cutter, then a foreman and finally becoming the proprietor of his own operation. Along the way he obtained a university degree. Before he was thirty, he'd made his first million. At some point early on, Bea wasn't too clear on the date, he'd shortened his name from Rosenberg to Rose. The flower had become his trademark. He'd worn it in his suit lapel and, when celebrations were called for, offered them by the dozens to friends and business acquaintances and to his wife, Deirdre.

Michel Allaire noted all this with his chewed ballpoint pen. He observed, amiably, that Sol's daughter had inherited her father's entrepreneurial spirit. "The yoga studio," he said, smiling at Bea, "is a great little business."

Bea suppressed an impulse to wince. She wasn't about to announce to her agitated, hospitalized father that she'd given up on that business. Michel had paid her a compliment she didn't deserve. She was a good teacher, but business eluded her. Gaya Pal had saved her from the anguish of closing the studio altogether.

"Cara's the real entrepreneur," she said, trying not to sound miserable. "She's the one who inherited the business gene."

Sol smiled.

"Does she work at Rosebud?" Michel asked Sol, trying to keep the conversation flowing.

The smile dropped from her father's face. Michel had entered a forbidden zone. Sol had always thought Cara would take over the company. That had been the plan. While studying for her commerce degree, Cara had spent summers working at Rosebud, beginning as a salesgirl and then taking on administrative tasks. To be fair, Sol had offered jobs to both of his daughters, but Bea had no interest in women's fashion. Cara was the one who was passionate about it. After graduating she'd managed one of the outlets and began helping with overall management. But five years ago, when she and Didier opened Crudivore, all that changed.

Michel must have sensed Sol's discomfort; he gracefully changed tack and asked about his health.

"I'm fine," said Sol, his mood lightening as they returned to safer ground. "For a man my age, I'm still going strong." He turned unexpectedly and addressed her. "Right, Beatrice?"

She nodded, her cheeks growing warm. So he did know who she was. He'd been speaking so cogently that it made sense, but this was the first time he'd said her name. It startled her to think how much his recognition still mattered. It had mattered since her early childhood, when only Deirdre had been able to look past her misshapen face and see the girl underneath.

For years Bea had been convinced she was her mother's favourite, as Cara was her father's. She and her mother had the same tastes. They both loved to read. Deirdre taught Bea how to string syllables on the page together at the age of four, two years before most kids mastered this skill. Bea used to sit on her mother's lap at the breakfast table, eating from Deirdre's plate and crowing out the newspaper headlines while her parents drank their coffee. And until she turned five and had to go to school, she accompanied Deirdre everywhere. They sang songs in the car and dreamed up word games.

In the dark years following her mother's death, when she was eight, when Sol had taken refuge in work and a series of nannies had taken over the girls' upbringing, Bea had clung to her belief in being Deirdre's favourite. Then one day, when she was twelve, she discovered, wedged between two dusty volumes in her father's den, a little booklet in which her mother had recorded Cara's baby data. The care with which each detail and date had been entered— Cara's first smile, her first tooth, her first syllable, her first step— put an end to that myth. When Bea handed the book to Cara, her sister had wept. Bea had to accept that there had been no favourite. Deirdre had been so skilled at loving that she made everyone feel special. Even from the grave.

Sol had turned talkative. "I still go to the office," he was telling the doctor, when Bea's attention returned to the room. "I still drive my car and wash down my dinner with a glass of Cabernet Sauvignon. I do what I please. Anyone who doesn't like it can go to hell."

Michel took all of this down. Then, taking advantage of Sol's improved mood, he mentioned a test he needed to administer. "You'll laugh when you see how easy it is," he said, offering Sol a pencil and the clipboard that, Bea now saw, held photocopied sheets. The test had several components, Michel explained: verbal, pictorial and mathematical. It would take only a few minutes to complete.

Sol struck the clipboard with his fist, knocking it and the pen from Michel's hands. "I don't need any *tests*," he said as the young man bent over in his chair to collect the fallen things.

Bea stooped down to help. As Michel straightened, Sol tried to grab the clipboard again, but this time Michel was prepared. He swung it out of Sol's reach. Sol sat back heavily in his chair. "Forget the test," he said, breathing hard and glaring at the doctor. "I need three things from you. My clothes, my car keys and directions to the street."

Michel Allaire was unfazed. "That's the plan, Mr. Rose. We want to release you. But first you've got to complete the tests."

"*Release* me?" Sol repeated contemptuously. "What am I, your prisoner? Is that what you're saying?"

Michel didn't deny it. In theory, Sol could leave the hospital any time, barefoot and bare-assed in his periwinkle gown. In practice, that wasn't about to happen and everyone, including Sol, knew it. He finally agreed to cooperate, putting on a pair of reading glasses that made him look a little more like his usual self. From the neck up, at least, he could have been in the living room of his home on Melville Avenue, reading *The Economist*.

The first task was to copy a drawing of two intersecting polygons. Sol set to work with the pencil Michel supplied, but the forms he produced looked more like circles. And they did not touch. Michel watched with a neutral expression. The next task required Sol to write the names of four pictured animals: a lion, a camel, a rhinoceros and a zebra. He filled in the blanks beneath the pictures correctly and quickly, sighing audibly, as if the whole thing were an insulting joke. Farther down the page, he was asked to draw a clock set at ten minutes to three. Bea watched with quiet shock as he drew both clock hands to the right of the twelve. She quelled an urge to point out the error. Surely he must see it. She glanced at Michel, but the doctor was studiously avoiding her gaze. He urged Sol on to the next question.

"Now we'll do some math."

Sol's eyes narrowed.

"I want you to count backward from one hundred by sevens."

Bea grinned. It reminded her of the games her mother used to devise. She'd reached seventy-two in her head when Sol grunted, as if clearing his throat. He picked up the clipboard and gripped it so tightly that Bea wondered if he intended to throw it at Michel's head.

The young doctor was as pleasantly calm as ever. "You've been in retail all your life, Mr. Rose. I'll bet you're good with figures." He began counting backward out loud, coaxing Sol to try.

But Sol shook his head. He'd always prided himself on his talent for math. At inventory time down at the flagship Rosebud store on Sainte-Catherine Street, he often didn't bother with a calculator, performing flawless mental arithmetic instead. Bea stared at him. She'd never seen him in such disarray, never imagined that such an integral part of him could be lost.

Michel didn't press any further. They moved on to the verbal section and Sol relaxed a little, lowering the clipboard to his knees. If Sol's math was strong, his verbal skills were stronger. Advice, judgment, rivers of opinion had flowed from him for as long as Bea could remember. His words had inundated her child-hood. Much of the time, they dwelled on her appearance—specifically her cleft, on which subject Sol was tireless. He would read up on the latest treatments and scientific research and tell her what he thought was best, whether she wanted to hear it or not. This was paternal attention, she couldn't deny it, but in her teenage years it began to feel like harassment, crowding out all other forms of communication they might have shared. His other subject was clothes. How, he had asked her, could the daughter of someone in women's wear have so little fashion sense? It was, he said without any attempt at kindness, one of the world's great mysteries. She was thirteen years old when it started, suffering through her pimply, self-conscious second year of high school, hiding her body in oversized men's flannel shirts and baggy army-surplus pants. Sol called her an eyesore.

Michel asked him to write a sentence.

"What kind?" he asked, suspicious.

The doctor smiled. "It can be anything you like, Mr. Rose. You choose."

Her father bent over the sheet and scribbled with great concen-tration. Bea watched the words appear: "When will this torment end?" That task, at least, had presented no difficulty. But when Michel moved on to the next item, giving Sol a list of five simple nouns and asking him to recall them, Sol got two. He stood up and threw the clipboard, discus-style, at the wall. His fists were clenched again and he was panting audibly. "I've had enough."

"All right," Michel said evenly. "You did fine, Mr. Rose. You can leave the rest if you want. We've got enough to work with." He retrieved the clipboard and laid it once more on his lap. "We should have the results from your MRI by tomorrow morning, and then, with what you've given us here, we should be able to come to a decision pretty quickly."

Sol's expression darkened. "It's not your *decision* to take." He turned to Bea. "Call my lawyer."

When she held his gaze, saying nothing, he got agitated, shoving the table into the wall. After that, he tried to take his test back from Michel.

Michel pried the old man's fingers loose from the clipboard and gently steered him back onto the bed. As Sol paused to catch his breath, Michel reached past him and pressed a red button on the wall. Outside in the corridor a code white was announced over the intercom, followed by Sol's room number. Seconds later an orderly appeared in the doorway, a gigantic man in green hospital scrubs.

Bea braced herself for what was coming. Sol tried to get off the bed, but it was too late. The orderly pinned him to the mattress. Bea watched unhappily as her father was sedated. It took four people: Michel, a second orderly who came in as backup and a nurse with a syringe.

After her father lost consciousness, Michel led Bea out of the room.

Sun was coming in through a window at the far end of the empty corridor, bathing the walls in honeyed tones. Quiet once more prevailed.

"I'm sorry you had to witness that," he said. "Has he always been so angry?"

Bea shook her head. "He wasn't violent. He never threw things."

"But the anger?"

Bea said nothing. She felt sick. And disloyal. She had no idea how to answer the question. What was appropriate in a situation like this? Could she be a trustworthy witness? Sol had been prone to anger from her earliest memory. But then, there'd been plenty to be angry about. His wife had died at the age of thirty-two, killed in a car he was driving, leaving him to raise two young daughters on his own. Nothing had been easy.

As a child, Bea had seemed to elicit his tirades. She never knew why. She'd tried to be good, to do well in school, to avoid getting in trouble. But her efforts never seemed to be enough. The only reason she could think of, was reminded of every time she looked in the mirror, was the cleft. Her face must have been an affront to this man whose business was making women look good. And Bea's nature hadn't helped. She was a dreamer, not practical and task-oriented as he was. In university she'd majored in religious studies. After that, she'd further irritated him by leaving for eight years to backpack through Asia.

But that was within the theatre of family. In the wider world, Bea knew, her father was known to be a good and reasonable man. "He's never angry at his store," she said.

It was true. His employees revered him. He was widely praised for his philanthropy.

The young doctor was watching her. "What about with you?"

Bea's face grew warm. "That came out wrong. I didn't mean . . ." She fell silent, unable to make things clearer.

Michel didn't press the issue. "Did he have trouble sleeping while you were growing up?" he asked unexpectedly.

She looked up with surprise. Yes, sleep had definitely been an issue, all through his life. She told Michel how her father had never slept more than four or five hours a night. He was famous for it. And she suspected that sometimes what he called sleeping was lying in bed, staring blank-eyed at the television set he kept on his bedroom dresser after Deirdre died, never turning it off.

"Did he ever talk in his sleep? Or leave the bed and walk around?"

This was getting a little uncanny. Her mother had preferred to call it "night wandering," as though the note of poetry would make it less frightening. Deirdre had taught Bea what to do when it occurred. You simply took him by the hand and led him back to bed. It was the oddest thing. His eyes were open, but he showed no awareness of Bea or her mother as they guided him, shepherd-esses leading a stray lamb.

"Yes," she said, "he sleepwalked. Not often, at least not when I was living at home. But when it happened, it was pretty odd."

"For as long as you can remember?"

She nodded. "And he talked. Whole conversations, staring in front of him as though someone was there."

"We'll have to wait for the MRI results," Michel said, "but from what you're telling me and from what I've observed today, I think I know what the issue may be. The fact that he was unconscious when they found him threw us off initially. We thought it was a concussion. But except for that bruise on his cheek, there are no signs of injury." He glanced down the corridor. "It's never wise to offer a diagnosis without seeing the tests. I'm not reaching any hard conclusions, I'm just speculating for the benefit of a friend. It looks to me like your dad may have DLB."

Bea looked at him blankly.

"Dementia with Lewy bodies," he said. "The shuffling gait is also a sign. I assume that's recent."

Bea had been wondering why Sol had been dragging his feet. She thought maybe he'd injured his leg on the night of the storm.

"Trouble with sleep is often the first symptom to present, long before people notice anything else."


Bea cycled home. She spent the rest of the day searching medi-cal websites. Millions of aging North Americans, she learned, had been diagnosed with DLB; millions more probably had it but were either undiagnosed or misdiagnosed with Alzheimer's or

Parkinson's disease. Bea read a long description of protein clumps and damage to a section of the midbrain called the *substantia nigra*. What she'd thought was an idiosyncrasy—her father's strange nocturnal comportment—was in fact a medical condition. It was progressive. There was no cure. A cold tide of fear flowed into her chest.

# 7.

WHEN HER RADIO ALARM went off the next morning, Bea had trouble opening her eyes. It was the start of her first full week of rehearsals and she'd barely slept, tossing all night and then falling into a dreamless doze at five in the morning. Now the room was soft with grey light. It was raining. On the CBC, someone was saying the rain would only stop that afternoon. Bea slapped the top of the radio with her palm and the room went silent. Her arms and legs felt like bags of wet sand. She didn't have to be at rehearsal until noon, but Michel had asked that she and Cara meet him for a "family council" at ten.

So she staggered out of bed, got dressed, drank a cup of tea and headed out the door. Her bike stood in a pool of water, chained beneath the dripping front steps. The prospect of cycling across the mountain in this weather was too much. *With heigh-ho*, she thought glumly, remembering the funny song sung by the Fool, and trudged down the wet sidewalk toward Park Avenue to wait for the 80 South. It showed up ten minutes later, long and wormlike, with an articulated middle that she kept imagining would detach and leave her stranded in the soggy street. But the bus stayed intact until the Place-des-Arts metro station, where it disgorged her and the other passengers into a damp tunnel that smelled of piss. Bea stepped gingerly around a man lying on the stairs, an arm covering his face. On the step below his inert body were an empty brown bottle and the sticky contours of a puddle where beer had spilled. Bea focused on her sandals.

At the hospital she checked the piece of paper on which she'd scribbled Michel's office number. Her wet feet squelched as she mounted the stairs. Her hair stuck to her face. Her shorts and windbreaker clung disagreeably to her body. On the first floor she gave up and rode the rest of the way in the elevator.

She had arrived fifteen minutes early, hoping to have a moment alone with Michel so she could ask about the things she'd read online. But when she reached his office she heard a familiar laugh through the half-opened door. Cara was sitting across the desk from him, smiling her brilliant white smile and expounding upon the health benefits of eating raw.

"You feel the difference immediately," she was saying. "The digestion clears up. The skin starts to shine. I haven't eaten anything hotter than thirty-three degrees Celsius in five years."

Cara did look wonderful. But then she always looked wonderful, even when she used to eat meat. She had inherited the rangy, athletic build of their mother's side of the family, along with the McMaster clan's iron-clad immune system. She'd probably live past a hundred.

"Wet out there," Cara said cheerily as Bea walked in. She herself was perfectly dry, her clothes and makeup as pristine and elegant as ever.

Bea gave her a kiss. Then she kissed Michel. "We met through yoga," she said in answer to her sister's inquiring look.

"She used to tie me in knots every Sunday," Michel offered. He pulled up another chair and the council, such as it was, began. The good news, he informed them, was that their father didn't seem to have sustained any physical trauma. Sol's brain scan showed no trace of a lesion or bleeding. If he had suffered a concussion on the night of the storm, it was, medically speaking, nothing to worry about.

Now came the bad news. Sol was presenting symptoms of moderate to advanced dementia. There was no reliable way to identify the cause, but on the basis of the medical history Michel had taken, the neurocognitive testing that had been done and Sol's pattern of emotional responses, he was confident about the diagnosis.

"Alzheimer's?" Cara asked quietly.

"We can't rule it out," Michel said, "but your father's symptoms are more consistent with another form of cognitive and affective decline."

"Dementia with Lewy bodies," Bea said. The words had been bouncing in her head like ping-pong balls all night long.

Cara looked at her in surprise.

"Bea and I spoke about it when she was here to visit your father." Michel listed its main symptoms, which Bea now knew by heart: sleepwalking, fluctuations of lucidity, incoherent speech, periods of altered consciousness, fits of rage, and even visual hallucinations. Sleep-related symptoms could manifest early in the patient's life, he said, which distinguished the syndrome from Alzheimer's, along with the rapid onset of other symptoms later in life.

Neither Bea nor Cara spoke.

"Not all of these things need to be present for a positive diagnosis," Michel continued. "The disease expresses itself uniquely in each person. Typically two or three symptoms can be detected at any one time."

Cara looked thoughtful. She leaned forward over the unnaturally bare desk, which Michel was likely sharing with other doctors. "So you can't be absolutely sure what he's got? Is that what you're saying? There's no way for you to be one hundred percent certain what he's suffering from?" She sounded exactly like Sol.

From what Bea had read online, the only definitive way to diagnose any of these aging brain disorders—DLB, Alzheimer's or even Parkinson's—was an autopsy.

Michel explained the diagnostic process one more time, avoiding explicit mention of the word "autopsy" but making it clear that certitude was possible only after death, in a "research context." Meanwhile, care had to be offered to people living with the symptoms. Diagnosis, even if only tentative, was an important first step.

"Drugs are available to help with some of the symptoms," he added, "and we can talk about that further down the road. But right now the main thing is to ensure your father's safety." Michel didn't seem boyish anymore. He was speaking fluently, with authority.

"Has your father granted either of you power of attorney?"

Cara shook her head. "He's not really that sort."

"No?" said Michel. "Well, even so, I advise you to take him to the notary. Soon. You need to discuss this with him. A power of attorney for now, but also, I'd say, a mandate of protection, which is a more all-encompassing legal instrument. The disease isn't in its early stages. Decline can be dramatic and quick. Much quicker than with Alzheimer's, although lucidity certainly fluctuates. I can do the medical paperwork, if you wish. You don't want to wait with something like this. It will get tricky for your family if you don't have notarial permission to oversee his affairs."

Michel withdrew two familiar items from the pocket of his lab coat—Sol's flat brown leather wallet and a key fob with the words RANGE ROVER embossed on a metallic strip at its base. "One of you will have to take these," he said, holding them lightly in an upturned hand. "Your father can't use his car anymore, for obvious reasons. I'm advising that his driver's licence be revoked. But even returning his wallet to him right now might be demanding too much. You'll have to use your judgment." He looked at them. "I know this isn't easy."

Bea stared at the little white fob. The car, bought last year when the first editions of the Range Rover Evoque were released in North America, was her father's pride and joy. He'd always loved cars. Early on it was sports cars, but after the accident he'd switched to sturdier models.

Cara took the keys and wallet and tucked them in her purse. Then, silently, each wrapped in her own thoughts, the sisters followed the young doctor down the hall to the patients' wing.

When they reached Sol's room he was sitting on the edge of his bed, feet dangling and torso tilted as if he were about to jump off the ledge of a building. Before him stood a stocky young woman in a pink jumpsuit. She wore a disgruntled look. A nametag identified her as "Noor." In her hand she held a small paper cup.

"Mr. Rose," said Michel. "It's good to see you again, sir. Your daughters have come to visit."

The tendons stood out in Sol's neck. His face was flushed. Both fists were pressed into the mattress. He and Nurse Noor had been having some sort of dispute.

"Pill time?" Michel asked the young woman, smiling.

She nodded. "He doesn't want to take them."

"Damn right I don't," said Sol. "I'm not sick! I want my car keys back. And my wallet. Cara!" he shouted, waving her forward. "They've detained me against my will! Tell them who I am! Tell them!"

Cara stayed by Bea's side at the door. Michel was the one who stepped forward. He took the pills from the nurse, allowing her to slip quietly out of the room. Then he walked to the foot of the bed and unhooked Sol's medical chart. "Hmmm," he said, perusing the notes. "These seem to be the meds you take at home. Anticholesterol, gout medication . . . does that sound familiar to you,

Mr. Rose?" With a bit of reassurance and a fresh glass of water, he convinced Sol to swallow them down.

"Now then," Michel said, straightening up. "I'd like to discuss your release."

"About time," said Sol. He was no longer shouting.

All three of them were standing around him now. "Look," Michel began, "I can release you today. I know that's what you want. Believe it or not, it's also what the hospital wants—we could certainly use the bed. But I won't be able to do that until a couple of conditions have been met. I know you're accustomed to calling the shots, Mr. Rose. It's normal. You've been calling them all your life." He consulted the file again. "But you'll be eighty years old next birthday."

Sol didn't respond. His face had tightened. His upcoming birthday was probably as shocking to him as it was to Bea. Eighty seemed impossibly ancient. Cara had talked about throwing a party, but so far neither she nor Bea had summoned the courage to bring it up with him.

"By eighty, most people enjoy some kind of help," said the doctor. "Help's not a bad thing. You live alone, right?" He flipped through the file.

"Yes, he does; our mother died when we were little," said Cara. She was freer than Bea on the subject of their mother's death, able to talk about it more easily. She had been so young.

"You didn't remarry?"

"He's an eligible bachelor," said Cara, smiling. "A cleaning lady comes once a week. Other than that, he's the king of his castle."

"Which is precisely how I like it," said Sol. "And how it will remain."

Michel's face stayed neutral. He removed the cap from his pen and wrote something in the file. After a moment, he looked up. "And you still drive."

Sol's look hardened.

"I'm afraid that can't continue," Michel said.

Sol's frowned. Then he let rip. Who did the doctor think he was? Sol had paid for a whole wing of the hospital. He'd drive if he damn well pleased.

Michel let him rant. Sol wasn't showing other signs of aggression. In fact, he was hugging himself. His voice squeaked like an upset child's. After a few seconds he released the hug to climb off the bed.

"You know Herb Litwin?" he asked the doctor. His arms were moving now, flapping like ineffectual wings. "You don't know Herb?" he repeated when Michel's expression failed to change. "You don't know the chairman of your hospital? You must be low on the ladder." Sol's body began to sway. "Herb Litwin. I sat on the board with him for over a decade. Call him. Mention my name. Tell him what you're trying to do to me. He'll let you know what's what."

"Dad," Bea said softly. She touched his shoulder. Herb Litwin, one of Sol's oldest friends, had died two years ago. He and Sol had been board members in the 1980s.

Sol spun around. "You're in on this," he shouted. "Don't deny it! Both of you. Otherwise, how would this guy, Doctor Whatshisname, get my keys?"

"You left them in your car," said Cara. "With the motor running and the doors open in the middle of a rainstorm. The police impounded it, Dad. You're lucky nobody stole it." Her voice broke as she spoke.

Michel listened quietly. Ownership of the Range Rover would have to be transferred to one of the daughters, or to anyone else Sol chose, he said after a pause. And Sol would be wise to make provisions for his business, too, although that would obviously take more time.

Finally, he came to the most delicate point of all. Sol would need round-the-clock care.

There was a moment of shocked silence. Then Sol seemed to wake up. "On the basis of what?" he shouted. "Counting backward by sevens? Drawing pictures of cubes? This is how you decide a man's fate?"

He turned on Cara, crimson with rage. "Say something! Speak up, for God's sake." His hands waved. Spittle flew from his mouth. Cara stared at him.

Michel moved to the head of the bed. His hand hovered over the red button.

Sol looked desperately at Cara and then at Bea. "No!" he shouted. "It's okay. Tell him not to do it."

Michel lowered his arm, and Sol climbed back into bed. He drank some water from the glass that Michel handed him.

Sol could be released that day, Michel said, if he convinced him that adequate care was arranged at home. If Sol and his daughters could work something out, then Michel would hand over his clothes and other possessions and he'd be free to go. Michel's tone was curt now. The only language that Sol Rose could understand, he seemed to have concluded, was firmness. He left the family alone to sort out the logistics.

Once the door closed, Sol leaned back heavily on the bed. His hair was in disarray, exposing his baldness. And he was still half-naked in the blue gown. Even so, he managed to take charge. It was just the three of them now: Sol and his girls, the old, familiar triangle. All he wanted, he said, pulling the sheet over his skinny thighs as if suddenly aware that he had a body, was to be released. If that meant giving the hospital what it wanted, so be it. Someone would have to move into the house.

Bea was struck by his lucidity. The desperate, raging man who minutes before had shouted at Michel Allaire was gone. The transformation was stunning. This sliding in and out of coherence was, as Michel had said, one of the hallmarks of DLB. Sol was cradling his arm now, scratching at the bruised, flaking skin around the little loop they'd inserted in him in case he needed an IV.

Cara spoke. "I'll see if Mrs. Szabó can help out."

Mrs. Szabó was Sol's housekeeper, a matronly woman, originally from Hungary, who had worked in his employ for over twenty years. In addition to cleaning, she prepared a weekly casserole. Sol liked her cooking, which was heavy on meat and paprika. More importantly, he trusted her. She had a husband, but her kids were grown so there might be a chance she could do nights.

Sol scowled. "She's a cleaning lady."

"And a good one too," said Cara. "She's honest and smart. You've said so yourself." When Sol kept on scowling, she switched tack. "There must be agencies that specialize in post-hospital care. I'll do some research." She forced out a smile. "Don't you worry, Dad. We won't consider anyone without references."

"References?" Sol repeated.

Cara nodded. "For the person who moves in."

"Whoa, whoa, whoa." Sol raised his hands. "There isn't going to be a *person*." He looked at her pointedly. "Unless it's you."

Cara stared at him. "You can't be serious. What about Didier and the kids? I have a family, remember? I can't just drop everything."

"There's plenty of room for all of you," said Sol. "The place is big. Space isn't an issue."

Cara blinked. Then she looked at Bea with her ice-blue eyes. *Do something*, those eyes said. *Volunteer. Save us from this madness.*

Her father turned toward Bea too, his expression thoughtful. His shape had shifted again. "Vulnerable" was no longer the right word. He looked crafty, as though he had a plan. He could have been in the board room at his store instead of in a hospital bed.

Her gaze shifted from the calculating eyes down to the thin blue cloth of the gown covering his knobby knees.

Mrs. Szabó was the obvious choice. But Sol wouldn't hear of it, and besides, after what Bea had seen in the hospital yesterday, she couldn't in all conscience expose the kind, old woman to the possibility of her father's wrath. An agency, where presumably the staff would be trained for such contingencies, might work better. But Bea's instincts rose in revolt at the thought.

A face appeared in her memory. A narrow, humourless face. Madame Huppert. Sol had hired her after their mother died from an agency that specialized in placing French nannies with North American families. Madame Huppert had come with a long list of references and qualifications. What she hadn't had was generosity of spirit. She'd lived with them for five years, inflicting a host of small miseries on Bea and her baby sister. Sol had not been a solicitous father. He hadn't coddled his daughters when they were young and in their adult lives he hadn't offered much support either, emotional or otherwise. Yet now he was vulnerable. And there was something in Bea, something unreasoning and irreducible, that wouldn't let her do to him what had been done to her and Cara.

Bea had no children or man in her life. And her days in the apartment on Saint-Famille Street were numbered. She'd be forced to move out soon, regardless.

"Okay," she said. "I'll do it. At least until we come up with a better solution."

Sol smiled, and she felt a thrill of self-congratulation. It was nice to be the hero, even for a few delusional seconds. She looked at her watch. "I have to go," she said. She and Cara had twenty minutes to firm things up before she'd have to set off for rehearsal.

They decided that Bea would take the Range Rover to work. Cara would use her own car to drive Sol back to the Melville Avenue house, where she would spend the day with him. They could go grocery shopping and pick up the girls in the afternoon from daycare and school. In the evening, Bea would take over.

"Bea's moving in with him," Cara told Michel when he looked in. "He'll have to stay on his own for a bit during the days while we're at work, but the nights will be covered. I think we'll be okay."

Michel smiled at Bea and nodded. From the bed, Sol watched with narrowed eyes.

# 8.

THERE WAS AMPLE SPACE outside the building on Young Street, but it took Bea three tries to get the Range Rover properly parked. When she opened the car door, a smell of rot assailed her. The sidewalk was overflowing with garbage for the Monday pickup, ripe-odoured from the rain. Animals had gnawed holes in the bags. Soggy pizza crusts and coffee grinds lay scattered across the pavement.

Someone was smoking in the shelter of the building's entrance. Jack DeVries stepped out into the drizzle, smiling. He must have enjoyed the display of her parking ineptitude. "This is yours?" he asked, tapping the car's shiny wet hood. "Nice." He pressed his face against the tinted glass to examine the plush interior. Bea explained that it belonged to her father, whose driving privileges were in the process of being revoked.

Jack made a face. "I'd fight back if I were him." Dots of wet were darkening his T-shirt, but he didn't seem to mind. He turned and called out to another figure standing in the entrance. Bea hadn't noticed he wasn't alone. "Check it out, Mimi."

Mimi flicked her cigarette butt into the street. "I have to get upstairs," she said, and went into the building. Bea sighed. It was hard to imagine Mimi Meir liking the idea that her underqualified ASM drove a Range Rover.

The day's rehearsal went badly. Two cast members, including Phil Burns, who was slated for every scene, had called in sick. Bea and Dave had to reorganize not only the day's rehearsal schedule but the schedule for the entire week. This took precious time away from everything else Bea was supposed to do. Her shift was extended. At five, as the actors began to leave, she was only halfway through her assigned tasks. While Dave emailed the new schedule to the cast, she cleaned the bathroom. *Not what I'd been hoping for,* she thought, crouching on a floor littered with paper and stray hairs, scrubbing the filthy toilet bowl. The bathroom stank. Someone in the cast must have had diarrhea: the rim of the bowl and the underside of the lid were flecked with brown. She wiped up the mess and threw the paper towels into an overflowing wastebasket, which she emptied into an industrial-size garbage bag.

Once the bathroom was done, she scrubbed her hands and forearms with soap and steaming water. Then she took out her phone. It was six o'clock, the hour she had promised to relieve Cara. She quick-dialled her sister's cell, just as Dave had taught her.

"Where are you?" said Cara.

Bea explained.

"Tell them it's a crisis," said Cara. "They need to cut you some slack."

Bea looked at Dave, still bent over his laptop. "There's no *they*, Cara. It's me and one guy. And there's a lot of work left to do."

"Tell the guy you have to leave. The girls are here, Bea. I have to take them home and feed them."

She promised to do her best. But by the time she got out of the building it was seven o'clock. The rain had stopped completely, and now a yellow sun dangled in a hazy sky. The air was as hot as it had been in the rehearsal room. No hint of a breeze.

The parking ticket was the first thing she saw. It was folded in two, tucked neatly under the windshield wiper on the driver's side. The Range Rover was the only car on the street to get hit. Bea's heart sank. Her first day at the wheel of her father's car and she'd been ticketed. When she unfolded it and took a look, the checked-off box said that she'd exceeded the statutory parking time limit. It didn't mention what that limit was. She looked up and down the street but saw no sign. Her ignorance of the mystery limit had cost her forty-five dollars.

She was leaning dejectedly on the car hood, digesting this fact, when she noticed something else. Her father's car had elaborate wheel rims whose metallic patterns made them look like silver-petalled flowers. In the centre of the flower on the front left wheel was a hole. She checked the rear left wheel, then went around to the passenger side. All four caps were gone. Bea's stomach gave a little lurch. It was a detail, she tried to tell herself. The wheel caps were small. They weren't even particularly attractive. She thought they'd been stamped with the Range Rover name, but she couldn't really remember the design. In any case the wheels looked weird without them, and when it came to his car, Sol had sharp eyes.

Bea climbed into the driver's seat and put the ticket in the glove compartment. She wouldn't tell him. She'd just make sure it got paid. The wheel caps would be harder to hide. Perhaps Sol wouldn't come out when she arrived, or be too distracted to notice.

When Bea pulled into her father's driveway on Melville Avenue, Cara's two daughters, four-year-old Yasmin and seven-year-old Elle, came running down the porch stairs. They'd been sitting outside with their mother and grandfather, watching for her. Cara got up from one of the weather-beaten Adirondack chairs that had graced their father's porch through all seasons for as long as Bea could remember.

"Do you know what time it is?" she said, her features hard.

Bea tried to explain about the day's problems at work, but Cara cut her off. "You need to talk to them, Bea. Let them know the situation."

Sol came down the steps as the sisters were having this exchange. He was definitely walking differently, barely lifting his feet as he approached them over the patch of lawn. He noticed the missing wheel caps instantly, squatting without ceremony to poke at the holes. His youngest granddaughter, grave-faced, squatted beside him. "When did this happen?" he asked, looking at Bea.

"It must have been while I was working," she said. "The car was parked right outside the rehearsal hall."

"In broad daylight, and you saw nothing?"

Bea lowered her gaze. She couldn't have watched it all afternoon, but the truth was she'd forgotten about the car. She'd been so busy she hadn't thought to check.

Cara laid a hand on Sol's shoulder. "She was at work, Dad," she said. "It's no big deal. Kids steal them all the time. I'll get you new ones."

Sol shook off her hand. "I don't want new ones. This is unacceptable. You take my car away and you bring it back like this!" He pointed an accusing finger at Bea. "I trusted you!" He was shouting now, his face reddening.

Yasmin reached for her mother's hand and Cara stooped to pick her up. Elle edged in closer.

"You're frightening the girls, Dad," said Cara. Yasmin watched him with round eyes. Her older sister had buried her face in her mother's waist. A group of boys who'd been splashing in the wading pool in the park across the street came around the bushes to see what the commotion was. Westmount wasn't a place where one often heard shouting.

"Dad," said Cara, aware of the growing audience, "you've got to calm down. We'll call the dealer tomorrow. I promise."

"Fine," he snapped, "but from now on I don't want her to touch it." He snatched the fob from Bea's hands. "Here," he said, passing it to Cara.

Cara and Bea exchanged a look, and Bea nodded. She didn't care if she never saw the car again. Cara and Sol got into a discussion about logistics, and Sol's voice returned to a normal decibel level.

Yasmin, still in her mother's arms, made a grab for the shiny metal rectangle, but Cara held it away from her. "It's not a toy, Yas," she said, depositing her daughter on the lawn. Yasmin continued to lunge.

"That's right," agreed Sol, but he was smiling now, enjoying himself. "Look at her jump," he said with admiration.

The little girl smiled too and jumped more energetically. Cara rolled her eyes, but it was clear she was pleased. Yasmin was an eager little copy of herself. Their colouring differed, but their bodies and spirits were one. Elle stood a little apart from them, watching quietly. Bea put an arm around her. She stiffened at the touch, but seconds later, when Bea didn't withdraw, her thin shoulders relaxed.

Then Cara announced she had to pick up Didier. The girls clamoured to accompany her. "No," she said firmly, crouching down to look her youngest in the eye. "Mummy's got errands to do. You're staying put with Auntie Bea. It's simpler this way. I'll be right back with Daddy."

Bea, who was already holding on to Elle, took Yasmin's sticky fingers as well. The child tried to break away but Bea held tight, kneeling on the grass to quiet her while Cara walked to the Range

Rover. Bea and the girls stood and watched with Sol as Cara backed the car into the street. She looked like something out of a TV commercial, her golden hair glinting in the evening sun. She opened the window and promised to be back soon, then blew them all kisses and sped away.

Sol watched with satisfaction. He was still pale from the hospital ordeal, but the simple fact of wearing his own clothes—a tailored shirt and neat linen trousers that hid his emaciated legs—gave him at least a semblance of normalcy.

Yasmin was whimpering.

"Hey," Sol said, "what's this?" He picked Yasmin up and looked into her teary eyes. "Come come, now," he added with a note of impatience. "Are you a winner or a whiner?"

How many times in her childhood had Bea heard the same question? It had worked then, as it worked now. The whimpers stopped. Yasmin fell into a thoughtful silence as her grandfather carried her up the porch stairs. Bea and Elle followed.

Sheets of paper and crayons were strewn over the porch floor. A green T. Rex with a huge, egg-shaped head and triangular teeth grinned up at Bea. Elle had drawn him. Drawing came easily to her. Reading, too. Quiet activities for a quiet child. Elle knelt down and was soon absorbed in colouring the dinosaur's clawed feet.

Yasmin's spirits revived. She tried to mimic her older sister and draw a dinosaur, but her effort wasn't very convincing. She examined her drawing briefly, then abandoned it and began to pelt Elle with crayons.

"Hey," said Sol when Elle yelped. He'd settled back into his old Adirondack chair, staring dreamily at the lengthening shadows in the park across the street. Now he leaned forward, giving Elle a stern look. "What did I say about whiners?"

Elle froze and fell silent. Bea gave her a hug. When she began to draw again, Bea led Yasmin into the house, away from her sister, to make lemonade. Sol always had a supply of concentrate in the freezer. The girls loved it, and despite the artificial flavours and chemical colouring, so did Bea. She let Yasmin mash the sticky pink ice with a wooden spoon—there were worse ways to channel aggression—tasting it as she did and squealing at its sourness. Then, after Bea found some crackers, Yasmin proudly carried them to the porch while Bea followed with four glasses of lemonade on a tray. The Range Rover had been forgotten when, half an hour later, it returned.

As Cara and Didier got out, Yasmin and Elle ran shrieking to greet them. Didier laughed and opened his arms. In his white button-down dress shirt with the sleeves rolled up, he looked good—tanned and slim. They were the same age, almost forty, but Didier seemed younger all of a sudden. He lifted his daughters off the ground, grunting dramatically, a girl hanging from each fist as though they were free weights at the gym. He raised them both to shoulder level then lifted Yasmin higher, straightening his arm over his head. She dangled in his grasp, kicking and squealing in terrified delight.

"Me too, me too!" Elle pleaded—to no avail. She was too big now, too heavy.

Sol watched from his chair. His ill humour had returned when he noticed that Didier was driving his car.

"Who is that?" he asked sharply.

Bea turned. Someone else was in the Rover.

"That's Gen-vie, Dad. You know her. She works at Crudivore."

Sol huffed. In the fading light, his features looked strangely chiselled. Bea remembered Cara's description of their father skulking around the restaurant, scaring poor Gen-vie in the dark.

Yasmin and Elle were now clambering into their parents' aging Renault parked in front of the house. Didier strapped them in.

Then he kissed his wife ostentatiously on the mouth and got back into the Range Rover with Gen-vie. The girls, who'd thought they'd be driving home with him, started to complain.

Sol got out of his chair and began to shuffle down the stairs. He was halfway down when the Range Rover's engine roared to life and the car sped away. Sol halted abruptly. Everyone watched the departing car. At the corner of Sherbrooke Street it paused at a stop sign. Its horn tooted twice, then it turned east toward downtown Montreal and was gone.

"Cara!" Sol shouted. At first Cara didn't hear him. Half her body was now hidden in the Renault, where she was reattaching the straps Yasmin had undone in her effort to get out and be with Didier. "Cara!" Sol shouted again.

She turned and looked up at him, frowning.

"The car . . ."

"Don't worry, Dad," she said in a tired voice. "Didier's an excellent driver." She climbed into the front seat of the Renault and revved the old engine, producing a stream of black fumes. "We'll talk tomorrow," she said through the open window. "I'll come in the morning after Bea goes to work."

Bea and Sol watched her disappear around the corner with the girls in the same direction Didier had gone. For a while, Sol stood there surveying the deserted street. The sun had dipped below the tops of the trees. Finally he climbed back up the steps with Bea. They carried the crackers and glasses inside, leaving the dinosaurs to their fate on the porch floor.

The interior of the house smelled musty, an old-man smell, like bread gone stale. Everything was the same as it had always been—the stained wood floors, the heavy furnishings, the sagging beige corduroy couch her parents had bought in the seventies. The curtains were drawn and the windows closed in an attempt to keep out the day's heat.

Bea opened the curtains. Only a waning glow remained in the western sky. Her face was reflected in the window, yellow and startled.

"Close them!"

Her father had come up behind her, his reflection blocked by her own. She did as she was told, shaken by the harshness of the command. Sol watched her reclose the curtains as he might have watched a sales clerk walking the floor at one of his stores. Then he went upstairs with his new old-man's gait and vanished into his den.

Bea retreated to the kitchen, where Cara had left a sheet of instructions for their supper along with a package of ground veggie meat she'd bought. In the pantry Bea found a red onion and rows of tinned Italian tomatoes; Cara had planned an ersatz Bolognese. After their mother died there'd been a lot of spaghetti dinners. Pasta had been Sol's fallback every Saturday night when the nanny was off—minced red meat with never the addition of, say, a green pepper or a mushroom. Bea wondered if this was a sly joke on her sister's part. A remembrance of things past.

The dining room table looked too big for the two placemats lying on top of it. In Bea's youth there had been four: Sol, the two girls and the nanny, whose job it had been to cook and serve and clean up before retiring for the night—to do, in other words, the work that Deirdre would have done. But a nanny's competence was no substitute for a mother's warmth. The first of them, Madame Huppert, whose five years of service had made her the longest lasting, was also probably the worst. Cara hadn't minded her, but then again, Cara had known nothing else. Madame Huppert had been a slender, delicate-looking woman who'd never married and who wore skirt suits and heels, even to the park. She had been a superb cook, preparing *boeuf bourguignon, coq au vin, petits pois aux lardons* and even, once, a *boeuf en daube*. It was to the preparation of such delicacies that she had devoted her afternoons. She and Sol drank wine with dinner, a ritual of civility from which Sol seemed to draw comfort. Sometimes, if the vintage was exceptional, he would pour a thimbleful for Bea and Cara, to cultivate their taste. Bea had come away with a fine palate, she supposed, but at a cost: Madame Huppert lacked enthusiasm for anything but haute cuisine. She didn't play games, didn't read to the girls and disliked the park. Every day after school Bea would stay outside for as long as she could, playing with whatever children she found there, knowing the park was the last place Madame Huppert would come looking. In winter, she took refuge in the library located on the park's western perimeter.

Sol never noticed there was a problem. He was home only in the evenings, after homework and afternoon activities were done. He saw the lavish dinners and nothing else. On weekends, when he took over, Madame Huppert wasn't around.

Bea had opened a Côtes du Rhône. When Sol took his customary place at the head of the table, she lifted the bottle from the little silver plate on which he liked to place his vintages and stood over him.

"Good?" she asked, after pouring the first mouthful and watching him sample it.

"Good," he agreed. He held out his glass so she could fill it. He looked happy. Restored.

She poured a glass for herself. It would help the bogus Bolognese go down.

It was after ten when Bea climbed the stairs to the attic. She'd moved up here when she started high school, ostensibly to give herself more privacy but really because she and Sol had begun to fight.

It was stifling under the gabled roof. The day's heat seemed to have accumulated here, trapped by the low, sloping ceiling. Bea opened the window, releasing grimy flakes of paint.

The attic was unchanged since she'd left it, except that her bedroom curtains had been removed. A twin bed stood beside the window—the same bed she'd slept in throughout her childhood and adolescence. At its centre, where she'd sat and read and played games and done her homework, the fabric of the white bedspread was so thin the blanket could be seen through it. Sol had obviously seen no reason to redecorate. Nor had he repainted the walls, which were the same dingy yellow they'd always been. Pinholes marked the spot where Bea had tacked up, over Sol's objections, a brooding portrait of a young Patti Smith.

When Bea sat on the bed, the frame creaked. She bounced experimentally; puffs of dust rose into the air. Mrs. Szabó hadn't been up here in a while. Across from the bed stood a bookcase holding the stories of Bea's childhood: Beatrix Potter, *Alice's Adventures in Wonderland*, the Narnia series, various adventures of the Famous Five. Her mother had bought her these books— the ones she hadn't owned herself as a child. They were British, because Britain was the land from which Deirdre's own family came. Her legacy, such as it was, lay here in this dusty corner. It was, almost, a shrine.

At the foot of the bed stood a small rocking horse. Bea remembered the sensation of swinging a child-size leg over its back and sitting on it. How she had loved that little horse. Her father had been a rider. In his boyhood, there'd been stables just off Côte-des-Neiges Road at the base of Mount Royal from which riders set off along the tree-lined paths of the park. By the time Bea was born, the stables were gone and Sol had stopped riding.

But his love of the racetrack had endured. Every summer he would drive down to Saratoga Springs for the August meet. Bea was four the first time she went with him. Deirdre had been alive, Cara not yet born. It was one of Bea's happiest memories. Sol had taken her to the paddock to meet the jockeys and see the horses up close. He told her, laughing, that the animals were all younger than she was. They were huge and sleek and they ran so fast their hooves thundered, kicking up great clods of earth.

Later, after the races were over, her father brought her to the gift shop and let her pick something out. She'd chosen the wooden rocking horse, with its soft string mane and embroidered-cushion saddle. It was by far the most extravagant toy on display. She'd thought Sol would scold her, but he laughed as he carried it to the sales counter, promising Bea riding lessons when she was older. In the end, she hadn't learned to ride. The rocking horse was as close as she ever got. After the accident, the plan for riding lessons had, like so many things, been lost in the chaos of grief.

She was sticky with sweat. She opened the attic door, hoping to create a cross-draft, but the air wouldn't move. She unzipped her shorts. Here was another problem with the hasty plan she and Cara had dreamed up. Bea had no clean clothes for work. After perspiring through one of the hottest days of the spring, she'd have to rinse out her underthings and T-shirt if she wanted to be even halfway decent for tomorrow's rehearsals.

As she stepped out of her shorts, something fell to the floor. Sol's wallet. Cara had handed it to her before leaving with the girls. Michel Allaire had suggested they hold on to it, at least for the first few days as Sol adjusted to being home. "Adjusted" was a euphemism. The fear was he would bolt. Michel had explained that wandering was a risk. It might not be as effective as taking his car keys, but confiscating his wallet was an added precaution.

Bea opened it. There was some cash. Eight twenties, new bills so crisp they were difficult to separate. She felt like a thief. Behind the bills was a piece of newsprint, folded in two. She extracted it, taking care not to damage its crumbling edges. When she unfolded it, a ghostly face stared up into hers. It was an obituary. She squinted in the weak light to make out the name: Avi Rosenberg. Half a second passed before she realized what she was holding.

The clipping was dated 1987, the year before Bea graduated from high school. She would have been fifteen. How could she have no memory of this death? She turned on the bedside lamp and the features jumped into relief. Yes. She knew this face. She'd seen it only once, but it had made an indelible impression. This was her grandfather.

He was born in Ożarów, Poland, she read, and had arrived in Canada in 1927. This much she already knew from Sol. His parents had been spared the horrors of the war in Europe. Avi's profession was listed as "tailor," and his spouse as the "late Chava Birenbaum," two facts that were new to her. He was survived by his son, Solomon Rose, and by two granddaughters. Her name and Cara's closed the spare biography.

She recalled the encounter precisely. She even remembered the month, October. Rosh Hashanah always fell in the autumn. She was seven years old. She'd spent the day at home and at the reform synagogue with her parents, listening to Rabbi Stern give a sermon. The whole family had gone, as they did every year for the high holidays. "Showing the flag" was what Sol called it. Her mother was roasting a *gigot* of lamb. It was what she always cooked for Rosh Hashanah dinner to welcome in the new year. Lamb and mint jelly. Her parents had invited guests: a supplier of Sol's who was Greek, not Jewish, and his family. He had two small children whom Bea had never met, and her mother had told her she would be responsible for looking after them.

That was why Bea had been looking out the bay window at the street that day when the strange man stopped in front of their house. She was waiting for the guests. But this man didn't seem like a guest. He looked old, for one thing, and for another he was alone, without a wife or children. His complexion was dark. He seemed uncomfortable in his oversized suit, just as Bea felt at that moment in the starchy tartan dress she'd been forced to wear. His nose was flat, like hers. But most shocking of all, a white line shimmered on his upper lip, dividing his face in two.

Bea had never seen this on an adult. She stared down at him from the big bay window. He saw her, and for a moment their gazes locked. Then Bea ducked below the window ledge, her heart hammering, and crawled commando-style to the kitchen to alert her mother.

It was Sol who went out to greet him. Bea was told to stay inside with Deirdre. From the window seat in the living room they watched the old man's face light up in a crooked smile when he saw Bea's father. Bea felt sure Sol would invite him in; she was eager for a better look at his mouth. But Sol stayed on the sidewalk, talking to the stranger as the shadows deepened and the streetlamps on Melville Avenue flickered on. Finally he took the old man's elbow and steered him up to Sherbrooke Street. The old man didn't seem happy. He looked back at the house with what seemed like distress. Bea's mother said it was sad.

"What is?" Bea asked, though in some dim way she already knew.

Deirdre took Bea into her arms, and Bea inhaled a heady mix of Lily of the Valley, her mother's favourite perfume, and the smell of roasting lamb.

"They're estranged," her mother said, releasing her. "Come." She held out a hand, resuming her customary air of practicality. "You and I have a dinner to prepare."

But Bea stayed in the living room, her face pressed to the cool glass, creating white circles of condensation with her breath. Eventually her father reappeared. He was walking quickly, alone. Bea drew back from the window so as not to be seen. "Estranged," she whispered, trying out the word. In her child's mind, it became mixed up, in a foggy way, with the image of a scarred lip.


Bea woke with a start. A voice was calling her. For an instant she didn't know where she was. Then, in the faint light of pre-dawn, she made out the sloped ceiling and furnishings of her old bedroom. She pulled on her still-damp T-shirt and underwear, left to dry for the night on her chair, and then sat motionless on the narrow mattress, listening. The call came again, faint but unmistakable. It was her father.

She got into her shorts and ran down the attic stairs, making what seemed like a terrible racket in the stillness of the house. The second-floor landing was deserted. Her father's bedroom door was ajar. She looked in. He wasn't in his bed. He wasn't in the bathroom either. She ran downstairs, but the first floor seemed deserted too. She checked every room, including the pantry off the kitchen. She was cursing herself now. She should have slept in Cara's old room, next to his. She'd been selfish by opting instead for distance and space, and now he'd forgotten himself, forgotten the instructions they'd given him, and wandered outside. Then a third call came.

She found him in the basement, where it was always cold and damp, even in the heat of summer. In the unfinished section that housed the furnace, Sol stored his golf clubs and skis and the neatly labelled cardboard boxes that contained his tax papers. The nearer room contained a couch, a TV and a DVD player, as well as a stationary bike that hadn't been used in decades. Sol was standing beside the bike. His eyes were open. He was facing Bea, but he didn't seem to see her. It was unnerving. Still, she wasn't alarmed because she had seen it many times before. She knew he was somewhere else, neither asleep nor awake, wandering in a world to which she had no access.

"Dad?" she said softly, taking his hand.

He was bare-chested, wearing only thin cotton pyjama pants, the drawstring tied in a clumsy bow. His skin was clammy. He pulled away from her touch and shuffled off in the direction of the furnace room. At the door he paused, then went inside. Bea followed him into an impenetrable, dimensionless darkness. The cement floor was rough against the soles of her feet. She put her arms out and walked gingerly, taking tiny steps, trying to remember where the furnace was.

Then he spoke. A single word—if it could be called a word. It might have been the nonsense syllables of a baby. Ah-bah. He repeated it with growing urgency.

Bea stepped forward. When she touched him his arms rose, knocking her hand away. But then they reached out and encircled her waist. It was the strangest thing. Her father was not a physical man. He'd never held her like this before, not even when she was small. She had stepped into a dream. She could see nothing; she felt only the heat of his skin and the gentle pressure of his hands resting on her. At last he let her go. She led him back upstairs to his bed, where he lay down obediently and was still.

# 9.

BEA ROLLED ONTO HER SIDE and opened her eyes. After five nights in the attic, she now knew where she was when she woke up. She took in the familiar furnishings and the dull yellow walls. Her skin was damp, and not just from the heat. She'd had the dream again, the same one she'd had her first night in her childhood home. She'd fallen asleep in the silvery early-morning light after seeing her sleepwalking father safely back to his room. The dream had shaken her, but she had assumed it was her exhausted subconscious trying to process a disturbing experience. But her subconscious wasn't done with it. The dream had come back.

In it, she was sitting on her bed in the attic of the house, as she was now. Only, the house was in ruins. The ceiling was pocked with holes that let in pale beams of moonlight. The bedroom floor was disintegrating too. Through gaps in the broken boards, Bea could make out the eroded floors below, all the way down to the dim skeleton of the foundations. The light was feeble, making it difficult to see. In the semi-darkness things seemed to be hanging: old ropes, coils of wire, swaths of cobweb coated thickly with dust. The old house seemed vaster than it was in reality. From her seat in the attic, Bea seemed to be looking down from a vertiginous height. The internal structure felt precarious, as if movement of even a millimetre on her mattress would result in catastrophe.

Then, far below, in the bowels of the house, something moved. She wasn't sure at first that she'd actually seen it, but she kept watching, straining her eyes in the dull light. And she saw it again. Someone or something was down there, flitting through the gloom. The dream had ended inconclusively, with her frozen on her little childhood bed, unsure what to do. She'd woken in terror, her arms and legs rigid, heart pounding.

As she sat on this same bed now in the reassuring light of day, she became aware of a mechanical whine drifting in through the open window. It was strident and high-pitched, although distant. Perhaps this was what had roused her—a strange noise intruding on her strange dream. She finally recognized the whine: it was racing cars. The Formula One racers were on the track at Île Notre-Dame preparing for the weekend's Grand Prix, the scream of their engines wafting up to Westmount on the June breeze.

Drops of water ran down the windowpane. It would be a wet weekend. Not a safe environment for racing cars. Or bicycles. She'd have to take the metro to rehearsal today, which meant an extra half hour each way, not to mention the fare. Still, it was a Saturday, and she wasn't expected in until noon.

Her clothes lay in a heap on the desk. She hadn't put them in drawers: her way of reminding herself that the stay in her father's house was temporary, a stopgap measure until they found a better solution. This arrangement couldn't go on forever. Her nightly fear that her father would wander was taking a toll. She knew it made more sense to sleep downstairs, nearer to him, but something in her couldn't face the idea. And so she'd lie awake in the attic, afraid to surrender to sleep, and then, when she finally managed it, she was assailed by unsettling dreams.

She reached for her T-shirt and a pair of the clean underwear she'd brought from her apartment a few days earlier along with her yoga mat and cork block. Emergency rations. She was back to a daily Ashtanga routine, which helped mitigate the effects of lack of sleep and made her feel more like her adult self again instead of a trapped and helpless child.

The situation wasn't likely to resolve itself soon. Sol had flat-out refused to hire Mrs. Szabó or anyone else to watch over him, but even if he had been open to outside help, bringing it in wouldn't be simple. A hired hand could hardly be expected to follow Sol down to the basement in the dead of night and submit to his antics.

Bea listened for signs that Sol might be awake. It was almost nine o'clock. Usually he got up before she did, but today all she could hear was the distant wail of the racing cars. Her neck ached. She turned her head slowly from one side to the other. When she looked left, the discomfort became intense. There was a knot in her trapezius muscle. The *trap*, she thought, with grim irony. She would have to stretch tonight, take a hot bath.

She walked to the attic's bathroom, a stuffy little space with a window that refused to open: a room that held unhappy memories. When Madame Huppert had come to live with them, Bea's hair had become a point of contention. It would get tangled when it was washed, and she'd howl when Madame Huppert tried to comb it. Cara's hair was fine and easy to manage, but Bea's was *"un nid de rats."* Around six months after her arrival, Madame Huppert cut it all off in the bathtub. Bea remembered the event distinctly. She'd stood on newspapers laid down on the porcelain, weeping as the scissors snapped. Within minutes, she was ankle-deep in black strands.

She looked at the tub with its lion paws and rust-stained drain, remembering. Bea's hair had not been a rat's nest. It was just thick and wavy. Ever since that sad year, except for a time in India, she'd worn it long. A pipe clanked as she splashed water on her face at the little sink. The plumbing was old. The house was hardly as dilapidated as in her dreams, but it was still ancient, stained, creaking under the weight of its memories.

When she turned off the faucet, she heard the faint metal twang of a pot in the kitchen. She knew her father's routine by heart. The pot was in the cupboard beside the stove. He used it for his oatmeal, steel-cut, which he mixed with maple syrup and five percent table cream. He made coffee in the drip machine and drank it black and strong.

A moment later the front door slammed. Sol was probably just bringing in the *Gazette*, but Bea's heart clenched. She came out of the bathroom, her face still damp, and tore down two flights of stairs. When she reached the ground floor, Sol was waving a newspaper.

"They're out of their minds."

The big headline on the front page was about a mob of student protesters who'd tried to disrupt the previous day's Grand Prix time trials. A photograph showed a line of policemen in riot gear advancing toward an angry crowd.

"I could do without the noise," her father said. "And the crowds. But you won't see me marching with a sign. Don't those idiots know how much money the event brings in? The Americans come up here in droves. They'll stay away if this keeps up."

Something in the photograph caught Sol's eye. He stopped waving the paper and took a closer look.

Bea looked too. In one corner, her chin jutting defiantly as she faced the helmeted hulk of a riot squad officer, was someone Bea recognized: Gen-vie Roy. Every time a confrontation occurred, she seemed to be there, right in the thick of it. The papers couldn't get enough of her. This photo was particularly striking: a slender female David glaring up at a uniformed Goliath. At least, Bea noted with relief, there was no sign of Didier. She hoped he'd had the good sense to stay home with Cara and the girls, but she suspected he hadn't. Her father was gazing darkly at the photograph. "Gen-vie is young," Bea said, hoping to defuse his anger. "You can't blame her. She works for a student group."

Sol looked up. "No," he said, "she works for Cara."

They were eating breakfast when a call came in on Bea's phone. It was her sister. "There's been trouble," she said. Gen-vie was in the hospital. She'd taken a burst of pepper spray in the face. "She can't see out of one eye. Didier is with her. I found a sitter, thank God, so the kids are covered, but I have to hold the fort today at Crudivore."

"Holding the fort" was one of Sol's turns of phrase. "What about the fort on Melville?" Bea asked.

Sol looked up from his oatmeal. Cara was expected later that morning so Bea could go to work.

"Extenuating circumstances, Bea. And weekends are our busiest time."

Bea took the phone into the living room. "I'm not sure he ought to be left alone."

Cara was silent for a moment. Then she erupted. "Look, Bea, we're doing what we can. I can barely cope anymore. I'm already having to deal with his Rosebud stuff, and I've got a business of my own to run, not to mention a family." The phone went crackly as she exhaled.

"So what do we do?"

There was a pause. Then Cara spoke. "Nothing."

Bea picked at a nail, letting the word hang between them. "I can't stay here today, if that's what you're getting at."

"It's not. You can't stay and nor can I. He'll have to go it alone. Read him the riot act, Bea. He wants to be home alone? Let him. Let him prove he can do it. He's got to remain indoors and out of trouble from the moment you leave until you get home from work. He has my cell number if he needs anything. If he can manage it today, fine. We'll hold off on the agency. If he can't, then he knows the consequences."

Bea nodded. Coming from Cara, the plan sounded rational. But the moment Bea hung up, she knew it was wishful. Dangerous even. Unfortunately, there didn't seem to be an alternative.

She went back to Sol and relayed Cara's message. His eyes lit up when he heard it.


The rain had put everyone in a bad mood. Even Dave Samuels was ill-humoured. Bea had been washing coffee cups when he asked her to prompt the cast members that day. It was the first time she'd been invited to involve herself directly with the actors. The day before, they'd gotten bogged down in Act One, Scene Four, in which the king's loyal advisor Kent, banished in a fit of royal pique, returns to his side disguised as a poor labourer. Dave had been prompting them, as he'd done every day since rehearsals began. Prompting took skill and sensitivity, given that some actors were liable to take any intervention as a sign of criticism. Phil Burns didn't belong to that category. His grasp of the text remained highly tenuous. Whenever Dave caught his lapses, which was often, Phil welcomed it. Stan Garroway, on the other hand, playing a thin-skinned Kent, had stalked off the stage when Dave tried to help him.

At his best, Stan was prickly. Today he was being openly hostile. The moment Bea began to supply a line he was stumbling over, he raised a hand and ordered her to stop. Mortified, she fell silent.

Artie stepped in. "Lighten up, Stanley. She's doing her job." He spoke in an easy tone, without aggression or emotion, but the underlying message was clear: he was defending Bea.

Bea reddened, her mind hurtling back to Princess Lea. The roles they'd once played.

Instead of cooling Stan's fire, the remark seemed to fan it. He erupted in a tirade, spewing hot complaint. If Bea had been doing her job competently, he said, referring to her in third person, there would be no problem. But there was indeed a problem, because Bea was not doing her job competently. She didn't know the difference between a dramatic pause and a dropped line. By screwing up her job, Bea had made him screw up his. He was on a roll now, shrill and invigorated by his bruised dignity. There was nothing to do but wait until the tantrum burned itself out.

In theory, Mimi had authority as director to take Stan in hand; instead she just sighed and looked away. Bea felt the stab of an older abandonment, one in which a far more important woman in her life had failed to shield her. Her eyes pricked dangerously. But then yoga practice kicked in. She felt her legs strong and sturdy, the soles of her feet solid on the ground. She took a breath. She hadn't been in this job long, but even she could see that when an actor like Stan was feeling slighted, the worst thing to do was slight him some more.

Artie offered Bea a tiny complicit eye roll as Stan's rant went on. He was attacking Artie now, accusing him of meddling in matters that didn't concern him. As he spoke, Bea remembered another confrontation, from years ago. It had happened during the awful year that followed Deirdre's death. Few events from that year lingered in Bea's memory; an obliterating unhappiness shrouded the weeks and months, covering them in a miserable, eventless fog. Yet one April morning stood out. It had been a cold, sunny morning; the children in the schoolyard were wearing their winter jackets. Johnny Mackenzie, who was older than the other children in Bea's class, had cornered her at recess. Johnny was a big boy, slow and strange. He had repeated grades and would eventually be moved to another school. It was obvious in retrospect that he was developmentally challenged, but to eight-year-old Bea Johnny was a nightmare. She was still in the intensive phase of her speech therapy, before her pharyngeal correction, agonizingly aware of the barely comprehensible manner in which words came out of her mouth. That morning, Johnny had decided to taunt her. He clamped his nostrils shut with his fingers, amusing himself with a crude imitation of her nasal speech. But the amusement didn't last more than a minute. Out of nowhere, Arthur White charged him, pinning him to the ground, pounding his face furiously with both fists. By the time a teacher pulled Arthur off, Johnny was dazed and bloody, a lumpen, snotty, crying mess. Both boys ended up in the principal's office. Notes were sent home to their mothers. And Johnny Mackenzie never went near Bea again.

At last Stan's tantrum was extinguished. The rehearsal resumed. Bea had survived the incident, but it left her hesitant to offer further prompts. She fell quiet, intervening for no one but Phil, who was dropping so many lines something had to be done.

At the break, Bea followed Dave outside onto the roof and watched him smoke. The rain had let up. Below them the streets looked freshly washed. "You can't take it personally," Dave said, sucking on his cigarette and, in the careful etiquette of twenty-first-century tobacco use, scrupulously blowing the smoke away from her.

"Oh yes I can," she answered. "How do you get called incompetent and not take it personally?"

Dave gave her a sidelong glance. "It's not about you, Bea. That's stage management. That's life. If a guy starts yelling, you have to know it's about him, not the person he's yelling at. Stan is a total perfectionist. He's super hard on himself. That's what it's really about."

Bea looked at Dave, with his billowing hair and his pierced brow and the smoke rising in wisps from the corners of his mouth. He was right. She saw it now so clearly. Dave Samuels was a wise man, even though he preferred to call himself a mother.

# ACT TWO

KING LEAR.

*Who is it that can tell me who I am?*

FOOL.

*Lear's shadow.*

$(1.4.236-37)$

# 10.

MONTREAL WAS IN the grip of yet another heat wave, this one so intense that the green seemed to have leached overnight from every plant in the city, leaving the island a listless, overcooked brown. Bea was crouching in the shade of a tree in Westmount Park. Directly before her was the stage, erected the day before by the technical crew on a patch of trampled, sunburnt grass. It was their first day of outdoor rehearsals.

The portable stage looked like something a clever child might construct. Three small white melamine platforms ascended like steps on the left side. Balancing them on the right was a larger platform. At centre, a third platform perched atop a twelve-foot-high framework of metal pipes. To reach it, you had to climb a ladder backstage.

Artie White had designed it. This task was not in his job description as artistic director for Bard in the Parks. That function was mostly administrative, involving grant-writing, promotion and overseeing general operations, although he also got to pick the play each year. In addition to his training as an actor, however, Artie had a diploma in set design. In Montreal theatre circles, he had a reputation for structural inventiveness.

Bear and Maggie from the tech crew were up in the tower he'd conceived, reinforcing it with cables. Bea took a tepid sip from her water bottle, watching them. The tower was high, looming majestically above the area of grass where the audience would sit, but it also wobbled every time anyone standing on it moved. Phil Burns had refused to climb up there that morning for the opening scene, claiming it was unsafe.

Bear and Maggie looked miserable, but not for fear of falling. They were wearing black. The colour was great for turning theatre people working behind the scenes invisible at night, but under a blistering sun, surely it was less than optimal. Bear's face was tomato-red. He'd tied a bandana over his hair, but even so he had to pause every few seconds to wipe the sweat from his eyes. He and Maggie looked like a pair of crows baking on a transmission tower.

Bea licked the last lukewarm drops from her water bottle, put her floppy, wide-brimmed sun hat back on and walked to the spanking new stage. The actors were on lunch break. Most had gone to Sainte-Catherine Street, a block away, to buy Popsicles at the local dépanneur. It was Bea who'd told them about the store, earning her a smile from Dave. His smiles had grown dishearteningly rare as rehearsals progressed and he discovered just how little Bea knew about theatre.

She did at least know the neighbourhood. Dave had toured the area, noting stores and restaurants and other amenities, but for some reason he'd missed Anthony's, a block south of the park at the bottom of Melville Avenue. As a child, Bea had spent her first pennies there. It was where the kids went after school, first for blackballs and licorice, later for beer and cigarettes. And for Popsicles when the weather turned warm. Anthony's had a five-foot-long freezer full of flavoured ices, chocolate Drumsticks and bright orange Creamsicles. Bea had revisited the place for the first time last week, when she picked up a carton of milk for Sol. A Korean family owned it now. Apart from that, nothing had changed.

A hedge and a gigantic pine tree blocked Bea's view of her father's house, but she could sense it hovering on the park's eastern perimeter. She'd spent much of her life trying to escape this neighbourhood. For the eight years that she'd been a nomad in India and Thailand, she had owned only what she could carry. Returning to Montreal, she'd rented an apartment in a neighbourhood as far removed from Westmount—atmospherically if not physically—as possible. Jean-Christian had moved in with her and they'd founded Om Sweet Om. Yes, it had been sweet. Not that Sol understood. But Bea had been truly happy. Now she was literally back where she'd started.

They would rehearse here for two more weeks before opening in July. After that they'd take the show to parks all over the island and even up to the Laurentians. For a good part of the summer, though, Bea would be here, in a place she'd known all her life. She felt like the butt of an obscure, slightly malicious cosmic joke.

The sun beat down on her until moisture ran between her breasts. The heat of the platform stung her palms as she climbed onto it. There the light was even more blinding than down on the grass, the sun's rays bouncing off the bright white surface and making her wince, despite her drugstore sunglasses. She reached for the scrub brush she'd left in a jam jar of solvent. The graffiti was pale now, a ghost of the black letters that had greeted her that morning. You could still see the writing, though, despite her best efforts.

She squatted down and resumed her scrubbing. There were four fat letters—DOGO, or OGOD, if you read it backwards. She'd spent the morning trying to make it disappear. The tag had been sprayed on all five stages, even the top one, where the techs were now roasting. Dave had been beside himself when he discovered it.

Sweat gathered in the fine cracks around Bea's eyes, making them sting. She was in her Indian whites, a cotton tunic over paper-thin pants—clothes she'd bought years ago in Delhi—but even so, she was suffering. An extreme heat warning had been issued and people were being urged to stay indoors, or to seek refuge in air-conditioned malls and movie theatres. Apart from the actors and Westmount's impressive population of fat grey squirrels, the park was deserted.

Wisps of fluff hung suspended in the soupy air. A strand wafted down and then was borne up again on an invisible current. The cottonwoods were in seed. The white fibres spread across the island of Montreal, catching on gables and hedges and gathering on blades of grass like a fine dusting of snow. Bea watched a strand turn on a descending air current, its glide terminating in the puddle of solvent before her. She poked at it delicately, trying to free the fine wisp, but all she managed to do was drown it.

Something moved at the periphery of her vision. A figure in a cream suit and Panama hat was approaching along the path. Bear and Maggie raised their heads to watch.

She did a double take. It was Sol. He had been so good over the past while, sticking to the daytime rules about staying inside, that she'd ceased worrying. A mistake. For here he was, shuffling down the park's main path toward her, looking determined and not the least bit contrite. As he came closer, Bea saw the anger on his face.

They'd had a difficult night. He'd wandered again, waking her out of a dead sleep with his moans and nonsense syllables in the pre-dawn hours. The cause of his distress, this time, had surely been the notary they'd visited the previous morning. Sol was outraged. He'd denied any need for a power of attorney, accusing her and Cara of conspiracy. He even told the young professional to his face that he was a blight on his profession. Bea was used to the outbursts by now, but the notary's look of shock and affront had reminded her of how irrational her father was becoming.

Sol drew close to the platform on which Bea knelt. "We have to talk," he said in a stage whisper. Beneath the rim of his hat, his face was pale and sweating.

Bea could see the actors returning. They'd just passed Westmount Park School, on the park's south border, the one Bea and Artie had attended. Now they were crossing the grass schoolyard where Artie had pounded the daylights out of Johnny Mackenzie. Their stomachs were full, their spirits high. The three young women who played Lear's daughters led the way, sucking long tubes of brightly coloured ice. Phil Burns trailed a half-step behind them, talking loudly and laughing at his own jokes.

Bear and Maggie were looking down from the upper level at the incongruously suited gentleman as if he might be a mirage. The actors spotted him now. Phil Burns stopped telling jokes and turned his full attention to the stage.

Bea was on her knees on the platform, but she was still uncomfortably high in relation to her father. He didn't seem to notice. He placed his forearms on the platform and leaned in confidentially. "I'm sick of this. You have no right to keep me prisoner in my own home."

He straightened and gazed directly at her. He'd trimmed his beard and had knotted his tie impeccably.

"We can talk about this later," Bea said in a low voice. She resisted the temptation to add that no sane person, let alone someone ill and frail and about to turn eighty, should be out in this heat.

"You have no idea what it's like. It's intolerable." He was talking fast, slurring a little. The words rose and quavered as he spun into rage. "It's de*meaning*," he continued. "De*human*izing."

Phil strode up behind him. "Everything okay, Bea?" His voice boomed. He sounded like God.

She looked down at the two old men and felt her ribcage contract. "Phil," she said as steadily as she could, "I'd like you to meet my father."

Phil's expression betrayed a fleeting moment of surprise. Then he extended his hand. "It's a pleasure and an honour, sir."

Sol didn't take the hand. "Who are you?"

With uncharacteristic modesty Phil said that he was in the show with Bea.

"Not just in the show, Dad," Bea said. "Phil *is* the show. He plays King Lear." She heard herself start to narrate the actor's career: his years at Stratford, his Broadway credits, the movies he'd appeared in and the stars he'd worked with. She spoke with impressive enthusiasm, if not outright reverence.

Phil drank it in. She'd studiously kept her distance from him since the first day of rehearsals, refusing to acknowledge any special familiarity. But Phil hadn't given up. At every opportunity he sought her out, offering jokes and stories and, one morning, a bag of Medjool dates after hearing her mention to Dave that she loved them. He was courting her. Everyone in the company saw it. He flirted with the other women, too—no female within hailing distance was safe—but Bea was his special target, perhaps because almost every other woman was so young that he didn't stand a chance.

Her praise today had nothing to do with Phil. It was aimed at her father, and it was working. His brow had smoothed. He was looking at Phil with interest. He offered Phil his hand.

Phil shook it heartily and the two men began to talk. Phil explained that he was originally from LaSalle, the working-class district that overlooked the Lachine Rapids. He loved Montreal, he said. Came back whenever he could.

"Roots," Sol said quietly. "There is nothing more important in this life."

Heat rose in punishing waves from the square of melamine on which Bea knelt. Were her father's words an indirect rebuke? Had Sol registered her reluctance to move back into his house? Had he been hurt by the fact, and it was a fact, that Melville Avenue was the last place on earth she would choose to call home? The four fat letters, OGOD, shimmered backwards below her.

Spots were appearing in her visual field, darting like water mites across the white surface of the stage. Not a good sign. It was time to get out of the sun. "I should take a break," she said, nodding to her father. "Let me walk you home."

She lowered herself carefully onto the grass beside him. Under his Panama hat, Sol's cheeks were now flushed. "His house is on Melville," Bea explained to Phil. "It's a two-minute walk."

Sol looked as though he might refuse, but Phil took hold of his free arm. "With your permission, I'd like to tag along," he said affably. "Do me good to stretch these old legs."

Sol allowed himself to be guided back to the house, entertained along the way by Phil's stories about Hollywood. Ten minutes later, he was safely re-ensconced in the dark cave of his curtained living room, with Itzhak Perlman playing a Beethoven sonata on the stereo. Bea made a big pitcher of lemon water, drinking half of it herself before she left him. As she and Phil crossed the soccer field on their way back to the stage, Bea confided to him that Sol had been diagnosed with dementia. Phil slowed his pace, his face full of alarm as she listed the symptoms: memory loss, mood swings, sudden eruptions of rage. "There can even be hallucinations," she said, "although so far that hasn't been an issue."

"He seems perfectly sane to me," said Phil, rolling down his sleeves to protect his forearms from the sun.

"He *is* sane," said Bea. "Mostly."

"But he's got it? The Lewy body thing? You're sure?"

"You can never be sure," said Bea. "Until the autopsy."

They walked the rest of the way in silence. It was a sad story to hear, but especially, perhaps, for Phil. He was sixty-nine, which surely meant he had a few health issues of his own. When they got back he hurried away, presumably in search of cheerier companionship.

Bea found Dave Samuels at the lean-to he'd set up as their new headquarters. It was a crude structure, a broad tarpaulin secured to tent poles and stretched over a table and two folding chairs. On the table were their scripts, open to the first act, where they'd stopped before lunch. Beside the scripts were Dave's office supplies, along with two enormous tubes of sunscreen and several cans of insect repellent. Lying beneath the table was a big first-aid kit with a red cross clumsily taped on either side. Dave was sitting in his chair, bent over his script. He looked up.

"Can you call everyone?"

She nodded. She felt better. The spots in her vision had filled in after she'd drunk the lemon water, but now her head ached.

She wandered to the women's changing tent, which she and Dave had erected that morning. "Ten-minute call," she announced, lifting the flap at the entrance. The tent was made of a white synthetic fabric dense enough to repel rain. Sunlight, however, it trapped. A wave of oven-force heat hit her in the face.

Ann O'Neill, who'd been cast in the role of Lear's scheming eldest daughter, Goneril, was bent over an open cloth bag, wearing a bra and cut-off shorts.

"Ten minutes," Bea repeated, although Ann had obviously heard.

"Right," she said irritably. A scarlet V stretched from her neck to her sternum above a soft white midriff. That morning she'd slathered her nose with zinc oxide, but had neglected her chest.

Bea withdrew and dropped the tent flap. The rest of the actors were sitting under a tree behind the tent, slapping themselves listlessly. The little grassy area where the stage had been set up was flat, which was good for outdoor seating, but drainage was a problem. The ground was wet and spongy. Even at midday in this overpowering heat, it teemed with insects.

Bea did a quick head count. Seven actors were needed for the scene they were about to rehearse: Lear; Kent; a knight in Lear's retinue; the Fool; Goneril; Goneril's husband, Albany; and their malevolent servant, Oswald. Including Goneril, she counted only six. She looked at the faces of the five men in front of her, trying to figure out who was missing, but her brain was sluggish from the heat.

Artie winked amiably, seeming to read her mind. He cocked his head at the men's tent. "Don't forget His Highness."

Bea thanked him, although she registered a certain wariness in his expression. Ever since the meet-and-greet he'd been tentative with her, and when Phil came around to flirt she'd often catch Artie looking watchful. Despite her best efforts to prove otherwise, he still seemed to believe there was something going on between them.

She looked inside the men's tent: empty. She checked all around the stage, but could find no trace of Phil. He did this from time to time, vanishing when he was needed. She hoped he hadn't gone off to the store. Just as her hope was turning into full-blown fear, she spotted him walking jauntily up the path from the public washrooms. When she called his name, he stopped and grinned, holding out his arms to her as if she were a long-lost lover.

"Ten minutes," she said, trying for a businesslike tone. "At least, you had ten minutes when I first started looking for you. Now it's more like two."

He hooked his elbow with hers, still grinning, and swung her around like a square dancer so they were both headed in the direction of the stage. "Let's go!" he said, goose-stepping as though it were all a big joke. Phil tacked sideways, listing toward her like an old schooner in a stiff breeze. His breath smelled odd. Not unpleasant, it was sweet and minty, but with a faint metallic undernote.

Everyone was waiting. Artie White's face was no longer amiable. She couldn't see his eyes behind the small round sunglasses that made him look like a blind man, but she knew he was upset with her. So was Dave. Bea had disappeared before the five-minute stage call, leaving him to handle it, and now here she was, arm in arm with jolly Phil. She pulled her elbow free and went to Dave's side.

Mimi, who'd risen from her seat in the shade to join them, clapped her hands. "Okay gang," she said. "Let's get to it." She nodded at Bea, more in dismissal than absolution.

Stan Garroway had the bulk of the lines at the top of the scene. By now he had the play's first half pretty much memorized, which made her happy. Bea, as the designated prompter, didn't want another tirade. She found a strip of shade by the side of the stage. Her cover would recede as the sun dropped in the sky, but for now it offered a little comfort. Behind her, in a tall cedar hedge, starlings had gathered. There seemed to be an awful lot of them. A convention of some kind, or did they like Shakespeare? She looked toward the stage again and tried to ignore the birds. She could see the actors only from behind, but there was an advantage to this. They couldn't see her either unless they craned their necks. They could hear her, though: a disembodied voice, a net to catch them if they stumbled.

Stan kicked things off with grace and assurance, a relief because this was Act One, Scene Four, the exact spot where Bea had had that first, awful run-in with him. As the Earl of Kent, he was in disguise in this scene, posing as a serving man in search of work. The king, who didn't recognize his old friend and ally

dressed in peasant clothes, was questioning him, trying to dis-
cover who he was. The play was full of disguises, something Bea
hadn't realized when she first read it in school. Here Kent was
trying to protect the life of his king, and later, noble young Edgar
would don the rags of a beggar and pretend to be mad in order to
save his father, the Earl of Gloucester. And at the end of the play,
King Lear himself would strip off his royal robes and bare himself
before the audience to deliver wrenching lines about who he was
or wasn't. Bea hadn't made up her mind what Shakespeare
was trying to say, but the play seemed to turn on the question
of appearances and what, exactly, lay beneath.

So far, she hadn't had to call out any lines. Phil had brought his
dog-eared script onto the stage. He carried it around everywhere
rolled like a baton, sticking it in his back pocket when he rode his
Harley. It was so mangled it wouldn't lie flat. He was slow reading
his lines because the pages kept curling, but at least he was saying them without prompts.

Ann O'Neill watched impatiently as Phil plodded through the
next pages. Speaking of appearances, she didn't look exactly
regal—she'd wrapped a damp T-shirt around her head and her
nose was still plastered with zinc oxide—but her delivery was
convincing. Her annoyance at Phil actually helped the scene.
Goneril was supposed to be impatient with her father here, treat-
ing him like a doddering fool. Her saucy servant, Oswald, came
onstage next to berate the old king and, now that he was at his
daughter's mercy, insult him shamelessly.

Finally, the Fool entered. Bea felt a tingle of pleasure. She
enjoyed watching Artie for many reasons, not all of them artistic.
He had been given a jester's hat by the costume lady. It had four
brightly coloured prongs, each tipped with a silver reindeer's bell
that jangled when he moved. He swept the cap from his head
now, holding it out to Kent and the king and dancing around

them on the stage while he cracked jokes about coxcombs. He still moved like a boy, nimble and quick, although his body was clearly that of a man. Muscular forearms flashed before her, waving the cap in the sunshine.

He was a good actor. Not in-your-face like Phil Burns, but the restraint made him all the more interesting to watch onstage. He looked confident and in command as he strode up to Phil and began to banter, warning him with a cutting wit against trusting those who were unworthy. He moved easily through his speeches and then launched into the famous lesson to the king. *"Mark it, Nuncle,"* he said, winking at the older actor,

*"Have more than thou showest,*
*Speak less than thou knowest,*
*Lend less than thou owest,*
*Ride more than thou goest,*
*Learn more than thou trowest,*
*Set less than thou throwest,*
*Leave thy drink and thy whore,*
*And keep in-a-door,*
*And thou shalt have more*
*Than two tens to a score."*

The whole thing was delivered pitch-perfectly, not a word and not a gesture out of place. Bea was grinning with the pleasure of it. Mimi, who was sitting with Dave in the shade of the tarpaulin, started to clap. But Artie didn't notice them. He was completely caught up in his role, dancing around the aged king, excoriating him for handing over everything he owned—his lands, his regal title, all his worldly wealth—to his daughters.

Phil regarded him in amazement. He lifted the rolled script over his head and shook it, his face stiffening with rage. *"Dost thou call me a fool, boy?"* His arm swung down, narrowly missing Artie.

The spell broke. Artie jumped back, his eyes opening wide. The sparring in this scene was supposed to be verbal only. He delivered his next line watching the king's hands.

Bea understood his confusion. She also found it hard to tell sometimes where real life left off and acting began for Phil Burns. He was, in the jargon, a method actor—which, as Bea understood it, meant he drew on wells of personal experience for the emotional authenticity of his performance—so the line was necessarily blurry, but at times it was uncanny how seamlessly he was able to merge his personality with the irascible old king.

There was a pause while Phil tried to find his page. Bea gave him the prompt, which he took greedily.

Half a minute later, Ann O'Neill swept back onto the stage. She still didn't look remotely royal. Nevertheless, she marched imperiously over to Phil and jutted her hip, waiting for his cue.

*"How now, daughter?"* Bea supplied, breaking the silence. Lear was supposed to go on to remark on Goneril's frown, but Phil had lost his place in the script again. Bea gave him the rest of it.

Artie and Ann had several lines after that, which ought to have allowed Phil time to figure things out, but he'd given up. His expression was blank. His mangled script hung limply in his hand.

*"Come, sir,"* said Goneril, taking his wrist and shoving the script in front of his startled eyes. In iambic metre, she urged him to snap out of his humours. Bea mouthed the familiar exhortations in silence.

> *"I would you would make use of your good wisdom*
> *Whereof I know you are fraught and put away*
> *These dispositions which of late transport you*
> *From what you rightly are."*

In the cedar bush, the starlings began to chatter again. Something was making them agitated. Bea turned around.

"Line!"

She spun back to face the stage. Mimi Meir was looking at her with impatience. Bea didn't even glance at the script in her lap. She knew this section cold.

"Does any here know me?"

She paused for a second, waiting to see if Phil would pick it up from there, but the script remained rolled like a baton he'd lost the will to pass.

"Give it to him," Mimi ordered. "The whole thing."

The birds had gone quiet. In one quick burst they took off, rising over the stage in a single body and veering west, wings flashing in the afternoon light. Bea's voice rose with them, cracking the silence.

Artie's face, already pink from the sun, was getting redder. As Bea delivered Phil's lines, Artie glared in fury at the distant treetops. And this was why, when Phil tilted, Artie was the last person onstage to notice. Bea witnessed it all from behind. It was the strangest sight. Phil leaned slightly in Artie's direction, and then leaned a little more. His old head floated for a moment and dipped gently, like a balloon leaking helium, onto Artie's shoulder. It was so slow and graceful that Ann laughed, mistaking it for a joke. Artie recoiled, but only for a second. When Phil's knees buckled, Artie managed to grab him around the chest.

"Whoa," Artie said. He was a smaller man than Phil, a good three inches shorter and much thinner. Weighed down by the old actor, he dropped to one knee and, using his shin as a lever, lowered the great mass of Phil's body to the hot surface of the stage. "He's out," he said, crouching to shield Phil's face from the sun. His expression was worried, almost tender, as he stroked Phil's cheeks and called his name.

Mimi ran to the stage. "Oh no, oh no," she kept saying, her voice wavering as if she might start to cry.

Bea ran to the nearest water fountain to fill a water bottle. She was pretty sure it was heatstroke, but for a man of Phil's age, losing consciousness could be serious. She remembered a St. John Ambulance course she'd taken, the signs of heart attack. By the time she made it back to the stage, sweaty and out of breath, he was sitting up, although his face was the colour of putty. He was trying to shoo Dave away, waving his hands as though he was swatting at gnats.

"Better," he said, after drinking from the bottle Bea gave him. He wiped his mouth with his shirtsleeve and gave her a wink. "Okay, ladies and gents," he told the circle of actors that had formed around him. "Drama's over. Back to the tragedy." He rose to one knee, wobbled, and promptly toppled over.

Dave dropped to his knees beside Artie to help him.

Mimi took out her telephone and announced that she was calling 911.

Colour rushed back into Phil's cheeks. "Oh no you don't." He raised himself up on one knee again, groaning prodigiously, and by some miracle made it to a standing position.

This time neither Dave nor Artie dared touch him. Phil began to walk off the stage with odd, jerky steps, his face tight with concentration.

Mimi bounded away, and in the grassy patch between the back of the stage and the hedge, she intercepted him. She was no longer tearful. Though she was half his size, she didn't hesitate to place herself squarely in front of Phil, blocking his path. Then, in a voice everyone could hear, she said she'd smelled the booze on his breath and wasn't fooled by his pathetic attempt to mask it with mouthwash. In her not quite Southern drawl, she told him that if he was bent on destroying himself, he could go right ahead. But not until after the show had closed.

Artie disappeared backstage, his expression grim. The rest of the troupe, Bea included, stood for a moment, stunned. Finally, Ann jumped down from the platform and headed for the tents. Only Bea and Dave were left standing in the sunshine, watching this real-life drama unfolding below them on the grass. After another minute, the intimacy of it was too much even for Dave. "C'mon," he said, taking Bea by the arm. "Mimi's got it under control."

"Control" wasn't the word Bea would have used. Phil was no more controllable than the weather. She and Dave retreated to their lean-to, resisting the impulse to look back. Bea's head was pounding now. She sat down in one of the folding chairs and finished off the last of the water in her water bottle. A line of sweat trickled down the side of her face and dribbled onto her neck. When she looked back toward the stage, Mimi was standing alone on the grass. She looked smaller than normal, hunched and sad. She was shielding her eyes, watching something on the street to the south of the park.

There was a sudden roar. Bea scrambled to her feet in time to see Phil driving off on his Harley, his helmet flashing like a mirror in the sun.

I I .

THE STREETLAMPS HAD JUST gone out and the sky was starting to glimmer when Bea heard a noise.

She lay still, trying to listen, but the house settled back into
silence. It was probably a cat down in the street, or a squirrel
nattering at someone. She hadn't been sleeping, just lying there
dry-eyed and exhausted, consumed by thoughts of Artie White.
Watching him on stage the previous day had stirred her. It was his
hands. Objectively they were pleasing, not meaty like a lot of
men's, his fingers long and slender. But they kept coming to her
with an insistence bordering on obsessive, waving the jester's cap
in the scene with Kent and the King; catching the body of Phil
Burns as he collapsed; stroking Phil's cheek with surprising
tenderness as he sprawled upon the stage. Whenever Bea shut
her eyes, there they were, lying in wait.

It was ridiculous. She barely knew a thing about him now.
And the things she did know weren't encouraging. He didn't
have a girlfriend. At first glance, this could seem positive. For
Bea, it raised suspicions. Margo Indongo had told her Artie
hadn't had a long-term romantic partner in years. He liked
women well enough, that wasn't the problem. In the local acting
community, he was considered a catch. He dated and had plenty
of women friends who adored him, like Mimi Meir, with whom

he'd collaborated on half a dozen productions. So what was the problem?

He wasn't an easy guy to read. Sometimes warm, then inexplicably cold. He pushed her off-balance. But somehow, perhaps because of their shared past, or perhaps because she hadn't felt the touch of a man in six months, he'd gotten under her skin.

The noise came again. Faint, but recognizable. It was her father. In the semi-darkness she pulled on shorts and an undershirt and crept downstairs. Her father was standing in the doorway of his bedroom. His feet were bare. He was wearing blue silk pyjamas, top and bottom. He didn't react when she appeared; he was repeating his nonsense word over and over, staring through her, his voice tight with alarm.

Bea swallowed. "It's okay," she said with as much reassurance as she could muster. "It's okay." But when she reached for him, he flapped his arms and shook free. She followed as he descended two flights of stairs to the basement, muttering relentlessly. When he came to the furnace room, he paused in the blackness. Bea took a deep breath. She wanted to believe her presence made a difference. She stood there, trying to dispel the panic, trying to be calm and not emit clouds of fear molecules into the dank, close air. His mutterings grew softer. Minutes later, they stopped altogether and she was able to lead him upstairs. Back in his bedroom, he lay down and sank into sleep.

She returned to the attic. There would be no sleep for her, what with the survival hormones that had just flushed through her. The sky had brightened and over in the park, birds had begun to chirp.

There was no rehearsal that day, a Sunday, so at least she wouldn't have to go to work. On the little attic desk, beside a heap of dirty clothes, was her laptop. Next to that lay a cheque made out in her name. It was for seven hundred dollars, not a bad amount, except that it represented her entire contract: all the work she'd done for Bard in the Parks Theatre so far and all the work still to do until end of the run in mid-August. She was, she calculated, earning about ten dollars a day. Her hours were long now, and would only get longer as opening night drew near.

Seven hundred dollars. She owed her landlord, Zorba, five thousand. Or at least, that's what she'd owe him on the first of September, when her lease formally expired. She'd already given him notice that she was leaving. He hadn't bothered to disguise his relief. She was a terrible tenant, months in arrears. At the moment, she wasn't even earning enough for groceries, let alone rent. She knew exactly what her father would say. Why the hell was she working there? In his present condition, with his emotions more volatile than ever and the indignities of his restrictive new life still fresh in his mind, there was no way he'd have offered to pay Bea's debts had he known about them. Which he never would. Bea would see to that.

She opened her laptop and began drafting a letter to Zorba, apologizing once again for her unpaid rent and offering him five hundred as a step in the right direction. A very small step. She doubted he would rejoice. It didn't come close to covering her debt, and she had no idea where she was going to find the rest.

She logged into her old email account. Dozens of messages flooded in. It had been a while since she'd opened her laptop; lately she'd been using only her phone for communications, consulting it many times a day to keep tabs on cast and crew through the new Yahoo address Dave had helped her set up, as well as through voice mail and text messages. This was how a person got hooked, she supposed. It was Dave who'd told her about "nomophobia": the no-mobile phobia that made people clinically anxious when deprived of their devices, even for a matter of minutes. Since Bea had gotten her phone, her anxiety levels had certainly shot up. There were plenty of other reasons for this, of course, but she was now, thanks to Shakespeare, part of this jabbering, finger-pecking world.

Emails were still pouring into the laptop. Fifty, fifty-one, fifty-two . . . The stream stopped, at last, at fifty-four. Bea sighed. She began the laborious work of sorting and deleting.

She clicked on one email and a beautiful face appeared on the screen: burnished skin and black hair braided to the waist. The face was looking off to one side, laughing as if someone had just whispered an intimate joke in the sculpted seashell of her ear. It was Gaya Pal. Arching over her head in the photo were the words OM SWEET OM in orange and pink. Gaya had kept the yoga studio's name. Bea's spirits soared for a moment, then soured. She and Jean-Christian had chosen that name together, back when she'd been full of hope. Could someone appropriate a business name just like that? Wasn't there legal protection of some kind? The name was too personal to be handed off like a yoga mat or bolster. It wasn't just another asset. Gaya must not have understood that.

She read on. Below the beaming face on Gaya's e-circular was a list of events she'd be leading in the upcoming months. Things were going well, Bea saw, and despite herself she felt a jealous twinge. Gaya was among the teachers slated to lead the Yoga White-Out, a massive rally held every August in Mont-Tremblant Park. Cash-toting enthusiasts flew in from the States and gangs of yoga teachers and their acolytes car-shared from Montreal to camp out, contort and cavort for three days in the Laurentian hills. It was like Burning Man, but with lakes and trees instead of desert sand. Bea had seen clips on YouTube: a gigantic field of white-clad people prostrating themselves in downward dog. Being asked to teach at the White-Out was a huge honour.

Bea scrolled down. She had to read the next item twice to

grasp its meaning. A five-day residential retreat would be held at a spiritual centre near Saint-Jérôme, in the southern Laurentians. The event's title was Five Gateways to Ecstasy: An Introduction to Tantra. Accompanying the description was a photo of a stone carving from India depicting a woman and man entwined in an erotic embrace. She hadn't realized Gaya was into this type of thing. What stopped her, though, wasn't the word "ecstasy," or even the suggestive carving. It was the name beside Gaya's: Jean-Christian Dubois.

Bea clicked on the link for Om Sweet Om in the email. When Gaya's elegant new website came up, she clicked on the course schedule. And there he was, his name listed as the instructor for two evening classes and the Saturday morning early riser. She scanned the schedule and saw Jean-Christian's name in a fourth box. Friday nights. A new course called Partner Yoga, to be taught collaboratively with Gaya.

Bea felt ill. She knew she ought to close the webpage, turn her mind to more productive thoughts, but something in her, something abased and self-lacerating, wouldn't let it go. She clicked on "More About Om" and found him. A bandana was tied around his head to hide the thinning hair; his sensitivity on that subject had once struck her as touching. In any case, he was still sexy. He'd be sexy until his dying day. He was smiling, one bushy eyebrow raised. She used to call that his flirt face.

Looking at it now, she couldn't help tormenting herself with questions. The India trip. Jean-Christian's mystery companion. Had it been Gaya? And when Bea signed the studio over, had Gaya just been a front for Jean-Christian himself? Bea scrolled down the list of teachers and stopped at Gaya's head shot. She was breathtaking.

Bea rubbed her eyes. Rosy orange light was filling the sky outside her window, matching the palette in which the website's name was lettered: Om Sweet Om. The old, stale words were fresh again in the colours of a brand-new day.

Bea closed the browser and Gaya and Jean-Christian vanished from her screen. She deleted the letter to Zorba she'd begun and shut down the laptop. She would deal with the unpaid rent this afternoon, after she'd slept. She might talk to Cara about a loan, though her sister had a habit of revealing secrets to their father. Sol's anger was more than Bea had the strength to face right now. It was six o'clock. Sunlight had touched the treetops in the park. Bea was tired and utterly dejected. She lay on the bed and shut her stinging eyes.

Four hours later, the sound of clattering metal woke her up. When she came downstairs, Sol was in the kitchen, scrubbing out his oatmeal pot.

"Yours is in the fridge," he said, not turning to greet her.

Breakfast he could still handle. He'd been eating the same thing for as long as Bea could remember. Deirdre had scorned sugary cereals; Sol had honoured her memory after she died by refusing to buy the Cocoa Puffs and Cap'n Crunch his daughters pleaded for. In three and a half decades, he'd made oatmeal thousands of times. Now, even as he lost the competence for other tasks, this one still came easily. It was muscle memory.

Bea went to the fridge and took out the bowl her father had prepared for her. He'd sprinkled the oatmeal with blueberries and pecans. For all its inconveniences, moving in with her father had improved Bea's diet.

"Coffee's still hot," he said. "Put your dishes in the machine when you're done." He started to shuffle out of the kitchen.

"Dad, what does *abba* mean?"

He stopped. "What?"

"Abba. It's a word. Or a name. Anyway, you said it. More than once."

Sol frowned. He was aware Bea was watching him. He would not meet her gaze. "When exactly did I do this?"

"Last night. It's happened before, though. At night, in your sleep."

He still wouldn't look at her. "I said it last night?"

She nodded.

"Abba," he repeated softly. He stood there, contemplating the scratches and stains on the floorboards of his kitchen.

Bea knew better than to press. Sol would talk if and when he wanted. He left the room and climbed the stairs slowly to his den. Bea put her bowl of oats in the microwave.

She was finishing breakfast when Cara arrived, trailing Elle and Yasmin. She looked harried. Didier's first court appearance was coming up; his lawyer, Cara told her, had just arrived at their place to strategize. Needless to say, it had thrown off their schedule and now Cara had to assume restaurant duty. Could the girls stay with Bea for a while? Not for long, Cara promised. She'd be back around three, as soon as Crudivore's midday rush was over.

Bea felt like howling in protest. It was her day off. She'd been waiting all week for this and had been counting on Cara to stay with Sol while she went to Sainte-Famille Street. She hadn't been home in days. She needed clothes. She needed to pick up her mail. She needed to talk with Zorba.

"I can't . . ." she began, but her sister looked suddenly so overwhelmed and forlorn that she couldn't continue.

"Please," said Cara.

There was nothing for it. She inhaled deeply and nodded. "But only till three," she said. "I've got to get home."

"I can drive you when I get back. We'll all go, right girls?" She looked over at them, but neither paid her any heed. Yasmin had climbed onto the back of the living room couch and was straddling it cowgirl-style. She'd kicked off her sandals and knocked the corduroy cushions to the floor. With one plump little hand raised above her head, she was a miniature rodeo queen. Meanwhile Elle was over in the corner, examining a pair of decorative antique pistols that Sol kept on a side table.

Cara turned back to Bea. "It'll be easier in the car than by bike. It'll save you time. We could even bring Sol along if you like."

Just what Bea needed. So much for a day of rest. She remembered, fleetingly, her plan to ask Cara for a loan. This was obviously not the time. It would seem calculated, crass.

"So we're good?"

Bea nodded curtly. The maddening thing about her sister was how fast she rebounded. Cara was smiling, all trace of helplessness gone. She picked up her purse and turned to the door. "You're the best, Bea."

Realizing that her mother was about to leave, Yasmin ran to her.

"No," Cara said in a calm voice, prying the child's fingers off her sleeve. "You're staying with Auntie Bea. Mama has to work. And I expect you to be good."

Yasmin looked at her aunt, then at her mother. She shut her eyes and began to wail.

"Come on, now," Bea said, trying to soothe her. She'd looked after the girls before, of course, but not enough to know how to handle their outbursts. When she tried to take Yasmin in her arms the little girl lunged for her mother's legs. Cara pried away her fingers a second time and, before Yasmin could reach for her again, hurried out the door. The wailing grew frantic, accompanied now by panting and hiccupping. Yasmin clawed at the brass handle on the front door. In her anguish, she no longer had the presence of mind to resist Bea, who enfolded her in her arms. The touch seemed to calm her. The wails grew less piercing, subsiding finally into sobs. Elle had come up behind them, and now

Bea gathered her into the embrace too. Then the three of them went to the living room window to watch as Cara sped away in the old Renault.

Sol called from upstairs, wanting to know what all the fuss was. The two little girls looked at her, wide-eyed.

"It's fine, Dad," she said, loud enough that he would hear. "The girls are here." She winked at them, smiling, and reached for their hands. What was the best way to distract children? Food, Bea decided. She informed her nieces there was a nice old cookie tin in the pantry. She didn't mention that the cookies in it were boring oatmeal ones: what else could they be, in Sol's house? And the cookies had raisins in them, which Bea and Cara had detested as kids. But the girls were delighted anyway. They stood at the counter, chewing happily. Elle told Bea that all cookies—all that were baked or contained sugar, at any rate—were forbidden in their home.

Printed on the sides of the cookie tin was a poem that dated back to Deirdre's girlhood. Bea helped Elle decipher the words as they read it out together.

> "*Monday's child is fair of face,*
> *Tuesday's child is full of grace.*
> *Wednesday's child is full of woe.*
> *Thursday's child has far to go.*
> *Friday's child is loving and giving.*
> *Saturday's child works hard for a living.*
> *But the child that is born on the Sabbath day is bonny and*
> *blythe, good and gay.*"

The girls asked Bea which days they'd been born on.

"I'm not sure," she said. "We'll ask your mum when she comes back."

"Do you know your day?" Elle asked.

Bea nodded. "Thursday." Deirdre had told her so, in this same room, thirty-five years ago.

Elle looked at the cookie tin and frowned. "Far to go," she said. "What does that mean?"

Bea smiled. "My life will be a journey. I'll have to go searching for the things that make me happy." That was the explanation Deirdre had given her. It hadn't been wrong.

Elle looked at her aunt dubiously. Thursday was clearly not the top choice on the tin.

After their snack, the girls followed Bea up the stairs, stopping at the den to say hello to their grandfather and then climbing eagerly to the attic, where Bea had promised toys. Yasmin squealed with joy when she saw the wooden horse. She climbed on its back and began rocking blissfully at the foot of the bed. Elle went to the bookcase, squatted down and started pulling out books. Sun poured in through the open window. In its honey glow, dust motes swirled.

Elle sneezed. Then she sneezed again. Bea opened the window as wide as she could, to little effect. The room was covered in a twenty-year layer of dust. She'd been sleeping here for a week, but her movements had been slight. The dust had lain largely undisturbed. Stirred by two active children, it was filling the air.

Bea hurried downstairs to the kitchen and came back up with a mop, a pail of water and an armful of rags. As the girls rocked and read and found new joy in the amusements of her past, Bea set herself the long-neglected task of making the space bright again.

# 12.

THREE DAYS LATER, Bea woke to the gong of her phone. The noise had become familiar; she always responded to it now, even from the depths of unconsciousness. She'd been troubled by insomnia once more. And when sleep finally came it had brought with it the recurring dream, which had been more harrowing than ever. The shadowy intruder had started climbing the stairs, advancing toward her in the attic. Her phone had actually been a deliverance.

She reached over the side of the bed and retrieved it from the floor, which was solid. Hole-free, she noted with relief. The ceiling, too, was intact. It was her sister. "Yes, Cara," she said, her voice husky from sleep.

"Did I wake you?" Cara sounded more surprised than apologetic. Yasmin was clamouring in the background. She wanted to talk to her aunt.

The air in the room was heavy with trapped heat. For days smog had hung over Montreal, growing denser and more malodorous as all the emissions of the city accumulated under its dome.

"In a minute," Cara said to her daughter. "First, Mama has to ask Auntie Bea a question."

Bea lay back on the bed. Above her, a strand of cobweb she'd missed in the cleanup wafted gently. She closed her eyes, hoping the question didn't involve a favour.

Cara needed her to go to the Palais de Justice in Old Montreal and help out with Yasmin. Didier's court date was at nine that morning and she had to be there. The trouble was, Yasmin's day-care had become infested with lice; the place had shut down for the week while they dealt with the situation. "Of course they close their doors when I need them most," Cara said. Elle was at school, but Yasmin had nowhere to go, and it was impossible for Cara to find a sitter on such short notice.

"I can give you a couple of hours," Bea said. "But only two. I've got to be at work by noon."

Cara said there was no problem. "It's just the preliminary hearing. They're quick. And don't worry," she added. "Yas doesn't have nits herself. I checked. But even if she does, you won't catch them unless you do something really silly, like share a hat with her or use the same brush."

Bea ran her fingers through her hair. She'd had lice once, on an ashram in India. Her scalp had itched ferociously, and then the nits hatched. Tiny black insects had crawled from the thicket of her hairline down to her cheeks, shocking her boyfriend of the day, a fastidious Israeli whose name she could no longer recall. She'd had no choice but to shave her head.

"What will I do with Dad?" she asked.

"Explain the situation. He knows the drill. He'll just have to stay alone."

Ninety minutes later, as Bea approached the Notre-Dame Street entrance of the Palais de Justice, she saw Cara hurrying in her direction, pulling Yasmin behind her.

"Thank you," Cara said, passing Bea her daughter's hand. "We were in a real bind." She didn't look as if she'd slept any more than Bea had. She had put on makeup, but it didn't hide the dark circles under her eyes. She kept glancing over at the courthouse, her brow furrowing in preoccupation.

Yasmin had gone shy again, or maybe she sensed that she wasn't her mother's principal concern at the moment. She looked up at Bea miserably and started to howl.

Cara knelt down in front of her. "Yas," she said, holding the little girl's shoulders. "Yas, honey . . ." She glanced at Bea for help, but Bea wasn't sure what to do. The howling intensified. "Yasmin!" Cara said a little more sharply. "You've got to stop this. You've got to try to be a big girl for Mama."

Yasmin shook her head furiously.

Cara stood up and gave her a nudge in Bea's direction, which only made things worse. Passersby were now looking at Bea with disapproval, apparently assuming that she was the mother because of their similar colouring.

Had Yasmin been her child, Bea would have taken her into the courthouse. She wanted to be with her mom, hardly an inappropriate desire. What harm could it do? For that matter, the presence of a four-year-old in the public gallery might soften the judge's attitude toward her father.

But Yasmin was Cara's child. And at this moment, Cara was starting to walk away. Yasmin darted after her, grabbing her leg and holding on for dear life.

"No, Yasmin," Cara muttered, trying to disengage herself. "It will be boring if you come with me. You'll have much more fun with your auntie. You had such a good time on Sunday."

Yasmin's mouth had formed a pink O from which howls streamed forth unimpeded. Bea could actually see her uvula trembling. It was like something out of a cartoon.

Cara groaned. "Of course this has to happen now. It's the nits, and also this legal thing with Didier. She's been acting out all week long."

Yasmin had switched her grip to Cara's arm, continuing her shrieks. Her eyelids and nostrils had turned red in an otherwise pale face, as if the anguish had chosen to concentrate there.

Something had to be done. Yasmin was working herself into a frenzy. Bea resorted to sweets again, just as she'd done on Sunday. It was a cheap gambit and a violation of Cara's dietary code, but it caught Yasmin's attention. She stopped crying. Cara didn't say a word as Bea promised they would go in search of candy. Old Montreal swarmed with tourists; eye-catching treats for children should not, Bea reasoned, be hard to find.

Looking nearly as distraught as her daughter, Cara seized the opportunity to hurry away. She went into the courthouse with only one backward glance as Bea kept up her enticing patter. The ploy worked, more or less. Yasmin's chin kept trembling even after they set off together into the sunshine, heading east on Notre-Dame, but at least the tears had stopped.

Tourist season was near its height. The buskers were out, and there, standing in front of a fountain beside City Hall, was a clown. His painted red lips were downturned. Blue tears hung on his cheeks under each eye.

He was selling hugs. A dollar each, according to a homemade cardboard sign printed in English.

Bea and Yasmin slowed their pace and came closer. When the sad clown saw Yasmin, he squatted down so that his tearful eyes were level with hers. He was dressed in billowy green pants and a bright yellow shirt emblazoned with a rainbow. He held out his arms to the little girl.

"Hug?" he said hopefully. He was younger than Bea had thought. Barely out of high school.

Yasmin shook her head.

The clown pretended to cry. It was very convincing. He reached into the pocket of his billowy pants and extracted a white hanky.

A whole chain of handkerchiefs followed, appearing one after the other as though from an infinite supply. When the last of them finally flipped into the air, he caught it with a flourish and blew his nose, producing a loud honk.

Bea and Yasmin laughed. The clown's closed hand emerged from behind his back. He opened it. On his palm lay a little brass horn with a red rubber bulb. His fist closed and the horn honked. He did it again. He winked at Yasmin and offered her the horn.

Yasmin didn't hesitate. She grabbed the horn and honked repeatedly, her bubble-gum pink running shoes dancing on the wide sidewalk.

The sad clown stood up. "She should join my act," he remarked. His painted lips were still downturned, but the real mouth beneath was smiling. He said his name was Steve. He'd hitchhiked across the country from Vancouver, hoping to join the Cirque du Soleil. After a few minutes' conversation and a great deal of honking in the sunshine, Yasmin handed him back the horn. Then she threw her little arms around him and squeezed with all her might. Bea hugged him too. He was a foot taller than she was, with a firm, boyish body that made her feel young and tender.

She fished a dollar out of her pocket, but he waved it away. "Forget it," he said. "No charge for the real thing."

In Place Jacques-Cartier, they stopped to watch a second busker who was juggling plates. He was an older man, clearly a seasoned professional. Six plates were spinning high in the air as he darted back and forth in a continuous jig, catching them on sticks and sending them aloft again.

By now Yasmin had forgotten about the candy, but Bea had given her word. She led Yasmin down to Saint-Paul Street and into the cool interior of the Bonsecours Market. They were buying bottles of water when they spotted the holy grail: in a pot outside one of the boutiques were immense multicoloured lollipops arranged to look like fresh-cut flowers. They were outrageously expensive—ten dollars a pop—but it was as if Bea had planned it. Minutes later, Yasmin's tongue was bright green and she was as happy as she could be. She'd hugged and honked and seen plates fly, and now she was riding a wave of sugar-fuelled euphoria.

Steve the sad clown had disappeared by the time Bea started leading Yasmin back to Saint-Laurent Boulevard. But ahead of them, in front of the courthouse, there seemed to be a new attraction. A crowd had assembled. Bea wondered if it was another busker. She held her niece's sticky hand in her own as they advanced, playing "I Spy." Bea was looking for something red, Yasmin's favourite colour, and not paying the crowd much mind when she saw a familiar figure standing on the courthouse stairs. No, two familiar figures: Didier and Gen-vie Roy, with a black patch over one eye. Jérémie Canton, the student leader, was beside them, holding a megaphone. All three had squares of red felt pinned to their chests.

"Red!" said Bea, pointing.

The child followed her aunt's finger. She released Bea's hand and started running, waving her lollipop and calling her father's name. Bea started running too. The gathering consisted mostly of students, but a group of men stood near its edge, dressed in dark clothing and conferring in low voices, their expressions serious. Unable to follow Yasmin, who was far ahead now, weaving adroitly through the adult legs, Bea edged around the back of the crowd, away from the reporters who had congregated at the front, their cameras and microphones held high. A media scrum was in the making, the focus of which would be Didier Ignace Malraux, the man toward whom Yasmine was running, full tilt.

She had by now almost reached her father. There was no sign anywhere of Cara. Didier bent close to Jérémie Canton and spoke feverishly into his ear. His face was tense. As he straightened, Yasmin made it up the courthouse steps and barrelled into his knees. Bea saw a way through and hurried to help him.

Didier was wearing a black T-shirt with the Crudivore logo on it, as was Gen-vie. With her eye patch, it gave her the look of a sexy pirate. The logo stretched over her pert little breasts, a seedling with fluorescent green leaves cupping the word CRU. It would get considerable air time, judging by the cameras pointing at her. Crudivore would be linked forever more in the public's mind with springtime and protesting students.

Didier was holding his daughter and looking around, bewildered, when Bea touched his arm. "Take her," he said urgently. "I thought you were looking after her. Take her, now!" He held out Yasmin's hand. When Bea tried to comply, Yasmin withdrew it, her green lips opening in plaintive protest.

"Okay, okay," Didier said, pressing the child's head to his leg in an effort to soothe her. *"Arrête de pleurer, trésor."* He squatted down, taking her shoulders in his hands and looking into her streaming eyes. That quieted her.

*"Il faut que tu sois sage, Yasmin."*

He looked out again at the surging crowd. "You don't want them to see you in tears, do you?" he said, nodding at the television cameras. He released his hold on her.

From this vantage point, the cameras looked like bazookas trained right on them. Bea started to edge away, but her brother-in-law gave her a look. "You stay." Again he passed Yasmin's hand over. The little fingers were sticky. Didier also handed Bea the half-sucked lollipop, which he'd been holding gingerly, upside down, away from his clothes. He winced, wiping his fingertips on his shirt. The candy had perhaps not been such a great idea after all. Bea spotted a trash can near the courthouse door, but when she tried to pull Yasmin toward it, the child whimpered.

Didier looked down sharply at her. *"Fais un beau sourire, ma puce,"* he said, and smiled to set an example.

To Bea's surprise, Yasmin complied. Despite her green lips and sticky fingers, she became a model of four-year-old grace. The sun beamed down on the entire scene. They were on show. Now that Bea was up here in the revolutionary lineup, she had no choice but to remain for whatever was to come. There was still no sign of Cara. Bea kept checking behind her, hoping for her sister to appear. She got rid of the lollipop, planting it discreetly in a nearby flowerbed.

After another whispered exchange with Didier, Jérémie Canton raised the megaphone and thanked everyone for coming out. The protests were winding down for the summer, he said. This was natural. The academic year was now officially over. But the fight would continue. *"Nous ne lâcherons pas!"* he shouted, raising his fist.

The crowd cheered.

There had been casualties, Jérémie said, and gestured gravely at Gen-vie. "The authorities have offered ample demonstration of what they're made of—flash-bang grenades, tear gas, pepper spray used against peacefully marching civilians."

Again the crowd roared.

Canton passed the megaphone over to Gen-vie. She turned out to be a gifted speaker. The demonstrators had always been peaceful, she declared with conviction. Untrue, Bea thought. A couple of government offices had been ransacked and there'd been street fights and some looting, for which the student organizations refused to take responsibility. In Quebec, Gen-vie continued, the right of peaceful assembly was sacred. The government was showing its true oppressive nature in criminalizing public protests.

There was more cheering. A number of people had brought pots and pans, which they now beat in approval.

Gen-vie waited through the noise, her youthful face pale with purpose. "We need to send the authorities a message," she proclaimed, after the clamour had died down. "We need to tell them this is no way to run a nation, no way to treat their young."

The crowd opened its collective heart to her. She was in her element. Her passionate voice captured the grievance these people felt in their lives and reflected it back to them in a way that made it seem significant and noble.

She'd spent a night in jail, Gen-vie went on. Why? Because she had dared to speak out. And for this act, for the simple act of expressing her convictions, she'd been summoned to court. Treated like a criminal. Was this what Quebec had become? Was this the nation the Québécois people dreamed of building? She raised her fist into the air, her eyes shining. Beside her, Didier did the same. Bea caught her breath. It was impossible not to be moved. The air filled with waving fists. Even little Yasmin joined in.

Bea was on the verge of raising her own fist when she felt a nudge from behind. It was Cara, breathing hard, her face strained and anxious. She squeezed into the lineup beside Bea and took her daughter's hand. With the return of her mother, Yasmin lost interest in the general goings-on. The sticky little fist came down and she ducked behind Cara, burying her face in the backs of her legs.

Gen-vie wasn't done yet. On the day of her arrest, she said, she'd been thrown to the ground and pepper-sprayed. She could have been blinded. Her black eye patch was stark and vaguely obscene in the sunlight. Was this justice? Her face retained its calm even as the crowd erupted in shouts of solidarity. The police were the criminals, she answered in a clear, almost childlike voice. They were the ones who were out of control. Bea found herself applauding, compelled by the urgent appeal for a better world.

Gen-vie's expression changed. Her posture stiffened, the confidence she'd exuded a moment before evaporating. Bea wondered if she might be overwhelmed by the energy and emotion of the crowd, but then she saw that Gen-vie was no longer looking at it.

She was gazing past it at something in the distance. She gripped Didier's arm and he, too, looked.

Bea followed their gaze. A line of men in black boots and body armour was moving north on Saint-Laurent Boulevard from the direction of the river. They wore white helmets, their visors sparkling in the sun. They carried dark shields marked with the word POLICE in large white letters. They were advancing slowly and deliberately.

Bea froze. Until that moment, she had carried an unexamined, unconscious conviction of her own security in the world. That as a human being, she was at the very top of the food-chain—a predator, not a prey. Yet here she stood, immobilized, her body quaking like that of a small hunted animal, a squirrel or maybe even a mouse. Standing beside her, Cara seemed to be in a similar state. She'd swept Yasmin into her arms at the first sign of trouble, but now she, too, stood there immobile.

The entire crowd appeared to have frozen. It was the oddest thing. For two or three seconds, no one moved. And then, in a mass, they snapped out of it. Didier started running north, pulling Gen-vie behind him. Jérémie Canton sped away east along Notre-Dame with most of the other protesters, splintering off onto side streets that led to the river. As they fled, they shed everything extraneous and incriminating in a trail behind them—banners, signs, bandanas, carnival masks, little red squares.

Cara, who by now had recovered her wits, began walking toward the courthouse entrance. Her pace was measured. She held Yasmin with seeming insouciance, her hands clasped under the little girl's buttocks, and didn't look back. Bea followed. Astonishingly, no one stopped them. It was a brilliant tactic: walk softly and carry a child.

When Cara got to the Palais de Justice, instead of going in she skirted the front of the building until they came to a little tree-lined walkway directly to the east: the Allée des huissiers. There, she began to run. Bea ran too, hair flying, face and neck cool in the breeze. Beside them was a park, a pleasant green place shaded by leafy elms, with a life-size statue of two children running and leaping just like she and Cara were doing. She had no idea where her sister was headed, no idea where the Allée des huissiers might lead. They clattered down a set of stairs to Saint-Antoine Street, where, it turned out, Cara had parked the Renault.

There had been a plan, after all. Cara handed her daughter to Bea and calmly retrieved her keys. Yasmin didn't protest, seeming to sense that this was no time for a fuss. It was only once she was strapped into her seat and her mother and aunt were sitting in front of her with the doors safely closed that she allowed herself a tentative whimper.

"None of that," her mother said sharply. The whimpering stopped.

As they rolled along Saint-Antoine and descended the on-ramp to the Ville-Marie Expressway, Yasmin stared out the window, wide-eyed and silent.

Fifteen minutes later, Cara parked in Sol's driveway and cut the engine. She turned around to look at her daughter, and for the first time all morning, she smiled. "You are one brave girl, Yasmin. I'm proud of you."

Before they walked into the house, Cara pulled out her phone to text Didier. The three of them waited in the sunshine for a minute, but no answer came. Now Yasmin's chin began to tremble.

"It's okay," Cara said, bending down to give her a hug. "Your daddy knows how to handle himself."

Bea glanced at her sister, but Cara didn't register it. She was rocking back and forth, holding her daughter tight against her.

Sol didn't come downstairs to greet them. He was in his den, watching television. He didn't even turn when Bea poked her head in the room to check on him. Bea didn't mind. She was grateful. He had come through for them. He'd honoured his side of the bargain and behaved. And because of it, they were together now, more or less safe and sound.

Cara was wiping Yasmin's hands and face with a damp cloth, setting her up in the living room with a video game when Bea came down the stairs. A minute later, she joined Bea in the kitchen.

"Shit, shit, shit," she said in a low voice. "What a nightmare."

It wasn't just the police breaking up the crowd, or the fact that Didier might yet again be in the lockup. Apparently the court appearance had gone badly. Formal charges had been laid, and not just for illegal assembly and rioting; Didier was also on the hook for mischief and damaging public property. Something had happened to the monument at Park and Mount Royal. Didier hadn't inflicted the harm himself, but he'd been involved. Then there was obstruction of justice: he'd tried to restrain the police officer who arrested Gen-vie. Not only that, but in court, while pleading not guilty, he'd made a political speech and only narrowly avoided a contempt charge. "And now this fiasco," Cara said, shaking her head in disbelief. "He'll be charged again, for sure."

Bea frowned. "Is it a crime to run away?"

"It's a crime to protest without a permit now, remember? It's totally fascist, but it's still the law. They were on the courthouse steps. In front of TV cameras." She covered her eyes with her hands. "He's lost his mind."

Bea pictured her brother-in-law hurrying from the protest with Gen-vie. He hadn't given Cara so much as a backward glance. "It's Gen-vie," said Bea. "She's so into the protest, so passionate." She searched for a tactful way to put it. "And Didier's spending so much time with her."

Cara went silent. Then she faced her older sister. "Is there something you want to say, Bea?"

"I think I just said it."

Cara leaned on the sink and gazed into the greenery of the backyard. "Look, Didier does what he does. He told me it's nothing, that there's nothing to worry about. What can I do? Do I really need to know more?"

Bea didn't hesitate. "Yes, you do."

Cara stared at her. Bea was no less surprised at her own bluntness. Confrontation was not exactly her style, especially with her opinionated sister. But the events of the morning had shaken something loose. Bea kept imagining the face of Gaya Pal. "I've been where you're standing, Car," she said. "I've been through it. Believe me, not knowing isn't a refuge."

A light of acknowledgment flickered briefly in Cara's face. But then she threw up her hands. "I can't push it, Bea. Not right now, not with Sol in the state he's in, and the kids and everything else that's going on. It's too much. It's too precarious. I'm sorry."

"I'm the one who should apologize," said Bea quickly. The giddiness that had surged when she'd spoken out was gone. Remorse flowed in to replace it. Bea was suddenly aware of the faint pinging sound of Yasmin's video game in the living room. Cara was right. There was a lot at stake: a decade-long marriage, two children, a flourishing business. Bea took a step closer and put her hand on her sister's arm. She did feel truly sorry.

# 13.

TEENAGE BOYS WERE PLAYING soccer on the field in Westmount Park. The shirtless players ran back and forth tirelessly, hooting and laughing in the sunshine. Normally Bea would have stopped and watched for the sheer pleasure of it. Not today. She'd stayed longer than expected with Cara, and now she had to hurry to make it to work on time.

The weather was dry and clear. The humidity that had plagued the city for weeks had finally lifted. Bea was following the footpath that ran along the southern edge of the field when Jack DeVries pedalled by on his mountain bike. Seeing her, he stopped.

"Hey, riot girl," he said.

Bea didn't know what to say to that.

Jack laughed and fished his phone from his shorts pocket. He was a good-looking young man with a flashy smile. "You're on YouTube. Racking up the views."

He whipped off his aviator shades and squinted at the phone, swiping screens with his thumb while he balanced the bike between his legs. He found what he was looking for and held the phone up for Bea, shading it with one hand so she could see.

There she was, standing with Didier and Gen-vie on Notre-Dame as they raised their fists in solidarity. She looked awful. Her scar, glaringly white on her sun-flushed face, rose from the worried line of her lip and disappeared up her nostril. Her nose looked more skewed than usual. Was this what she had become? A tense, crooked creature with a crack in the middle of her face? She'd never liked photographs of herself; video was a thousand times worse. She looked thinner than she'd thought. And older. Gen-vie's smooth, youthful features made for a painful comparison.

"You know Gen-vie Roy?"

Bea nodded. She had to make an effort to look up from the phone. "Didier is my brother-in-law."

Jack's mouth opened in surprise. "Gen-vie is your sister?"

"No, no," Bea said. She explained that Gen-vie was Didier's employee at Crudivore, the restaurant that Didier owned with her sister, Cara.

Jack looked at her blankly. "O-kay," he said, pausing on the second syllable as if he still didn't understand. "But you're in with that crowd. You're a *casserole*."

Bea wanted to tell him that it was more complicated than that. Or simpler. She'd just been babysitting.

But Jack had already taken back his phone and was swiping again. "You saw this one, right?" He held up a photo of a girl in alpine gear hanging from a rope, rappelling down the angel statue on Park Avenue. The photo must have been taken at night, because both the statue and the girl's face were obscured by shadow. The girl's sexy pirate body was, however, unmistakable.

"It was in all the papers a couple of weeks ago, here and in Europe," he continued, oblivious to Bea's dismay. "She's the face of the *printemps érable*."

Only you couldn't see her face. Bea squinted at the little screen. At the statue's base another shadowed figure caught her eye. It was a middle-aged man, gazing upward as he secured the girl's ropes.

Jack was rambling on, praising Gen-vie's courage. "It's like the

Salt March, you know?" He was surprised by Bea's blank look. "You didn't see *Gandhi*?"

Bea shook her head. She had no idea what he was talking about, and anyway she was definitely late now. Dave wouldn't be pleased if he saw her standing here with Jack when she should be helping him set up.

"You've got to see it," Jack insisted. "Kingsley. Gielgud. Total A-list cast."

Jack walked his bike alongside Bea as she hurried toward the stage, edifying her with talk about Gandhi and long marches in sandals.

Mimi Meir was sitting on a folding chair beneath a wide multicoloured golf umbrella. She stood up when she saw them. Her smile was so unexpected that for a moment Bea couldn't believe it was directed at her. Then Mimi raised her fist. On the stage Jay O'Breen, the noble young Edgar, was warming up. He too raised a fist when he saw Bea. Beside him, old Gregory Pym—Edgar's father, Gloucester—just looked confused.

Mimi crossed the grass, followed by Dave Samuels. Bea started apologizing but Mimi waved a dismissive hand. It turned out that Gen-vie Roy was a personal friend. In fact, most of the cast knew her: before taking the job at Crudivore she'd waitressed at Rockabilly, a bar on Saint-Laurent, whose cheap beer and late kitchen hours made it the preferred hangout of Montreal's Anglo theatre community.

"I'm glad they're fighting the charges," Mimi said.

"Fucking cops," Jack muttered. "Pepper-sprayed her right in the face. That's the crime right there, if you ask me."

Everyone in the cast had seen the video of Gen-vie climbing the angel and her subsequent arrest. Both events had been posted on YouTube. Only Gregory Pym, who didn't own a cell phone, kept asking what they were talking about.

"She should file a civil lawsuit," said Mimi decisively. "The best defence is a good offence."

Bea smiled and said nothing. On the screen of her mind a shadowy girl hung in the air, her feet planted on an angel, while below her Cara's husband held the ropes.

The day's rehearsal schedule had been changed: Phil had called in sick again. Instead of Act Three the company would rehearse Act Four, which contained a fair number of scenes without him.

Bea took a seat beside Dave, whose long limbs were folded into a tiny plastic chair. His script was on his lap so that he could note the actors' movements onstage—their blocking, as Bea had learned it was called.

"What's wrong with Phil?" she whispered.

Dave drew a squiggle on a slip of paper and added a dot. A question mark.

"Could it be serious?"

Dave shrugged. The rings in his eyebrow rose and fell. "I asked him that," he whispered. "He hung up. When I called back, he didn't answer."

Up on stage Jay was delivering a soliloquy. Then Gregory Pym came stumbling on, led by Margo, her black braids tucked beneath a cap. She was doubling roles, playing a serving boy before Cordelia's return to the stage in the final act.

Gregory held his arms out straight. His face was contorted in a theatrical squint.

Dave turned to Bea. "Blood?" he whispered, cocking his head at the stage.

He was referring to Gloucester, whose eyes had just been gouged out by Goneril's evil husband. Gloucester ought to be covered in blood. .

Bea flinched. She was the blood lady. Dave had given her the recipe: cocoa powder, icing sugar, water and red food colouring—it was almost like mixing brownies. Bea was supposed to prepare it at home and replenish the stock nightly. She'd made a fairly successful trial batch; the cocoa had a pleasant smell and gave the blood a grimly realistic, purple-brown tinge. The actors were supposed to be using it now so that Gregory could get accustomed to the feel, but after the drama at the courthouse Bea had completely forgotten about it. She promised Dave in a whisper that it wouldn't happen again.

"Good," said Mimi as the scene ended. "Now let's do the cliffs."

Bea settled down on the grass. She loved this scene. Old, blinded Gloucester asks a mad beggar to lead him to Dover, where he intends to plunge off the chalk cliffs into the sea and die. What Gloucester doesn't know is that the mad beggar is really Edgar, the son he's wrongfully renounced, the child who will save his life by leading him in circles, and will open his blind eyes, at last, to the light of love.

Jay O'Breen recited his lines as the beggar-in-disguise, delivering the verse with such ease that for a second Bea forgot herself. *"Come on, sir; here's the place,"* he lied, leading his blind father to the top of a nearby knoll.

> *"How fearful and dizzy 'tis to cast one's eyes so low!*
> *The crows and choughs that wing the midway air*
> *Show scarce so gross as beetles. Halfway down*
> *Hangs one that gathers samphire, dreadful trade!*
> *Methinks he seems no bigger than his head.*
> *The fishermen that walk upon the beach appear like mice."*

A few lines more and he stepped backward, claiming his head was spinning from the height. Gloucester asked to be set where his guide had been standing. *"Give me your hand,"* said Edgar, reaching out. *"You are now within a foot of th' extreme verge."*

It was over in an instant. That's what happened when theatre worked, Bea was starting to realize. You stepped out of time and ordinary existence. Mimi was grinning. She'd felt it too. In her lilting accent, she heaped praise on the two actors—one green and eager, the other stooped and a little tired in the heat.

The remainder of the afternoon was spent on the play's last scene, which contained a fight to the death between Edgar and Edmund, Gloucester's legitimate and illegitimate sons. Mimi had hired a friend to coach Jay and Jack in swordplay. Their weapons were plastic and weighed next to nothing, but they did somehow produce great clangs when they clashed. The real prop swords— made of wood, slightly heavier, more realistic-looking—would arrive the following week.

"Put your back into it," the fencing coach said as Jack lunged. "I want to see you sweat."

Jack's eyes gleamed. He pinned Jay to the ground almost immediately, but Jay threw him off. The fighting between the young men was controlled, yet unhinged and erotic.

"Good!" said the coach. His accent sounded Australian. He whipped the air with his own sword. He was a seasoned athlete, and he obviously knew his weapon. "You're desperate, right?" he said, stepping between them. "One of you must die."

He whipped the air again. He had a cork tip on his sword, but that didn't stop him from disarming both actors and knocking them to the stage.

When the coach released him, Jack was angry. "Take it easy," he said. "All we have are toys."

After Dave had noted the blocking, Mimi released the cast for the day. Bea put the swords away and carried prop boxes to the company's rental truck, glad to be let off early. Something caught her eye lying in the dirt behind the stage. It was Phil's curled-up script.

Dave's face darkened when she showed it to him. "Would you deliver it to Phil, Bea? He's not far from here. He left Mimi's place a few days ago. One of us should make sure he's alive."

The new place was on Sherbrooke in the neighbourhood of Notre-Dame-de-Grâce, only ten minutes by bike from Melville Avenue. Across from it were a Salvation Army outlet and a guitar shop blasting Jimi Hendrix into the street through wall-mounted speakers. Phil's building was characterless, neither old nor new, with a glass front door. The entry was redolent with smells from the Polish bakery next door.

Bea punched in the apartment code Dave had given her. The intercom rang repeatedly, filling the entrance with its chirp before finally switching to a dial tone. Relief rippled through her. Perhaps he was out. She glanced through the glass at her bike, waiting for her a couple of metres away on the sidewalk, locked to a pole. Her relief didn't last. He could also be in there, so weak and ill he couldn't make it to the intercom. Bea read through the list of tenants. There was no superintendent or manager to buzz for help. She punched in Phil's code again, trying to retrain her imagination. On the third ring, he answered.

When he came out from the elevator his skin looked greenish in the fluorescent light and his hair was uncombed, but otherwise he seemed all right. He was dressed in a pair of purple shorts and an old T-shirt with an image of a sailing sloop on the front, its sails and masts half-effaced by the tempests of too many spin cycles.

With a sweeping gesture, he invited her in. She wanted to refuse, but he held the door open, gazing at her with such determination that she stepped past him into the lobby. She'd make small talk for three minutes, she told herself, check that he wasn't dying, and then get out. She'd be merciful to an old man.

The tiny, musty elevator groaned as it rose. Phil looked at Bea and smiled as though not quite believing his luck. They were standing too close for comfort. She could smell his skin, musty and metallic. She looked up, fixing on the floor numbers lighting up above his head. When they finally bumped to a stop, he placed a hand on her back to guide her out the elevator doors. If he was sick, he was doing a great job of hiding it.

The apartment he'd rented was a dismal studio. A picture window overlooked the cars and grime of Sherbrooke Street. At the base of the window, a small screened rectangle was open to let in air. Tinny music from the guitar shop drifted in, punctuated by traffic sounds. The furnishings consisted of a small bamboo table and a queen-size bed. There wasn't room for anything else, or for anyone. The bed was unmade: no blankets or bedcovers, just disordered sheets and a couple of indented pillows. Phil pulled at the sheets, half untangling them, and then sat down, patting the mattress beside him in invitation.

Bea's mercy dissolved. She stood where she was and held out the curled script. "You forgot this behind the stage. I thought you might want it."

He rolled his eyes.

"I mean," Bea said, "you might need it."

"Ah," he said, leaning forward over his knees. "*Need.* Now that's a different story."

He'd kicked off his shapeless brown slippers, revealing feet that were cracked and chalky. The purple shorts he was wearing, Bea now saw, were in fact plus-size boxers. He'd come to the front door in his underwear.

"We missed you today," she said, trying inanely to stick to her purpose. On the floor, half-hidden by the bedside table, was a makeshift bar: half-empty bottles of Noilly Prat and Beefeater gin.

Phil straightened, grinning at her like a naughty child, and patted the mattress again. "Come sit with me."

Bea shook her head. Then she took a half-step forward to put his script on the bed. As she neared him, he seized her hand. Their eyes met. He kept grinning as if it were all a big joke.

"Hey," she said. It wasn't panic, not yet, but she could feel her heart beating in her chest.

She shook free and stepped away from him. There was no way she could mother this man; he'd made that abundantly clear.

"I can't stay," she said. "I just dropped by to see if you were okay."

"Right." The grin faded, although his eyes were still twinkling. "And?"

"And?" she said, wary.

"So what's the verdict? Am I okay?"

She sighed. He was angling. And he was drunk. That was the problem here, not illness. He masked it like a pro, but she was starting to recognize the signs.

She looked away. On the little bamboo table was a framed photograph of a child of maybe four or five. Dark hair cascaded down her shoulders in natural ringlets. Her eyes were closed, making her look like a cherub. It was a lovely shot. Bea recognized her from the baby portraits on the wall in Mimi's flat.

Phil was still waiting for his answer. He noticed what she was looking at. "My long-lost daughter," he said, clearing his throat. Bea glanced at him. "Not literally," he said, shaking his unkempt head. "I know perfectly well where to find her." He paused and scratched his chest at the spot where the sloop's mast disappeared into white cumulus clouds. "She's in Toronto, running a gym for kickboxing."

He was estranged from her. That was what he was trying to say in his alcohol-tinged, discursive way. He looked at the picture, all the bluster gone. Her name was Angelina. Angelina Meir. She'd taken her mother's last name, he said, legally dropping Burns when she turned eighteen and was capable of doing such things. "The only hint of me that remains is in her gym, Burn Baby. Apparently, it's done well."

Bea remembered the pink canvas gym bag at Mimi's place. She wondered whether she should risk saying something sympathetic. She knew a fair bit about estrangement herself. But there was too much chance Phil would wilfully mistake sympathy for something else. She couldn't afford to feel sorry. She stood for a few more awkward seconds by the bed, and then said goodbye.

She didn't bother waiting for the creaking elevator. She couldn't wait to be outside again, free of him and the dismal building. For five flights down the metal fire stairs her feet clanged, loud and jarring.

Sol came outside onto the porch as Bea was locking her bike to the railing. He'd been alone again this afternoon. It was now part of their daily routine. So far, they'd been lucky. Sol seemed to be managing fine. Compared to Phil, he looked like an ad in GQ magazine—pink shirt and pale linen pants cinched by a belt of finely woven leather strands. The only thing missing was his Panama hat.

She greeted him with a smile.

He responded with a scowl. "Do you think I'm a fool?" His voice trembled with emotion. "Do you think I'm so old and stupid I won't find out what you do? Is that what you think?"

Before she could ask what he was talking about, he shuffled back into the house. She finished locking her bike and went inside. He wasn't in the front hall. Bea threw down her knapsack and called out for him, but there was no answer.

She found him at his desk in the den, glaring at the wide flat screen of his desktop computer. It was the YouTube clip of that morning's impromptu demonstration at the Palais de Justice. She saw herself, skinny and crooked-faced, in the background.

"What got into you?" he said, his eyes hard with judgment. "Where is your loyalty?"

"Loyalty? What are you talking about?"

"I'm talking about Cara," he said. "Your flesh and blood. Are you blind as well as stupid?" His right fist flew out and struck her shoulder. He gasped at the impact, as if he were as surprised as she.

"Stop it!" she yelled. "Dad! Look at me! Stop!"

He was squaring up to throw another punch when she caught his wrist. It was so thin her fingers encircled it easily. He began to struggle. She seized his other wrist and pinned his hands behind his back. Her father was about her height, five foot six. He'd been taller once, but the years had shrunk him. They stood together, panting, in a clumsy embrace. The bristles of his beard scratched her cheek.

Gradually his breathing steadied. His arm muscles relaxed. She let him go. "I'm sorry," she said. He went back to the desk and smoothed his clothes. "Did you hear me?" she asked. "I said I'm sorry."

She was hoping he would apologize too. He had hit her. They'd fought countless times in the past, but never with fists. Sol prided himself on his physical restraint. Words were his weapon of choice. Until today. Bea's hands were shaking. What a day it had been, first the awful encounter with Phil and now this. Bea wasn't afraid of her father; he'd hurt himself more than he'd hurt her, but she was shocked. Mystified too. He was like a different person. And what was that strange remark about loyalty to Cara?

He was staring at the screen now as if none of it had happened. He clicked Replay and the courthouse clip started again. Bea's body tensed. Over his shoulder, she saw that the video had been viewed nearly sixteen thousand times.

14.

IT WAS THE SUMMER SOLSTICE: a bleak morning of steady rain. Outside Bea's bedroom window, every trace of colour seemed to have leached from the world. She sat on the bed and punched "Montreal weather" into the browser on her phone. A bunchy cloud appeared, from which continuous lines of rain fell. The probability of precipitation was ninety percent. She'd thought Artie might cancel the day's rehearsal, but she hadn't yet received a text to that effect. It looked like she'd be working in the rain.

She had overslept. Sol had wandered again in the night. He'd been gentle as a lamb when she found him in the furnace room, all his fury over the courthouse clip gone. He'd called out his word again and embraced her. She'd stood in his arms, listening to the creaks and knocks of the old house, feeling the rise and fall of her father's thin chest against her own. The sensation of being held in his arms, of being clung to by this man whose embrace she'd so seldom felt, had been profoundly disturbing. And it had been blissful. Finally she'd led him back to his bed and watched as he turned his back to her, faced the wall and became still. Then she went back to her own bed and cried.

Sol's attack the day before—punching her, leaving her no choice but to restrain him—had made finding someone to look after him suddenly much more urgent. If his rages were to lead regularly to violence, Bea wouldn't be able to do it alone. She'd spent the evening online and found a number of companies offering care for older people, including one—Alert Eldercare Inc., on Décarie Boulevard—that specialized in geriatric dementia. The homepage showed happy white-haired men and women engaged in a variety of activities, everything from gardening to playing cards. When she clicked the "Meet Our Staff" tab she discovered a sadder reality. The Alert staffers were mostly female: no surprise there, given the working conditions and pay. Some were young, some older, their skins every colour of the human spectrum, but to a one they were tough-looking and grim.

That was what she was searching for, though, wasn't it? Someone tough, or at least tougher than she thought she was. A stand-in to take the blows. Bea covered her face with her hands. It was too horrible. She couldn't, in all conscience, demand this of anyone. She lowered her hands, wiping her eyes, and then drying her fingertips on her shorts. She didn't know what to do. She made a mental note to phone Michel Allaire. He was an expert in Sol's affliction and he'd also seen Sol in action. Perhaps he could advise them.

As Bea went downstairs, the whole house was reverberating with the strains of Mozart's *Magic Flute*. Sol was listening to the opera in the living room. It had always been his favourite. In Bea's youth, he'd played it on Sundays—the day he took entirely off from work. Bea and Cara had come to know the arias by heart.

This morning he'd cranked up the volume like a metalhead listening to his favourite band. It was so loud that Bea was tempted to block her ears as she passed the living room on her way to the kitchen. Sol nodded cordially to her as she went by. No sign that he recalled either yesterday's punch or his nocturnal rambling. They exchanged no words, but even if he'd tried to speak she wouldn't have heard him, not with the Queen of the Night exhorting Tamino to rescue her daughter from the evil sorcerer. *O zittre nicht, mein lieber Sohn!* O tremble not, my dear son.

Sol had made breakfast for her, as usual. A bowl of oatmeal sat on the counter. Coffee was in the pot. Bea took neither. The oatmeal had turned cold and lumpy; the coffee was surely sour by now. Instead, she made herself a fried-egg-and-ketchup sandwich, which she ate sitting on the couch across from Sol while the Queen of the Night's serving girls offered Tamino a magical gift for his journey—a flute that turned sorrow into joy. Bea hummed along. She used to love this part. Between bites of her sandwich she checked her phone for a message from Dave announcing the rehearsal had been cancelled. No such luck.

She did her yoga routine upstairs in her bedroom, which calmed her somewhat, and left the house just before noon in an old jacket of Sol's that might once have been waterproof but now leaked at the seams. She didn't mind rain. At least Sol would be less tempted to venture outside. Not that he'd been going out much, but the rain added extra security. Sol didn't even own an umbrella.

The soccer field in Westmount Park was sodden, half of it submerged by brown puddles. Bea had put on flip-flops and turned up the hem of her shorts under the jacket so they wouldn't get soaked. Water sluiced down her bare legs and ran in streams between her toes. It penetrated the gaps in the jacket. Warm drops were trickling down her neck and back.

Her phone was tucked safely into her back pocket. The breeze was rain-fresh and warm. There were, Bea thought, worse places one could find oneself on a damp day. *"With heigh-ho, the wind and the rain,"* she warbled in a low voice. The Fool's storm song had been in her head for days. Forget *The Magic Flute*. This was her theme song for the summer. Artie had surprised the music director by composing a catchy little melody, which he now performed engagingly in a sweet light tenor. She smiled, thinking of his many talents, and sang it through from the beginning.

> *"He that has a little tiny wit,*
> *With heigh-ho, the wind and the rain,*
> *Must make content with his fortunes fit,*
> *Though the rain it raineth every day."*

And then she sang it again, louder, pleased with herself. There must, she thought, be something in the Rose family genes that loved a lusty performance.

Wide filthy puddles lay ahead of her on the path. She skirted the first two as best she could. But when she reached the third she waded right in, belting out the Fool's song with gusto. The water felt good. Something bloomed inside her. She was becoming as fickle as the weather. She was happy.

The Bard in the Parks stage rose up on her right, an austere metal and melamine outcrop against the grey sky and rain-darkened vegetation. Another of Artie's collaborative creations. It was deserted. Bea walked toward it over the mushy grass, smiling as if it were an old friend. Her flip-flops squeaked. The main platform glimmered. It now bore only a ghostly shadow of the graffiti she'd worked so hard to remove. Raindrops had collected into little pools on the surface of the stage and rivulets ran off its sides. Under the platform they'd stowed the gear that wasn't likely to tempt thieves: folding chairs, the first-aid kit and various unexciting supplies. The company's rental trucks were nowhere in sight: the techs hadn't arrived yet. Bea fished out her phone, curving her body to shield it, and looked for the cancellation notice she was now sure she must have missed. Nothing.

She was wondering whether to head back to the house when she heard her name. Mimi was at the far end of the cedar hedge, holding her huge, brightly coloured golf umbrella and waving. "We're in the comfort station," she called in her odd half-twang. She pointed up the path and disappeared. Bea followed the rainbow hemisphere to the park restrooms and saw Mimi entering the men's half. Just then Bea received Dave's text. Somehow, her name got dropped from his list when he sent out the location. Half a minute later, Bea reached the door. As she opened it, thunder cracked like cannon-shot.

*"Singe my white head!"* boomed Phil Burns. Evidently, he'd recovered. He was dressed colourfully, as usual, in an orange sweatshirt, its rolled-up sleeves revealing two thick forearms. A pair of worn green army shorts completed the outfit. His hair was drawn back in a ponytail, accentuating the regal lines of his face. He rose from the changing-room bench where he'd been sitting beside Artie.

Bea didn't look at him.

*"Blow winds,"* he said, stepping uncomfortably close. The restroom window rattled.

Jay O'Breen, trying to light a match on an adjacent bench, looked up and laughed. Phil turned on him. *"Crack your cheeks. Rage, blow!"* The damp little room rang with his voice. He turned back to Bea and clasped one of her hands in both of his. "Cold," he said, and blew on her skin with soft warm breaths, watching her face as he did so.

Bea pulled her hand back. Mimi was looking on sternly. Artie White's expression was pained. The other two men present—Jay and old Gregory Pym—sat watching with bland speculation. Bea turned away, irritated and embarrassed.

Nasty smells permeated the building: shit and bleach and chemical lemon cleanser. Dave came in from the toilet area holding a pile of paper towels. "You're soaked," he observed. "You can dry off back here." He led her back the way he'd come, away from Phil.

The odour was stronger here than in the changing room. He swung open a cubicle door and they discovered its source. The bowl was brimming with a soup of disintegrated toilet paper and turds. He slammed the door shut again. "Forget you saw that." He made a sign with black marker on one of the paper towels and stuck it to the door with the gum he seemed to have been chewing for that purpose: HORS SERVICE.

When they returned to the changing room, a ribbon of smoke was curling from an incense cone on the grey cement floor. Jay had lit his match. He grinned with satisfaction. The shitty air was now laced with patchouli.

The group began to run lines from the heath scenes, where Lear encountered Mad Tom, the half-naked beggar who was in fact Edgar, legitimate son to the Earl of Gloucester, in disguise. Some of the most famous lines in all of literature were spoken here. These scenes were the crowd-pleasers, the crux of the play, according to Mimi. The mind of the old king was starting to unravel. She wanted them perfect. It would add a thrilling charge to run them during a thunderstorm, for in the play, too, a tempest was raging.

They started with what Bea privately called the strip speech— by the time it was over, not only was Mad Tom naked on the stage, but the king, too, had torn off most of his clothes.

Phil stood and faced them as he began the king's monologue, using Bea in particular for his audience. He was reading from her script, having neglected to bring the one she'd delivered the day before. It was obvious he'd done no work on his lines. Bea was on prompting duty again, so she sat beside Jay on the bench and bent over his copy.

*"Is man no more than this?"* Phil said, gesturing at Jay, who responded clownishly by pulling his T-shirt over his head. Jay's chest was smooth and hairless, with small pink nipples. Phil barely gave him a glance. His eyes were fixed on Bea.

He approached the bench and leaned over her. *"Consider him well,"* he said, as if this were a lesson and he were her teacher. *"Thou owest the worm no silk, the beast no hide, the sheep no wool, the cat no perfume."*

Jay stood up and began to mug, striking bodybuilder poses to illustrate Shakespeare's point.

Phil looked at him witheringly. *"Thou art the thing itself,"* he said. But the next moment, his shoulders sagged. His face too, as the meaning of the words he was speaking began to penetrate. His voice fell to a whisper. *"Unaccommodated man is no more but such a poor, bare, forked animal as thou art."*

Bea stared at him. She couldn't help it. Phil was no longer looking at her, or at his script. He was tearing at his orange sweatshirt, not in jest, as Jay had done, but in true tragic panic.

*"Off, off you lendings!"* he shouted, pulling the orange fabric over his head. His hands were desperate, fumbling. *"Come, unbutton here!"* The sweatshirt fell to the filthy cement floor. His breasts, now exposed, drooped from a mat of snowy hair.

The sight was so piteous, Bea forgot to breathe. She and the others sat riveted, unable to look away. Finally Artie stood to deliver his lines. *"Prithee, Nuncle,"* he said. *"Be contented, 'tis a naughty night to swim in."* His voice, and his eyes, were full of tenderness. As he spoke he took up the sweatshirt from the floor and draped it over Phil's shoulders.

Phil didn't appear to notice, even when it slipped off one arm and threatened to fall again. He was gone, staring into space, not registering Artie's lines as they came at him. No trace of the proud, vigorous actor remained. In his place was someone much older, someone utterly defenceless and exposed. The sight was so devastating, Bea wanted to run and throw her arms around him.

Artie finished his speech. He paused for a moment then sat down discreetly, averting his gaze. Everyone else looked away, too. Everyone except for Bea, who couldn't help herself.

Phil came out of it about a minute later, but by then the energy in the room had changed. They sat for a few moments more in silence. There seemed to be a generalized reluctance to re-enter the play, though they still had several more scenes to do, including another in the storm. The last storm segment was an important one. In it, the old king slipped into delirium. It was also the very last scene with the Fool.

Phil put on his sweatshirt. Then, instead of opening his script, he held up his hand. "I wonder if I might ask a question." He glanced at Mimi, who was standing at the door, watching him with concern.

"By all means," she said.

Phil then turned on Artie, who had stood up again in anticipation of his denouement. "You, sir," he said.

Artie turned. "Me?"

Phil nodded. "In your role as the Fool. Why do you disappear after this next bit, never to be seen again?"

Artie sighed. The point had been raised before. "We've discussed this, Phil. Don't you remember? Second or third rehearsal. You were definitely there. It's a technical thing," he said, his voice pleasant enough, although Bea suspected he must be annoyed. "In Shakespeare's day, as you are well aware, Cordelia would have been played by a boy. Shakespeare would have doubled him as the Fool. That's why the Fool and Cordelia never appear together onstage. It's a budget thing. Strip off Cordelia's skirts and put on a clown suit. One less actor to pay."

"Yes, yes," Phil said. "I've heard that theory countless times. But I don't buy it." His colour was back. His provocative streak, too. "When was Will Shakespeare ever a bean counter? I mean, seriously. His casts are always enormous. He doesn't give a shit about budgets."

Artie's spine straightened. He stared at the old actor. "You have a better explanation?" Over the past few days, he and Phil had had some exchanges over Phil's conduct. They were managing to stay civil, but not much more.

"Lear kills him."

Artie looked at him blankly. "What?"

Phil nodded. "You heard me. He beats him to death. Lear's got knots in his brain. A condition that unleashes rage." He turned to Bea. "Help me here, darling. It's that thing your father's suffering from. You know . . ."

Bea blinked. She'd told Phil about her father in confidence, not so he could announce it in rehearsal.

"It's a recognized medical condition," said Phil, unfazed by her silence. "*Something* bodies. What is it again? Lester bodies? Levi bodies?"

"Lewy bodies," she said quietly.

"Tell them the symptoms." Phil turned to his ex-wife. "You've got to hear this, Mimi. It's uncanny."

Bea took a deep breath. The smell of shit had reclaimed its ascendancy in the room. Jay's patchouli cone had burned down to ash. She imagined her father, frail and betrayed.

Phil was looking straight at her. Waiting for her to speak. So was everyone else. She had no choice.

"It's called dementia with Lewy bodies," she said. "People who suffer from it get emotionally volatile. They can be violent. They hallucinate."

"Like Lear with the mouse," Phil said eagerly. "I've always wondered why he speaks to a rodent. What is Shakespeare trying to say?" He paused a moment for effect. "That Lear is hallucinating, that's what. In the barn, he mistakes a milk stool for Goneril."

"And a chicken for Regan," Mimi said thoughtfully.

"Exactly! He sees things that aren't there. He's going mad!"

Bea was about to speak again, to tell them that hallucinations weren't always present with the condition. And that *madness* was, in any case, too strong a term. Lucidity came and went. It was a question of degree. In the corner, Dave shook his head. Nothing obvious, just a flick of his curls when he caught her eye. His own eyes had widened with import. You've gone too far, they were saying. You're trespassing into the creative camp. Watch your step.

"Hallucination isn't murder," said Artie, reasonably. "You can't make up plot points that aren't in the script. Nowhere does it say the Fool dies."

"So it's not in the stage directions," said Phil. "That proves nothing. Shakespeare wasn't one to spell things out."

"He left broad hints, though," snapped Artie. "Especially in this play. Lear doesn't turn violent on the heath. He does the opposite. He discovers his heart." He looked pointedly at Bea, but she couldn't meet his eye. Her own heart filled suddenly with confusion. Her cheeks began to burn. "That's what the play is about, by the way," he told her angrily. "Not dementia. Love."

Phil smiled. "Fair enough. But the heart is a troublesome thing. Lear is a tormented old bugger. He's lost his impulse control; he's constantly flying into rages. He's losing his mind. That much is on the page. Come on, Artie. Admit I'm right."

"Rage . . ." Mimi began. She didn't finish. She was thinking.

Bea wished they would stop. This was her father's illness they were talking about.

"Rage is what drives all the king's relationships," Phil said, warming to his theory. "He loves the Fool but he also can't stand him. The Fool knows too much, gets too close. Lear tolerates it at first, not sensing the danger. The boy is almost like a son to him. But then . . ." He turned on Artie and began rabbit-punching him with quick soft blows.

Artie stepped back, crushing the cone of patchouli ash with his heel, but Phil stayed in his face, doing a lumbering imitation of a boxer, dodging and jabbing. When Artie didn't fight back, Phil grabbed his shirt and tried to pull him into a clinch.

"Fuck off, Phil," Artie said, reddening and struggling to get free. "Seriously. Fuck off."

Mimi stepped between them and gave Phil a hard shove. She was a foot shorter than he was, but it worked. The old actor took a parting shot at Artie's head and dropped his fists. He was panting like an excited dog, lips drawn back in a snarling smile. Artie was panting too, his face still red. One of his shirt buttons was missing. Bea had never seen him so upset—not as an adult, anyway. He avoided her gaze and began straightening his clothes.

Mimi seemed already to have forgotten about the skirmish she'd broken up. "Rage," she said again. "You know, it kind of makes sense."

Artie tilted his head and gave her an are-you-kidding look, but she ignored him. "Okay, that's it," he finally said to no one in particular. "We're done here, right? Rehearsal's over?" When Mimi didn't say anything, he grabbed his jacket and walked out into the rain.

Mimi gave Artie a distracted wave. Phil was at her side now, still looking like a happy canine. The rest of the cast began to gather their things, not quite believing that rehearsal was so soon over. Mimi didn't stop them as they filed out.

When she got outside, Bea paused for a moment on the steps. The fresh, moist air came as a relief. She scanned the paths fanning out from the restroom, but apart from the other actors, now making their way in a clump of umbrellas to the bus stop, no one was in sight. Artie had vanished. She stepped gingerly onto the footpath, which, in the unceasing rain, had become a rushing stream. She could still see Artie's stricken face, his arms raised ineffectually against Phil's punches.

"I need to hear more about this disease." Bea turned to see Mimi approaching under her enormous umbrella. She held it higher to accommodate Bea, creating an intimate space for the two of them. "It fits," she said. "All that confusion and fury."

Her father's condition was the last thing Bea wanted to discuss right now, and yet she couldn't help feeling flattered by Mimi's attention, especially when the director offered to walk her home.

Her reserve soon fell away. Mimi was charming, and an excellent listener. Bea found herself describing Sol's disappearance on the night of the storm, his symptoms, and Michel Allaire's diagnosis. She told her about the night wanderings and nonsense babbling—things she hadn't divulged even to Cara.

"Abba," Mimi repeated. "How sweet."

They'd come to the edge of the park. They paused for a second on the curb and looked out along the deserted length of Melville Avenue.

"Like the band," said Bea.

Mimi glanced at her. "I thought you were Jewish," she said. Bea looked at her blankly. "*Abba* is a Hebrew word," she explained. "An endearment. It means daddy."

Bea's breath stopped. Her thoughts went instantly to the yellowed obituary. Avi Rosenberg, the man with the cracked face. Was it to him that Sol spoke in the night?

They came to the house. Bea's feet were soaked, as were Mimi's. "Come in," Bea said. "You can dry off. Plus"—was it an inducement or a threat?—"you can meet my father."

"Your *abba*," said Mimi, and smiled.

Sol opened the door as if he'd been waiting for them. As usual, he was dressed impeccably, in pressed summer pants and a loose-fitting silk shirt. He immediately won Mimi over with his considerable geniality, bringing her fresh towels and then tea in the good silver tea set—complete with clawed tongs to pick sugar cubes out of the little silver bowl—which Mimi said reminded her of her childhood.

He kept exclaiming over the way Mimi spoke, laughing at her Southern-belle expressions and comparing her to Vivien Leigh, who'd played Scarlett O'Hara in *Gone with the Wind*.

"She was a Brit," Bea pointed out.

"True," said Mimi, "but she beat out all her American rivals in the auditions for that role. And walked off with an Oscar. At the very least, she's an *honorary* Southerner."

Then Mimi talked about her own performer parents. Her mother was the true Southern belle of the family. She'd run off with Mimi's father at age nineteen after meeting him in Charlottesville, where he was touring. As she'd told Bea earlier, Mimi said, he was a French mime artist, Paris-trained.

"And a Jew," Sol added, guessing, most likely, from Mimi's last name.

"And a Jew," Mimi confirmed. "Although hardly an observant one. After they eloped, it took my mother a full year before she clued in to his ancestry."

"She never converted?" Sol asked.

"Nope." Mimi held up her hand as if to fend off further questions. "Which means I'm not a member of the tribe. I know. Believe me. You don't have to rub salt in the wound. Every Jew I've ever met has hastened to point it out after hearing my genealogy."

It was a link. Bea smiled at Mimi and said that her mother hadn't bothered to change her status as a lapsed Presbyterian either.

Mimi smiled too. Then turned back to Sol. "You're Jewish, I gather," she said.

Sol nodded.

"Born here?"

A second nod.

Bea held her breath. Her father didn't talk about the past. Certain stories were permitted, and these were repeated over and over until they attained a sort of legend-like quality. The rest was off-limits.

Ignoring Sol's reticence, Mimi continued the interrogation. "And your parents? Where were they from?"

"Poland. A town called Ożarów, about a hundred miles north of Kraków. Before the war, it was the biggest Jewish community in the country. No Jews live there now, not a single one." He shook his head. "My parents were lucky. They got out in the twenties, before the Nazis came. Their parents and all their brothers and sisters died at Treblinka."

Bea listened quietly. She knew this history, mainly from her mother. Deirdre had insisted on passing on Sol's heritage. But what came next Bea had never heard mentioned by either of her parents. Sol's father had been a tailor. This Bea knew from the obituary. Now Sol added something new. He had not been successful. In Canada as in Poland, his businesses had failed. "He was a generous man," Sol said. "Soft-hearted. Too soft to succeed in the world."

Later, after Sol had disappeared into his den, Mimi helped Bea clear the table. "He's a charmer," she remarked as she put uneaten cookies back in the cookie tin. "Truly, Bea, you are blessed."

Bea stopped rinsing spoons in the sink. She turned off the tap and looked at Mimi. "Blessed" wasn't the first word that jumped to mind. But perhaps Mimi had a point. Perhaps Bea was too weary and mixed up at the moment to see straight. Mimi was right: her father *had* been a charmer this afternoon. He'd been interesting, attentive and more relaxed than she'd seen him in ages. What would he be tomorrow?

Mimi held up the cookie tin, amused. "Where did you get this thing, Bea?"

"My mother. It was part of her good Christian upbringing. Are you Tuesday's child?"

"Oh, no," said Mimi. "I'm full of woe. My daughter is the one with the grace."

"Angelina?" Bea asked.

Mimi looked up in surprise.

"Phil has talked about her."

"Has he?" Mimi said, her voice hardening. "That's good to hear."

The question hung unasked between them. Bea knew she had to answer it. "I didn't sleep with him, Mimi. Or ever want to."

"It's none of my business."

"It is your business, though. You're the director. My sleeping with him would make things way more complicated."

Mimi shook her head. "Things are always complicated. When people work hard, when they spend long hours together, sex, or at least the thought of sex, is inevitable. It's natural. I'm not jealous. I stopped being possessive about Phil a lifetime ago. But I see him chasing younger women, chasing you, I see him ignoring your dignity, ignoring his own, and I think of my daughter. His daughter. She's so angry." Mimi put the lid on the cookie tin and pressed it closed. "Philip Burns is as fine an actor as I've ever met," she said slowly. "He's also a drunk and a lecher and an ass-hole. His only child hates him. He'll probably die alone and miserable. And try as I might, I can't help feeling that I'm partly responsible."

Bea watched Mimi struggle for composure for a second before finding the courage to reach an arm around her.

"Thanks," Mimi said, taking a breath.

Bea walked with her to the front door. The rain was still falling. Mimi stepped out onto the porch—then she paused. "It's hard, I know, coming back here. Living with your father. But you're doing it, Bea. You're doing it. And you'll have this to hold on to, after-ward." She opened her multicoloured umbrella. "I wish Angelina could connect with Phil somehow, like you're doing with Sol." She managed a smile and a wave before setting off up Melville Avenue in the shelter of her own little rainbow.

# ACT THREE

LEAR.
*When we are born, we cry that we are come*
*To this great stage of fools.*

(4.6.184–85)

## 15.

THROUGH THE SCAFFOLDING holding up the highest stage, Bea saw hundreds of faces, a sea of them, golden and laughing in the glow of a sun that was still high in the western sky. The first performance would soon begin. The crowd had already gathered around the stage in Westmount Park with lawn chairs and blankets and picnic baskets even though thirty minutes remained before show time. Children ran around, chasing each other and squealing as they wove through the archipelago of adults. Bea could see people's expressions quite clearly. And she knew they had no difficulty seeing her. There was no backstage to speak of, no place to hide. According to Artie, its principal architect, the stage was supposed to be an artistic statement, a repudiation of the artifice of the whole theatrical enterprise. The scaffolding was part of that statement. No illusions. No curtains to lull spectators into suspending their disbelief and thinking, even for a second, that this was a real castle, containing real people, living real lives. The design was clever, but it didn't make Bea's job any easier. She was dressed in theatre blacks, a long-sleeved jersey and jeans, her uniform for the rest of the run. She was supposed to be visible but inconspicuous. Yet on a hot summer's evening, with the sun so slow to set, black clothes were anything but inconspicuous.

Sol was sitting on a rented folding chair in the middle of the crowd, directly in front of her. Best seat in the house. Bea had placed him there well over an hour ago, after accompanying him from Melville Avenue. Cara had planned to bring him, but Crudivore was closing for two weeks of renovations and there was too much to do. Bea noticed that her father's hair had gotten long: a few white wisps touched his shoulders. His beard was longer too, giving him a vaguely biblical look.

The past week had been relatively calm on Melville. Bea's hours had been crazy; on successive nights they'd held the technical rehearsal, the dress rehearsal and finally the preview. She and Sol had been like ships passing in the night. But to her immense relief there'd been no night wandering and, more importantly, no new episodes of rage. Mimi's visit on that soggy afternoon of the solstice had released something in Sol. He seemed content, although he was displaying a couple of worrisome new tendencies. Early yesterday morning they were out doing errands and he'd forgotten where the dry cleaner was, a dry cleaner whose customer he'd been for years. Bea drew a little map for him, but even then he'd seemed lost. And last Sunday, when they went shopping together at the supermarket on Victoria Avenue, half a dozen blocks west of the house, he'd had no clue how to get home. These confusions, and his nonchalance about his hair, were new. She'd phoned Michel Allaire for advice, but he was away on vacation.

The sun was declining over the park, but not fast enough to bring any relief. All day the temperature had been punishingly high, wilting the leaves on the trees and yellowing the grass of the playing field. As they prepared for the show, the actors and crew had wilted too. Bea's skin prickled and itched in her dark, out-of-season clothes. And the mosquitoes were out. Dusk was feeding time. The ground was permanently spongy, and the mosquitoes it bred were big and hungry. They hovered around Bea, their whine filling her ears.

She finished the props check. Bea had printed out a list for herself specifying what went where for each scene. She'd used fourteen-point type so that she could read it in the dark and had encased the sheets in plastic to protect them from the rain. Tonight's forecast was iffy: a chance of thundershowers. Everyone was hoping the bad weather would hold off until after ten.

Dave walked over and gave her a hug. "All set?"

She nodded. To the general astonishment of the company, last night's preview had gone well. Phil had finally made an effort and memorized his lines. During dress rehearsal he'd dropped key passages and floundered, but in the preview he'd been nearly perfect.

Dave checked the time on his phone. "Can you give the half-hour call?"

This was something he usually did himself. After tonight, though, it would be Bea's job. Mimi's contract was up as soon as opening night was over. Her tasks fell to Dave, who would also continue to operate the lights and sound effects. The remainder of his former tasks now fell to Bea. She nodded again.

She was sad to see Mimi go. It had taken most of June to plant the seeds, but now a friendship was blooming. Mimi had even gone back to the house on Melville and asked Sol to join them for the final rehearsals. She'd ensconced him in a chair beside hers under the tarp in the lighting booth and plied him with lemonade and iced tea to protect him from the heat. She told Bea it was a pleasure, but Bea was sure it was to help her out, since she had to be away from home so much. During the most demanding week of rehearsals, Mimi had devoted precious energy to providing a diversion for her lonely father.

Bea wasn't the only recipient of such attentions. Mimi's daughter had broken her wrist and needed surgery. "And for a kickboxer, that's death," Mimi told Bea the day she got the news. She would fly to Toronto that night, right after she'd given the actors their final notes, to be with Angelina. Mimi had also brought Dave Samuels in as assistant director for a Noël Coward play she was soon to begin directing in the Eastern Townships. "My pinch hitter in case of complications with Angelina," she said, smiling. Not only would Dave have the chance to direct, but as he later confided, Mimi would be paying him from her own pocket.

Bea walked to the changing tents. The men's tent was nearest the stage, shielding the women's tent behind it. A flap hung down over the entrance, blocking the interior from view. Bea cocked an ear. All she heard were the distant cries of children. "Hello?" she called. No one answered. She called again.

The heat struck her as she lifted the flap and stepped inside. Phil was sitting alone on a hard-backed wooden chair, the kind found in schools and the basements of churches. He didn't appear to be doing anything except staring at the trampled grass at his feet. Nor was he in costume; he had on the camouflage vest he sometimes wore, the one with a great many pockets of different sizes. He patted his side as if checking for something.

"My dear," he said, rising. A sweet metallic smell hit Bea. Phil leaned on the chair for support. "Dearest dear." He gestured with one arm. "Welcome to my pleasure dome."

"Phil—" she began, but he put a finger to her lips. The finger was cold. His face shone with sweat. A flask-shaped bulge was visible in a front pocket of his vest. He was drunk.

Dave would be beside himself if he found out. Mimi would be homicidal.

Bea made up her mind. She would get him a coffee. The dépanneur on Sainte-Catherine had a machine. If she ran, she could be back in five minutes. Phil waved his hand in dismissal when she suggested it.

"Don't you worry," he said.

"Of course I'm going to worry."

She turned to the long line of costumes hanging between a pair of tent poles. The hangers were arranged in alphabetical order, each one bearing a white label printed neatly in Bea's handwriting. She found his robes and held them out; he took them from her roughly and laid them on his lap.

"It's fine," he said. "And I don't need any shitty coffee." His movements were steadier now, his voice carrying a little more authority. He waved his hand imperiously. "Off," he said. "Get thee gone, girl."

She promised to return after giving the other actors their call. It was a gamble, but there'd still be time to get the coffee if he hadn't improved. She found the rest of the men in a clump of trees behind the tents. All were dressed and in makeup. Some were doing vocal exercises, contorting their mouths to produce exaggerated vowel sounds, but most were just talking quietly. Margo Indongo was with them, splendid in her rose-coloured gown. Maggie the youthful techie was squatting behind her, trying to attach a microphone to her bodice and simultaneously hide the battery pack in folds of pink satin. They smiled at Bea as if all was right with the world and the show would be great.

Lear's other daughters were still in the women's tent.

"Half hour," Bea announced through the open flap.

Ann O'Neill was wearing only a bra on top. "It is so fucking hot," she said, narrowing her eyes as though Bea were somehow responsible. "I can't believe I have to wear velvet."

"And pancake makeup," said Claire Johnson. "It clumps in the heat. So gross." She was still in her street clothes, curling her eyelashes.

"You two need help?" Bea asked. She didn't expect a yes. Ann and Claire reminded her of girls she'd known in high school— haughty and self-reliant, girls who accepted help from no one, least of all social inferiors.

"Could you have a word with the guy upstairs?" Claire said over her shoulder. "Tell him to adjust the thermostat?"

Bea laughed and walked out. The crowd was growing. People were streaming into the park, setting up cushions and blankets and lawn chairs in whatever spots were left. Sol was still in his fold-up chair, surrounded now on all sides. Artie was making his way through this chaos in his three-pointed jester's cap, jingling and directing traffic, instructing people to keep their possessions clear of the two roped-off aisles. In another staging innovation, during several scenes the actors would be moving up and down those passageways through the audience.

Bea did a final check to make sure the actors' chairs were lined up in their correct places backstage, with the right prop box beneath each one. Then she checked that Phil's cardboard crown was in its spot beneath the tower. Phil considered its cheapness contemptible and had taken to leaving it offstage during rehearsals. Bea made a mental note to check it again before his first entrance.

At the fifteen-minute call, she returned to the men's tent. Phil was now in his robes. His cheeks were pale but there was a stateliness about his demeanour, as if the costume had sobered him. Clothes did, at least somewhat, make the man. The robes were a deep burgundy, lined with ermine. Weasel fur, Phil had told her, grinning, the first time he tried it on.

Today, he allowed Bea to brush out his hair. He'd been letting it grow since winter for the role. It was long and silky, the strands as thin and soft as a baby's. She brushed it straight back from his forehead, which gleamed up at her, dotted with moles and liver spots. "Thanks," he said, patting her hand, and for once there was nothing suggestive about the touch.

At the five-minute call, everyone but Phil was waiting behind the tents. Bea told them to form a line and, miraculously, they obeyed. She ran back to the men's tent just as Phil appeared. He blinked in the hazy sunlight and put a hand to his brow to shield his eyes. She circled him, making sure everything was in order. Maggie had fitted him with his mic and battery. "You good?" Bea asked.

He blinked again.

She followed him back to the others, walking a step behind as though she were a servant or Elizabethan wife.

"Nick of time," Artie said, his voice strained. Phil's lack of punctuality had always annoyed him; tonight it must have seemed like an affront.

It *was* an affront, Bea thought, remembering his condition in the tent. And here she was, leading him out to the line as though she condoned it. She tried to make eye contact with Artie, but he seemed to be studiously avoiding her. She got busy with the head count, but she couldn't help glancing back at him, wishing he'd turn, wishing she could explain the complexity of minding a man like Phil Burns. Eventually she gave up. She waved at the tech box, where Dave was sitting. They were good to go.

The trees were casting long shadows on the grass. The sun would set at eight forty-five and the moon would rise shortly afterward. There'd be light for another hour or so.

Dave gave a sign and Artie left the line, jingling in his fool's slippers and cap. The crowd fell silent as he hoisted himself off the grass, onto the shiny white stage. Bea's breath quickened in anticipation.

He looked great. Almost more at ease up there than down here in the real world. He gazed out at the crowd, scanning it, radiating a smile as if each individual were a personal friend. She loved his jester suit. The costume lady had stitched together bright diamonds of jersey that hugged his lean, athletic frame.

Bea couldn't help thinking of the little boy he'd once been, crown prince of their grade three class at Westmount Park Elementary. He'd even played the role of the Little Prince in the school play that year. All the girls had liked him. And whom had he liked in return?

Bea. Even with her scars and her strange manner of speaking, even though the boys mocked her and later mocked him for being her best friend, he'd stuck by her.

Artie introduced himself as the artistic director of Bard in the Parks and thanked Heritage Canada for the grant that kept the company alive. He thanked their corporate sponsors: a local law firm, a well-known west-end deli, a couple of other businesses. And finally he thanked the audience for coming to the season premiere. He explained that the theatre was run on a donation basis. At intermission, the actors would come around with their hats. He swept off his own cap, jingling it like a tambourine, to demonstrate. "If you like the show," he proclaimed, "please give generously. If you don't like it, give even more generously. So we can improve."

As the crowd laughed, Artie jumped nimbly off the stage and disappeared behind the tents.

The music started up, a Renaissance madrigal pre-recorded for the show by Lear's three daughters. Over the speakers, the song was tinny, marred by static. Dave was still fine-tuning the sound levels, not that it seemed to be helping. The crowd hushed anyway as the actors emerged from behind the tents in single file and walked to their chairs. They were completely visible in the dying light. No one spoke. They were under strict orders from Mimi to be seen but not heard, at least until they stepped onto the stage.

Bea sat on a small patch of dirt behind Phil, more or less out of sight of the audience. Her plastic-sheathed notes indicating costume changes and prop settings were spread before her. A star with exclamation points shone out from the margin beside the opening scene. She mustn't forget the crown. She was about to retrieve it from under the tower when someone hissed her name. It was Ann O'Neill, gesturing frantically. Bea bent low and ran to her.

The clip for Ann's battery pack had broken off. She held up the useless piece of metal and frowned at Bea like a child with a damaged toy. Bea stuck the pack in Ann's pocket as a temporary, precarious solution and went in search of Maggie. She had to creep around the periphery of the audience to reach the tech box. Maggie looked up sharply when she saw her, understanding instantly that something was wrong, and the two of them returned backstage as fast as they could. They arrived too late. The play had begun. Stan Garroway was already proclaiming Kent's opening lines.

The first scene took place on the high stage, visually establishing the king's status. This meant that the audience's eyes were raised. No one would see Bea and Maggie rooting around in the shadows. It also meant that Bea could see none of the action. Stan's voice floated down, slightly distorted by the speakers. Now she and Maggie stood perfectly still, listening. Phil was delivering his first lines.

"*Give me the map there,*" he ordered Kent. He explained to the court, including his daughters, that he had divided his kingdom into three equal parts. "*Tis our fast intent,*" he boomed above them, "*to shake all cares and business from our age, conferring them on younger strengths, while we unburdened crawl toward death.*"

Bea's lips moved in synch with the recitation. Her heart, which had clenched when Phil began to speak, relaxed now. He was nailing it. His tone was majestic, unafraid.

Through the scaffolding Bea could see the audience, heads tilted heavenward. Sol was there, his face rapt with wonder. Bea took a long, slow breath. Phil Burns had done it. He'd sobered up and somehow pulled it together at the eleventh hour. Her gaze drifted happily over the crowd, seeing and not seeing. Then she noticed a giant sun hat, a straw cone that looked as though it belonged on a Vietnamese rice paddy. She recognized it as Mimi's. Her chin was propped on one hand, her mouth partly concealed, but it was clear she wasn't happy.

At the tech booth, Dave was frowning too. Above them on the high stage, Phil was still going strong. Bea looked back at Mimi. The director was no longer watching the actors. She was looking directly at Bea, her face grim. Bea's heart tripped over itself. What was wrong? She mentally scanned her list of pre-performance duties. It was only when Phil came down the ladder that Bea saw what the matter was. His head was bare. He'd done the entire opening sequence—the one that established his royal status and showed the audience the innumerable things he stood to lose—without a crown.

Bea snatched it off the ground. Phil was back in his chair. When she placed it on his lap, his old eyes narrowed. "Shit," he said, loudly enough for the people in the front to hear.

Maggie replaced the battery case for Ann, who'd also returned to her seat. Bea was left on her own to look after Phil. He wouldn't be on again until Scene Four, and this time he'd be on the lower stage. There would be no ermine-lined robes, only his cooler, lighter royal riding clothes, and he'd been divested of his crown.

———

Bea made sure his second entrance went smoothly. She'd passed Phil her script so he could review his lines, and his opening exchange with Kent, his loyal courtier, was delivered without a hitch.

Then things unravelled. It started with the Fool's famous speech about having *"more than thou showest."* The audience recognized it immediately. Artie's delivery was so masterful that they broke into applause before he was through. He bowed, beaming. But the clapping threw Phil off his game. In the minutes that followed, he kept stumbling over his lines. Then, when Artie received fresh applause later in the scene for his song about how foolish the old king was becoming, Phil lost it altogether.

From that point on, he was unmoored. He forgot entire passages or mangled them so badly they were unrecognizable. And the puzzling thing was, his lines in this scene were simple and short. In the preview, he'd blazed through this part. Now he staggered about the stage, ignoring the blocking and mumbling all kinds of extraneous nonsense. Goneril ordered him to smarten up. This was in the script, but Ann's delivery was so acid-laced, it stung Phil awake.

He blinked into the stage lights. *"Does any here know me?"* he asked, bewildered. He paused, surveying the crowd, as if expecting someone to answer. The audience stopped fidgeting.

Phil took a shaky step toward them. *"This is not Lear,"* he said in a voice not much louder than a whisper. *"Does Lear walk thus? Speak thus?"* He looked like a toddler, unbalanced yet determined, learning how to walk. His hand touched his throat, then his eyes. *"Where are his eyes?"* he sobbed, and fell to his knees.

Even from behind he was riveting. The next lines were the finest in the play. The words rose up inside Bea in anticipation of Phil's delivery. She couldn't see his face, but she had a clear view of Artie in profile, turned toward his king. Artie's expression was tense, his eyes fixed on Phil's mouth as though by sheer willpower he could tear the lines out of him. The park was so silent Bea could hear the thudding of her own blood. Seconds passed.

Artie began to improvise. *"I suppose, regal sir, you'll say next that your brain is so addled, your discernment so muddled, that you forget your own name."*

When Phil didn't respond, Artie tried again. He circled the older actor, pricking him with questions, trying to help. *"What is it, sir? Do you forget who it is you are?"* The clue could not have been more blatant.

But it did no good. Artie began to grow desperate. *"Good thing you have a fool to tell you what you need to hear."* He ended up delivering all the lines, Lear's and his own, in this passage that Mimi insisted was crucial to the play.

*"Lear's shadow, sir. That is who you are! A shadow of the greatness you once were."* The verse was lost, but at least the words were spoken.

Artie and Ann stumbled through the rest of the scene with Phil, improvising furiously, trying without sucess to prod his memory.


The last scene of Act One was a brief two-hander, involving only the king and his Fool. They had just begun when Phil suddenly raised his hands in defeat.

"Ladies and gentlemen," he said. His voice resonated from the speakers with surprising force, as if he'd suddenly remembered his noble origins. He grabbed a handful of his own hair and pulled it high above his head. "I'm an old man, as you can see. White-haired, white-bearded and bent. I'm not saying this for your pity, but to beg forgiveness for bludgeoning to death some of the greatest lines in all of Shakespeare."

There was a moment of shocked silence. And then, from the

front of the crowd, someone began to clap. Others followed, one by one. Someone shouted bravo and gave a whistle. Phil shook his head. Amid the clamour he placed a hand over his heart. "God bless," he cried. "God bless you for your kindness."

Instead of finishing the scene he retreated off the stage, hunched and miserable, abandoning Artie to the night. Artie closed the act as best he could.

By now the sun had set, shrouding the back of the stage in shadow. Phil was in his chair, his head in his hands. Bea hurried to him with a water bottle. Artie came up behind her and bent over the older actor, their faces inches apart.

"What the hell is wrong with you?" he whispered.

Phil didn't move.

"Are you sick or drunk or what?"

"I'm fine," Phil said through clenched teeth.

Artie took Bea's arm and led her over to the hedge. He and Phil had eight minutes until their next scene. He was breathing hard. His jester's cap had slipped sideways. It looked like it might fall, at any moment, off his glistening head. "That man is not fine," he said gruffly. "Come with me a moment." He stalked off in the direction of the changing tents.

In the men's tent he went straight to where Phil had piled his street clothes. Within seconds he found the flask in the breast pocket of the camouflage vest. He unscrewed the top and sniffed. Grimly, he emptied the contents into the dirt. He screwed the top back on and held it out to her.

"Did you know about this?"

She didn't dare speak.

"You did, didn't you? Goddamn it, Bea!"

He tossed the flask onto the small, sad heap of Phil's clothes. "It has to stop," he said quietly. "You think you're doing him a favour covering for him, keeping his secret. Well, you're not.

Believe me. I've known men like him before. There's no help for them. They're beyond that."

He drew in a breath, let it out and faced her squarely. "There will be no more alcohol on this production," he said. "None. Are we clear?"

She nodded.

"I should fire him, but I have no replacement. We're stuck. You'll just have to watch him. From the moment he arrives in the park until the moment he walks off the stage in the last act, you're his shadow. Got it?"

She nodded again. Artie walked out of the tent, leaving her alone and ashamed.

# 16.

THE NEXT DAY Bea woke to a flood of light pouring in through her window. The room felt like an oven. She groped for her phone, which she'd set on the floor at two in the morning, and saw that it was noon. She'd slept ten hours straight. She jumped out of bed, pulled on her clothes and hurried barefoot down the attic stairs.

The second floor was absolutely still; not even city noises could be heard. Sol kept the windows closed all day and curtained against the heat. She checked his bedroom first, although he never slept this late. The bed was empty and unmade. Since Bea moved in Sol had stopped making his bed in the morning, abandoning this and other daily household chores to her without any discussion. She passed on quickly to the den. It too was empty.

Bea ran down the main staircase. She'd slept like the dead. The moment she lay down exhaustion had crashed over her in a dark, obliterating wave. If Sol had wandered in the night, or even beaten pots and pans outside her bedroom door, he wouldn't have disturbed her.

He wasn't in the living room, or the kitchen or the basement. She called for him in a tense, shrill voice. Sol was her responsibility. She'd come to her father's house precisely for this reason, to keep him safe from danger.

She grabbed her house keys from the hall table, strapped on her sandals and hurried out the front door. And there he was, sitting calmly on his Adirondack chair in the sun, reading *The Economist.*

"He's too old," he said, laying down his magazine and gazing at the park. It was the last day of June and everything was shimmering. Leaves hung in clusters on the great, towering maples. The air smelled of cut grass.

Bea slipped her keys into her pocket and focused on slowing her breath.

"That man," Sol said, after a pause. "Your friend. The one who plays the king."

"Phil?"

"I forget his name."

"Philip Burns."

"He was terrible. A catastrophe. I left halfway through."

"I know."

That, for Bea, had been the other catastrophe of the night: her father's empty chair. At intermission she'd been so intent on Phil that she paid no attention to her other charge. Once Lear was onstage again, more or less remembering his lines, she looked out at the audience and saw that Sol had vanished.

She couldn't go look for him. Phil was offstage for much of Acts Three and Four, and this was precisely the time he needed a minder. Artie had been clear. So she'd sat miserably on her patch of dirt behind the old actor, scanning the audience, row by row, in the desperate hope that her father was still out there. He wasn't. The instant the play ended, without waiting to explain to anyone, Bea had sprinted across the unlit soccer field to Melville Avenue. The front door had been left unlocked. The first-floor lights were on. A gesture of consideration or a lapse? She found Sol in his bed, sound asleep. Shaking with fatigue, her burst of adrenalin exhausted, she'd gone back downstairs, turned off the lights and slipped out the door, locking it with trembling hands. Only then did she return to her duties at the park.

"He screwed up all his lines," Sol said. Oh, the harshness of the old toward the old. "I've never seen anything so bad. Shakespeare must be rolling in his grave. Whose brilliant idea was it to cast him?"

"Mimi Meir's."

That made Sol pause. He'd spoken of Mimi repeatedly, and very favourably, in the days since their afternoon tea.

"Phil is a fine actor," Bea said. "I told you about all the films he's been in."

"Maybe he was before," Sol said. "But whatever talent he had is gone." He looked at her. "Come on. Admit it. He was appalling. That's how it goes." He stopped. A new thought had occurred to him. "And where were you, anyway? I didn't see you."

"You're not supposed to see me," she said. "I work backstage."

Sol snorted. "The whole point of theatre is the limelight. Why do it if you don't want to shine?"

"I do want to shine," she said, "in the sense of doing a good job. I'm not an actor though, Dad. It's a question of temperament."

Sol shook his head. "Ridiculous. Backstage is terrible, whatever your temperament. Why hide in the dark when you could be out front? Even in a production like this one. Risk a little, Bea. Show your face."

Bea leaned against the wall. The sun was shining directly in her eyes. She felt the bricks against her spine, solid and warm through her T-shirt. Her father was right. The whole summer had been a mistake. She wasn't even a mother to these actors. She was a glorified maid, a drudge, picking up their props when they dropped them, gathering their soiled costumes after each performance, washing and hanging them in neat rows so they could be soiled again. And now she was also to be a nanny—or whatever the equivalent was for old men—her nights spent minding an erratic, faded actor, her days enduring the criticisms of a frail, querulous father. She glanced sideways at Sol, who was frowning. He wasn't even the worst of it. The worst was Artie White, her childhood ally, who now couldn't stand the sight of her.

17.

THE WIND HAD RISEN, swirling grit into Bea's eyes as she walked across the playing field to work. A week had passed since the premiere. The show had found its rhythm. Phil had pulled himself together, albeit too late for the single theatre critic who'd bothered to show up on opening night. The play had been savaged in Montreal's sole English-language daily, the *Gazette*, largely because of Phil's lamentable performance.

It was Friday, which meant the crowd would be big, despite the windy weather. Fridays and Saturdays brought the best audiences. And tomorrow promised to be their biggest night ever. They'd be performing in La Fontaine Park, on the east side of the city, near the apartment Bea had hardly seen in weeks. It would take a lot of effort to pack up the equipment and set it up again in a day, but that was their mandate—to bring Shakespeare to English-language communities across Montreal and, later, off-island. Mimi was coming to see the La Fontaine Park show with her daughter. She'd texted Bea to say the surgery on Angelina's wrist had gone well.

Dave was standing in the shade of a big maple near the stage, finishing a cigarette. As the branches shook over their heads, he took a last drag and tried to drop the butt into a Starbucks cup he was holding in his left hand. It never landed. The powerful wind sucked it into an upward vortex, scattering sparks and making it glow deep orange.

Bea and Dave watched it disappear while nearby the cables securing the upper stage sang plaintively. Bea's hair whipped at her eyes. She'd fixed it in a braid before leaving the house, but the wind pulled at it, loosening strands. Conditions were less than ideal for Shakespeare. They'd have to secure everything that could move.

The tents were the first priority. The wind was beating their canvas flanks and threatening to lift them off the ground altogether. When Bea and Dave walked over to inspect them, they found uprooted pegs littering the grass. Dave began stamping the pegs back in, but as soon as he did the wind yanked them out. Bear had to come over and drive them in with a hammer. Even then the tents didn't offer much privacy. The wind kept raising their corners and pulling at their flaps.

Bea's efforts to contain this disorder soon attracted an audience. On a Friday afternoon, lots of people were hanging about the park. Bea was inside the women's tent, trying to retie the strings more tightly to the tent poles, when she looked up into the face of a teenage boy peeking in. He recoiled in surprise, then ran off laughing with his friends. Minutes later an older man appeared where the boy had been and began to tell her his life story through the gap. Dave arrived to inspect her work and put an end to the discussion. "This won't do," he said, frowning at the man's retreating form. "We'll have to cover corners with tarps. We're putting on a play, not a peep show."

It was six o'clock when Bea finally emerged from under the canvas, sticky with sweat, her shoulders aching. From the footpath, yet another man was watching her. She ignored him as she circled the women's tent, checking her work. The tent corners were now reinforced, which pleased her. But when she'd completed her circuit, there was the man again. He'd left the path and was standing on the grass, in full sunlight, only a couple of feet away.

He didn't look like a Shakespeare buff out for a night in the park. He was wearing a dark suit and carrying a briefcase. On the other hand, he didn't seem dangerous: a short middle-aged guy with thinning hair. But he was gazing at her with an unnerving steadiness.

"Madame Rose?" A gust of wind blew the plastic skin of a jumbo Freezie through the air between them. The little man cleared his throat. "Beatrice Rose?" He looked at her intently.

When she nodded, he handed her a printed form.

"Consider yourself served."

The document said what she already knew. She owed five months of back rent minus the five hundred she'd recently paid: a total of four thousand dollars. If she failed to pay it in full by the last day of July, the notice said, eviction proceedings would be taken against her. Zorba had finally run out of patience. When Bea looked up the man was already on the park path, walking quickly toward the street.

She'd known this was coming. Zorba could have evicted her in February, but he'd waited. He was a kind man. And he knew who she was. Or rather, who Sol was. What he didn't know was how impossible it was for Bea to approach her father for help. How she dreaded it. But now she had no choice: she would have to ask him for a bailout. Cara was her only other option, but she was stretched thin with the renovations at Crudivore, plus there were all those legal worries with Didier.

Artie rode into view on the bike path. He was leaning low over his handlebars, intent with effort as he pedalled against the wind, an oversized cotton shirt billowing behind him. But when he spotted her at the tents, his face loosened into a smile. Bea's heart rose like a balloon. But then his smile disappeared. Bea turned to see what he was looking at. Phil was sitting on a bench beneath a line of chokecherry trees, chatting with a woman Bea had never seen before, his hands waving expansively.

She folded the eviction notice into her pocket. The woman beside Phil wore a brilliant yellow sundress. She was no longer young, but not old, either: somewhere in between, like Bea. Her hair was black. At their feet a flock of pigeons milled about, pecking at the dirt. Someone, perhaps the woman herself, had tossed down some bread. Sunshine glinted on metal as the woman raised a flask to her lips. Then she passed it to Phil, who screwed it closed.

Bea glanced quickly back at Artie. He hadn't noticed the transaction. He was locking his bicycle to a pole. So what had upset him? Was it just Phil sitting there in the sunshine? Was it that Bea wasn't by his side, supervising? Did that man never think of anything but the play?

Phil spotted Bea and waved. The flask vanished into one of his many pockets and he stood, pulling his collar up against the wind. He said something to the woman and came over to the tents.

He walked across the grass in a straight line. His hair was mussed, but then so was hers. His eyes were more or less focused. Maybe he was okay. Maybe he was just being magnanimous with a new friend while he abstained. Still, though: he had a flask in his pocket. He knew it was a violation. He stood before her in the sunlight, relaxed and smiling. A couple of tent pegs had popped out again. Bea was trying to jam them back into their holes with the heel of her sandal.

"Allow me." He was wearing his cowboy boots and came down on the pegs with his full weight, driving them deep into the dirt again. Then he took her arm and pulled her into the women's tent to escape the wind. Inside, he and Bea watched the canvas sides heave. "It's like being inside a lung," he said.

"Or the belly of a whale."

That earned her an approving look. "A simile worthy of the Bard himself. I do love you, Beatrice Rose."

He took out his flask and offered it to her.

She stepped back in surprise.

"Oh go on," he said, grinning. "Cut loose. I promise I won't tattle."

*Cut loose. Risk a little.* What was it about old men that made them urge perversity on the very people whose good sense they relied on? Was it mockery? Did they scorn the timid little souls without whose sober service they would surely die? Did they scorn her especially? Obedient Bea? Ugly Bea? She was sick of it.

Phil was still smirking, his face flushed. She hesitated, and the fact that she could even consider accepting astonished her. What was wrong with her? Dave would have confiscated the flask in an instant. But then, she thought, Dave was a good mother.

She took the flask and drank. The liquor seared her throat. Bea stood there, eyes watering, and fought the urge to cough. She did not want, at this moment, to look weak. By the time the alcohol's heat bloomed in her stomach, the satisfaction of her private rebellion had dwindled to nothing. This was what betrayal tasted like: fiery and metallic, tainted with the spit of strangers. She regretted instantly what she'd done. But regret, of course, always came too late.

Phil smiled. "You're some broad, Bea." He took back the flask and raised it to his lips.

"No," she said, putting a hand on his arm. "No more. Not for the rest of the show."

His smile wavered. "Oh come now," he said. *"Sois gentille."*

That had been Jean-Christian's phrase, the precise wheedling formula with which he expressed his desire for sex.

"I mean it, Phil," she said, trying to keep her voice steady. "If you take one more drink I'll report you."

The smile vanished, but Phil bowed his head in obeisance as if some part of him was actually relieved. Without a word, he screwed the top on the flask and slipped it into his vest. They walked to the men's tent in silence, and she stayed with him while he dressed. Although she had resisted it, Artie was right: Phil required constant supervision. Bea didn't leave even when the other men arrived—and nor did they expect her to, having become reluctantly accustomed to her presence. Stan Garroway made a pointed joke about wanting a dresser too while Jay O'Breen changed quickly in a corner and then went outside to do his makeup.

Phil and Stan began talking about Los Angeles, where they'd both lived for several years in the 1980s. For Stan, the experience had been a disappointment. "Dog-eat-dog," he said. "Everyone you meet is in the business. Every waiter, every janitor, dreaming of fame while cleaning toilets or flipping burgers or doing whatever it takes to make ends meet. It was as depressing as hell."

Phil had been luckier. "*Malice* made all the difference," he said. "That role made me. Three whole seasons, and it led to other things." He stretched out his legs. "When it's good in L.A., it's really good. You feel like it will go on forever." He smiled ruefully. "Which it doesn't. I just wish I'd appreciated it while I had it." He turned to Bea. "That's the saddest thing about this life, my dear. No one pays any attention to the good times. Not until they turn bad."

His speech wasn't slurred. It was louder than it had to be, but that was par for the course with Phil. He sounded like an after-hours blowhard in a bar. And he looked old, suddenly, even compared to Stan, whose highlighted hair was dry as straw and whose belly, above his Elizabethan breeches, looked like a misplaced pillow. Phil's eyes were moist. Tiny blue blood vessels snaked down his cheeks.

Bea put the crown on his head herself, as she had since their second night. As he mounted the ladder to the upper stage, a wave of relief passed through her. For a full hour and a half she'd watched him, making sure the little flask stayed untouched. Now he was safely onstage. Her job, the most important part of it, was accomplished.

Artie was in his chair, waiting for his entrance. As Bea took her seat on the grass behind him, he turned around and smiled, full and warm. She ducked her head, pretending to sort through her notes. Blood pounded in her ears. He was a conundrum. When she glanced up again, he was still watching her. It couldn't just be the job, could it? The fact that, thanks to her, Phil had made it to the stage on his feet and sober? She met Artie's eye. She could taste the liquor's faint residue at the back of her mouth. She was sorry for what she'd done in the tent, but not that sorry. It had been instructional to cut loose and see that the world kept right on turning.

The performances that night were solid. Not brilliant, like some of the moments she'd witnessed in rehearsal, but all of the actors, including Phil, held their own despite the distraction of the wind gusting periodically across the stage and grabbing at their costumes and hair. The tents remained miraculously upright, as did the poles supporting the stage lights. Not one of the actors' microphones cut out. The cast even received a standing ovation, although Bea suspected it was as much about people wanting to stand up and stretch their legs as anything else.

Artie and Bea were among the last to leave the park; he'd helped her load the final prop boxes into Bear's rental truck for the night. "May I walk with you?" he asked as she was getting ready to go.

She looked up, startled. "It's not far."

"I know," he said, and smiled his enigmatic smile.

Bea reddened. "I mean, I can get home fine on my own." Then she reddened even more, because it sounded like a rejection. "It's perfectly safe, I mean," she said, flustered. "There's no problem."

"No, I know." He pressed a button on his watch and the dial lit up. "But it's almost midnight. I'd like to walk you, if that's okay. It's on my route."

Her hands were in her pockets, balled into fists. It was crazy how flustered she got around him. A mere look from him turned her into a blithering fool. She uncurled her fingers. "Sure," she said. "I'd like that."

She stood beside him as he unlocked his bike. He was wearing an old black T-shirt, the one he used for working on the set. Underneath it she could see his ribs and the muscles of his shoulders flexing as he lined up the numbers on his combination lock. Bea knew this body—or the child's version of it. From the age of four till she turned eight, she'd played with him nearly every afternoon. Seeing him so close as an adult was a strange experience; it was as though she were looking at one of those trick drawings she'd loved as a child, her brain flipping back and forth between the ambiguity of two equally viable but opposed perceptions—young woman and old woman, flower vase and lovers' profiles. Sometimes, when she relaxed, she could register both at once.

Artie freed his bike and they began walking down the unlit path. The wind that had plagued them earlier in the evening had dropped. The park was quiet again, and peaceful. He was silent for a bit. Nervous about something. "I've been wanting to talk."

Bea tensed. She thought again, guiltily, of Phil's flask. But it had nothing to do with that. He wanted to apologize. "You were right," he said shyly. "About killing the Fool. It works."

"Not my idea," she said quickly.

"Maybe not," said Artie. "But you told Phil and Mimi about that condition, the one your dad has. It's actually quite a brilliant addition to the play." He paused, eyeing the pavement. "Not that it makes it any more bearable. I hate that final scene in Act Three, when he beats me up."

"I can imagine."

He stopped walking. "Do you remember my father?"

Bea nodded. She pictured a tall, grave-faced man, quite a bit older than Artie's mother and somewhat bald. He wasn't gregarious like his wife. Bea had mostly stayed clear of him.

"He's dead now. We worked out a lot of stuff when he got sick. But when I was young, I couldn't stand him. He used to do that."

They'd started walking again. With no lamps lighting the way, Bea could barely see the edges of the path. What was he saying? That he'd been beaten? She looked at him, but his face was shrouded in darkness. The only sound was the ticking of his bike as he wheeled it along beside them.

"He thought it would toughen me. That's what he told me, anyway, before he died." They were approaching the road, and a streetlamp suddenly illuminated Artie's face. He attempted a smile. "I wasn't a tough child, as you might recall."

He looked suddenly young again. "You were beautiful," she said.

Artie gave an embarrassed laugh and they walked in strained silence until they reached his former house. A red tricycle sat on the front porch, upended between two wicker chairs. A young family had moved in a year ago, but Bea hadn't met any of them yet. "You remember this place?" said Artie.

Bea nodded, not trusting herself to speak. In the games she had played with Arthur White, she was usually male. When they played cowboys, for instance, she was a cowboy too. When they played war, she was a soldier just like he was, grunting into the cheap walkie-talkies his father had given him as a gift one Christmas. There was one game they played, however, in which she was a girl: their *Star Wars* game. Deirdre had taken them to see the film as an end-of-school treat in kindergarten. Bea and Artie had called their game Han Solo. Arthur was Han; Bea was Princess Leia.

As a rule, Bea detested princesses. They never did anything of value. They tended to be captured or locked up or placed under magic spells that put them to sleep. Princess Leia was an exception. She was abducted in the movie, but she was also a fighter. The film posters showed her holding an impressive black ray gun, or blaster, as she called it. Bea and Arthur usually played the game outdoors, whooping through the park, evading and outsmarting Imperial stormtroopers who lurked behind every tree. But they also played it indoors, in Artie's basement. Here, they could wear costumes: swords, cloaks made of satin, a rhinestone tiara for Bea's hair that Arthur's mother had bought one year for a costume party. The basement was big and unfinished, unencumbered by furniture. The floor was cement, painted oxblood red and peeling around the drain in its sloping centre. It was often damp and there was no natural light, but its ugliness was its greatest asset: Artie's parents almost never ventured down there.

It was in this basement that Bea and Arthur had first kissed. Neither of them had any idea that tongues were part of it. They did what they'd seen actors do onscreen, pressing lip to lip.

# 18.

AFTER WAKING LATE and doing her yoga routine, she fixed
an egg-and-ketchup sandwich for herself and a stir-fry for Sol to
reheat in the microwave later that evening. Then, at four o'clock
in the afternoon, she got on her bike and rode to work. She hadn't
brought up the matter of a loan with Sol. She still wasn't ready to
face that discussion.

She hadn't ridden her bike in the weeks they'd been based in
Westmount Park, but tonight they'd be performing in La Fontaine
Park, in the Plateau. She cycled straight up Westmount's slope
to the boulevard and east to Côte-des-Neiges Road. Then, hoist-
ing the bike on her shoulder, she climbed the staircase from
Côte-des-Neiges and pedalled uphill to Chemin Olmsted, the
dirt road that ran through Mount Royal Park. To her surprise, she
wasn't out of breath. Scrambling around on the set, combined
with yoga, had kept her fit. On Olmsted the ride was a breeze: a
long downhill coast with a warm summer wind drying the sweat
from her face.

Although there wasn't a cloud in the sky, she hummed the Fool's
storm song. But when she came to Park Avenue and the Cartier
Monument, the song died in her throat. Clusters of tourists and
young people were about, many of them lounging on the grass in
the late-afternoon sun. The angel's verdigris wings rose, as always,

into the sky. The expression on her face was as peaceful as ever. But she'd been mauled. Extending down her front was a long red slash. Bea pedalled over for a closer look. On the pale granite obelisk on which the angel stood, someone had painted the word NON! in sloppy red letters.

Bea's first thought was of Sol. He hadn't been raving all those weeks ago. He'd seen this on the night of the protest: he'd witnessed this terrible thing the protesters had done. That was why he'd been going on about angels at the hospital, first to Cara when he landed in the emergency ward, and later to her and Dr. Allaire. Her second thought was of Didier. Was this the property damage Cara had been so upset about? The red letters had been sprayed on at a hurried slant. Paint had bled in ugly streaks from their contours down to the statue's base. She couldn't believe Didier had been part of this desecration.

The Théâtre de Verdure in La Fontaine Park was a Greek-style amphitheatre, its seats laid out in a semicircle on a gentle slope rising from the stage. The stage was a permanent one, owned by the City of Montreal, with dressing rooms behind that had makeup tables and even a couple of toilets. Everyone—performers and audience alike—would be exposed to the elements, just as in Westmount and in the parks to come, and the seats weren't great—hard metal benches—but even so, it felt like luxury. Bea knew the theatre well. She'd come here many times with Jean-Christian for worldbeat concerts and contemporary dance shows. The city sponsored a whole series of artistic presentations every summer, free of charge. This was her neighbourhood—or at least, she thought sadly, looking at the empty seats, her former neighbourhood.

The stage backed onto a little stream that filled the air with the calming sounds of running water. Bea had been enchanted when she'd first discovered it, but she realized now that, like their soggy field back in Westmount, the whole area bred swarms of mosquitoes.

People were beginning to file in through the gate at the top of the hill. Her first priority was, as always, the king. She hadn't seen Phil yet, and it was already forty-five minutes to show time. She slipped backstage to the dressing rooms. Here he had his own private accommodations, complete with a yellow wooden star nailed to the door. When Bea knocked, there was no answer. She opened the door a crack. The dressing room was barely larger than a closet, but it had its own toilet and a makeup table with a mirror bordered by lightbulbs. And there was Phil, sitting in his undershirt and boxers, staring into the mirror. His back was to her, but she could see the reflection of his face, chalky and ill. His makeup kit was unopened. Beside the kit lay a bouquet of red roses, wrapped in plastic, wilting in the heat.

"Hi there." She'd taken to hiding behind a girl-Friday mask of cheerful practicality.

He stared blankly at her reflection.

"You okay?" she asked.

Now she caught the odour: a mix of sourness and the artificial mint of mouthwash.

"Phil—" she began.

He held up his hands. "Please," he said. "No lectures."

He sounded all right. No slurring or running his words together. But when he stood up he had to push hard with both fists against the red surface of the dressing table. Sweat beaded at his temples and ran down his neck.

"I'm fine," he said. "It's the heat."

Panic rose in her. This was their biggest night of the season. Well over a thousand people would be out there. He couldn't let them down. She was about to lay it out for him when his knees gave way.

He collapsed back into his chair. He was coated in sweat now, trembling, his gaze vacant. She took his arm and tugged, then guided his limp, compliant body to the floor. There, she rolled him onto his back and raised his thick legs in the air, clutching his ankles at the level of her armpits. It took a minute, but his gaze came back into focus.

"Better?" Bea asked, but she already knew. His skin had regained its colour. His eyes were clear again. They stayed in this odd, intimate posture for another minute or so, with his old bare feet cradled against her chest.

"That was marvellous," he said as she helped him stand. "What a manoeuvre. *You're* marvellous." He winked. The old lion, unvanquished. But as she helped him peel off his soaking undershirt, he put his hand on hers to still her. There was no threat this time, no sexual posturing. "It isn't the heat, you know," he said. "Angelina's here. She and Mimi are out there."

"But that's great," said Bea.

"No." Phil shook his heavy white head. "No, it's not great. It's not great at all." He looked at her, his blue eyes watery and pleading.

Phil was terrified at the prospect of facing his child, the little girl with the ringlets. It was hard to believe, but it was true. This larger-than-life, louder-than-life man was quaking over his daughter. Bea gave him a sympathetic hug. He didn't resist; he just stood silently, passive and grateful.

Then he thanked her, a bit gruffly, not moving away. A line from the play came to her. She whispered it into the space between them. "Thou art the thing itself."

Phil's spine straightened. He chuckled. The line was from the strip scene on the heath. *"Unaccommodated man,"* he said, stepping back and spreading his naked arms wide. *"A poor, bare, forked animal."* He smiled. "Here I am."

She helped him into his king's robes.

"You can do this," she said at the door.

"We shall see." But he winked. The focus was back. The old gleam.

Bea hurried to the wings on stage left. Because this was a real theatre, she'd be able to act like a real assistant stage manager for once, talking with Dave through an intercom system. The green light on the base station was flashing. She took down a pair of headphones from the nail on the wall and flicked the switch Dave had shown her.

"Where the hell have you been?" he yelled. The actors in the first scene had already assembled, unsolicited, for their entrance. They were watching her now with curiosity.

The headset took getting used to. It was basically a walkie-talkie, like the ones she and Artie had once played with as kids. Only this one was attached to a wire long enough to allow her to move around while receiving Dave's commands. She pushed the switch one way to listen to him, the other way to talk. Impossible to do both at once.

She flicked the switch and said that she'd been helping Phil Burns dress.

"Is he there?" Dave asked when she flicked the switch back.

Before she could answer, Phil came around the corner and joined the lineup behind Stan Garroway. His face was pale, but he'd made it. On his head he wore his cardboard crown.

"Yes," said Bea, sending Phil a prayer of gratitude. She took a breath and did the head count. "Everyone's present and accounted for."

"Good." Dave's voice had returned to its ordinary mellow pitch. He told her to give the five-minute call. Then he cut the connection and the light on the box went red.

———

The first half of the show went beautifully. It was a Saturday night in early July. The weather was good and the audience huge. Dave estimated total attendance at just shy of two thousand. People laughed heartily at the Fool's lines and clapped along when he sang.

Bea scanned the crowd for familiar faces. All kinds of people she knew from the Plateau and Mile End would be here. The first face she recognized was Mimi's. She was sitting three rows from the stage, sharing a bag of popcorn from the concession stand with a young woman sporting a buzz cut. The sun hadn't set yet, so Bea could see the two of them with perfect clarity. This must be Angelina Meir, *sans* ringlets. She was pale and small like her mother but seemed to have inherited Phil's regal cheekbones and forehead. She looked tense, almost mouse-like, as she nibbled snacks and watched her father perform.

At the far end of the same row, a red-and-black bandana caught Bea's eye. Her breath stopped. It was Jean-Christian. She'd known that a meeting was inevitable. The Plateau was such a tiny, incestuous place, there was no way she could avoid him forever. His bandana was pulled low, covering the hairline that Bea supposed had retreated further over the winter. Then she noticed the person beside him—golden-skinned, straight-backed in her seat. It was Gaya Pal.

Jean-Christian put his arm briefly around her and nuzzled her hair. He looked happy. But then, he always looked happy; happiness was his default state. Bea hadn't known anything was wrong until the day she stumbled upon that telltale Visa item. All those years, obliterated in an instant. He and Gaya had probably been involved with each other for months by the time Bea found out, she realized with a jolt. How cool she'd been negotiating the purchase of the studio. Not a wrinkle of remorse on that smooth brow. Not a hint in her eyes of what was really going on.

Bea returned to her principal duty: watching Phil Burns. He seemed to be doing fine. Better than fine. He was acting his heart out. The others were, too: the first acts had flowed as easily as water. Dave had told Bea about this—the moment in a production when things fell naturally into place, when the actors switched from self-conscious effort to artistry. She realized that they were doing it now. Making art.

The technical side of the production could not have been going better, either. None of the microphones had broken down. The music, fed through a high-quality sound system, sounded good for a change. The lighting was subtle. No one had missed a single cue.

At intermission, Bea crossed paths with Phil as he came off the stage. "Brilliant," she whispered, raising her hand for a high five. He grinned as their palms made contact. She couldn't attend to him immediately, though; first, she had to add some spruce boughs to the hovel where Lear and his Fool would take refuge on the heath. "I'll be by in a bit," she said.

She pressed her baseball cap low over her eyes and stepped onto the stage. With any luck, Jean-Christian would be so wrapped up in Gaya he wouldn't notice her. She'd barely taken two steps when he called out her name.

She kept walking, pretending she hadn't heard.

"Bea! Beatrice Rose! Hey, *chérie*! Over here!"

He was on his feet, waving his arms as if he were actually glad to see her. Night had fallen, stretching vast and silent over La Fontaine Park. He kept calling to her, impossible to ignore. A lot of people had left their seats to buy snacks at the concession stand. Now Jean-Christian left his seat too and moved toward her down the empty aisle.

"I thought I was hallucinating," he said in French, the language they'd always spoken together. He was gazing up at her rapturously, his forearms resting on the stage. He was as handsome as ever. His eyes—hazel-coloured, striking against the pallor of his skin—studied her for a moment. He had the gift of making everyone he looked at feel desirable. Even now, even after betraying her, he couldn't help himself. Perhaps it was a tic, a mechanism for his own survival. Whatever it was, it worked. The lump of hurt and outrage that had lain in her throat, choking her all winter and spring, felt like it might dissolve.

"What are you doing up there?"

"Setting props," she said flatly.

"No way," he said. "No more yoga, then? None at all? I figured you were still teaching somewhere."

Bea shook her head. "Nope." She looked carefully at this man whose life she had shared for seven years. His eyes skittered this way and that, like water bugs across a pond's surface. "Stop it," she said.

Jean-Christian's eyes stilled for a moment. "What?"

"Stop lying." It was, suddenly, very important that she say this. "I know about the studio. I know about Gaya. You don't have to do this anymore."

"Bea," he said, smiling his most winning smile. "You mustn't think badly of me. It's not what it looks like. She invited me back there to teach. I accepted an opportunity, that's all. After the sale, I mean. Everything was honourable. Believe me."

From the edge of the bandstand, Gaya Pal was watching them. She didn't wave or smile. Bea took a moment to breathe. The sweet spruce smell of the boughs she was holding wafted up, their needles prickling her arms. She'd spent the winter feeling like the unluckiest woman alive. She'd been wrong. Gaya Pal had saved her.

His step less buoyant, Jean-Christian went back to his seat. Bea got to work, placing the boughs on the hovel and fastening them with wire clips from her pants pocket. It was exacting work, especially now that the branches had dried out and the needles were starting to shed. She gave it her whole attention, blocking everything else out. By the time she looked at her watch, intermission was nearly over. Up in the lighting booth, Dave was glaring at her. She rushed to her station in the wings, where the green light on the base station box was flashing in a fury.

As soon as she got her headphones on, Dave's voice assailed her. "What were you doing out there for so long? We start in five minutes!" He asked if the actors were assembled.

Four of them were present. Bea removed her headset before he could start yelling again and took off at a run.

The door to Phil's dressing room was closed. Bea stood for several seconds listening, but no sound came from inside. The little yellow star was homemade, she noticed, cut with a hacksaw. One of its points was longer than the others, making it seem off-centre, precarious.

On the other side of the door, Phil coughed. She knocked and walked in. The dressing room itself was empty. She found him kneeling over the toilet.

He appeared to be in the same dazed state he'd been in at the top of the show. Bea wasn't even sure he recognized her. His long hair stuck damply to his cheeks. His skin was pallid. The flowing white robe that made him look like an Old Testament patriarch was askew.

Bea offered him her arm. "You're on," she said, helping him get up. A bright welt ran the length of his right cheek down to his lip. "Did you fall?" She scanned the floor for his flask but didn't see it. There was no whiff of liquor on his breath. She wondered suddenly if she should call an ambulance. She tried to remember the warning signs of stroke.

As she straightened his clothes, however, he began to come around.

"Bea," he said, shaking his white head, "I don't think I can—"

She didn't let him finish. "Forget that," she said. "Thinking's highly overrated."

He laughed feebly.

"Just act," she said. "Do what you were born to do." She felt like a football coach, only way more tender. Motherhood. That singular mix of toughness and care. Maybe she was capable of it after all. "I'll be with you every step of the way," she told him. "You know that, right? I'll be back here, cheering."

The rest of the cast were assembled in the wings. Bea escorted Phil into the line, edging past Artie, whose face was white with apprehension. The light on the base station was flashing again. Dave's panic flooded her ears the instant she got the earphones on. There was no time to tell him what had happened, but there was also no need. Everyone was there. Phil was upright and functional. He'd bounced back in the play's early acts; he'd have to bounce back again. Bea informed Dave that they were ready to roll.

When Dave gave the cue for the king's entrance, Bea turned to Phil. His back was to the others, so only she saw his terror, the blankness in his eyes. A condemned man. The moment passed. He cleared his throat and strode onto the stage.

His post-intermission performance that night was the best of the entire run. The lines came from him with the immediacy of truth. He was not an ailing old actor. He was a king, desperate and raging in the teeth of a storm. He no longer paid a whit of attention to the blocking. He was in the grip of something much bigger and more urgent. Bea watched from her hiding place behind the boards, and as she did this, she watched his daughter watching.

Gregory Pym joined Phil onstage, his eyes blindfolded, the cocoa-powder blood that Bea had mixed that morning staining his cheeks. He fell to his knees before the old king, wanting to kiss his royal hand.

Lear wouldn't let him. *"It smells of mortality,"* he said, pulling his hand away and wiping it.

Bea began to cry. For Lear and Gloucester and the two old men playing them. But also for Sol. And for her own broken heart.

Artie approached her. After being bludgeoned to death at the end of Act Three he would often roam backstage, offering a hand to the other actors. Bea wiped her cheeks, but he'd seen her tears. She hurried past him, averting her face. The walk home from Westmount Park last night had been sweet, but it had stirred her up. There had been no kiss, in the end. Not even a two-cheek *bisou* at her door. It made her realize how badly she wanted one.

And now she felt like she'd been turned inside out. She stumbled through the dark to the seclusion of the women's washroom, where she soaked two paper towels under the tap and pressed them to her eyes. Dave would kill her if he knew. She wasn't supposed to leave the set. Ever. It was a cardinal rule. But rules could be bent. Wasn't that what drinking from Phil's flask had shown her? With her or without her, the earth would keep right on spinning. The show would go on. For a long moment she stood in the darkness, letting her emotions settle.

She was still at the sink when the door opened. It was Claire Johnson, Lear's second daughter, Regan, needing to pee.

Bea stared at her, incredulous. "You're already dead?"

"As a doornail," Claire said.

Bea threw the wads of damp paper in the trash can. Four scenes must have passed since she'd fled the stage. It felt more like four seconds. She hurried back to the wings. A moment later, Claire joined her. The play was over. People were starting to applaud.

The actors lined up behind the set and prepared to take their bows. Artie, his jester's cap back on his head, rushed up to Bea, breathless.

"Where is he?"

He meant Phil. Bea felt her face go hot. She had completely forgotten about him. She ran to his dressing room, pulled open the door and found him collapsed in his chair, staring into space, his face slick with sweat. He'd taken off his robes, for some reason, and was sitting bare-chested in his underpants. His skin was a strange pasty colour. He was shaking.

Through the plywood walls, the applause sounded like water crashing from a great height. It went on and on, interspersed with yells and whistles. People began chanting a word that at first Bea didn't understand. "Wah-lire, Wah-lire!" It sounded unfamiliar and strange. Finally it dawned on her: *Roi Lear*. They were calling for the king.

Artie burst into the room, jingling. Bea was clasping Phil tight, trying to stop the shivering. Artie stopped short. "What are you doing?"

She let go of Phil and started searching for his shirt. It was suddenly crucial to her that Phil be covered. She dug among his clothes, pushing aside his jeans and less-than-clean socks. His teeth had stopped chattering and the shudders were subsiding, but his skin was damp and clammy to the touch. She found the shirt. "He's sick," she said, draping it around his shoulders.

Artie frowned at her. He bent over Phil. "Come on, Phil. You can't abandon us now."

Stan Garroway chose that moment to push his head through the door. "Where is the bastard?" He was grinning, but his eyes didn't look friendly. "They want you, dear. Get off your old arse and put some clothes on."

Phil didn't move.

"He's sick," Bea said again. She turned to Artie. "You'll have to announce it."

Stan was pumped with adrenalin and not about to be denied. "Nonsense!" he said. He took Phil's arm and pulled. The shirt that had been draped over Phil's shoulders fell to the floor. "You outdid yourself," Stan said, not seeming to notice. "Fucking brilliant!"

Bea had to intervene. She pushed Stan toward the door. Artie, who finally understood that something serious was going on, came to her aid. He led Stan away to take part in the curtain call. The applause thundered on.

Phil's flesh was covered in goosebumps. Now that they were alone, Bea began to dress him. He showed no resistance, but neither did he offer any help as she guided his arms into the sleeves of his shirt. It was like dressing an oversized child. She wondered whether he really had suffered a stroke. He was certainly the right age for it. She looked closely at his face. No signs of drooping.

"Can you say your name?" she asked.

He looked at her, startled.

"Your name," she repeated, loudly and clearly, as if he might have gone deaf as well.

"What are you talking about, Bea? You know perfectly well who I am." He frowned at her as though she was the one in difficulty.

She laughed with relief. Outside in the corridor there were footsteps and shrieks of delight. The actors were coming off the stage, elated. The night was over. Phil, who seemed to have woken up, began fastening the buttons on his shirt.

There was a knock at the door. When she opened it, Bea saw the brush-cut hair, the plaster cast on the arm, and knew she was looking at Angelina. Her mother stood behind her. Mimi moved deftly in front of her daughter and drew her into the room, closing the door and taking charge.

"What's the matter, Phil? Are you ill? Is something wrong?"

He didn't answer immediately. He was staring at his daughter as if she weren't quite real. He stopped buttoning his shirt and his hands fell to his sides. "Please forgive me." He seemed to be referring to his state of undress—his legs and feet were bare; his shirt half-open—but there might have been more to it. His daughter chose to interpret the words widely. Her chin started to quiver.

Phil seized Bea's arm. She managed to sit him down on one of the aluminum folding chairs at his dressing table. "What is it?" said Mimi, bending over him. "Dizziness?" She looked into his eyes. "Are you having a spell?" She sniffed at his face discreetly, then put a hand on his forehead. "He's feverish."

Phil didn't respond. He gripped the sides of his chair and rocked, his eyes fixed on the floor. Pearls of moisture gleamed at his hairline.

"He's about to faint," Bea said decisively. "Let's get him on the floor."

The three women manoeuvred Phil down onto the cement. Bea grabbed his feet while Angelina knelt and cradled his head. Mimi put a hand on his chest. His arms and shoulders, which had been rigid, as though in spasm, began to relax. The sweating stopped, too. Colour seeped back into his cheeks.

Bea told Mimi that he'd been shaky all night.

"It could be simple dehydration," Mimi said. She went into the bathroom and filled a glass with water. "Drink this," she instructed as soon as he was able to sit up.

When he was more himself, she began to scold him. "This isn't normal, Philip. It's the second time you've fainted on my watch."

"Your watch, my dear, is over," he said.

"The second time on the show, then," she said, irritated. "At least that I've seen. It isn't something to joke about. What if it's your heart? Or one of those mini-strokes. I think we should go to the emergency ward."

Phil snorted contemptuously.

"I'm serious," Mimi said. "Your life could be in the balance."

Angelina stepped in, physically coming between her squabbling parents. She moved gracefully. "Leave it, Mimi," she said. "Give him a chance to catch his breath."

Phil smiled warmly at her, then turned to his former spouse. "Listen to your daughter."

"She's your daughter too," Mimi said. "She's got the Burns stubborn streak, that's for sure. Not to mention her daddy's mistrust of doctors. She spent a month with a broken hand before deciding to have it looked at."

"And?" Phil asked Angelina.

"And," she said, "they told me I'd made things worse. The bone atrophied. The surgery was more complicated."

"But you're all right now?"

"I guess. Although the surgeon says my kickboxing days are over."

Phil went silent, his eyes dark with concern.

There was a knock at the door. Artie hurried in, followed by Dave. "What's happening?" Artie asked, visibly worried. "Is he okay?"

"Tip top," Phil said, smiling.

"Bullshit," said Mimi. "He almost fainted, and apparently it's not the first time this evening. Something is definitely wrong. You're back in Westmount tomorrow?"

Dave nodded. "We've got a matinee at two."

"Cancel it," said Mimi.

Phil tried to protest, but Mimi was unwavering. "You have to rest. Two shows in a day is too much for a man who can barely stay upright. And you're coming home with me tonight."

To Bea's surprise, Phil didn't object. Angelina fished through the pile of clothes on the floor and found his pants. She passed them to him shyly and offered him a steadying arm as he pulled them on.

Getting his pants back on seemed to help. His dignity restored, Phil walked over to the dressing table and picked up the bouquet of roses that had been lying there all evening. They were limp now but still looked impressive in his arms: twelve long-stemmed burgundy blooms. He held them out to Angelina.

"For you," he said. "I was hoping you'd drop by."

Angelina was caught by surprise. Her tense, narrow face lit up almost in spite of herself; suddenly she looked like a child. "You didn't need . . ." she began, although it was obvious to Bea, and to everyone else in that hot, cramped dressing room, that exactly such a gesture *had* been needed. Angelina pulled open the plastic wrapping and buried her nose in the petals.

# 19.

THE NEXT MORNING Bea was in the kitchen, scrubbing the tarnish off Sol's silverware, when her phone rang. With fingers covered in grey suds, she pressed Talk and stuck the phone between her jaw and shoulder. It was Mimi. "Bea?" she said. Her voice was low. "I won't keep you. I just wanted you to know: they're talking. Angie's in the next room with her father, and they're talking. My daughter slept under the same roof as her father last night. The last time that happened she was four years old."

"Oh, Mimi, that's great. How's Phil feeling?"

"He just ate two bagels with lox and cream cheese, which I guess is encouraging. But overall, he's not good. The drinking is out of control. He'll spend the rest of the run at my place. I told him I'd book him a visit with my GP."

When the call ended, Bea rinsed her hands. Forks and knives lay gleaming on a white dishtowel on the counter before her, each handle engraved with a stylized *M*. The twelve-place dining set had come from her mother's side of the family; generations of McMasters had used it. The candlesticks, still in the sink and covered with acrid polish, bore the same monogram. Deirdre had used them every Friday, for Shabbat dinner. Bea reached for them now and scrubbed them. When they too were gleaming she took them into the dining room and placed them carefully on the table.

"What's the occasion?" said Sol, coming downstairs and noticing the extra placemats. Bea had reminded him the day before that Cara and her family were coming, but he'd forgotten. It was happening more frequently now. Losing track of appointments. Not knowing what day of the week it was.

"No occasion," she said. "We're having a family brunch."

"Who's having brunch?"

"Cara's coming. I told you already. Cara and Didier and the girls. I was supposed to go to work, but the matinee was cancelled."

He frowned. "They're coming today?"

"Yes, Dad. It's Sunday. We always have brunch on Sunday." She paused. Had it sunk in? "They'll be here any minute."

"Who will?"

"Cara."

"Just Cara? Why so many placemats?"

She was putting out the plates when she heard Cara's key in the door. "Auntie Bea!" Yasmin cried, running headlong into her. Bea clasped her niece's hands and laughed as little feet climbed up her thighs and belly.

"Yas!" her mother called from the door. "Your sandals! Take them off before you climb your auntie!" Yasmin flipped over like a trapeze artist and landed gracefully on her feet. She sat on the rug and tugged off her sandals, eyeing Bea unblinkingly, as if willing her not to disappear. "Again!" she ordered, once her feet were bare. She reached out with chubby fingers. And now Elle came over in her quiet fashion to say hello. Cradled in her arm was a book from the attic that Bea had lent her, *The Lion, the Witch and the Wardrobe.*

"I finished it," she said proudly. "It took five days."

"That's got to be a record."

"It's the first chapter book she's read on her own," Cara said. "She barely stopped to eat."

"Well you can make up for that now," said Bea. "We've got good things to tempt you."

Bea had been cooking since early in the morning. She'd made a grated carrot salad with walnuts especially for Cara and a frittata with a bunch of asparagus she'd found in the fridge for her and Sol. She'd also baked a *tarte tatin*, a dessert her father adored. She was hoping Cara might relax the rules for the day and allow the girls to try it.

Didier headed for the kitchen carrying a cardboard box.

"Our contribution," said Cara, watching as he passed. "Or rather, hers." She smiled as Gen-vie entered the room. "Gen-vie's off work today," Cara added quickly. "We all are. The never-ending renovations, remember?"

Bea did remember. Crudivore was growing. Cara and Didier had opened a new section at the back of the restaurant for more tables and refurbished the cellar for food storage. They were painting the place as well, Cara had told Bea, whitewashing the walls, giving it a whole new look. They'd bought tables covered with blue ceramic tile in honour of Quebec's national colours. But the chair cushions would be red, a wink to *la République*. The grand opening was set for Bastille Day—or Bastille Night, to be precise. It was less than a week away.

Still, even with an enforced day off, it was surprising to see Gen-vie here. And odd that Cara hadn't mentioned it on the phone this morning, when Bea said she'd be joining them. They were one place short at the table; Bea would have to add another chair. For the first time she had a chance to look at Gen-vie up close without distraction. She was attractive enough, though not all the elements of face and body sat easily with each other. Her skin was as smooth as fine china, but dreadlocks swung down her back like long blond burrs. Her build was delicate and childlike, just a hint of breast and hip, and she was clothed like a child in a pink T-shirt and jeans. Yet her expression was cool and knowing. At least she'd dispensed with the eye patch and no longer looked like a pirate. Yasmin grabbed Gen-vie's hands; she wanted to climb her too. She seemed at ease with the young cook, as though they were in the habit of spending time together.

Bea added a new place setting, and they all sat down at the table. Gen-vie had brought veggie sushi with avocado centres, sprouted buckwheat crackers, nut spreads and a bright purple mound of grated beets. Cara and Didier had supplemented this with bagels and smoked salmon from the Fairmount Bakery.

"Only two?" Sol asked, looking at the bagels Cara had set out.

"One for you and one for Bea," she said.

He looked at her in confusion.

Cara sighed. "We don't eat them, Dad. Remember? They're baked."

"Well, yes," he said, his eyes narrowing. "That is how bread is made." He looked at Yasmin's plate, with its single piece of untouched sushi. "Get over here, darlin'," he said, pushing his chair back so she could clamber onto his lap. He picked up a bagel, cut it and began slathering it with cream cheese. Then he topped it with a generous slice of lox. "Try it. Go on. You'll see why human beings invented the oven."

"Sol," said Cara in a warning tone.

Yasmin glanced first at her mother and then at Didier, who was watching with quiet disapproval. He shook his head. "It's a fish, you know," he said quickly in French. "It was once alive."

Sol scowled. "Don't you worry about that," he told Yasmin. "It's food. Highly nutritious. And it tastes good." Yasmin paused, considering these contradictory exhortations. They didn't seem to faze her. On the contrary, she was enjoying the adult attention. She took Sol's bagel in both hands and bit lustfully. *"Miam,"* she said, chewing. She shut her eyes to avoid the sight of her irate father. *"C'est bon!"*

Sol laughed. "Case closed."

No, it wasn't. Didier was fuming. In stumbling English, Gen-vie intervened on his behalf. "It is not *nutritif,*" she said. "It is smoke."

"Smoked," said Cara. "Not to mention farmed. Teeming with antibiotics."

"Antibiotics?" said Sol. "What are you talking about? It's lox and bagels. The food of her ancestors. What's bad about that?"

"She is pure," said Gen-vie. "She has eaten raw food her full life. You will . . . *vous allez la contaminer.*"

Sol's jaw tightened. He hadn't addressed Gen-vie directly, nor would he even look her way. Now that Bea thought about it, he hadn't said a word to her.

In the end, she and Sol barely made a dent in the frittata. The apple tart, which she'd thought would really please him, was completely ignored. Gen-vie had brought another dessert—strawberries from the market. Bea could see her in the kitchen, piling them deep in Deirdre's china bowl with the blue willow design of Chinese pagodas and songbirds on its sides.

Didier was standing in the passageway to the dining room as Gen-vie carried the bowl through to the table. He put out an arm like a toll barrier and stopped her. He must have supposed he wasn't visible from the dining room. Plucking a berry from the bowl, he brushed it against Gen-vie's lower lip. The berries were locally grown—small and sweet and deeply red. Gen-vie, who had a view of the dining room and knew they could be seen, ducked her head in refusal and brushed past him. The incident was over in an instant, and yet it had been so flagrantly intimate that Bea felt her face flush. She glanced at Cara, but Cara was gazing out the window. Sol, however, was staring straight into the passageway, his face twisted in fury. He threw down his napkin and rose to his feet.

"How dare you?" he said, leaning on the table for support. He was addressing Didier, but Gen-vie also froze. "In my house," he said, his voice tightening to a croak. "In my own house."

Yasmin, who'd been playing with Elle under the table, poked her head out and stared with frightened eyes.

"Dad," said Cara. "Don't. Please."

She took the bowl from Gen-vie and set it on the table. "It's okay," she said to no one in particular. Then she picked up a serving spoon, one of the large silver ones that Bea had polished that morning, and sat down to serve the fruit.

Sol watched her do this. His face was still a mask of anger. He seemed on the verge of another outburst, but he restrained himself. Without looking at his son-in-law or at Gen-vie, he left the room. A minute later, his bedroom door slammed so loudly they all jumped.

## ACT FOUR

KING LEAR.
*Blow, winds, and crack your cheeks. Rage, blow!*
. . . . . . . . . . . . . . . . . . . . . . . . . . . . . . .
*Crack Nature's molds, all germains spill at once,*
*That makes ingrateful man.*

(3.2.1–9)

20.

THE NEXT WEEKEND was sunless and grey. An evening storm had been forecast for Saturday, but no cancellation notice went out, so at five o'clock Bea kissed her father goodbye, put on his ratty old rain jacket and walked the dozen blocks to Girouard Park in Notre-Dame-de-Grâce. The company was back in town after a week spent carting their gear about to various suburban green spaces in Montreal's West Island. When Bea reached the park the stage had been assembled on the baseball field and the actors' tents put up. It had been smart to leave her bike behind at her father's house. Thunderheads were scudding in from the north.

Dave, trying in vain to control his wind-blown hair, was talking to Artie on the knoll at the north end of the field, where the audience would sit. Bea knew better than to ask about cancellation possibilities. Artie hated being pestered about the weather. If he decided to cancel the show, he would inform people in his own sweet time. Until then, they had to zip their lips and pray to the weather gods.

Bea waved and smiled, but before Artie could wave back Stan marched up, grimacing under a stylish new straw fedora. Lately he'd been taking a great deal of care with his clothes; today, for instance, he was in a loose silk shirt that billowed in the wind. It was probably for the benefit of Jay, whose lack of interest seemed evident to all but Stan. Jay's feelings weren't the only thing he was blind to. He was also surprisingly oblivious to Artie's ways. Every night the weather was doubtful, he'd ask the same useless question.

"We're on, I take it?"

Artie didn't respond.

"You saw the forecast?" Stan persisted, looking up at the threatening sky.

Artie still didn't react.

Stan frowned. Clearly wanting to say more, he checked himself. Theatre, Bea had learned, was in many ways like the army. You did not argue with the generals, even when you thought they were crazy or even possibly suicidal. Reluctant as he was, mouthy, obstinate Stan Garroway would do as he was told. Still, it was obvious to him and to the rest of the cast arriving at the little park that no audience would materialize. Putting up a stage that night just to take it down again seemed a colossal waste of effort. According to the hourly forecast, the storm was now a certainty.

As Stan walked away to grumble to the other actors in the men's tent, Bea and Dave set off for the tech trucks parked on Girouard Avenue. They unloaded the prop boxes and carried them to the stage. Then, after Bea had found the microphones and checked their batteries, she went to fill the actors' water bottles in the park's washrooms. They were filthy. On the women's side the floor was wet, a large puddle lapping at the base of the sinks. The walls were smeared with dirt, or worse. Bea shoved a bottle under a tap and ran the water, trying not to breathe.

When she emerged from the bathroom, a couple of teenage boys with skateboards were nosing around the stage. Apart from them the only people in sight were the Bard in the Parks cast and crew. It was just past six now; the sky was black and the immense maple trees lining the field were thrashing in the wind. Bea glanced over at Artie sitting in the lighting booth, but he didn't look her way. Ever since Phil's collapse in La Fontaine Park, he'd kept his distance. She didn't know what to make of it. He'd seem interested in her, but then the interest would drop away. Perhaps he still thought something was going on between her and Phil. Or maybe he was just plain perverse. She frowned, unable to make up her mind. Phil, at least, was doing better. Now that he was back at Mimi's place he was eating and sleeping more regularly. He'd been to her family doctor, who had diagnosed anemia and certain vitamin and mineral deficiencies, to which aging men were apparently prone. Gin was also a factor, which came as no surprise. Bea scanned the park for any sign of him.

Later, midway through her checklist, she felt a drop. Then another, exploding on her scalp like a tiny bomb. Within a few moments rain was crashing down around her in sheets.

Dave came splashing through the grass. "Everything that isn't nailed down goes into the trucks!" he yelled, his voice muted against the roar of the cascade. He sprinted off to find the actors. Soon the baseball field was alive with activity. Artie tore off his shirt and, bare-chested, supervised the stage's dismantling in the driving rain. Water streamed off his bald head and down his neck and shoulders. A tool belt hung low around his waist, leaving red marks on his slender hips. The main challenge was the scaffolding's steel pipes, many of which were too long for a single person to take down; the biggest of them required the combined efforts of three or four of the male actors. Artie shouted directions and warnings like a foreman on a construction site. The men worked diligently, securing the heavy, rain-slippery metal parts and collectively lowering them onto the grass. Then, in twos and threes, cast and crew carried them to the trucks.

Dismantling the stage wasn't in the actors' contract, yet every night they all pitched in. Every single one, young and old, male and female, joined the effort. Even Phil, who was under a doctor's care and had entertained the cast with tales of vitamin B₁₂ megadoses being injected into his backside by his young and pretty GP, managed to do his bit. They were a troupe, a tribe, bound by traditions of solidarity that were ancient even in Shakespeare's time.

Bea stuffed dripping canvas tent walls into duffle bags. All that was left of the women's tent was its peaked top, mounted on four collapsible steel poles and sagging under the weight of accumulated rain. These tents—called pop-ups, Bea now knew—were designed to fold into a compact package at the flick of a little metal lever on each pole. But as she released the first two levers the top wobbled and then emptied several gallons of water down upon her. The next time she knew to jump clear, but she was already drenched. Her fingers were soon stiff and clumsy with cold. Margo Indongo helped her take the remaining tents down, shivering in her shorts under a cheap rain poncho that kept ripping. At last both the women's and men's tents were packed away. Bea and Margo worked as a team, hauling the heavy bags, one by one, to the truck.

They were halfway across the baseball field with the first bag when the sky lit up. All around them people tipped back their heads, their faces going blank and white. Thunder detonated with such a tremendous crack that a few of them dropped the poles they were carrying. Some lifted their hands to their ears. Others swore.

After the flash, the park went black. People stood there, stunned, for what seemed like a long time, although it couldn't have been more than a few seconds. Artie brought them back to life, shouting at them to hurry. Bea and Margo resumed their forward movement, dragging the soaked deadweight of the tent between them. More flashes came, followed almost instantly by crashes of thunder. The stage, built of highly conductive metal, was the tallest structure in the open playing field. Bea didn't know much about electricity, but she knew enough that her skin prickled with fear.

By eight-thirty, the stage was put to bed. Cheers resonated through the park. Fists were pumped, and the company began to disperse.

Now Artie walked over to her. "Come on," he said without ceremony. "I'll get you home."

Once inside his little blue Toyota Echo, Bea pulled off her father's old jacket and waited, fogging the windows, while Artie did a final check of the field. The storm had been frightening, but now that she was sheltered, she was grateful for it: she'd be able to make it to the Bastille Night party at Crudivore. Through the streaming windshield she watched Artie line a park trash can with a fresh green bag, having thrown the old one onto the pile of Bard in the Parks' garbage that Bear would later load into the truck. He was as scrupulous as ever, even in the driving rain. He jogged back toward her.

His chest and shoulders gleamed as he climbed into the car and slammed the driver's door. He reached behind his seat to put his dripping tool belt on the floor, then grabbed the towel and shirt that lay folded on the back seat. "Some night," he said, drying himself. Then he noticed her drenched state and gave her a sheepish look. He held out the towel. "Sorry. I should have offered it to you first."

She shook her head.

Artie put on his dry shirt. Almost instantly the shirttails turned dark from his soaking shorts. He fished for his car key. "Melville Avenue, I presume?"

Bea nodded. "But only for a minute. Then I'm going to your side of the mountain. Would you mind giving me a lift?"

She explained about the party.

"Crudivore," Artie said. "Sure. My condo is half a block away."

"You can come if you want," she said, finding it hard, suddenly, to look at his face. She hadn't planned to invite him, but now that she had, she was glad. Glad and nervous. It wasn't a date, strictly speaking, but it was certainly a move in that direction.

"Sure," he said. "But I'll have to drop by my place for clothes." He pulled at the hem of his shorts. "I can't go like this."

Artie started the engine and turned the defogger on high, relieving them of the need to talk. With one hand he wiped a hole in the condensation, which slowly widened as he drove. They inched down Girouard toward Sherbrooke, marvelling at the storm's power, Artie's windshield wipers flailing.

When they reached Melville, the lights were on in the house. With Artie behind her Bea hurried up the stairs to the porch, anxious for her father. She found him peacefully seated in the living room, listening to Mozart and flipping through last week's *Economist*. Relief swelled at the sight of him, touched with a shade of dread. She had been hoping he'd be in bed so she wouldn't have to tell him where she was going, or introduce Artie. No such luck. Here was her father, wide awake, rising from the couch to greet them.

"Dad," she said, "this is Arthur White."

Artie offered his hand. "We've met. Years ago. I'm Joe and Johanna White's son."

Sol nodded. "Sure, I remember your parents. They lived next door." He frowned, eyeing Artie. "Can't say that I recognize you."

Artie smiled. "I used to have hair."

Bea left them talking in the living room and ran upstairs to change. She was beginning to feel a tingle of elation, as if she were young again and this really was a date. Or was she just feeling echoes of her past, her father in the living room interrogating some young man she'd had the temerity to bring home? She was glad he hadn't asked where they were going. Cara had been categorical: she told Bea that after Sol's behaviour at brunch, he couldn't come. She'd told him simply that the Bastille Bash would be a party for young people, full of loud music and strangers. He'd be much happier at home with his Mozart and a glass of Chablis.

Bea changed in a hurry to spare Artie too much paternal grilling, but when she got downstairs again the two men were sitting on the couch like old friends.

"Your father was telling me he was born in the Plateau," Artie said. "His house was just around the corner from where I'm living."

"Only we didn't call it the Plateau then," Sol said. "It was the Jewish ghetto. And I couldn't wait to leave it. All of us wanted out. But now everybody and his brother wants to buy there. Go figure."

"It's a great neighbourhood," Artie said.

"You want great?" Sol said. He made a sweeping gesture with his arm. "This is great. This is where you want to be. With the trees, with the silence. I keep telling my daughters."

"Oh, come on," Bea said. "You love the Plateau. Admit it. Saint-Viateur bagels? Schwartz's smoked meat? It's the food of your ancestors, I thought."

"I don't love it," said Sol. "I have ties there, history. That's different from loving." To Bea's dismay he began to elaborate.

"Your street, for instance," he said to Artie, "was once a hub of Jewish culture. In the forties, when I was a kid, practically every Jewish institution of note in Montreal had an address there. The Jewish library was on the corner at Mount Royal. One door down from it, a woman called Ida Maze held these famous literary salons. The Jewish Aid Society was also on that block. And around the corner was the Jewish school I went to."

He stopped for breath and smiled at Bea as if talk about his past was a regular occurrence. Where had this impulse come from? And why now, with Artie, whom he barely knew?

"And then there was Fat Charlie." His smile widened. "Did I ever tell you about him, Bea?"

"Never," she said in amazement.

"I never met him. I was a toddler when he died, and besides, he was a gangster. His surname was Feiganbaum, which I happen to know because his nephew was my best friend in grade school. Anyway, Charlie Feiganbaum was shot dead on your street."

Artie's eyes widened. "By the cops?"

"No. By criminals. Jewish ones, as it turns out." Sol grinned at them. He seemed to be trying to score a point against Artie by mentioning this dark moment in the Plateau's history, challenging Artie's rosy take on the neighbourhood, but his tone remained relaxed and conversational. Bea didn't sense even a hint of anger. He rose to his feet and held his hand out to Artie. "It was a pleasure to meet you again."

As he shuffled off to the kitchen for a glass of water, Bea shook her head. He hadn't lost his charm. He'd flashed it first with Mimi and now, once more, with Artie. Happiness filled her, followed by relief. He seemed almost normal.

As they were letting themselves out the front door, Sol walked up quickly behind them. "You're going there now, aren't you?" he said, breathless.

Bea swallowed. His jaw was jutting. So he hadn't forgotten what night it was.

"To the Plateau. The restaurant. Don't try to deny it."

It was a strategy that worked with Bea every time. Accuse her of lying, and she'd blurt out the truth.

"Yes. Okay. You're right."

His face darkened, but he held his peace. After an awkward

pause, Bea stepped out onto the porch, pulling Artie's arm so he would follow. Her father's moods blew without rhyme or reason these days, like the weather. She couldn't let something so unruly rule her life. She turned back to say goodbye, but before she could utter a word the door slammed in her face. She and Artie stood and listened as the bolt clicked.


Now she was worried. She stood there, wavering. Artie was a few steps beyond her, at the edge of the porch, his body silhouetted by a streetlamp. They had a date, sort of. And he looked like he wanted to go through with it. Sol would be fine, she told herself. He'd stayed on his own for six weeks without a mishap. Never at night, but that wasn't such a big deal. He'd been so wonderful just minutes ago, telling all his stories.

She took a breath and went to Artie's side. The rain was still falling, but more lightly now. Artie was quiet as they got into the car. To save time and avoid the traffic lights on Sherbrooke, he drove up Westmount's leafy slope to Cedar Avenue. Bea knew instantly where he was headed. She thought about saying something, suggesting another route, but in the end she kept quiet. Three decades had passed. She ought to be able to handle it.

They looped around the southern face of the mountain. Rain sprayed the windshield, temporarily obscuring the outside world.

As they approached the intersection at Pine, agitation began to rise in her. She had always avoided this place. Always. Whenever she rode her bicycle from Westmount to the east end, she took long detours rather than confront it. The physical look of the place was changed, of course. The underpass had been demolished, the street ripped up, revamped, repaved—but still, this was the place.

Artie slowed to a stop at the traffic light next to Molson Stadium. Bea felt her chest constricting. Raindrops were drumming on the roof of the car. Quite suddenly, the words came out of her. "My mother died here."

Artie turned.

"Not here precisely," she said. "A little farther along, between here and the next traffic light." She watched rivulets snaking down the windshield. "October sixth, 1979."

The traffic light turned green. Then it turned orange and red again. Artie put on the hazard lights.

"I remember her," he said. "She told me I'd grow up to be an actor one day. She said I'd be famous."

"My mother said that?"

"Also that it was okay for boys to cry."

Bea told him the story of the accident. Her parents had been coming home from dinner at a Greek restaurant on Park, Sol at the wheel of his Triumph TR7 convertible. The road conditions were fine that night. Sol had drunk two glasses of wine with his meal: he wasn't even slightly impaired. He'd been driving at a good speed, but there was no evidence that it was over the limit. As he negotiated the curving underpass that led from Park onto Pine Avenue, he'd lost control of the car and it skidded, bounced against the concrete divider and flipped. Long black streaks were left on the asphalt. Bea had seen the photos, years later, when she looked up the police report.

"He must've died too," Artie said quietly. "Part of him, anyway. The guilt . . . can you imagine?"

She couldn't, really. Her father had never talked about it. Not once. Not to her.

The Echo started to move again. Artie crossed the intersection and headed north, accelerating past the place of the accident, driving fast up Park. What an odd night this was turning out to be, with all these confessions and stories. When Bea surfaced from her thoughts they'd already turned onto Duluth and were making a left, northward again, onto L'Esplanade.

Artie's condo seemed even bigger than the first time Bea had visited. There were plants everywhere, in pots on the floor and hanging from the ceiling, their leaves and fronds reaching to her like open hands. During the party, Artie explained, he'd stored them next door at his neighbour's place. Now they made the space an indoor jungle, sweetening the air and softening the noises that came up from the street.

Artie took a shower, providing her with a chance to explore. On the wall beside his bookcase, three small photographs were arranged one above the other. His mother, Johanna, smiled from the top frame. Her hair was black and lustrous, her skin unlined. This was the woman Bea had known in her childhood. Beneath her was a young man in his late teens, with tousled dark hair and soulful eyes: Artie, while he still had hair. The third and final picture was of a little boy, perhaps three years old, perched on the shoulders of a large, florid, fair-haired man. The father. Joe. The violent one. From the photograph, it was hard to believe. Little Arthur was having the time of his life, his arms outstretched, his head thrown back in laughter. Only his father's grip on his ankles was holding him in place.

"*La sainte famille,*" said Artie, coming up behind her. "You recognize any of them?"

Bea nodded. "All of them." She pointed to the picture of the laughing child. "You look like a happy little boy, Arthur White."

He looked at the photo thoughtfully. "I do, don't I? In my version of the story I tend to forget that. There was happiness too."

———

By the time they left the apartment, the sadness that had descended on them both had lifted. Artie held a big black umbrella above their heads and adjusted his steps to match hers. It wasn't hard: their legs were more or less equal in length. Even before they turned onto Rachel Street they heard the music. Big-band swing. The blare of trombones cutting through the rain. Parked in front of the restaurant was Sol's Range Rover, its driver's side now bearing the Crudivore logo. Bea walked over to investigate. It had been professionally spray-painted, a discreet green sprout with the restaurant's name arcing above it in Day-Glo green. She was glad her father wasn't there to see it.

A few of the braver partygoers were clustered on the sidewalk having a cigarette under their umbrellas. They were all young, most of them wearing shorts and flip-flops; in her trusty pink kameez, Bea suddenly felt overdressed. Inside the door more young faces greeted her: Gen-vie's protest crowd. The music was deafening. Bea looked around for Cara but couldn't find her. On the other side of the room she spotted Gen-vie, holding a tray aloft as she navigated the sea of bodies.

The restaurant interior was transformed—a wall had been knocked down and it was much more spacious than before. Bea shouted Gen-vie's name across the cavernous room, but her voice was swallowed by the din. She kept waving, though, and eventually Gen-vie saw her. She too was transformed: her dreadlocks had been pinned back and adorned with a flower, and her usual jeans had been replaced by a short, flared white skirt. She nodded at Bea, but it was to Artie that she offered a smile. They were exchanging greetings when Didier, a fluorescent Crudivore sprout stamped on his T-shirt, materialized out of the crowd. He air-kissed Bea and took two cocktails off Gen-vie's tray, handing them to Bea and Artie. The drinks were bright green and came in stylish jumbo martini glasses.

"Not bad, hey?" he yelled as Bea took a preliminary sip.

She winced. It tasted like the paint thinner in Phil's flask.

Didier patted her back. "It has a punch." He smiled. The word came out as *paunch*. Shouting to be heard, he told them that it was a kombucha-vodka mix sweetened with concentrated apple juice. The apples were local and organic. No carbon footprint. The colouring was natural. *"Chlorophylle,"* he yelled. *"Complètement naturel."*

*"Délicieux,"* Bea yelled back, trying to sound sincere. She gestured at the renovations, which she could praise honestly. *"Super beau!"* She gave Didier a thumbs-up.

The music made sustained conversation impossible. Didier and Gen-vie slipped back into the crowd, leaving Bea and Artie with their psychedelic martinis. Bea scanned the crowd again for her sister and took a second sip of her cocktail. It was less awful than the first. She took another. A sizable dance space had been cleared a few steps away, where couples were happily bobbing. Bea glanced at Artie. He didn't seem like the dancing type, which was too bad. Her feet were tapping. The music was hard to resist: big-band numbers, swing. A Benny Goodman song was starting up. Didier had hired a DJ, a young man with a bushy red beard. Bea took another swallow of greenery. Heat had begun to radiate from her scalp. Her hips were swaying. Just then she saw Cara come out of the kitchen with a tray of food. Bea grabbed Artie's hand and pulled him toward her sister.

"Hey-ho," Cara proclaimed when she saw them. She'd put the tray down on a counter and was gracefully slicing sushi rolls with a knife that seemed to sparkle in her hand. A kitschy strobe light that had been suspended above the dance floor began to flash, making the white walls of the restaurant explode with light at half-second intervals. Cara put down the knife and high-fived Bea, her hand moving in strobed jerks as it approached Bea's, almost spilling the remains of her chlorophyll. "You're actually drinking that stuff?" she shouted.

Bea nodded. Her sister's surprised face lit up and vanished repeatedly. "Brave!" she yelled.

Bea introduced Artie, but talking was too difficult. They just stood there, watching Cara work. Artie grinned at Bea, then nodded at the dance floor. He must have noticed her restless feet. The song wasn't one she recognized—a sassy female vocalist was belting out bad rhyme—but she didn't care. She was itching to move. They put down their drinks and pushed their way through the crowd. When they reached the dance floor, they began to do a rough approximation of a jitterbug. It was clear that Artie knew nothing about swing dancing, but neither did she. They were both happy enough to see what worked and go with it.

Artie tried to twirl her around, but their arms got tangled and they had to stop and rewind. Their second effort was more successful. They started innovating, clumsily but with energy, grinning at each other through the noise and flashes of light. Bea's limbs felt loose. Artie's bald head strobed in and out of view in dreamlike staccato glimpses. The number came to an end and a new one started up: Count Basie's fast-moving "One O'Clock Jump." On impulse, Bea stepped into Artie's arms. He smelled of soap, and beneath it was another aroma, more intimate: yeasty and subtly sweet, like freshly baked biscuits. She closed her eyes and breathed.

When she opened her eyes again, a familiar figure was directly in front of her: Didier Malraux. Bea had never thought of her brother-in-law as a physical man. Yet here he was, moving sinuously on the floor, his feet in perfect synch with Count Basie's brilliant rhythms. He wasn't dancing with his wife. His partner was Gen-vie, her dreadlocks flying as he whirled and twirled her, once even flipping her over his shoulder. Bea stopped to watch. Artie did the same.

Now Bea understood Gen-vie's white skirt. It was flaring and falling, shining brightly in the strobe. Beneath the skirt she wore a pair of silver shorts that caught the light with each twirl. A circle opened up around her and Didier. Soon the whole room had become their audience.

When the number ended, everyone clapped. Didier took Gen-vie's hand and held it up, drinking in the applause.

Artie turned to Bea. Another song was starting, an even faster one, with blaring trumpets and trombones. They couldn't talk, but it was clear that Artie was as impressed by Didier as she was. She glanced at the counter where her sister had been slicing sushi. There was no sign of her. Artie reached for Bea's hand and they began to dance again, a little more shyly this time, intimidated by her brother-in-law's exuberant style. Didier himself was still dancing with Gen-vie.

But the music was good, and the chlorophyll cocktail was now singing in Bea's veins. She was losing herself in the pleasure of the swing-time rhythms when she realized that Artie had stopped moving. He was looking out the front window of the restaurant. Bea followed his gaze and saw her father standing there in the rain. He was dressed in his white linen suit, his face pressed to the glass.

She hurried outside, followed by Artie. Sol made no attempt to greet them. He was muttering to himself, his face taut with anger. She thought maybe it was the Rover, but he didn't even glance at it. He ignored her questions and wouldn't explain why he'd come, or how. He must have dressed and called a cab soon after they left. Bea's ears were ringing; the raindrops were cool on her face. Through the glass, the restaurant throbbed with music and shouts. Her father kept muttering and trying to see inside.

"I'm going to take you home," Bea said. "Let's go in. I'll call us a cab."

"Forget the cab," Artie said. "I'll drive you."

As Artie walked away to get his car, Bea led Sol into the restaurant to see Cara, who was now back at the counter, slicing a fresh platter of Gen-vie's sushi. When she saw her father, her mouth fell open. She looked at Bea accusingly.

Bea raised her hands to show that Sol had simply appeared, but Cara gave no indication that she understood. Bea tried shouting Artie's name; she mimed steering a car. Cara's face remained angry, empty of comprehension. The brief elation of the cocktail was fading fast. Bea's temples ached. Then she began to feel a low, creeping sense of panic: from the tightness of Sol's features, she could see that rage was rising in him. She found an empty bar stool and sat him down. The strobe light was beating on his white suit, turning him into a tremulous on-and-off spectre. He looked around, searching for something.

Why had he come, after Cara had expressly told him to stay home? He was lucid. Lucid enough, evidently, to call a taxi; to give the driver directions; to pay the fare. Yet something was wrong. He'd said nothing to Bea, or to anyone else, since arriving. All he'd done was mutter in anger. He was there but not there. As the pain in her temples grew steadily worse, she felt suddenly, overwhelmingly weary.

The floorboards were bouncing beneath her. Sol's eyes narrowed. He'd seen something behind her. It was Didier. Regrettably, he was still dancing with Gen-vie. The circle had formed around them again. People were clapping and laughing. Gen-vie was smiling.

It took Bea a moment in the fragmented light to realize that Sol had gotten up from the stool. Moving with a speed and purpose that caught her off guard, he went to the counter where Cara was still slicing sushi. Bea tried to follow, but the dense crowd slowed her down. She saw Sol seize Cara's wrist. Cara reacted, the alarm on her face frozen in a strobed instant. Then Sol was gone again, swallowed up in the seething mass of people. Bea scanned the room, dread rising in her throat. She saw her father's white suit flash as he pressed himself into the massed dancers who'd formed a circle around Didier and Gen-vie. He was struggling to get through, his arms flapping.

She tried to shout; the music drowned her voice. Now Cara was fighting through the crowd as well, but she was too far away to catch up. The dread in Bea's throat crested and broke. She dashed forward, aiming not at the place where her father was but at the place where he was going. People strayed into her path and yet she kept her body low, elbowing them aside as she went. At the edges of her vision she saw surprised faces, affronted mouths yelling protests she couldn't hear.

And suddenly Bea was there. The packed people gave way and she was in the empty circle with Didier and Gen-vie and Sol, who'd got there half a step ahead of her. He was directly behind Gen-vie, who was fully absorbed in the music. Bea placed herself between them. She wanted to protect her father. She had always wanted to protect him.

The room went black. It went white. Sol's beard was so near she could have kissed it. His mouth opened, forming a perfect *O*, but all she could hear was the swing-time's brassy wail. Her father's arm was poised in the air. Something was shining. She reached out, wanting to reassure him. The room went black.

"It's all right," she tried to shout. She was touching his shoulder. "It's me."

There was a tap on her chest. And then a second. Two light knocks, as though someone were trying to get her attention. Her hand slipped from him. She groped to find him again.

The room went white. His face was right there, but something was wrong. Half of him had disappeared. Where his right cheek should have been, black dots appeared and were growing. Cara arrived. Her hands went to her mouth and she stepped back.

The room went black. It went white.

New black dots appeared. Bea reached out to touch her father's face, but he wouldn't stay in focus. He was melting, dripping onto the floor. She wanted to whisper to him—he was so close he would hear—but she couldn't. There was a stitch in her side. She couldn't draw breath. Inside her head, her heart was beating louder than the music.

Then Bea understood. The dots weren't part of him. They were coming from her. From her mouth, from her nose. The knowledge calmed her. She sat down on the floor, and the room went black for good.

ACT FIVE

*When thou dost ask me blessing, I'll kneel down*
*And ask of thee forgiveness: so we'll live*
*And pray, and sing, and tell old tales, and laugh*
*At gilded butterflies, and hear poor rogues*
*Talk of court news; and we'll talk with them too,*
*Who loses and who wins, who's in, who's out,*
*And take upon's the mystery of things.*

(5.3 10–16)

21.

A FACE WAS GAZING down at her. It was autumn and she was six years old, sitting with her mother on the porch overlooking Melville Avenue. The light was fading, turning the sky a dusky purple colour, like plums. The park—the whole city—had fallen still. Bea was perched on her mother's knees, wrapped in a caftan that smelled familiarly of the kitchen and of her mother's hand lotion.

The sun was sinking behind the mountain, lighting the clouds from below. Her mother loved watching sunsets. She would often call to Bea to come and join her. The face over Bea came into focus. It was her sister's.

"Welcome back," Cara said.

Bea was on a bed, in a place she couldn't identify, surrounded by a pale blue curtain. There was no sign of the sun—no window, even, through which to see it. A translucent tube snaked out of her left arm. Behind her, something beeped. It was a sound she recognized. How many rooms like this had she known in the years when her mouth was being made whole? How many times had she woken from a dream, hemmed in by curtains, tasting her own blood?

She tried to speak.

"Don't," Cara said. Deep rings circled her eyes. She looked thin and haggard. "Don't even try. I'll go find—"

A young woman stepped through the curtain before Cara could finish. Her hair was thick and black, woven in a braid. The stethoscope snaking around her neck disappeared into the breast pocket of her surgical greens.

"How are we doing?" She introduced herself: Dr. Essakhri. She had performed the surgery. She was pleased to see Bea coming around so quickly. "In cases like this, you can never be sure until the patient wakes up."

Cases like this?

Bea tried to speak again, but Dr. Essakhri shook her head. There was kindness in her eyes. Bea had been lucky, she said. The wounds could have been far more serious. Only one organ had been touched.

"Which is why you've got the tube," said Cara. "Your lungs—"

"Lung," Dr. Essakhri corrected. "Just the left one. Thankfully."

Bea stared at them both, trying to remember. She'd been dancing with Artie. That part was intact. And then her father had shown up. She tried to shape a question.

Dr. Essakhri patted her shoulder. "Everything's fine, Beatrice. There's no need to talk just yet. Please don't exhaust yourself."

Exhaustion did seem to be an issue. Every movement she made took a huge effort. The simple act of turning her head sent ripples of pain through her chest. Each breath was a challenge.

The doctor smiled. "The lung is holding. That's the good news. We released the air trapped in the pleural space and now your body is taking over. You'll have to rest for a few days, of course. Time's the big healer. We've got you booked in here at the Sam Rabinovitch Spa for at least a week. You may as well enjoy it."

She poured a glass of ice water from the plastic jug beside the bed and inserted a straw. "Here," she said, putting it in Bea's hands. She adjusted the bed to a sitting position. "You're probably pretty parched. Drink all you want. But don't overdo it on the talking. In fact, don't overdo it, period."

She turned to Cara. "Your sister will need quiet. One visitor at a time. At least till she's out of the ICU."

The young doctor slipped out through the blue curtain, leaving Bea alone with her sister.

Cara told her what had happened. Her eyes stayed on Bea as she spoke. Their father had attacked her. "He totally lost it. It could have been the strobe on the dance floor." Cara's eyes turned shiny for a moment, but she swallowed and continued. "The doctors aren't sure what triggered it. And he's gone mute, so there's no way to find out." She took a breath and looked into Bea's eyes. "He stabbed you twice. Here and here." Her finger hovered over the points on Bea's chest.

"It was my knife," Cara continued. "He grabbed it out of my hands. I was too surprised to stop him."

Bea remembered the sushi. She shook her head, wanting to speak. Cara put a finger to Bea's lips. "No," she said. "Be a good girl. They just patched you up." She set Bea's glass aside and produced a ballpoint pen and a steno pad. "Here. The nurse suggested we use these."

Bea could barely grip the pen. Her fingers refused to do what she wanted. Her handwriting came out in rickety spikes. But she persisted until the anxious question had taken shape on the page. She passed over the notepad.

"Oh," Cara said. "Sorry. I should have told you right off the bat. He's fine. Physically, at least. He's being detained at the police operations centre on Crémazie Street in the north end. He's in the infirmary, not a holding cell. I just came from there."

Bea took back the pad and scratched a new question.

Cara read it and looked straight at her. "They had to arrest him, Bea. That's how it works. The important thing is, he's safe. The infirmary people understand the situation. He'll appear in court Monday morning. I found a good lawyer. He says not to worry, there are precedents with dementia. He doesn't even think it'll go to trial. Dad will probably be declared unfit."

Bea's head was churning. A nurse came through the curtains at that moment, putting an end to the conversation.

"I'll be back this afternoon," Cara said, gathering her bag and sweater. "I have to check on the girls. Please don't worry, Bea. Dad's in good hands. All you need to think about is getting well. Oh," she said, pausing for a second despite the nurse's evident desire to see her gone, "there's someone else out there. He'll be happy to hear you're awake. He spent the entire night in the waiting room."

The blue curtains parted and Cara left. It was an odd feeling, being mothered by one's baby sister. Odd, but not disagreeable. Cara was carrying the whole load right now: Sol, the kids, Bea. Not to mention a marriage that appeared to be disintegrating. An image of Didier swinging Gen-vie across the dance floor rose in her mind.

After taking Bea's temperature and blood pressure the nurse continued to fuss, fluffing pillows and straightening covers. When things were finally to her satisfaction, she disappeared through the curtains. Bea listened to her footsteps receding and then to voices somewhere close by conversing in hushed, insistent tones. She must have drifted off, because when she next looked up, Artie was sitting beside the bed, gazing at her intently. He grinned when he saw she was awake. Then he leaned in and cupped her chin in his hand.

The gesture was so simple and intimate that she winced.

Artie pulled back in alarm. "Did I hurt you?"

She shook her head, but immediately her neck went into spasm, triggering hot stabs of pain that radiated down into her back and chest. She winced again, in spite of herself.

"I'm sorry," he said, looking miserable.

She lay still, resting her eyes on him as the pain receded. His own chin was covered in stubble, the hairs an earthy mix of rusts and grey. He was wearing the same white T-shirt he'd been wearing at the party, crumpled after so many hours of use. A brown crust of blood was smeared across its front. She couldn't help staring. When Artie realized what she was looking at, he blushed.

"I was with you till the ambulance came. They wouldn't let me ride with you, but I followed in my car. I haven't had a chance to change." He blinked. "I told them I was your fiancé." He looked around furtively as if someone might be hiding behind the curtains, listening. "Don't disabuse them, okay? Otherwise they won't let me in here."

She nodded, more slowly this time, taking care.


A vase of roses stood on her windowsill: bright red, their blooms starting to open. Artie had brought them several days before, after she was wheeled to a private room: her suite at the spa, Dr. Essakhri had called it. Bea liked Dr. Essakhri.

Her room was on the same floor as the ICU, but in a quieter wing, tucked away from the bells and the bustle. She was surrounded by walls now instead of a thin curtain. And she had a window, although the view was hardly inspiring—an exterior brick wall and, if she sat up, a flat gravel roof. But at least there was daylight. A glimpse of bright summer sky.

Artie came every day that week, arriving punctually at ten and staying until mid-afternoon, bringing greetings from her friends in the company. She hadn't asked him to. Then again, she hadn't asked him to stop.

The visiting rules here were more relaxed. He'd dropped the pretence of being her fiancé. He was her walking partner. Dr. Essakhri had instructed her to walk as often as possible to get her lungs back in shape. Every half hour he would accompany her out of the room and they would amble through a slow lap of the corridor. She also had to do a series of breathing exercises involving an apparatus called an "incentive spirometer." It was a simple device with a clear plastic shaft into which she breathed, suspending a little yellow ball on a column of air. As her lungs grew stronger, the ball rose higher and stayed up longer. Artie helped her with this as well, joking and badgering her like a personal trainer. In the evenings, Cara would come with back issues of *The New Yorker* and takeout soup from the Tonkinoise place across the street; she'd also give her an update on Sol, who'd been declared mentally unfit, as his lawyer had predicted. The lawyer, whom Cara now spoke of as a personal friend, secured Sol's transfer to the geriatric unit at the Riverview Mental Health Facility, where he would undergo further psychiatric evaluation. There would be no trial, and no possibility of any criminal record.

At Bea's request, Artie brought newspapers. The story of the attack had been on the front page of both the *Gazette* and *La Presse*. Everyone in the city knew the Rosebud store and its philanthropist owner, so his violent act was major local news. Cara had been besieged with media calls. A reporter from the *Gazette* even came to the hospital looking for Bea, but the staff chased him away. Interest was intense for a few days; then it died down and the world moved on.

Bea's body was healing. Her chest no longer hurt when she moved, and she could take deep breaths. But she hadn't resumed talking. If she needed anything, she scribbled a note. She could make sounds well enough; she'd tested her voice at night when no one was around. But in the daytime, silence felt safer. She had always preferred silence to speech, probably because of her cleft, and so far no one seemed to object, least of all Artie, who sat by her bed each day, filling the space around them with stories. He gave her daily tidings from the show: who was feuding with whom; who was out, who was in.

The play was running smoothly. It was too late in the run to hire a new assistant for Dave, so the entire cast had absorbed Bea's duties. They ironed their own shirts and dutifully spritzed vodka on the armpits of their costumes to suppress their own odours until laundry day. Dave was doing the laundry himself, twice a week, in the machines in his apartment building. It wasn't ideal, but that was life. The actors also set their own props, checked their microphones and helped each other through the costume changes. Artie had stepped into the role of Phil Burns's keeper. "I'm actually beginning to like him," he confided one morning on one of their strolls through the hospital. They were exploring new routes as she grew stronger. Today, they had decided to venture down to the coffee shop on the first floor. At the elevator, Artie pressed the button. "He wants to come and see you."

The next morning, Bea's fifth at the Sam Rabinovitch Spa, instead of Artie, a troupe of actors showed up. Phil was the first to enter her room, with an enormous helium-filled Mickey Mouse face fastened to a stick and a fruit basket encased in crinkly cellophane. Bea couldn't stop smiling. No one seemed fazed by her silence. Phil and Stan started in at once with anecdotes and jokes, keeping Jay and the others laughing. Phil kept popping cherries in his mouth after Bea removed the wrapping from the fruit basket. Of the women, only Margo and Bea's favourite tech, Maggie, had come. Apparently, Ann had fought with Claire at the previous night's performance. They were both still licking their wounds. And Mimi was in Toronto. Bea didn't mind. The tribe had shown the flag.

Artie arrived late the following day. He and Bea went on their default circuit through the hospital ward, the first one she'd ever walked with him.

"How did it go?" he asked. They were walking more slowly than usual. He seemed preoccupied, almost listless.

"Fine," she said carefully. She had begun to speak again, but only to him and Cara, and even with them it was sparing. "Everyone seems in top form."

"Hah," said Artie with a strong hint of sarcasm. "Never trust appearances. Not in this business, anyway." He went on to describe the row between Ann and Claire, and how Phil had been late for yesterday's show. "No apology, no explanation, no nothing. I've had it. He can bloody well change his own royal robes."

They stopped in a little glassed-in alcove. "There's nothing between us," she said quietly. "Just so we're clear."

Artie searched her eyes in a panic.

"Between me and Phil," she clarified.

He rubbed a hand over his scalp. "I actually know that. Or at least this part of me does," he said, knocking his head with a knuckle. "My body is a little slower to come around." He paused and turned toward the window. "It's not just that he hits on you, though. He reminds me of my father." He fell silent and they resumed their walk.

Joe White, Bea learned that day, had been a very troubled individual. There was the violence, but there had also been women. A parade of them, throughout Artie's boyhood. Artie looked away from Bea as he told her this. He walked like a man in deep shame, his eyes on the floor. "If my mother went out of town, he'd bring them home. Sleep with them in their bed. I'd wake up in the morning and there would be some person I'd never met before brushing her teeth in the bathroom. It was pretty messed up."

Artie's father had died alone the summer before, in an apartment overlooking the Lionel-Groulx metro station. "It was sad at the end. He had no one. Except for me, I guess. We made up. At least there was that. He told me he loved me, which is more than many fathers get around to doing. But I have this thing about feckless men. That's why Phil drives me nuts. It's not just the beatings he gives me in the play. Although that's hard to take, believe me. It's how he is in real life. The carelessness with other people. His utter lack of responsibility, of shame. And the fact that he gets away with it. When I look at him, all I see is my father."

They were passing the nursing station. A couple of heads looked up to watch them, but Bea didn't care. She took Artie's hand in hers. He was startled, but she didn't let go. She kept right on holding it all the way back to her room.

## 22.

A MAN IN A GREEN UNIFORM was driving a tractor-mower across the hospital's bright green lawn next to the traffic light on Légaré and Côte-Sainte-Catherine Road. Artie held Bea's elbow to cross the street as if she were a child or an invalid. It irritated her slightly, even though, strictly speaking, she *was* an invalid, released moments before after seven long days at the Samuel Rabinovitch Hospital. She filled her lungs down to the deepest recesses.

Artie was driving her home to Melville Avenue. There was nothing left in her Sainte-Famille apartment except for a few stray possessions she'd have to collect by the end of the month. Cara had insisted that Bea needed help—she was under strict instructions from Dr. Essakhri not to lift anything weighing more than a kilogram. Cara had moved into the Melville house as well, not merely for Bea's sake. She'd confronted Didier about Genvie. Two days later, following a series of tense exchanges, she'd packed suitcases for herself and the girls and driven over the mountain in Sol's Range Rover. She was staying in his bedroom, with Elle and Yasmin sharing her old room down the hall.

Bea unlocked the front door and led Artie into the house. "Hello?" she called out in a voice that sounded almost normal. Leaving the hospital had meant dropping the remnants of her silence. She was back in the world. It felt good to be in voice again.

She knew there would be no answer. The girls were at the YMCA day camp a few blocks away, and Cara was at the Riverview with Sol. A note in the front hall ordered Bea to eat. The fridge was full of food.

The climb from the first floor to the attic proved more challenging than Bea had anticipated. Artie carried her knapsack and the roses he'd given her, their stems swaddled in a wet paper towel and their heads just starting to nod, like sleepy children. Every couple of steps, Bea had to stop. Her chest cramped the way it had in the first days of her recovery. After the flat corridors of the hospital, stairs presented a whole different experience. She experimented with shallower breaths. When they finally reached the attic landing, she clasped the handrail, swaying.

"Whoa," said Artie. He put down the knapsack and supported her the rest of the way. "You all right?" he said once he'd sat her down on the bed.

She was panting. "Fine."

"You sure?"

She wasn't sure. Her vision was tunnelling and there was a straining sensation in her chest, as if a hand had reached inside her and was trying to pull her ribs out.

"Lie down," Artie said.

She did as she was told. Her breathing grew easier. The tunnelling stopped and the pulling at her ribcage subsided somewhat.

He sat at her side. For a minute they were silent. Then he looked around the room. "This is a little weird," he said. "Kind of a time warp."

She slapped the mattress. A few motes rose into the air, but not the thick clouds of her first days here. "You should have seen it before I dusted. My father hadn't touched a thing." She glanced at him shyly. Did he remember Han Solo? Princess Leia practising her kisses on the solitary smuggler?

Artie faced her. Then, as if reading her mind, he leaned in. She wasn't sure whether he was aiming for her cheek or her mouth, or which, in that confused moment, she would have preferred. She turned her head and their noses collided. He pulled back abruptly.

"Sorry," he said.

"That's okay."

"Well. You look better now. If you need anything . . ."

"Yeah. Thank you. Really."

He hurried off. She heard his feet clattering down the attic stairs, then silence as he reached the rug on the second floor. Half a minute later, the front door closed and her father's house fell into its customary hush. Bea shut her eyes. The hand inside her chest was still pulling. In her ears, faint but steady, was the sound of her own pulse.

She awoke two hours later in the grip of fear. Somewhere far below her children's voices cried out. It occurred to her that the girls' day camp must be over. She blinked into the hazy late-afternoon light still half-immersed in dream, then shut her eyes. It had come again.

The house had been more derelict than ever, the floors so rotten it was a wonder the bed could stand. She'd knelt on the narrow mattress, looking over the edge. If she climbed down, she'd fall to her death; if she stayed put, she'd likely suffer worse. Through the gaps in the boards, she could see the ghostly figure coming up a huge, spiralling staircase that rose like a coil of DNA through the hollow centre of the house. The figure was making quick progress, mounting the stairs with a relentless animal focus. Panic gripped Bea. Her chest was so constricted she couldn't breathe. When it reached her room, Bea screamed, even as she realized there was no reason to be afraid. For hovering in front of her in the dusky light was a woman: shifting and insubstantial, no more threatening than herself.

## 23.

BEA WOKE THE NEXT MORNING to the sound of rain. The matinee might have to be cancelled. She reached for her phone to check the weather, then her hand stopped. She sank back onto her pillow and pulled the covers over her chest. She didn't have to think about that. Her phone was off. It lay in a drawer in her desk.

She went back to sleep.

It was ten o'clock when she came downstairs. The house was empty. Cara had left a note saying she'd taken the girls back to the condo on Villeneuve to see their dad and to get some of their toys. Bea fixed herself a green tea and stepped out onto the front porch. The rain had stopped and the sun was emerging. It was the second to last Sunday of July; Quebec's annual construction holiday had started. The only sound she heard was the chirping of sparrows in Sol's forsythia bush. Melville Avenue was deserted. And so was the park: no children in the wading pool, no soccer players on the field.

She sat in her father's Adirondack chair and sipped her tea. Her mother had done this, drifted out here on Sunday mornings to drink tea and enjoy the silence. It felt good to be still, to remain motionless in the midst of a quiet summer day. She realized her chest no longer hurt. The only lingering reminder of her injuries was a pulling sensation on the left side, where the intercostal drain had been. It wasn't pronounced, just a twinge whenever she stood up or sat down. Dr. Essakhri had assured her that it too would pass.

Sunlight was starting to freckle the trees in the park across the street. A noise made her turn. The front door of the neighbouring house opened—the house where Artie and his family used to live. A little boy of four or five came out onto the porch. He stopped when he saw her.

"Hello," said Bea.

His eyes were a lustrous dark brown, framed in an olive complexion. A beautiful child. He ran back inside. A moment later, he reappeared with his mother and an older girl.

"Oh," the mother said. She and her children paused and contemplated their neighbour. The girl was sturdier than her brother, her features a shade broader; both were variations on the theme of their mother's loveliness. "Well," the mother said. "I was wondering when we'd get to meet you. I'm Ariela." She extended a hand over the balustrade.

Bea took it. "Bea Rose."

"I know," Ariela said. "Who doesn't? How are you feeling?"

She had a slight accent. Middle Eastern? Bea assured her that she was fine.

"And your father?" Ariela asked.

The two children were staring openly. Bea smiled at them. Instead of answering their mother's question, she addressed them.

"There are two girls living here," she said. "My nieces. Just about your age. They're out right now, but one of these days you should come over and play."

The girl looked up at her mother. The little boy studied Bea, unblinking.

"What are your names?"

Ariela laughed. "What am I thinking? Poppy," she said, pointing to the girl. "And Eitan."

Bea shook the children's hands ceremoniously, and Ariela and her children continued on their way.

As they walked down the street, Mimi rode up on her bicycle. "I called the hospital and heard you'd been released," she said. "I tried your phone, but there was no answer." Bea started to apologize, but Mimi cut her off. "It's good that there was no answer. It gave me an excuse to come over."

They retreated to Sol's kitchen, and were soon carrying a fresh pot of tea and a plate of apple slices back out to the porch. The sun was climbing steadily through puffs of cloud above the park, its light creeping up the porch steps, nibbling at the base of the chairs. Mimi sighed luxuriously as she sat down beside Bea. From her bag she extracted a small bouquet: half a dozen small-faced sunflowers. "You're a Leo, aren't you?"

Bea nodded. Her birthday was a week away.

"But you're a bit of a closet lioness," Mimi said, looking at her thoughtfully. "A quiet member of the pride. You don't roar much. Philip's a roarer." She blew on the hot tea in her cup. "He'll be seventy in August." She sipped reflectively. "Hard to believe."

"I'm turning forty," Bea said.

Mimi smiled. "And you think that's a big deal, don't you, darlin'. It's not. You're young. With any luck at all, you're not even halfway through your life." She rolled her eyes. "I remember forty. I cut off all my hair. It was starting to go grey, and I couldn't stand it. When I think about it now, it seems so ridiculous. Fifty, on the other hand . . . well, fifty's a whole 'nother can of worms. Hormones and all. But that's a decade away, and even fifty isn't so bad. To me it felt like shedding a burden. The unimportant stuff I'd lugged around for years finally dropped away—the self-consciousness, the worrying that I wasn't good enough, the silent terror that something was fundamentally wrong with me and that I had to make sure no one ever saw it—all that nonsense was finally off my back."

Mimi began to talk about a play she wanted to produce that coming winter. It was about an Ojibwe girl in trouble with the law, living in a group home. "She's murdered. It's very topical," Mimi said. "But it's poetic, too. That's what drew me to it. It's about the deeper strains of cruelty and suffering that run through us all. The killer isn't the white man you suspect all through the play. It's the girl's own mother. The playwright is Ojibwe herself, a brilliant artist." Mimi smiled. "She's in her fifties. No more tolerance for bullshit."

Bea remembered her dream: the terror of the figure stalking her, who had turned out to be a woman. She described it to Mimi.

"Ohhh, great dream," Mimi said. The sun had continued its upward creep. It was shining on their laps now. Mimi took off her shoes and wiggled her toes in the light. "It sounds like the flip side of the play I just read," she said. "The murderer in the play is a true threat. She's confused, blinded by hatred for herself and the world that has damaged her, and in her anguish she kills her own daughter. But this figure in your dream is . . ." She paused. "Jung might say she's you. The shadow of you. Unable to show her face, yet desperate to confront you. Climbing up from your unconscious, bearing news you need to hear." Mimi's hands were fluttering. "She's actually not a threat at all. She just feels that way."

The fluttering hands settled back into the sunlight on Mimi's lap. She was smiling, full of goodwill, mildly exhilarated by her own insight. And Bea, for no reason she could think of, wanted to cry.

———

Cara and the girls returned in the middle of the afternoon. They'd spent the day at their old home visiting with Didier. Yasmin's wails rose two storeys to the attic, waking Bea from a dreamless doze. By the time she got downstairs, both children were sobbing. Cara was in the kitchen emptying the dishwasher, slamming pots, homicide in her eyes. Bea took one look and told the whimpering girls that she had something for them upstairs.

She couldn't lift Yasmin up, though the little girl desperately wanted to jump into her arms. Doctor's orders. Bea reminded her about her hurt lung and knelt gingerly to offer her a hug instead. Then they climbed the stairs to the attic single file, the girls leading the way. They were in a state of upheaval, all of them, adapting to changes they hadn't wanted or foreseen. Adapting, also, to new intimacies and proximities. To Bea's surprise, she was finding happiness in the experience. Her nieces had taken over the room directly below hers, but they didn't often use it. At night they climbed into the bed that had belonged to Sol and slept with their mother, the three of them curled beneath a single blanket, like refugees.

Bea's room looked cheery and calm. Afternoon sunlight was pouring through an open window like honey, turning the walls gold. There was always a sense of stillness up here at the top of the house. A sense of security from the world below. The girls raced across the room and jumped onto the unmade bed. Bea went to the bookcase and squatted down. She studied the titles for a few seconds before pulling out a yellowed volume. She held it up to her nieces, smiling, and took her place between them on the bed.

Like a cat, Yasmin wound herself onto Bea's lap.

Elle gave her sister an irritated look. "Get off her. She hurt her lung. Remember?"

"It's okay," said Bea, balancing the book lightly on Yasmin's knees. "I'll manage."

The choice was *Alice's Adventures in Wonderland*. Her mother had bought it when Bea was five. She still remembered the delight she felt as Deirdre read it to her: the story's hilarious logic; the warm music of her mother's voice. The memory was almost as palpable as the book in Bea's hands. It was a vintage edition, cloth-bound, with gorgeous illustrations protected by sheets of translucent onionskin paper.

She turned to page one.

Bea was stretched out, still clothed, when Cara came up to her room that evening. Her bedside lamp was on, although she wasn't reading. She wasn't doing anything, really, just feeling the lingering weariness in her bones and a faint pinch in her side every time she breathed.

"Am I bugging you?" Cara said from the door. She was wearing a faded blue sweatshirt. Her eyes were pink-rimmed. "I really lost it with the kids today," she said. Then she looked at the floor. "It's final, Bea. He's not giving her up. He told me at the condo."

Bea rose from the bed. They didn't speak. Cara stepped over the threshold into Bea's arms. The feel of her body was a shock. Bea had always known her sister to be tough, athletic. Now she felt like a bird. Bea was afraid to crush her.

Cara clung to her hard. Their chests touched, and then, after they both relaxed, their bellies. Cara hiccupped and began to cry.

"I'm so sorry," she said afterward, when they were sitting side by side on the bed. She was bunching Kleenexes into both eyes. "I'm the one who should be taking care of you. But look at me." She gestured at her mottled face. "I'm a mess."

Bea took her sister's jaw in her hand and held it. "No," she said firmly. "Trust me. You're just fine."

## 24.

BEA LEFT THE HOUSE at nine on Tuesday, after the girls had gone to camp. She was to take the green metro line to De l'Église station in Verdun. From there, she'd take a bus west along LaSalle Boulevard to the hospital. Cara had printed the directions from Google Maps, not trusting Bea to find them on her phone. She'd wanted to drive her, but Bea refused. Then Cara proposed going with her on the metro. Bea refused that too.

On the porch, she took a cautious breath and gazed out at the park in which she'd spent so much of the summer. The play and the actors and her stage-managing responsibilities now seemed like details from someone else's life. The morning was cool, with a light breeze blowing from the west. The sun lit up the grass on the soccer field as she walked down to De Maisonneuve Boulevard. The grass was a deeper shade of green than was usual this late in July. It had been a record year for rain. Poppies and roses were blooming in front of the gracious Serbian Orthodox church at the south end of Melville. Bea had walked this stretch of road thousands of times. Never had it been so beautiful.

Just as her body was starting to tire, she reached Atwater station. The coolness of the underground revived her, and now that rush hour was over she was able to find a seat in the metro car. By the time she arrived at De l'Église, she had recovered her strength. She decided to skip the bus and walk along the waterfront instead. The first blocks of LaSalle Boulevard were an eyesore: a treeless strip of asphalt with no sign of the river. She passed a barn-like municipal auditorium and several fast-food outlets, including one for barbecued chicken with a parking lot full of little yellow cars with red coxcombs on their roofs.

But soon enough, the buildings to the south of her fell away and Bea caught a glimpse of the water. She climbed a shallow slope of grass to see better and found herself on a strip of parkland that extended for miles up the shoreline. The air changed. River midges swarmed her and gulls circled overhead, calling mournfully. The leaves on a grove of poplar trees shivered and danced in the wind.

Bea followed a ribbon of bike path west. The river was narrow at first, hemmed in by Île de Soeurs, but when the island ended small boats came into view, and then a cargo ship far out in the seaway. Sun shone from a cloudless sky, making the waves glitter.

She passed through playgrounds and a water park, where a couple of teenagers were chasing each other through the spray, shrieking with pleasure. Bea stopped to watch them, no longer thinking about the time or the distance she had to cover.

The sign for the Riverview Mental Health Facility stood at the entrance to a tree-lined driveway so long it resembled a public road. It wasn't obtrusive, but it was impossible to miss if you were on the lookout.

The Riverview wasn't one building, it turned out, but a collection of buildings scattered across a tract of prime real estate in Verdun. People working there used the word "campus" to describe it, as if it were a school and not an asylum. The layout was sort of school-like, Bea thought, as she entered the grounds. To her left was a football field, to her right a string of small red brick houses. The larger administrative and residential pavilions lay up ahead.

But the campus was too quiet for a school. On the playing field, the only sign of life was a flock of Canada geese sitting in the sunshine and pecking languidly at white heads of clover. On its far side a man was bouncing a beach ball for the entertainment of a child. They were the only human beings in sight.

She had no trouble finding where her father was being housed—the Sheldon Horowitz Pavilion, three storeys of blond brick fronted by a parking lot. There appeared to be several entrances. Bea chose the main one. She walked up the stairs and then stopped in front of a glassed-in receptionist's desk. No one was there. A door leading farther into the building's interior was locked. She pressed a buzzer at the door and waited. A minute later, a woman pushed the door open and greeted her. She was older than Bea, with short dark hair and startling blue eyes. She knew exactly who Bea's father was, and presumably who Bea herself was. She'd know the whole story, in all likelihood. It would be in Sol's case history, and if she hadn't read that, she'd surely seen it in the news. If she was surprised at seeing Bea, she didn't allow it to show. She asked for a piece of photo ID.

Cara had warned Bea about the ID but said the nursing staff were mostly kind. Once they got to know you, they allowed you to pass freely in and out of the building. The Sheldon Horowitz Pavilion was, apparently, run on hope and trust in human goodness.

"He's not in the best of shape," the woman said, returning Bea's driver's licence. "Your sister has told you, I assume?"

Bea nodded. She was relieved that a woman like this was in charge of Sol. A woman who could manage the delicate balance between discretion and forthrightness.

"I'll show you to his room," she said, turning down the hall. "He's probably asleep. To tell you the truth, he hasn't done much else since he got here." She paused. "I wonder if I should get a nurse in there with you, even so. I'd do it myself, but I'm with another patient just now. He's on his own. You understand that? You'll be on your own in there with him."

Bea said she understood. But suddenly she wasn't sure what, exactly, the nurse was getting at. Should she be worried about visiting her father unescorted? Cara had said that in the first days after Sol's arrival he'd been under "constant care," a term used by the hospital to denote twenty-four-hour watch. It was because of the assault. But it soon became clear that the only threat posed by Solomon Rose was to himself. He was in a state of deep lethargy, refusing to speak to his psychiatrist or to any of the Riverview staff, refusing food, and now even refusing to open his eyes. He'd been awake during the police detention and, initially, after his move to Riverview, but even then, in those first days, it had been hard to know what he understood. He recognized Cara. With everyone else, he'd been unresponsive.

The nurse, whose name was Shelagh, led Bea down a narrow corridor. Paintings hung on the walls, and there was a small kitchen, Bea noticed, where you could make tea and sit down in armchairs to drink it. A large-print calendar had been tacked to the kitchen wall, with the month and day marked in red. Efforts were clearly being expended to make the place less institutional. But no one was around to enjoy them. Silence prevailed. The doors to the patients' rooms were sealed. Had Bea not known better, she would have thought the place was deserted. The nurse stopped outside one of the doors and spoke to Bea in a whisper.

"He's barely opened his eyes today. I had to rouse him just now to take some juice. There shouldn't be a problem, but you never know. Follow your intuition. If you feel the least bit uneasy, just come out into the hall and call my name. I won't be far."

Sol lay in bed, completely motionless. That was a relief after the nurse's warning, but an instant later the relief evaporated. Nothing could have prepared her for the change in him. The figure on the bed was barely recognizable, a desiccated remnant of the man who'd once been her father.

She moved in closer. His beard had grown unruly, creeping up his sunken cheeks to cover half his face but for the one small patch of scar tissue. A smell she couldn't immediately identify, a wet, mushroomy odour, wafted from the bedsheets. She touched his cheek and he turned to her, eyes closed, his mouth opening reflexively. She said his name, not loudly, but close enough to his ear that he'd hear. His eyes stayed firmly closed.

She sat on the visitor's chair. The happiness that had buoyed her as she walked beside the river in the sunshine was gone. She felt hot. She'd walked for almost an hour to get here. A little warmth was natural. But there was something else. Her chest was tight—a tightness that had nothing to do with her exertion or her injury. She was angry.

This man lying before her on the hospital bed had hurt her. He hadn't known what he was doing. She understood that. Yet she couldn't suppress the outrage that rose up in her now, heating her blood. Violence had been done. Her father had done it. She needed him to open his eyes.

Cordelia had journeyed back to England from France to be with her father. For days Lear had lain on his sickbed, unconscious, yet she had only to utter his name and the old king opened his eyes. Mimi had wept with Angelina as these things happened on stage. Bea had wept too, night after night in the dark. In the play, when Lear woke and saw Cordelia alive and well before him, he thought he was hallucinating. He couldn't believe it was really her. But his vision was clear, possibly for the first time in his life.

Bea took a fistful of Sol's pyjamas and shook him. His emaciated body rose from the bed like a rag doll in a dog's mouth. He weighed next to nothing. His arms hung limp by his sides, wobbling like cooked spaghetti. His eyelids fluttered. His slack mouth

fell open. Bea kept shaking, trying to ignite a spark of consciousness in him. "Wake up," she said, shaking and shaking until the
pain in her ribs jolted her to her senses. Her father was hanging
in her grasp, helpless and utterly unaware.

Panting, she eased him back onto the mattress, smoothing his
pyjama shirt, laying his arms flat, resettling the sheets. Her chest
ached. Her cheeks burned. She was terrified that she'd hurt him.

This summer Bea had learned that there was a moment in clas-
sical tragedy known as the reversal—a moment of acute human suffering during which wisdom has a chance to enter. In Shakespeare's
last and greatest tragedy, after King Lear had lost everything he'd
held most dear, he arrived at it. Solomon Rose would not. And no
amount of hope or stubborn wishing could change that. Sol's mouth
had closed again. In repose, in the frame of his white beard, his lips
curved naturally into a frown. This, she supposed, was what would
stay with her. This unhappy, downturned mouth was the image she
would carry through the rest of her life.

When Bea got back to Melville Avenue, it was noon. Cara was
unpacking groceries in the kitchen. "That was fast," she said,
coming into the front hall. She looked into her sister's face. "Oh,
Bea. Was it that bad?"

They went into the living room and sat on the corduroy couch.
"He looks so awful," Bea said quietly. "Like he's preparing to die."

Cara nodded. "He knows what he did. Maybe not in any normal way, but that knowledge is somewhere inside him. I mean,
imagine doing that to your own child. I can't stop thinking about
it. I'd want to die too."

"I'd rather he lived and faced me," Bea said.

Cara took her sister's hand. "He didn't open his eyes at all?"

Bea shook her head.

286 | CLAIRE HOLDEN ROTHMAN

"You can still talk to him, you know. One of the nurses, this really nice one named Shelagh, said he could hear us. It's different from sleep, whatever state he's in. The body's immobile, but the brain's still processing. Thinking. She said that talking helps." Cara shrugged. She was wearing her faded sweatshirt again. Its pale blue brought out the more vivid blue of her eyes. "I don't talk. I sing. Folk songs, blues, *The Magic Flute*—not that I remember all the words." She raised her hands speculatively. "It beats sitting there in silence. You should try it. He hasn't objected yet." She smiled.

"Oh," Cara added, heading off to the kitchen again. "I found something you should see." She came back with a cardboard shoebox. "Here."

Something rustled inside as she placed it on Bea's lap. It didn't weigh much. Bea removed the lid and saw that the box contained envelopes, perhaps a dozen of them. All of them slit neatly up the right side. This was how Sol opened his mail: one quick slash with the blade of his silver letter opener. The envelopes bore his name and the Melville address, written in blue ink in a hesitant, almost childlike hand.

"Each one has a cheque in it," Cara said. "A returned cheque."

Bea picked up the envelope on top and pulled out its contents: a letter in the same clumsy handwriting and a cheque, dated September 18, 1981, for two thousand dollars. The cheque was signed by Sol and made out to Avi Rosenberg.

"It's his father, right?" said Cara. "I recognized his name from the obituary you found. Dad seems to have sent him money every month. And every month, Avi Rosenberg sent it back."

She looked at the envelopes huddling sadly in the box. "Why did we never meet him, Bea? Why did Dad keep us from our own grandfather?"

Bea contemplated the cheque in her hand. Sol's handwriting

on it was the opposite of his father's. It was bold and smooth, as befitted a man of education, a successful man. "Our grandfather was damaged," she said slowly. "There was no place in Dad's life for damaged things."

# 25.

THE FACE WAS YELLOW, smudged and shadowy, a monstrosity. At the age of three, Bea had tried to destroy it with a black felt pen. In vain. The ink had beaded ineffectually on the slick surface of the photograph, and the image, one of the first pregnancy ultrasounds ever performed at Montreal's Samuel Rabinovitch Hospital, had endured. When Bea's mother discovered what she'd done she didn't get angry; she put the photo album out of reach on the top shelf of the bookcase in the living room, where it had remained, part of a growing pile, ever since. No one looked at them anymore; but Bea had done so tonight, carrying them upstairs in secret after Cara was in bed.

The air in the little attic room was suddenly hard to breathe. The revulsion she'd felt at three was still there, trapped inside her like a malicious spirit. Next to the ultrasound was a second photograph, less smudged and shadowy. In this one, Bea was out of the womb and in her mother's arms, a newborn wrapped in a flannel blanket, a little white cap covering her hairless head. Her mother had pulled down a corner of the blanket to expose her for the camera. Right in the middle of Bea's face gaped a hole. Her eyes were closed, as if she'd already intuited what lay ahead and wanted no part of it. Her parents had evidently watched for signs, that was why they'd ordered ultrasounds. The family albums contained grainy *in utero* shots of both daughters, a rare intervention in the 1970s. The one of Bea had confirmed their fears. In this photograph taken a day or two after Bea's birth, Deirdre smiled bravely, displaying her newborn daughter to the world as though everything were fine.

Sol had lost no time hunting for solutions. Two pages farther into the album, Bea came to pictures of her face post-surgery. She was still a newborn, six weeks old, according to the date printed in her mother's careful hand. A strip of brown adhesive tape stretched the width of her face, gluing it together just beneath the nose. Her eyes were still closed.

A fly buzzed in the window. Bea got up from where she'd been kneeling on the floor. The photographs horrified her. They were her deepest shame. She stood up too quickly, and for a moment felt light-headed. She gripped the windowsill to steady herself. The fly bounced frantically back and forth in the narrow space between the screen and the glass. It landed on the screen and went quiet, twitching its wings over a shiny green back.

Slowly, Bea raised the window as high as it would go. Then she turned the latches securing the screen and pushed. The screen gave way, and the little creature flew into the night.

For some minutes she tried, unsuccessfully, to reattach the screen. The nights were cooler now, the insects fewer, but still. She gave up on the screen and pulled it back inside. A sliver of moon hung over the park. With no wire mesh in between, it seemed near enough to touch.

The sound of chimes startled her. Her phone was on the bed, where she'd left it after returning from the Riverview. She looked at the caller ID and saw it was an unlisted number. She answered it anyway, even though it was late.

Artie White began to talk. The company had been in Côte-Saint-Luc Park for two shows, he said hurriedly. Tonight had been their last performance there. They'd just finished packing up. He sounded breathless.

Bea held the phone away from her ear and checked the square of light: twenty-three minutes past midnight. Some intuition, not quite at the level of conscious thought, made her move to the window. In the line of parking spaces reserved for park visitors, she saw Artie's Echo glinting under a streetlamp. He was leaning against its hood, his legs crossed at the ankle, his phone cradled to his cheek. He was looking up at her.

The line went quiet. "I saw your light," he said after a moment. "Can I come up?"

He took off his muddy workboots on the porch and she led him inside. They climbed the stairs without saying a word. Cara and the girls had gone to bed hours ago. She closed her bedroom door softly behind them, feeling awkward. They hadn't spoken since Saturday's not-quite-kiss.

"You're better," Artie said with a smile.

Bea realized he meant how easily she'd managed the stairs.

He walked over to the albums spread across her floor. "What are these?"

Before she could stop him, he'd knelt down and was gazing at images of her babyhood. Bea stood frozen as he began to turn the pages of the album she had just put down. The photos started with Deirdre pregnant. Sol had loved taking pictures: his wife's bulging belly was the subject of several shots.

Several pages following those documenting Bea's birth dwelled on the surgery. She'd been a month old. Her eyes were closed in every picture. Her post-operative face looked like a tiny boxer's, swollen and bruised, divided horizontally by surgical tape. By four months the incisions had healed, and for the first time in the album, her eyes were open. She was practising a smile.

The face wasn't lovely to look at, not by any means, but at least it wasn't monstrous. At two years old she'd perfected her smile, although her jaw was still a bit skewed and her nose flat. She looked happy, though, squatting in the sandbox in Westmount Park, gazing up at whoever was behind the camera. A happy, damaged little face. Those had been her best years, she realized now: the years spent at home with Deirdre, before she started kindergarten and learned that her cleft made her different from everyone else. At school she'd been regularly taunted, especially by boys. The only one who hadn't, ever, was Arthur White.

He kept flipping pages. When he came to the end of the first album he picked up the second. She stood silently beside him, trying not to feel humiliated. She remembered the day the first photograph in this album was taken: it was the first time she'd been allowed to hold the new baby without her mother's help. She was seated on the living room couch. She looked worried, but baby Cara, slumped in her arms, was full of smiles. Cara was looking directly at the camera, waving her chubby hands.

The contrast between the two sisters was stunning. Cara's face was perfect. A delicate nose extended straight down its middle, separating two absolutely symmetrical halves. Her hair was the colour of new corn, so light it looked almost white. Offsetting the hair was a pair of electric blue eyes. But it was the mouth, open in laughter, intact and unmarred, that undid Bea. The rest of the book was devoted to shots of the little girl splashing in her bassinet, seated in her stroller, bouncing happily in her Jolly Jumper. Artie flipped quickly through the remaining pages. He closed the album and placed it carefully on top of the others. Then he stood up.

"I think we ought to try again."

Bea didn't react. And then his fingers were moving slowly across her upper lip, feeling the tiny ridge of scar tissue, registering it as if he were blind.

"I've wanted to do that forever," he said.

He gazed straight into her eyes. There was no collision this time when he leaned in.

They did a a sort of improvised waltz toward the bed. After a moment Artie's face took on an expression of concern; she was still recuperating, after all. He started to say something, but Bea didn't want talk. Her hand covered his mouth. She felt the wet contact of his lips on her palm as he kissed her again and then they tumbled sideways onto her old white bedspread.

She had imagined he'd play the director in bed, leading the way, but she was wrong. He lay by her side, watching her closely, waiting for her to give him the cues. He was a boy. This was his secret. There was a boy in there, wide open and ready for anything, just waiting for someone to notice.

She took off her T-shirt and sweatpants. She didn't feel shy, which surprised her, but then they weren't strangers, she and Arthur White. Long ago, she had made friends with this body. They kissed again and he reached for her. Not her breasts, not first thing. He ran his fingers down her side, feeling the ribs and the indentations between them, feeling also the bandage still covering her wounds. Only then did he move to her breasts. He sucked on the nipples, tugging with lips and teeth until she could hardly bear it. He didn't take his own clothes off. Instead, he rolled her onto her back and slowly, with lips and tongue and fingers, made his way down to find her.

She came quickly and hard, crying out so loudly that he pulled away, startled, before she was quite done.

She lay on the pillows, happily spent, and he crawled on his elbows to join her, wiping his mouth on his sleeve. "And here I thought you were the silent type."

# 26.

THERE APPEARED TO BE a hole in the wall of her bedroom
through which the great glowing ball of the sun had just entered.
It hung above the bed, dousing her with light. Bea's eyes opened
and the glowing ball changed shape, transforming into a face. It
was Cara. She was carrying a tray with toast and a pot of tea. Elle
and Yasmin were with her, two smaller orbs staring at Bea from
the bedside. Their jaws were slack with surprise. There was a confused flurry of feet and apologies as Cara reversed direction and
ushered the girls back out onto the landing. The door banged shut.

Bea was now fully conscious. Beside her on the bed, Artie sat
up, pulling the sheet protectively over his chest. The flesh on his
shoulders was speckled with goosebumps. Bea took his fingers
in her own and kissed them. They were cold. She pulled him
toward her, covering him with the bedspread, which had slid off
their bodies during the night.

"I should go."

She stopped rearranging their bedding and shook her head.

"No?"

His erection bumped against her hip. "No," she said, and
reached for him. The girls would be fine. Their mother could
explain things. Right now, there was some unfinished business to
attend to.

Artie was circumcised, unlike Jean-Christian and almost every other man she'd slept with. Rising from between his skinny legs, his penis looked vulnerable, especially the tip, which was as soft and pink as a rose petal. Her tongue darted experimentally and a drop of liquid squeezed out, a tiny tear. She licked again, tasting salt, and then traced the whole head, carefully, with her tongue.

An hour later, when they came downstairs, Yasmin bounded over to them, grinning. "Is it true that he's your *boy*friend?" she asked Bea, forgetting the prohibition against climbing up her front.

"Are you a monkey?" Artie asked, sweeping her up in his arms and lifting her high over his head. "Bea never told me she had monkeys in her family."

Yasmin squealed in delight. When he put her down on the rug she grabbed his hands and began climbing again.

"What's your name?" he asked as her feet clambered up his legs.

"Monkey!" she shouted. "Monkey, monkey, monkey!"

"And you?" Artie addressed Elle, who was standing by the couch, watching her fearless younger sister. "Are you a monkey too?"

She shook her head and looked away.

"She's a girl!" Yasmin shouted. Her feet had reached Artie's chest. Her head was pointing downward at the rug now and her face was red. "I'm the only monkey," she said joyfully. "And you're my tree."

Cara came in from the kitchen, wiping her hands on an apron patterned with bright red peppers. "I'm so sorry," she said. "Get down, Yas! Now! He is not a tree!"

Artie said it was okay. He was honoured to be a tree.

The girls were home from camp that morning for their annual pediatric checkup. Yasmin had been up since six and was bursting with unspent energy. "I apologize about earlier," Cara said to Artie. "I had no idea Bea had company."

"We made you breakfast in bed," shouted Yas, still hanging with her back against Artie. Her legs flipped down and she landed facing him on the rug. She executed a theatrical bow and then reached out for his hands.

"Again!"

# 27.

PHIL BURNS LOOKED SURPRISED when he saw Bea in the
back of the car. He was standing on Saint-Joseph Boulevard in
front of Mimi's flat. "What are you doing here?" he demanded
when Bea cranked down her window. Artie's Echo had manual
windows. It was hard to believe such things still existed in the
twenty-first century. Phil manoeuvred himself into the front seat,
frowning. "I thought you were recovering."

"I am," she said.

Artie turned the key in the ignition, checked his mirrors and
pulled sharply out from the curb, throwing Phil back in his seat.
It was eleven in the morning, the last Sunday in July. They'd be
playing their final out-of-town engagement of the run. Bard in the
Parks was going to the country for a two-show day. The matinee
was to begin at one-thirty.

"She's a spectator today," Artie said.

Bea had consulted Dr. Essakhri, who'd said it was all right to
go as long as she didn't lift things. Exertion, the essence of stage
management, was prohibited.

Phil tried to turn around to look at her, but he was a big man
in a small car, and Bea was seated directly behind him. After the
second attempt he gave up.

"I'm feeling much better," Bea said.

"Oh, come on," Phil said, addressing the windshield. "You could be doing anything you want today. Sleeping, for instance. Doing the *New York Times* crossword puzzle. Reading Chekhov. And what do you choose? To drive out to the middle of nowhere in this junk heap"—he turned to Artie—"no offence intended, old man, to watch a show you've seen a hundred times? Pardon my bafflement."

"But I haven't seen it a hundred times," she said. "In fact, I haven't even seen it once." This was strictly true. She'd heard the lines. She knew the play so well she could recite it in her sleep. But she'd never actually sat in the audience, facing the actors, and watched them perform.

Artie stopped at Mont-Royal Avenue, his turn signal flashing as they waited for the light. He'd slept over at Melville Avenue again. He was becoming a fixture—the tree Yasmin liked to climb was putting down tentative roots. Now they were crossing the mountain once more. They'd had to detour across town to pick up Phil after Dave Samuels called Artie early that morning and asked to be replaced as the irascible star's driver; apparently, the two had had one too many ill-tempered exchanges during Saturday's show. As the light changed and the Echo sped across Park Avenue before veering left to climb Camillien-Houde Road, Bea craned her neck to catch a glimpse of the angel. She wanted to check whether the graffiti was still there, but all she could see was trees.

She sat back to enjoy the panorama directly in front of her. The weather was perfect. The sky was cloudless. The smell of sweetgrass wafted in through Artie's half-open window. Even the asphalt looked beautiful, glistening and sparkling in the sunlight. Theirs was the only car on Camillien-Houde. Only at the belvedere did they come up behind another vehicle, the number 11 bus, black exhaust puffing out as it strained to climb the slope ahead.

This was surely the city's most scenic bus route. Mourners sometimes took it to the Mount Royal Cemetery. Families and students also used it to reach the park for picnics and walks. As Artie passed the bus, Bea noticed an ad extended along its side: the familiar green logo gleamed in the sunshine next to a photo of a blond girl sitting cross-legged on the ground, eating a plate of salad. CRUDIVORE.

Didier was now running the place singlehandedly. No, not quite singlehandedly. Gen-vie was still there, although not in the kitchen anymore. She'd graduated to marketing. The bus campaign was no doubt her inspiration. But Cara was gone. She'd quit her position as joint CEO. Their lawyers were working out the particulars.

Fifteen minutes later, Artie joined the line of cars waiting to roll onto the Décarie Expressway. Their destination was the Laurentian town of Morin Heights, an hour's drive north of Montreal.

"We're in for a twelve-hour day," Phil said to the windshield, his humour soured by the thought. He attempted once more to turn around, but again his bulk defeated him. "You realize we're stuck there till midnight, my dear Bea. If not later."

"That's life in the theatre, Phil," Artie said. "You, of all people, ought to know."

"What I know is exploitation when I see it. I have rights like everyone else."

Artie laughed. "Since when were you remotely like everyone else?" He accelerated onto the highway. "Seems to me you've spent a lifetime trying to prove you're *un*like everyone else."

Phil decided to take that as a compliment. He laughed. "You've done the same."

"True," said Artie. "But I don't go around complaining about exploitation."

Phil addressed Bea in the windshield, jerking a thumb in Artie's direction. "When did he get so smart?"

As the Echo merged with the river of northbound traffic, they fell silent. Artie's window was rolled shut now. The air conditioning kicked in. Bea leaned back on the faux leather and sighed.

Artie checked her face in the rearview mirror. "Everything okay back there?"

She nodded. The sky was paintbox blue. Things weren't just okay. Despite her aching wound, despite the fact that the father who'd inflicted that wound was now locked up in a mental hospital, her mood was oddly buoyant. Her veins hummed in harmony with the air-conditioning system in Artie's no-frills car.

Bea was in love.

She wondered whether the company had noticed a change in their artistic director. He was funnier, more direct and yet more tender than before. He'd asked her not to tell Mimi about them. Bea understood. She knew from bitter experience how difficult things could get when you mixed work and romance. And she was still hoping to return to the company and help with the last few shows.

"You'll drive me home tonight," Phil said to Artie. It wasn't a request.

They were behind a long silver dairy truck. Artie raised his eyes to the rearview mirror and found Bea's. Then he turned to Phil. "Actually, Dave will be taking you back to Montreal."

"Goddamn it, Artie," Phil said. "Dave is always the last to leave. He also happens to be very tiresome."

They shot past the truck. "Sorry, my friend."

Phil looked at him. "Who's taking my place on the ride home?" he said in an aggrieved growl.

"No one." Artie's voice was calm. "I'm staying up north tonight."

Phil's eyes narrowed. "Nice. He drives us into the wilds then makes us find our own way home."

"Not Bea," Artie said quietly. "She's staying up north too."

Phil digested this piece of news. For long moments the only sound was the air conditioner's mechanical sigh and the sibilance of tires on heat-softened asphalt. Finally, he laughed. "Aren't you clever, for a fool."

"Clever? Moi?" Artie was unable to suppress a smile. "More like blind luck, if you ask me."

"Luck, indeed," said Phil. "As for the blind part, I certainly didn't see that coming, not after your depressing sermons on the perils of combining sex and work. You total scoundrel. I suppose you had her lined up from the first day."

Bea didn't appreciate the proprietary edge. But if Artie was maintaining his restraint, she would do the same.

This time, Phil wasn't going to be denied the satisfaction of looking at her. He unbuckled his seat belt and with a mighty effort turned around at last. "And you, little Beatrice. What have you got to say for yourself?"

Her cheeks reddened. Had he just called her *little*? She was about to object when Phil pre-empted her: "How long has this courtship been going on?"

The word was so prim, so antiquated, that she lost hold of her indignation and laughed.

"Not long," she said. "A few weeks, maybe." But even as she said it she knew it wasn't true. She hadn't fallen for Arthur White a few weeks ago. She'd first loved him in another age, in a life dimly remembered.

Mont-Bellevue Park, in the Laurentian town of Morin Heights, wasn't an ideal location for putting on a play. It wasn't a park at all, in the conventional sense of the word. There was no playground, no wading pool, no baseball diamond or soccer field. It was just a tract of land on the outskirts of a rural town, covered with coarse, prickly grass that pierced the skin of your feet if you wore sandals and was unpleasant to sit on. The stage had been set up near the road to alert cottagers and attract passersby. It was visible but totally exposed, without a single tree to offer shade.

Nevertheless, Mont-Bellevue Park was celebrating its official opening that weekend. Festivities had been organized to mark the occasion, and Bard in the Parks was part of the lineup. The hope was that the site would draw people in for cultural events and boost the flagging tourist trade.

As soon they parked the Echo Phil headed for the concession tent, where cold drinks and corn on the cob were on offer. By the time Bea found him he was chatting up a blond girl in heavy makeup working behind the counter. He gave Bea a broad smile and, in bad French, introduced the young woman, whose name was Francine. Phil's cheeks were flushed. Bea glanced discreetly at the drink in his hand and saw with relief that it was iced tea.

"*Dis-moi,*" Francine said to Bea. The tent had a pleasantly sweet smell from the boiling corn, overlaid with the vanilla in Francine's perfume. A chunk of butter sat melting on a plate before her. "*Est-ce qu'il a vraiment travaillé avec Penélope Cruz?*"

Francine was attractive. A pair of very short cut-off jeans showcased her tanned legs. Her toenails were summer-sky blue. She cocked an eyebrow, waiting to be informed that Phil had never been in the same time zone as Penélope Cruz; when Bea confirmed the story, her wide eyes opened a little wider. Bea bought a lemonade, and as she walked away she could hear Francine's excited giggles. Phil had started in on his celebrity stories.

Dave had already arrived with the other actors. The stage and the dressing tents had been set up. Everything seemed to be in order. Bea poked her head into the women's tent. Margo was ironing a blouse.

Bea was still cool after the air-conditioned ride, but Margo's dusky face gleamed with sweat. The iron was on high; the blouse was cotton.

"Bea!" she said, smiling broadly. She put the iron down to hug her. "We heard you might be coming."

"I wish I could help," said Bea, pointing at the blouse. "It's hellish in here."

Margo laughed, making her face a half-shade darker. "Don't apologize, girl. Now I know what it felt like to be you, all through the heat wave, ironing our clothes. You're tough as nails, Bea Rose."

Blushing, Bea turned and pinned up the tent flap to allow in a breeze. "I can see the headline now," she said. "Actor Broiled Alive in the Laurentians." Margo nodded, grinning, and Bea felt a surge of affection. She liked this particular princess, and apparently, it was mutual.

"I'll be back in a minute," she said.

Phil was still at the concession stand, well into his second iced tea. He grinned at Bea and wheedled Francine into giving her a bottle of water free of charge from the tin washtub full of ice.

"Catch," Bea said when she got back to the tent, tossing the water to Margo.

Margo groaned with pleasure. "You are a *goddess*." The frigid bottle was dripping with condensation. She rolled it down her neck and chest.

After Margo had finished her ironing they stood outside in the shade of the tent, letting the breeze cool them. "There's a rumour circulating," Margo said, looking up coyly from her drink, "that the artistic director has been spending his nights in Westmount."

The mix of surprise and mortification on her face made Margo laugh again, but when she saw that Bea really was uncomfortable, she softened. "There's nothing to be ashamed of, Bea. You're not the first woman who's asked Artie White into her bed. But you're the first I've heard of"—her voice was low now, and appreciatively lewd—"who's gotten him to say yes."

The room was small, but the starry pre-dawn sky visible through the window gave Bea a sense of space. The Clos-Joli inn had once been a farmhouse. Its bedrooms, most of them modestly proportioned like this one, were prettily decorated and furnished with taste. The bathroom was tiny but immaculate. They'd talked a little with the owner, a man with wind-lined skin and kind eyes who'd stayed up late to let them in. His family, they learned, had once farmed this unyielding land.

A digital clock sat on the night table: it was almost four a.m. Bea rolled onto her side. Artie was lost in a dream, breathing softly and steadily through his mouth. She put her hand experimentally on his shoulder. His eyelids moved but didn't open; his lips pursed and then released a puff of air.

Deirdre had told her once that what you did on your birthday, at the precise hour of your birth, was significant. Four o'clock was usually a bad hour for Bea, the hour when sleep became fretful. Her father was the same. Four o'clock was when he wandered.

In the clock's glow Bea gazed at the curve of Artie's lips, the harmony of his features. She was lying beside a beautiful man in a country inn. She'd just watched one of Shakespeare's finest plays. So what if it had been performed in a field with only twelve other people in the audience, including the stage manager and the mayor of Morin Heights, who had no choice but to be there? She kissed Artie's forehead. His eyes opened. She kissed him again, on the mouth.

Apart from them, the dining room was empty. It was Monday morning, the construction holiday over and vacationers suddenly scarce. Chef Marie-Josée, who owned the inn with her husband, had prepared crêpes with a coulis of berries from her garden and crème fraîche from the milk of her two nanny goats. When she brought Bea's crêpe out from the kitchen, it had a sparkler in the centre. She carried the blazing offering to the table, singing:

> "*Chère Béatrice,*
> *C'est à ton tour*
> *De te laisser parler d'amour.*"

Her husband came into the dining room to join them. They sang the song three times, beaming, as if they meant it.

A call came in on Bea's phone while she and Artie were still at breakfast. She'd switched the ring tone from Tibetan chimes to an actual, old-fashioned ring. It was Cara, who said she was at the Riverview visiting their father. She noted the beautiful weather. Perfect for a birthday. She wished Bea a year full of love.

"That's all?" Bea said, laughing. "No fortune or fame?"

"Those too. I wish you all of it. But without love, the rest isn't worth much. Believe me." She sounded weary. She'd been visiting Sol every day, singing him songs, reading him the papers, praying, even bringing in his cherished recording of *The Magic Flute* performed by the London Philharmonic with Elizabeth Vidal as Queen of the Night. She'd tried everything to rouse him. And everything had failed.

"How's he doing?" Bea asked.

"Same old," said Cara. "He's sleeping."

All he did now was sleep. He had barely opened his eyes in a week.

"Still not eating?"

"No. The nurses are getting juice and water into him, but he's starting to resist even that."

Bea looked guiltily at her plate. Sol hadn't taken a proper meal since the night of Cara's party. Hope was getting hard to sustain.

"He may have to go to the hospital for rehydration this week. His doctor says it's a near certainty if things don't change." Cara stopped herself. "We'll discuss it later, Bea. It's your birthday. You shouldn't have to think about this."

They said goodbye and Bea sat back in her chair.

How contradictory life was. Her father was in a mental hospital, bent on dying. And here was Arthur White, her new-old lover, sitting with her on this flawless morning, finishing his crêpe and drinking his coffee, reviving all her joy in life. Should she grieve or give thanks? Her heart seemed to be doing both.

Her phone rang again. She glanced anxiously at Artie, not wanting to offend him. He smiled and raised his cup.

"Beatrice?" It was a woman's voice, but not one she knew. The woman identified herself as Johanna Jacobsen. "You knew me as Johanna White, years ago."

"Oh," Bea said, flushing. Artie was no longer looking at her. "Of course. How sweet of you to call."

"I couldn't resist," she said, her Lancashire accent detectable now. "Arthur told me it was a special birthday. I hope that you don't mind." Bea remembered the once familiar voice calling Artie home from across the park when it was time for supper. "I was overjoyed when he said he'd found you again." There was a pause. "Your mum and I joked about this possibility, you know. You were so deeply in each other's pockets."

The room went suddenly still. Sunlight pooled on the blue-and-white checkered tablecloth. Outside the window, Marie-Josée was pulling weeds in her garden. Bea's gaze came back into the room. She laughed, then reached across the table for Artie to tell him who it was.

# 28.

VISITING HOURS AT THE RIVERVIEW had long since ended when they got back into the city after their Laurentians escapade. Artie drove Bea there anyway, leaving her at the front door of the Sheldon Horowitz Pavilion just as a church somewhere in the distance began to sound the Angelus. The day was waning, but there was still plenty of light.

"I'll wait for you," Artie said, as she stood beside the car.

"What about the costumes?" she asked. They were stuffed into a hockey bag in the back seat of the car. Artie was giving Dave Samuels a break from the additional duty. They'd planned to do the laundry that night at Sol's house. Now Bea wasn't sure there'd be time.

"What about them?" He grinned. "It'll get it done, Bea. No worries. Besides, you're still on medical leave; you're not allowed to help. I'll be sitting over there." He pointed past the empty parking lot to a grassy prominence shaded by a willow tree. "Take all the time you need. I've got a book."

She kissed him through the car window and walked toward the pavilion's main door. This was a novel experience: a man taking care of her.

The night shift was arriving. She showed her ID and followed an orderly and a young nurse inside. At the nursing station, Shelagh was packing up her things.

"Hey there," she said, smiling. "Bit late for a visit, isn't it?"

Bea explained about the trip to the Laurentians. When she said it was her birthday, Shelagh hugged her and waved her through.

Sol's lights were on. His room looked cheery enough, but the wasted figure on the bed was, as ever, motionless. He seemed even more shrunken than the last time Bea had visited. His head was tilted back on the pillows, hyperextending his sinewy neck and making his frowning mouth gape open. Bea's breath caught in her throat. It was a posture of death.

She sat down in the worn leather visitor's chair by his bed. The anger was gone. But now, even now, she wanted him to see her.

Bea leaned forward and traced with her fingertips the shape of the unhappy mouth. For forty years she'd believed she was its cause.

*Better thou hadst not been born than not t'have pleased me better.*

She'd believed it was her face that had hardened her father's heart, her damage he abhorred. There had been anguish in that conviction, but also a bitter satisfaction. To be abhorred was, at least, to be seen.

Yet the lingering memory of an old man being turned away from the door on Melville Avenue had always whispered to Bea of another, older, more bitter abhorrence. A yellowed obituary had given it a name. A dozen refused cheques wrapped in a dozen reproachful letters had confirmed it.

She couldn't struggle anymore, not after seeing the truth written in shaky blue ink. When Sol's eyes had burned with rage and frustration at the mockery of the cleft, it was not, after all, Bea he was seeing. It was his own father. *Abba*. The weak. The imperfect. The intolerable. It wasn't Bea he had embraced in troubled dreams in the basement of his house. It was *Abba*.

And he hadn't meant to hurt Bea. As soon as she had been able to think calmly about the incident, she knew it wasn't her he'd tried to kill at the party. It was Gen-Vie he'd lunged for, the girl who had defaced his angel and humiliated his perfect daughter. It wasn't much of a consolation, however. Bea was the one in the way. The one he looked past, or through. Her father hadn't seen her. Now he never would.

Cara had said that talking might help. Was this why Bea had come tonight? She began to tell Sol the story, the facts she'd pieced together over the summer. She talked for quite a while, allowing the narrative to grow and take shape. There was no sign of resistance from him. No sign of surprise. No sign of anything, really. Maybe he was listening, or maybe not. It didn't matter. The story was for her now, just as much as it was for him.

When Bea was done, she stood up. Then she bent over the bed and kissed him, gently, on the mouth.

# EPILOGUE

*EDGAR.*

*The weight of this sad time we must obey,*
*Speak what we feel, not what we ought to say.*

(5.3.325–26)

BEA SAT IN an Adirondack chair on the front porch, a bag of Cheezies in one hand and *Alice's Adventures in Wonderland* in the other. She passed the bag to Elle, who'd pulled the other chair close beside her. Yasmin, nestling on Bea's lap, cried out in protest.

"Sorry, Yas," said Bea. "I don't have enough hands to turn the pages *and* dole these out. She'll share them with you." She turned to Elle. "Okay?"

Elle nodded reluctantly.

Yasmin went quiet. Bea was getting the hang of this, learning how to intervene at the start of a conflict before it blew up into a fight. It was all about needs. Getting clear about one's own, learning to imagine those of another. Not easy at four years old; no easier at forty. This past week she'd spent a lot of time with her nieces, ferrying them to and from their camp so that Cara could meet with lawyers and accountants and oversee things at the Rosebud stores. Today was Saturday, meaning no camp, but Cara was off with Didier at the lawyer's office, trying to hammer out a mediation agreement.

Bea and the girls were well into Alice's story. She'd been reading a portion to them at the end of every day. It had become their ritual, something solid in the heaving seas of their family's dissolution. She opened to chapter five.

Yas started whimpering again.

"Your sister wants some," Bea said to Elle. "Can you pass her the bag?" You had to keep the voice calm. Speak to their higher selves. The bag was jumbo size, more than two little girls could possibly finish. They'd bought it that afternoon at Anthony's, a small detour on their way home from the park.

When Elle finally passed the bag, Yasmin plunged her hand in deep. She pulled out a fistful of Cheezies, stuffed them in her mouth and then reached for the book, her grubby little fingers coated with greasy orange powder. Bea caught her hand in mid-air, gave it a kiss and placed it safely on the little girl's legs.

Yasmin's hands instantly rose into the air again. "Is that a *worm*?" she asked, pointing at the illustration. Worms scared her.

"No," Bea said. The finger kept pointing but maintained a respectful distance. "It's a caterpillar," she explained, "sitting on top of a giant mushroom." She didn't mention the hookah.

The answer seemed to satisfy Yasmin. "Read," she instructed.

Despite that imperious command, Cara's younger daughter was not the Red Queen. She was Alice, trying to find order in a world gone suddenly and grossly awry. Bea had forgotten how moving Lewis Carroll could be. By chapter five Alice had already shrunk and grown and shrunk again. The girls loved the illustration of her gazing longingly at the miniature cake on which EAT ME was spelled out in currants.

Now the caterpillar was in Alice's path. "Who are you?" he demanded, his face puckered and stern. Poor Alice couldn't come up with an answer. She'd changed so many times since getting out of bed that morning that she no longer had a clue.

The girls listened intently. There were no more questions about worms, no more grubby pointing fingers. For them, it all made sense.

The distinctive muted boom of loud music in a closed car

intruded on Bea's reading. The Range Rover pulled into the driveway. "Someone Like You" drifted up to the porch.

"Mama!" Yasmin shouted. She slid off Bea's lap and followed her sister in a clamouring rush down the front stairs. The book and the bag of Cheezies were forgotten.

Bea watched them run. Events had unfolded exactly as Sol would have wished. Cara was the new owner of his house. The Range Rover had been restored to its rightful place, *sans* logo. All that remained of it was a faint leafy sheen visible only in direct sunlight, like an expunged tattoo, beneath the new paint job. Most significantly, Cara was the new Rosebud CEO. The paperwork was done. She was running the family business.

The music died and Cara got out of the car. Not only was she in an old pair of jeans and sneakers; she also seemed to have entirely dispensed with makeup. She crouched to hug her daughters. "What's this you've got all over you?" she said, taking Yasmin's hands and examining them.

"Cheezies!"

Cara, former hater of junk food, looked over at Bea and smiled. As she and the girls came up the steps in the soft August sunshine, despite everything, they looked happy. Cara kissed the top of Bea's head in greeting. "Cheezies," she said, reaching for a handful from the bag on her lap. "I always loved those things."

Mother and daughters disappeared into the house. The sun was going down, introducing a slight chill to the air. Summer was waning. The lawn had yellowed in spots, and in the park the leaves were beginning to lose their lustre. Next month, Yasmin would start kindergarten at big girls' school, the same one Elle attended.

An hour later Bea gathered her things and went to say goodbye before leaving for work. The company was back at Westmount Park now for their final performances. Tonight's would be their last.

Cara was in the kitchen preparing kale, pulling leaves off fat green stems in one clean motion. "Time to go," Bea said, touching her shoulder. The theme song from a Disney video drifted up from the basement. Bea nodded at the stairwell. "I'll just go and kiss the girls."

"No need. We're coming tonight."

"To the play?" said Bea, surprised.

"It's now or never, right? Your last hurrah?" Cara smiled, shearing a final feathery leaf. "We want to cheer you on, Bea. And I want to meet these characters you've been hanging out with all summer." She paused, raising an eyebrow. "Like the famous *Mr. Burns.*"

Bea let the comment pass. Her mind was too busy compiling objections to the plan. The production was two and a half hours long. Elizabethan English was hard for anyone to understand, let alone children of four and seven. And Cara, who'd watched Shakespeare's plays in London's West End, might not be so impressed by this local production. In the end, she said none of this. Who was she to predict her sister's judgment or her nieces' pleasure? Cara wanted to be there tonight. Bea would honour that.


Bea was squatting for the last time beside Margo in the dirt in Westmount Park. The stage lights glared before them through clouds of gnats swirling around the halogen bulbs. The first act had just begun. In the early weeks of the run, daylight had lingered well into the third act. No more. Bea could barely see Margo's hands or make out the features of her face.

Wordlessly, Margo took Bea's shoulders and turned her around. She was trying to read Bea's back. Dave Samuels had made them all T-shirts as a parting gift. It was a stage tradition, apparently.

The T-shirts were black, the theatre's signature colour, with quotes from the play printed on their backs in white letters. Most bore a line from the Fool's ditty: WITH HEIGH-HO, THE WIND AND THE RAIN. It would remind them of their long, wet summer of Shakespeare.

As the star of the production, Phil Burns had received a quotation all his own. It was one of his lines from Act One. A line he'd had trouble with throughout rehearsal: WHO IS IT THAT CAN TELL ME WHO I AM? When Dave had handed him his T-shirt, Phil smiled. When he saw the answer to that question printed on Bea's back, he laughed out loud.

LEAR'S SHADOW.

Margo squeezed Bea's arm, laughing as well. Phil and Artie had descended to the lower stage and were now directly in front of them. Moments before, the king and his Fool had arrived at Goneril's palace with a boisterous retinue of knights and horses. Phil was about to deliver the line on his T-shirt. From where she was kneeling, Bea could see only his back. It was stooped. Dishevelled white hair flowed down his shoulders. His hair had grown wild over the past two months; he looked every inch an aging monarch sliding into decrepitude. Was it just the role, or was Phil Burns himself growing old before her eyes? Bea didn't particularly trust her eyes these days. Mortality had become something of an obsession. Wherever she looked, she saw impermanence. Nothing was solid. Nothing would endure.

Phil's line came out perfectly, delivered in the slow, uncertain voice of a man who is aware that he's lost his footing. It was riveting. And then the Fool answered. Margo gave Bea's arm another squeeze.

It wasn't true that Phil Burns had faded to a shadow of his former self. A couple of weeks earlier, when Bea and Artie had stayed the night in Morin Heights, Phil had stayed over too. It was remarkable. In just days he would celebrate his seventieth birthday, and yet he'd managed to pick up Francine, the concession girl. Bea had bumped into them the next morning, drinking lattes together in the sunshine on the terrace of a café.

"They'll never take me alive, my dear," he'd confided when Francine disappeared to the washroom.

Bea looked out at the audience spread across the grass, their faces glowing in the reflected light. Cara and the girls were sitting near the sound booth, their eyes fixed on the stage. Even Yasmin seemed to be following the story. It was pretty dramatic. Lear was raging against Goneril for opposing him, cursing her with barrenness and worse. Bea's eyes blurred. It was too awful to watch: father and daughter locked in this blind, blundering two-step.

She stepped back from Margo's chair, taking cover in the darkness. The air was cooler by the bushes, comforting with its smell of sodden earth and cedar. A sole mosquito buzzed apathetically near her ear.

The king was alone now, his Fool at his side. Phil and Artie weren't acting anymore. They were being. The emotion was so pure that Bea forgot the verse and the archaic diction, forgot too all contrivances of plot. Phil was yanking the roots of his hair with both hands, imploring the heavens to protect him. He was going mad, he shouted at the awed, silent faces, at Cara and Cara's children, at Mimi and everyone else out there watching in the dark. He'd lost everything—his lands, his rank, his retinue and his royal family—and now he was losing his mind. The lines he spoke weren't lines. They were arrows, precise, merciless and true.

When Phil walked off the stage, Bea was waiting for him at his chair. He took the water bottle she held out and drank thirstily. Then he handed back the bottle, reached an arm around her shoulders and hugged her.

"I'm going to miss you, Beatrice Rose."

He called her by her full name, as her father used to. He was gazing into her eyes as if he truly did love her. But of course it wasn't love. He ran his fingers down her spine in a caress.

She shook her head and smiled. "You'll never learn."

Act Two was underway. A few feet from where they stood, Edmund was spinning falsehoods in a twisted desire to win his father's love.

Phil leaned forward until he was inches from her ear. "You're quite a broad, Bea."

She took his fingers in hers and kissed the tips chastely, as a daughter might. Then they got to work, removing his cloak and finding his boots for the next scene.

After the play was over and they'd struck the stage for the last time, Bea and Artie drove over Mount Royal to the cast party. Bea was still wearing her gift from Dave. Artie was wearing his too. WITH HEIGH-HO, THE WIND AND THE RAIN. The stars were out. The night was crisp. They were driving up Remembrance Road, passing the dark humps of the gravestones of Notre-Dame-des-Neiges cemetery, when he turned to her.

"I've been thinking about next summer."

Bea looked at him, astonished. The *King Lear* run had just ended. Her shoulders ached. Her right shin, which she'd banged on a metal storage box, was still throbbing. She hadn't yet begun to digest this summer, let alone consider what was next.

"I checked with Equity," he said. "All you need is five more shows as an assistant and then you can be a full stage manager, like Dave. Five shows, Bea. Think about it. If you're organized, you can do it in a year. That's what Dave did. One summer he was ASM for Bard in the Parks, and the next he ran the show."

Artie's hands danced in the air above the steering wheel. "You can do it, I know you can." He turned to her, his face shining in the dashboard's glow. "Everyone loves you. Especially Dave. He'll take you as an assistant this fall on anything he gets."

They'd passed the mountain's summit and were speeding down Camillien-Houde. The city's east end lay below them like a mirror of the starry sky. Artie pulled sharply into the belvedere.

"Think of it, my love," he said, easing to a stop between two parked cars. "You could manage us next season."

Bea had never stopped here before. They were on the edge of a precipice. Off in the distance, the Olympic Stadium shimmered. In front of her was nothing but air. She thought of her father. And of poor, blind Gloucester standing with his son on a mound of dirt, thinking it was a cliff.

"I think I know what I want to do," Artie said. *"A Midsummer Night's Dream."*

She frowned. "A comedy?"

He shrugged. *"Lear* was heavy going for summer audiences."

"But it was a success," Bea objected. "Do you really need to go light?"

"Not light," he said. "Shakespeare's comedies are full of truths, too. There are some great roles in *Midsummer Night's Dream.*"

Bea had a vague impression of lovers running around in confusion, of magic spells and things going generally amok.

"It's actually a romance," Artie said.

His hand was resting lightly on her thigh. On either side of them, lovers were holding each other in their cars' dim interiors. She stroked his long, slender fingers.

"I think I'm done with stage management," Bea said.

Artie started to object. She was hardworking, resourceful, calm in a crisis.

"It's not about competence," she said, a little surprised at how easily she'd accepted his praise. "It's about desire." She twined her fingers with his. "Don't worry. I don't mean this."

Bea didn't know what the future would bring, beyond a deepening intimacy with the man sitting beside her and visits to her father at the Samuel Rabinovitch Hospital, where he'd recently been moved. Cara's daughters would also need a lot of attention.

Artie kissed her. Then he restarted the engine and eased the Echo out of its parking spot and back onto the road. As they came off Camillien-Houde and turned south on Park Avenue, heading for the cast party, a familiar figure loomed above the trees. Her massive verdigris wings rose into the sky, her arms outstretched in blessing. The angel. Bea pressed her nose to the window, squinting. The city had gotten its act together and cleaned her up. In the darkness, she looked as good as new.

# ACKNOWLEDGMENTS

AMONG MY INSPIRATIONS for the play's depiction were Laurence Olivier's 1983 TV movie *King Lear* and the 2014 National Theatre Live version, directed by Sam Mendes with Simon Russell Beale playing Lear. All line citations in this novel come from the Signet Classic edition of William Shakespeare's *King Lear*, published in 1998.

Thank you to Jacob Holden for expertise regarding the criminal justice system, and to Dr. Ann Rothman, Dr. Caroline Vu, Dr. Serge Gauthier, Bernie Kelly Goulem, Dolly Dastoor and Susan Doherty for helping me understand aging human brains and bodies. Any legal or medical errors in this work of fiction are of the author's own making. I take full responsibility for them.

Thanks to Samantha Haywood, Stephanie Sinclair and Jennifer Deleskie for early reading of the manuscript and timely counsel. Many thanks to the team at Penguin Random House Canada: Nicole Winstanley and editors Shima Aoki, Alex Schultz and Lara Hinchberger for their keen intelligence and intuition.

Deep gratitude to my husband, Arthur Holden, for his good humour and love, and for being this book's first reader.

To the Conseil des Arts et Lettres du Québec and the people of Quebec, thank you for invaluable material support during the first year of the writing process.